THE BRIGHT PAVILIONS

A NOVEL

—————— BOOKS BY HUGH WALPOLE ——————

THE
LONDON NOVELS

SCENES FROM
PROVINCIAL LIFE

Fortitude
The Duchess of Wrexe
The Green Mirror
The Captives

The Young Enchanted
Wintersmoon
Hans Frost
Captain Nicholas
The Joyful Delaneys

The Cathedral
The Old Ladies
Harmer John
The Inquisitor

HERRIES

Rogue Herries   Judith Paris
The Fortress   Vanessa
The Herries Chronicle (*The four novels in one volume*)
The Bright Pavilions

———————

The Wooden Horse
Mr. Perrin and Mr. Traill
*The Prelude to Adventure
*Maradick at Forty

The Dark Forest
The Secret City
*Portrait of a Man with Red Hair
*Above the Dark Circus

* *An omnibus volume entitled* Four Fantastic Tales
includes these four stories

A Prayer for My Son
John Cornelius
The Sea Tower

Jeremy
Jeremy and Hamlet
Jeremy at Crale

———————

SHORT STORIES

The Golden Scarecrow
The Silver Thorn

The Thirteen Travellers
All Souls' Night
Head in Green Bronze

———————

Joseph Conrad (*A Critical Study*)
Anthony Trollope (*English Men of Letters*)
The Apple Trees (*Golden Cockerel Press*)
The Crystal Box

The English Novel (*Rede Lecture*)
Reading (*An Essay*)
The Waverley Pageant
The Cathedral (*A Play*)
Roman Fountain

———————

(*With J. B. Priestley*)
Farthing Hall (*A Novel in Letters*)

THE
BRIGHT PAVILIONS
A NOVEL

BY

HUGH WALPOLE

THE REPRINT SOCIETY
LONDON

THIS EDITION PUBLISHED BY THE REPRINT SOCIETY LTD.
BY ARRANGEMENT WITH MACMILLAN & CO. LTD.
1941

PRINTED IN GREAT BRITAIN
BY R. & R. CLARK, LIMITED, EDINBURGH

FOR
RONALD STORRS
IN FRIENDSHIP

A DEDICATORY LETTER

MY DEAR RONALD,

In dedicating to you this Elizabethan romance I feel that I am doing myself much honour. It is with great pleasure that I give you something that has for two years absorbed my imagination. I would wish at the same time to warn all those critics or others who detest long historical novels, and especially the Herries variety, that this book is not for them. I would wish also to apologize to the friends of the ' Herries Chronicle' in that this volume has a certain grimness. Many of us, educated on boyish romances, have looked back to the Elizabethan period as one of music, dancing, colour, and the gallant rifling of Spanish treasure. Gallant it certainly was, but even as our present times are gallant — gallant and grim.

For then, as now, the men and women of England were fighting a desperate and tenacious enemy. Then as now they were fighting for their lives. And, even as romantic novels go, I remember that ' Westward Ho!' painted the tortures of the Inquisition and that ' Kenilworth' is, with ' The Bride of Lammermoor,' the most sombre of all Scott's novels. The Elizabethan Age was ferocious, cruel, superstitious, greedy and courageous.

Before I end my letter, I would like to acknowledge the great debt I owe to ' The Tragedy of Fotheringay' by the Hon. Mrs. Maxwell-Scott — a delightful and thrilling work.

Your affectionate friend,

HUGH WALPOLE

The hills tell each other, and the list'ning
Valleys hear ; all our longing eyes are turned
Up to thy bright pavilions : issue forth
And let thy holy feet visit our clime !

To Spring
WILLIAM BLAKE

CONTENTS

PART I

PART IV

PART I

THE BROTHERS

AN ENEMY

On the grey afternoon of December 22nd, 1569, Nicholas Herries sat his lovely mare Juno on the moor inland from Silloth in Cumberland, every nerve alert because of the event that any instant might bring.

Nicholas, at this critical moment of his history, was twenty-five years of age, the son of Sir Michael Herries of Court Mallory, near Lewes in Sussex. He was a large young man, six foot four inches in height, of vast breadth of shoulder, a mighty chest, great thighs and a round, rosy-cheeked, merry-eyed head and a thick neck. He was not as yet fat, although later he might be. He was an exceedingly cheerful young gentleman.

Save for his attendant servant, Jack Oates, who sat his horse, obediently, at a distance, there was no other human body to be seen in all the visible world.

Nicholas wore a hat of green leather that sat firm and close on his head, round his thick neck a falling band, a green doublet close to his body, his boots black, long and close to the leg and the boothose some two inches higher than his boots and tied with points. The hilt of his sword was handsomely gilded. His mare and himself seemed like one. Not an inch of him stirred, and his servant, a little man with a cynical eye, was as still as he.

The scene was, at first glance, peaceful enough. A thin line of sea like a long attenuated skein of smoke was barely to be distinguished from the grey of the monotonous sky. The Scottish hills were like vapours of breath. In the bend of the moor close at hand could be seen the roofs of some hamlet. To the right like a mark of astonishment was a peel-tower raised many years ago against the Scots marauders.

Otherwise not a sound, not a sign, save a hawk quivering

3

above them, then suddenly plunging to its prey. But Nicholas, who was no fool for so big a young man, knew that there was more in the scene than met the eye. He was doubly engaged, for while he was so passionately alert for what was happening at his side, his mind was also introspectively moving around his own private personal world. Although he did not know it he was pursuing two opposite activities at one and the same time.

He was thinking first and foremost of his young brother, Robin, whom he was that night to meet in the little town of Keswick. His young brother was his great duty to the world. Ever since that day when at the age of five he had been shown the white, thin face of that helpless infant in its froth of lace and silk, he had sworn that no harm should come to it. The contrast between his own five-year sturdy ruddiness and that fragility had struck deep to his heart. ' Robin shall know no harm.' *That* was his faith, and equal with it was his worship of his Queen. For a man so young he had already a clear view of her as she was — whimsical in personal fancy, parsimonious, often cruel, often coquetting from vanity, often jealous, often absurd in her love of flattery — but always with a passion for her country's greatness which, however it might be confused with a passion for herself, was nevertheless a grand inspiration to all young men who sought to do great deeds even as Nicholas did.

To these two faiths he added a third, and that was for his own immediate family. The small junior branch of Herries to which he belonged, although allied to the great family of Howard and, on another side, to the Herries of Lowland Scotland, was the subject of his simple and even spiritual worship. He would not be a Duke of Norfolk or Northumberland or Earl of Leicester. He would not be my Lord Herries although he followed what he could hear of that bold Earl's doings with interest — but only Nicholas Herries, elder son of Sir Michael Herries of Court Mallory, and faithful member of that little group : his father's brother, Sir Martin Herries, whom now he was going to visit ; the Herries of Temple Guard near Salisbury ; and a stray or two like his old cousin Penelope Herries of Dover ; old Daniel Herries, a squire in Herefordshire ; and his numerous cousinhood.

Here were his three faiths and they were all that he had, save only, the greatest of all, his faith in himself.

Now, at this present instant, all four faiths were concerned, for during the last few weeks there had been stirring deeds in Northern England.

Young Nicholas was no politician nor a religious man either. Anything his Queen might choose to do was right in his eyes. He was nevertheless young enough, full-blooded enough, adventurous enough, to be moved by the knowledge that Mary of Scotland was prisoner in England ; lovely, helpless and, in spite of her forced resignation, a Queen. Some who had seen her said that she was not so lovely after all, others who knew her whispered that she was by no means so helpless — but there it was : she was a Queen and a prisoner. Nicholas cared nothing for the Roman Catholic religion nor very much for the Protestant either. This present world with its glories was sufficient for him. But there were others who thought differently, who had gone so far as to plan to marry the Duke of Norfolk to Mary of Scotland. The Duke of Northumberland with old Richard Norton and his seven sons and a number more hotheads with them had risen in the North, and on November 14th of this very year had entered Durham Cathedral, thrown down the Communion Table, torn up the Bible, raised two altars and restored the Mass. There were some thousand foot, ill-armed yokels for the most part, and fifteen hundred horse. For a brief while the North was in their hand. They marched towards Mary at Tutbury, and she, poor thing, was at once hurried away to Coventry. The rebels turned north again, took Hartlepool and Barnard Castle. By this time levies had been raised against them from all over England, the whole country standing loyal, they broke and fled, and on December 20th, only two days before this present, their leaders, riding for their lives, crossed the Border into Scotland.

Of this final issue Nicholas did not yet know. He had himself been staying for several weeks with Sir Timothy Curtis, a young man much of his own age, near Doncaster.

At the first news of the fighting his immediate impulse had been to go and have a cut at the rebels, for it was always his disposition to fight wherever fighting might be, but a certain sensible caution that was mixed oddly in his nature with his impetuous activity prompted him to remain where he was. Two days ago he had ridden to Carlisle to stay with a friend of his father's and now he was on his way to join his brother and see, for the first time for ten years, his old uncle outside Keswick.

This had been, in a small fashion, a northern pilgrimage for him : he had never been north before. He had felt at once, riding through Penrith, towards Carlisle, the stir from the northern strain in his blood rise within him. This bare, smoke-grey country widely open to the sky, with the fresh, wildly running streams, the long horizons with only a lonely little tower here and there to break them, the strong smell of the turf, the sturdy ugly sheep, and, soon, the gently rising, unoccupied hills, all these things belonged to him and he to them.

He was always happy when he was not angry, and so he was happy now, singing something out of tune as he rode and calling on Jack Oates for a chorus. There had been no adventures save for his beating a drunken hostler and rescuing a rather blowzy servant-maid from rape in a country barn.

In Carlisle, however, all had at once been different. His father's friend, Thomas Berwick, had a small manor-house in the suburb of the town, where, being now over seventy, he raised bees and a handsome garden. Berwick was a Protestant and a servant of his Queen, and had as deep a hatred of the Scottish Mary as it was possible for so gentle a nature to cherish. The obvious failure of the ill-judged insurrection rejoiced his heart, but already, although the rebellion was scarcely over, hangings and burnings were on the way, villages outside Carlisle were flaming and a number of young, self-important officers of the Queen were out to satisfy their own sadistic passions as a proof of their loyalty.

Nicholas was at once anxious for his brother, who was but twenty years of age and had travelled up by himself from Oxford. So, on the third day, he left old Thomas Berwick, who had been in perpetual astonishment at his size and vigour and appetite, and rode for Keswick.

Here he was, sitting his horse, motionless on the grey moor, listening for a certain sound to be repeated. His head was erect, his eyes searching, his hand on the hilt of his sword. Oates was as still as he, and Juno, the beautiful darling, as motionless as the little jet-black cloud that hung exactly above their heads.

The sound that he had heard was of a man frantically breathing. It seemed impossible in such a place, for nowhere at hand was there the smallest bush or tree. Nevertheless Nicholas said at length quietly :

' Come out and show yourself, whoever you are.'

There was no answer, but Nicholas, straining his gaze, saw come from the distant tower two figures and stand there. They were wearing armour which shone and glittered even in that dim light.

Nicholas said again :

' Come out and show yourself.'

There emerged then right from between Juno's feet a head of tangled hair, naked shoulders, the lean ragged body of a man.

' Stand up,' Nicholas said.

The man stood up and it was clear that he had come from a hole in the ground, a hole covered with twigs and fragments of dried bracken.

The man was indeed a wretched object. Hanging to one shoulder was a blood-stained torn shirt ; his thin chest was covered with grey matted hair, dank with sweat, and his bony hands were about his middle, for he was naked there ; long, stout hose still clung to his legs, but he had no shoes. His face with a week's growth of beard had charm beneath the terror, and Nicholas studying it (for he was even at his present age an excellent judge of men) caught the bright blue eye, the well-modelled nostril, the high intelligent forehead, under the dank hanging hair.

' Where are you from, and from whom are you hiding ? '

The man pointed with a shaking hand to the two distant figures in armour by the peel-tower.

' They'll be moving. They'll be coming this way.'

' Well — what if they are ? '

A shiver shook his body.

'They have dogs with them.'

Nicholas spoke contemptuously.

'You needn't fear.'

The man broke out passionately :

'By God I fear !'

'Where are you from ?' Nicholas asked again.

'I was in the sack at Durham. After, I escaped as far as Penrith. Since then they've been hunting me and several more.'

Nicholas moved Juno a pace.

'Against the Queen. I can do nothing for you.'

The man cried out with a shrillness like a hare caught in a trap.

'No — I swear not. I am a bookseller. I was travelling north to Edinburgh. I have no part in politics nor in religion neither. I'm for the Queen and her service whatever it may be. But the town was in an uproar, and like a fool I must see with the rest. I was with the mob in the Cathedral and a prayer-book fell into my hand marvellously illuminated. I kept it, and two days later was found with it at Barnard Castle. By good fortune and a friend's aid I got away and thought I was safe, but in Penrith was sworn against by a soldier and with five others was hunted on to the moors. I have had nothing to eat or drink for two days. I had been searching for a mountain stream when I heard them out with the dogs. I found this hole and covered it. I have been lying here for twelve hours. I am almost perished with the cold.'

Nicholas looked into the man's blue eyes and believed every word of this that had poured out in a breathless gasping torrent, the man's head turning again and again towards the two motionless figures by the tower.

'They are watching the moor,' he said. 'I know one of them. Philip Irvine. He is in charge here and is a devil.'

'What is your name ?'

'Peter Gascoigne. Bookseller by St. Paul's Churchyard.' The fellow sank suddenly on his bare knees, clasping his bony hands together. 'Save me from the dogs,' he whispered. 'Anything but that. Anything . . .' Then, the words tumbling over one another : 'I have a friend in the village there. I come north twice in the year by Keswick. Take me there under your protection and I can manage the rest.'

' Get up behind me then,' Nicholas said.

The naked, trembling creature caught at the stirrup and swung himself up, not without agility, and Juno moved forward. Nicholas could not tell whether the men at the tower had seen anything. They did not stir.

As they moved towards the hamlet, Nicholas cursed himself for a fool. His man's ironical eye had told him. Once again his impetuous temper had betrayed him. Although he could witness a bear-baiting, a burning, a hanging and disembowelling, without a twist of the heart, he was so made that he must help one in distress if that one were weaker than he. At least he must always take action and often enough his common-sense caution came after the deed. He had especially determined that he would not be mixed in this Northern business, and most certainly now he was about to meet his little brother Robin. And here he was, by one moment's ill-advised action, already mixed in it !

There was another thing. The name of Philip Irvine stirred something in his memory. He was in some fashion concerned with that name, and not pleasantly. He struggled to remember but caught only the idiotic scent of a carnation. A carnation. A room. A mirror. A monkey. These ill-assorted articles would not arrange themselves. Irvine. Irvine. There was a Sir Humphrey Irvine of Northumberland. A place near Alnwick. A carnation . . . a mirror . . .

Nevertheless, so uncomfortable an uneasiness stirred in him that he felt an impulse to turn in the saddle and tell the man to drop to ground, he could do no more for him. He must fend for himself. Even as he thought this, thin, slow flakes of snow began to fall, wetting his cheek, intermittent as though someone in the sky were letting them slide from his hand, counting them as they fell. At the same time the armed figures by the tower moved. Horses had been brought. They mounted and slowly started towards the hamlet. There were three great dogs that ran before them. He heard the man's whisper : ' Oh, Christ ! . . . Oh, Jesu Mary, save me ! '

Juno mended her pace. Nicholas must be in the hamlet

and rid of the man before those others reached it. The snow began to fall more swiftly.

The hamlet was quickly reached. Hamlet indeed it was. Some half-dozen cottages, made in the old style of wood posts and ' saddles ' covered with clay, mere ' wattle and daub,' and one place, better in quality, with a chimney and one window of glass. This had in front of it a wall. No human being was in sight. A dog lay in the mud scratching at fleas, not minding the snow that already was masking his coat.

Nicholas reined his mare.

' Now down with you. You must fend for yourself.'

The man slipped to the ground and stood there, looking up at Nicholas. Once again young Herries realized that this scarecrow had about him an original charm : his gaze was pure, unclouded, and he stood there as though he had some message to deliver. But he did not speak.

' I should waste no time,' Nicholas said kindly.

At that moment the two armoured horsemen were upon them. They must have ridden with great swiftness, Nicholas thought, from the tower. They must have seen this fellow from the first. The man stood there, without moving. He seemed to be crumpled with terror. The three dogs strayed behind the horses.

The foremost of the two riders and Nicholas then considered one another — their first survey and, by all the designs of heaven, not the last. And yet *not* the first survey, for Nicholas recognized him at once. In the preceding year he had stayed for a night, with his brother, at Sir Henry Sidney's, and, on his arrival, there had been several visitors departing. As they had passed out of the great hall a girl had thrown a dark carnation to a young man who had been teasing a monkey on a gilded pole. He had caught the flower, fastened it in his velvet hat, but not looked at her, only with his head up as though he were king of the world, strode out to the court-yard. He had not even seen Nicholas, but he, alone afterwards with his brother Robin, had asked whether he had noticed him.

' I know him,' Robin had said. ' His name is Philip Irvine.'

Why did I notice him ? Nicholas thought. The dark

carnation. The monkey chattering with rage. The girl in a heavy crimson dress. As he caught that flower I hated him. He did not even see me.

But he saw him now. He was a young man of great beauty. His jack or steel coat was, in its small overlying plates, of gilded metal ; his cuirass also of gilded metal, and his burgonet. His body was of perfect slimness and he sat his horse nobly. His complexion was dark and on his upper lip was a thin black moustache. His eyes were young, ardent, scornful. He was a very proper youth, as Nicholas at once acknowledged to himself.

He seemed at first glance surprised that Nicholas should be there and that he did not move his horse. Their mutual concentration had, indeed, something especial about it.

About Irvine's mouth there was a scornful curve as he regarded Nicholas' great body, contrasting undoubtedly his own slim proportions. But Nicholas was accustomed to jeers at his size. Irvine's voice, however, was gently courteous.

' Sir,' he said, ' this is my prisoner. I am acting under the command of Her Majesty.'

Nicholas raised his hat.

' Mr. Irvine,' he said, ' although we are not acquainted we have almost met. I have seen you at Sir Henry Sidney's.'

Young Irvine bowed

' My name,' Nicholas said, ' is Nicholas Herries.'

Irvine bowed again.

' This is a pleasant meeting, Mr. Herries,' he said. ' I fancy I know your brother.' Then, quite cheerfully, he went on : ' But I fear time presses. I have reason to be in Carlisle before dark.'

' I apologize for detaining you,' Nicholas said. ' But I am certain that you would not wish an injustice to be done.'

' Most assuredly not.'

' I have had some talk with this fellow and he assures me that he is an innocent bookseller from London who, travelling north on business, found himself in Durham at the time of the present rising, was involved there by no fault of his own, has been driven by fear——'

Irvine interrupted.

'It is certain he does not look an innocent man,' he said, smiling politely.

It was now intensely cold. The moor behind them lay under a skin of snow. The dark was coming on, but the snowfall gave a moonshine effect to land and sky. But what Nicholas felt and was afterwards to remember, was the peculiar silence. In the hamlet not a soul was visible. The buildings were like dead buildings. Their two voices rose and fell as in a dead world. The two servants, the three dogs, were without movement. Suddenly, and for no apparent reason, Irvine's servant struck a flint and threw, with a careless gesture, some lighted fragment on to the straw-covered floor of a mean barn that was just beyond the wall of the house. The flame ran along the floor and very quickly caught the bare rafters. A great light sprang upon the scene, and the crackling of the flames, as of peevish, quarrelling voices, broke the silence. Irvine made no motion. It was as though he had neither seen nor heard.

'I must have that man,' he said.

Nicholas, whose anger was steadily rising, answered :

'I assure you that he is innocent. He had been in no way concerned against Her Majesty.'

'You have his bare word for it,' Irvine replied. Then, more impatiently, he went on : 'Come, sir, as I have said, time presses. I have much to do. Harrison, show Mr. Herries the warrant.'

The man was feeling in his breast, but Nicholas broke out :

'I assure you I would do nothing against the Queen. Her Majesty has no more faithful servant anywhere. This man shall be examined at Carlisle if you will, and perhaps you will permit me to accompany you there. I had only feared some injustice out of hand.' Then he smiled his boyish, confiding grin. 'The cold is perishing and the fellow will die before our eyes, for as you see he is naked. You are right in this too, for this is certainly no business of mine and I am due to meet my young brother in Keswick — but somewhere the fellow's case has touched me. If I seem to interfere it is the last thing, I assure you, that I would wish.'

Young Irvine had listened to all this with that same intentness he had observed from the beginning. The lighted barn was now flaming to the dun sky, scornful of the snow, and all the scene was illuminated. Irvine's face, armour, body, horse, were gilded with fire.

He stayed for a moment as though to see whether Nicholas had more to say, then sharply and now with no courtesy answered :

' Mr. Herries, I cannot see that this is any business of yours. This man is a rebel and must be peremptorily dealt with.'

The man, who had not stirred, although his skin was purple with cold, gave a cry, turned, and for an instant Nicholas thought that he would leap into the fiery barn. He must have seen, in that illumined relentless face, no sign of hope. Bent, his head down, his rags fluttering, he sped past the barn, on to the moor.

Irvine called : ' Castor ! Caesar ! '

Nicholas shouted : ' No. No. . . . By Christ's body, no ! '

He thought that he had never seen a man run so fast. The flames showed an expanse of moor like a dirty cotton sheet. The dogs, baying, their heads down, were in pursuit. There was nothing for Nicholas to do, but he, who had already seen and even shared in so much cruelty, now sickened at the heart ; must stare because he must, and yet would have put his horse to the run and galloped from the place.

It seemed for a moment as though the man would out-distance the dogs. But indeed he had no chance. Suddenly he turned, curved in his step and then ran back towards the hamlet. Maybe his notion was that he would leap the wall of the house and beat on the door there for safety, or it might be that he was so desperately maddened by fear that he thought no longer about anything.

Nicholas, almost as though it were himself that was being pursued, cried out :

' Not back, man. . . . Not back ! Out, out to the moor ! '

As the wretch came into the full illumination of the fire again, the frantic stare of his eyes could be seen, his head thrust forward as though that would carry him the faster. Then, almost as he reached the flaming barn, the foremost dog was on him, leaping at his back. The man let out a great screech, then fell, the dog on his back. All the dogs were on him, as they would on a fox. They growled, they gobbled. Pieces of bleeding flesh were flung into the air.

Irvine called them off and they obeyed with reluctance. His man climbed down from his horse and bent to look.

'He's dead,' he reported nonchalantly. Then he picked up the remains and threw them into the blazing barn. Irvine dismounted from his horse and went over to the barn as though to make sure that his duty was completed.

Nicholas also dismounted.

'Before you go I must have a word with you,' he said.

They approached one another. They were of no great age and it may be that Irvine was truly astonished at the rage that Nicholas Herries showed. For he had, after all, but done his duty, and who cared for the proper punishment of some wretched nothing? A nothing moreover that had been in undoubted rebellion against the Queen. Now that the insignificant nothing was disposed of, Irvine wished to be on his way, back to Carlisle, for it was already dark and fiercely cold. So he was surprised at this huge irate young man facing him, and it was more surprise than irritation that he felt at first. He half turned towards his horse.

'I wish you good evening, Mr. Herries,' he said. 'It is very cold. I assure you that I have but obeyed my orders — although why,' he added, smiling, 'I should have to defend myself to you I cannot imagine.'

'Perhaps I can explain that,' Nicholas answered gravely. 'That poor fellow had placed himself under my protection. You offend me in your disregard of that.'

'I fail to see the offence,' Irvine replied. 'It was in execution of my duty.'

'Every man has a right to trial.'

'By God, man,' Irvine broke out. 'Where have you been? Do you know in what days we live, when the whole of the North is out against Her Majesty?'

'I am perfectly aware of it,' Nicholas said, coming a little closer. 'Nevertheless, it was the man's right to have trial.'

Irvine's temper was now up. This silly, clumsy, interfering fool!

' I could arrest you, Mr. Herries, for interfering with the Queen's justice.'

' Try it and see,' said Nicholas.

Irvine's hand moved to his short dagger beside his sword. But he spoke suavely.

' Now, Mr. Herries, I want no quarrel although it appears that you want to force one on to me. I have told you a number of times that I am out on my proper duty. The rebellion is not yet ended, and even now the whole of the North may be up. You say that you are a faithful servant of Her Majesty and I have no reason to doubt it. I will wish you a good night and we will both go about our several duties.'

' I am afraid, Mr. Irvine,' Nicholas answered, drawing yet closer, ' that it cannot be so easily settled. The man was in my care. I asked that I might go with you and him to Carlisle, much, I may say, to my own inconvenience. You refused me that courtesy. I request an apology.'

Irvine laughed.

' When you are more russet-pated, Mr. Herries, we will consider it.'

' It is sad,' Nicholas answered, ' for your excellent father to have had such a coward for a son.'

On that word both daggers were out. Irvine had his breast armoured, but his neck and arms were bare.

Both men stepped back and an instant later had sword in one hand and dagger in the other. Both servants had dismounted and were standing ready.

Nicholas, heavy although he was of body, was already an excellent swordsman and loved any kind of sword-play as well as anything in life. The movement alone, in this bitter weather, was a hearty pleasure, but also he had, unanalysed, a deep sense of shame that he had allowed so helplessly the poor man to go to so wretched a death. Beyond this again he felt a hatred for Irvine that he must watch lest it blind and confuse him.

He discovered at once that Irvine was no mean swordsman. As they felt their way, keeping sedulously their ward, their swords rasping and quivering, but still distant from one another, their personalities betrayed themselves. They had the eagerness of the young men they were and the wisdom of the long training they had received. The snow had made the ground slippery ; the fire was dying in the barn ; after a minute or two it seemed to Nicholas as though he were in a dream, as though he had been in this place and situation before. He wanted to finish it. He tried the thrust, the charging blow, with the right and reverse, with the edge, the back, the flat. Both men used the Italian play, forcing their weapons, as they had been instructed, ' with two edges and one point.' They moved round in a circle, advancing and retreating, both keeping their ward or guard with all proper elegance.

Then Irvine slipped and Nicholas pierced his arm. Irvine's sword dropped. Nicholas with a bow handed it to him.

' Mr. Irvine,' he said, ' I am quite satisfied.'

Blood dripped from the arm on to the snow. Irvine stared into Herries' face as though committing his features to memory for ever.

' This is a private quarrel, Mr. Herries. No question of my public duty.'

He turned on the snow as though he would fall. His man's hand was on his shoulder. He shook it off.

' Our next meeting ' — he bit his lip — ' shall be more fortunate.'

' As you will,' Nicholas said.

He mounted Juno and rode slowly away.

THE BRIGHT PAVILIONS

CHILLED to the spleen, mired with the filth of the uneven track under Skiddaw, Nicholas and his cynical man arrived late at the Keswick inn. The hour, the dark, the dripping melancholic snow made no difference to the welcome. The host was out in the yard, servants were running ; one took Juno, was for rubbing her, giving her her feed. But Nicholas, even before he saw his brother, must be sure that Juno was well suited, and so there he was in the stables, rubbing his stout snub nose on Juno's coat, murmuring in her ear, and she, in the sharp light of the held-high stable lantern, flashing her imperious, brilliant eye, her ears raised for a sound, her nostrils distended, then quietening as she knew that her friend and master was caring for her and would see that she came to no ill.

And so, back in the inn again, Nicholas was calling : ' My brother, Mr. Herries ? He has arrived ? '

' Four hours ago, sir. The room is ready, a fire burning, supper prepared.'

He ran up the wide oak stair, the host and a bundle of servants looking up after him in open-mouthed admiration of his size and vigour.

He flung back the door.

' Robin ! Robin ! Where are you ? Come from your pent-house. Where are you hiding ? '

Then, inside the door, he stood a moment lost childishly in the pleasure and delight of seeing his little brother again.

Robin Herries was there, warming himself in front of the fire. He was dressed entirely in black, with a diamond at his neck and diamond buckles to his shoes. He wore white cuffs of delicate lace turned back on the sleeve, his white ruff reaching up against his deep dark-brown hair. He bore no resemblance to his brother save for the Herries sharp bone formation that gave a kind of horse-strength to all Herries faces.

His features were almost delicate, saved from femininity by the strength of the eye and the strong broadness of the forehead. His face had much beauty of seriousness and grace of breeding, the eyes dark and lambent, the carriage of the head on the neck full of unconscious dignity, the cheeks delicately smooth. It was the face of a boy in a certain ingenuousness and purity, but the face of a man in its thoughtfulness and intelligence. His body was perfectly formed, slight and elegant but of a strong carriage and dignity. The ' Portrait of a Gentleman ' by Nicholas Hilliard has been supposed by some to be a likeness of Robin Herries.

Now his face was illuminated with pleasure at the sight of his big, joyful, bustling brother. The love that there had always been between them was indeed ' passing the love of woman.' They were the exact complement the one of the other, Robin's gentleness, passion for the arts, mystical spirit, love of all beauty, mingling perfectly with Nicholas' animality, out-of-doors eagerness, excitement in worldly adventure. Robin, like any other young gentleman, could ride, fence, play tennis, dance, be a proper courtier, but his heart and mind were already preoccupied with other matters. He gave himself with great difficulty to others whereas Nicholas was anyone's friend or enemy. He had not as yet fallen in love and Nicholas had been in love a thousand times. They shared a devotion to their home, their father and mother, but even here Robin kept something in reserve. Nicholas' patriotism was simple : whatever the Queen did was right. Robin, as Nicholas had of late, with concern, noticed, was moving towards the Catholic religion. At home there had been a priest, Stephen Rodney, frequently in his company. His father and mother were of the Queen's religion, Lutheran. Sir Michael detested extremes whether of Puritan, Calvinist or Catholic. Nicholas' own spiritual business was with this present enchanting world than which he wanted none better. There were many elements in his brother's nature that he did not at all understand. These were the very things therefore that he must protect. He felt often that Robin was his child, ignorant of the world although so brilliant, weak physically (but Robin wasn't weak).

Now he moved forward, caught him in his arms, held him to his great chest, kissed him, hugged him, stood him back with his hands that he might look at him, hugged him again.

' Robin ! Robin ! . . . I'm all of a muck, and you as elegant as though you were going to Court.'

' I've been here since afternoon waiting for you,' Robin said.

Nicholas threw himself on to a stool, stretching out his legs. Then he jumped up, opened the door, roared out into the passage for someone to come, then threw himself down again.

' We'll have supper here.'

He got up again, bent in front of the fire, rubbing his hands.

' It's been a bitter ride. And there's been another thing. On the moor I found a man, a fugitive. He said he was a London bookseller, wrongly suspected of a part in the rising. He was in Durham when they sacked the Cathedral. Poor devil, he was naked and eaten with fear. And he had reason, for, after I'd taken him on my horse, one Philip Irvine — you remember him at Henry Sidney's — came up and demanded me to deliver him. I tried what I could do, but the poor devil ran and the dogs had him. Then Irvine and I had a word or two and I ran him through the arm. Then I came on here.'

This was like Nicholas, who always must pour out all his own doings before he enquired of anyone else's. Directly after two servants came in, pulled off his boots, brought in a wooden tub of hot water. Jack Oates appeared with luggage. Nicholas stripped, bathed, dressed in an elegant silver-grey doublet and hose, had all cleared away and supper things laid before the fire. Through all of this he was talking, asking questions and not waiting for an answer, swinging his arms, slapping his chest, then scenting himself, combing his hair, fastening his points as delicately as a woman.

The candles were lighted on the table, food and drink appeared, Oates, with a friendly kick, was speeded down to the servants' quarters, and the two brothers sat down to their meal, under a delicate painting of Venus and Adonis. The snow had turned to sleet and now beat against the windows, which were of horn and so gave a smart but not uncosy rattling response to the weather.

Robin's questions were all of the Rebellion. How far had it gone ? There were stories in Keswick that the Northern Lords were defeated and fled to Scotland. Most of the better class in the North were Catholic. Moreover, in everyone's mind lay the thought of Mary of Scotland, who, however wicked she may have been, was a prisoner in England against Elizabeth's given word. Moreover for these young men the whole matter had an especial interest, for their own distant cousin, Lord Herries, had crossed the border with Mary and was intermediary between her and Elizabeth. They felt almost as though it were a family concern.

'I tell you what it is, Robin,' Nicholas said, taking a chicken bone in his hands and eagerly gnawing it. 'Mary will be no light trouble for our Queen. What's to be done ? They can't send her back to Scotland to the tender mercies of her brother. France has no wish for her. To keep her here in England as prisoner is to break the Queen's word and to rouse every Catholic in the country. To execute her is to repeat the murder that she herself committed on Darnley.'

'It is no certain thing,' Robin said, 'that she was privy to her husband's death.'

'She not privy !' Nicholas exploded. 'Was she to forget the Italian falling at her very feet, sixty daggers in his body ? Was not Darnley doomed from that very instant ? Did she not marry Darnley's murderer some bare months after his putting away ? Has she ever wished to bring him to any justice ? She may be a queen and fair, but she is no lady for my bedding.'

He laughed and, stretching out, took Robin's slight hand in his.

'There's a straight path and an easy, brother Robin. We have a Queen and we are her servants. There's no other duty for us but that.'

Then he told Robin some more of the things that he had heard in Carlisle about the Rebellion : how at Raby the con-

spirators had been all but scattered, forgoing their project, when Lady Westmorland, Surrey's daughter, threw herself among them ' weeping bitterly ' and crying that ' they and their country were shamed for ever, and that they would seek holes to creep into.'

How Mary of Scotland was moved from Tutbury but just in time ; that on November 23rd a courier dashed in from London with an order for the Queen of Scots' instant removal, and that Shrewsbury and Huntingdon then rode, with an escort of four hundred men, and conveyed her to Coventry, which town they entered at night to avoid the gaze of the people. Had the Northern Lords secured her at Tutbury the whole country might have risen.

It was here that Robin sighed. Nicholas looked at him in consternation.

' Robin . . . you don't mean——'

' It might be better for the country. God may be angry with us that this Roman religion——'

Nicholas jumped to his feet.

' Be quiet, Robin ! Think where you are ! Men suffer the rack for less. . . .'

Robin looked up at him, smiling.

' What do I care for politics ? That is not my world nor ever will be. My imagination works perhaps. That distraught Queen, hurried by rough soldiers, conveyed into a town secretly by night——'

' Don't waste your pity.' Nicholas sat down beside his brother, putting his arm around him. ' She's as tough as the horn in that window there. She'll ride or shoot or curse or murder with any horse-trooper in her company. I'll swear that my Lord Bothwell, now pirate in the Orkneys they say, was hided like a porcupine, stank of drink like an ordure-barrel and tugged her hair in his amorous ecstasy till the lady screamed again. Didn't she wear man's dress to bide with him, and scream from the windows of Holyrood like a fishwife and dance while the powder blew up Kirk o' Field. Waste no pity, Robin. She'd have her talons in our Queen's throat or pour poison down her royal gullet had she her way. Waste no pity, Robin. . . . Waste no pity.'

Robin, staring into the fire, said at last :

' Who knows the truth of it ? The letters they have in London are forgeries, no question. Moray, her own brother, hunts her to the death. I can only say that she is a sad, pursued Queen who, if she loved wildly, loved truly, and had her destiny in a country of bare stones and wild savages.' Then, smiling again, he pressed his brother's arm. ' Come, Nick. You look like a boy whose porridge has been taken from him. We are together and what else matters ? This is a pleasant, happy little place. I was by the edge of the Lake with the snow falling and a wan light on the opposite hills. It's a kind of fairy place.'

Nicholas sighed, looking perplexed.

' I don't know what it is, Robin. That man who asked me for protection. I think I shall never forget him. There was something noble about him although he was naked and blue with the cold. He asked me for protection and trusted me and I broke his trust. I feel as though there were evil in this meeting. There's a sort of foreboding in it. At least,' and his face suddenly lightened — he was happy and confident again — ' there is Mr. Philip Irvine to have a reckoning with. There is an enemy most happily made, and here,' he said, taking the flagon from the table, ' is to his merry and utter destruction.'

They were not due at their uncle's house, which was only a few miles from Keswick, until the following evening, so early in the next afternoon they strolled about the town. A lovely day, the sun glittered down upon the thin scattering of snow, sparkling upon the eaves and posts and wooden galleries, upon the colours and movement, music and shouting, as if it loved the world that it must illumine. They walked first down to the Lake and looked across it, with its dark studs of islands, to the hills beyond, now all carpeted with snow and silver-sharp against the cloudless blue sky.

What Nicholas felt at once was that this was a little world apart. Carlisle, and all the Border country, was alive with fear and anger. Raids and burnings and hangings were all in the day's work, but this present Rebellion had strained nerves to hysteria, and now that it looked to have failed who knew what vengeance might follow ?

Here in the little country town there seemed to be none of this. The Lake sparkled in the sun as though it were outside man's foolish history. The hills were so marked with quietude that only when one cloud for a moment invaded the sun and a purple shadow passed across the snow-flanks was there any change.

Nicholas drew in a breath of the sharp cold air.

' I love this place and always shall. I shall come back here, perhaps make my home here. From the moment I entered the North something happened to me. My heart enlarged.'

' Why, you're a poet ! ' Robin said, laughing.

' That I'm not,' Nicholas answered indignantly. ' But I am certain that there is sport here and the men hold their heads proudly and everywhere there's a sound of running water. If that's poetry then I'm a poet.'

' As thus,' said Robin, and staring on to the glittering water and beyond, he repeated, as though to himself :

' What sweet relief the showers to thirsty plains we see,
  What dear delight the blooms to bees, my true love is to me !
  As fresh and lusty Ver foul winter doth exceed—
  As morning bright, with scarlet sky, doth pass the evening's weed —
  As mellow pears above the crabs esteemèd be —
  So doth my love surmount them all, whom yet I hap to see.'

Nicholas was always unhappy when anyone repeated poetry, so he turned his brother up into the town again.

' All the more,' he said, ' that you yourself have no love — poor fish-veined brother that you are ! But I, now ! Before half an hour is out in this blessèd place I shall have a girl in my arms.'

It was a true prophecy and came about thus :

He was in a state of the highest animal spirits, with the sparkling weather, his own good sleep, ale and toast at six-thirty, and at midday a fine meal of venison and the best beef he'd ever eaten in his life and a tart of apricots ; moreover, he was greatly pleased with the Keswick inn, which was superior to most country inns he knew, for there was a big window of glass in the hall and some of the rooms had matting rather than rushes, and even where the rushes were they were fresh ones instead of stinking as they often did. Also he had slept like the doomed, in the naked bed, his arm across Robin's chest ; slept in a sweetness of love and charity to all the world, especially to his dear brother.

So he marched singing into the little Square and presently stood, Robin quietly at his side, lost in pleasure at the sights he saw. Charming was the place with the Town Hall with its whitewash and black timber, the houses, snow glittering on the eaves, and the fields and gardens leading down to the Lake, and the snow-crinkled hills guarding all.

It was but a day or two before Christmas, and a body of rogues and vagabonds had marched into town. Not far from them a man was fiddling and girls and boys dancing. There was a puppet-show with dolls showing the History of Charlemagne. Boards were laid out on trestles, and sweetmeats, trinkets, household goods, were for sale. To the left, at the side of the meadows leading to the Lake, there were games — football, wrestling and playing at the catch.

Nevertheless, besides all this noise and bustle and colour, common to any country town at Christmas-time, there was, both for Nicholas and Robin, something especial — the air and savour of a newly-opened world, as you might gaze in the opening of a shell to find glistening water and bright stirring colours. Everywhere there was the scent of the country. Sheep moved up the street, the dog barking at their heels ; a bull was led past the boards and trestles ; serious, grave-faced men, in rough clothes but with most unusual dignity and reserve, stood talking in groups. Moreover, not a soldier was to be seen, nor any burning buildings. The bells of Crosthwaite Church were ringing ; there was the stir of voices, laughter, the movements of the animals, the fresh breeze from the mountains and the sun shining on the water.

On the other hand, the natives of Keswick had not let the brothers go past without observation. The thews and sinews of Nicholas caused attention wherever he might be, and the delicacy and breeding of Robin marked him out as someone not in the ordinary. Even though Keswick might be aloof from the trouble on the Border, it was alive enough to what

was going on, and it eagerly speculated as to the identity of
these two gentlemen. Some thought that they might be
Recorders sent up from London or Commissioners with orders
for investigation : but, no, they were little more than youths,
and the one who was a giant was clearly by his laughter and
easy friendliness there for his own enjoyment with no thought
in his mind of Northern Rebellion or the hunting down of
fugitives.

Nicholas soon asked a stout farmer standing beside him
with two sheep-dogs how much liberty they gave the vagabonds
in Keswick. The farmer's brow wrinkled with disgust.

' Aye — 'tis Christmas-time and there's no reason to be too
hard on them this day or two. But we've the stocks handy,
and out by Druids' Circle there's two Clapperdogens hanging
to an oak tree that have been there these two months. There
was a man whipped through Keswick for counterfeiting only
last week.'

But by now Nicholas had noticed something else. Moving
in and out, standing watching the puppet-show or the game of
football in the meadow were men, women and children of quite
another breed from the Cumbrians. Nicholas had never, in
fact, seen people of their like before. They were plainly
foreigners, and even the roughest of them — and some of the
men were rough indeed — wore a quiet, almost stern aloof-
ness that marked them out. Plain and ordinary though their
clothes were, there was often something — the set of a cap,
the workmanship of a silver clasp, the fur of the coat or gloves
— that set them apart. Just then a man and woman of these
people passed by, and Nicholas, catching their guttural accent,
asked his friend as to their identity.

' They be Germans from Magdeburg and such towns.'

' What are they doing here ? '

' Working in the mines up at Newlands and other places —
silver and lead — sent here by the Queen to work for her and
make money for her.'

' Are there many of them ? ' Nicholas asked.

' Plenty enough. Foreigners is foreigners all the world over.'

' Do you Keswick people suit with them ? '

' Well enough when they're quiet. And for the most part

they're peaceful. 'Tis religion mostly causes the trouble, for
they're Lutheran and Protestant and there's plenty of Catholics
hereabout. There's times when something stirs in them and
they're like a swarm of bees, buzzing and whirring. Last
Whitsun feast there was a fight down on the meadows there
between a posse of they miners and fifty or more of our own
lads. Five of them were killed and two of them hung for
murder.

'For the most part they're quiet enough.' He spat and
then chuckled, deep in his throat. 'Their women are handsome time and time and our men are lusty as young men
should be, I reckon.'

'That's a strange thing,' Nicholas said. 'Are there none
of your own men can mine sufficiently well?'

'There's a trick in it, I reckon, and we men of Cumberland
have better things to do — above ground with the sun shining
on you and the rain in your face, walking the Tops gathering
the sheep . . .'

He broke off. He had been staring at Nicholas for a long
time.

'Pardon me, sir, but you're the strongest-looking young
gentleman I've seen in a score of seasons.'

'I'm strong as men go,' Nicholas said, laughing. He was
not boastful ; he looked on his size and strength as pleasant
accompaniments to daily life, nothing to his credit, but useful
and amusing features.

His body often moved before his brain, so that now, without
thinking at all, he strode forward to the trunk of a tree that
was lying in front of one of the trestle-tables where goods were
sold. It lay there, waiting to be used on a new building near
by. He bent down and without strain raised it in his arms,
held it above his head, then hurled it through space on to the
edge of the meadow beyond.

This feat attracted, of course, very general attention. He
was suddenly aware that he might seem vainglorious, so,
blushing like a boy, he turned to a round, rosy country woman
who, exactly in front of him, was selling cakes and sweetmeats.
He adored sweet things, and here were some of the best. He
stood eyeing them and grinning.

There was marchpane made of pounded almonds, pistachio nuts, sugar and flour ; sugar cake of rose water and oranges ; and, best of all, his dear Eringo which he had never hoped to see in a little country town. Eringo, Eringo, the candied root of sea-holly, whose sharp tang, soaked in sugar with a flavour of burning, he had enjoyed on summer nights at home, lying under the oak tree with a girl, stuffing her mouth with it and then tasting the crisp sugar on her lips.

He had been a great attraction to the rogues and vagabonds, who, gathered in a group under the Town Hall wall, were doing a brisk business in a diversity of ways. They were an odd company, very thick over England at this time because of the cessation of the monasteries as places of hospitality. The wars, too, had left a whole army of vagrants. Their headquarters was in London. They moved up and down England, their common purpose to live without work, their common end the gallows.

In this group there was an old bearded man frothing at the mouth and crying out. Soap was his aid. There were the one-legged and the one-armed. There was an Egyptian or two, with the dark visage, the gilt earrings, the shabby crimson coat. They were known as Moon-Men, and one of them now was busy telling the fortune of a mouth-open country boy. But quite close to Nicholas were three of the greatest rogues in all Christendom. He knew at once what they were about. They had a table in front of them and about this a small crowd was gathered. There was first the Taker-Up or Setter. This was a little man, like a weasel, in a torn, dirty doublet, a feather in his hat, his impudent, small nose seeking out his victim. Standing beside the Setter was the Verser, in this case a broad, stout fellow, dressed not too ill with gilt buttons to his doublet. It was he who, pretending not to know the Setter, was suddenly interested in the cards laid out on the table and thought that, in all innocence, he would have a try to discover the coin under the card. Discover the coin he invariably did, and so the rest of the innocent world was encouraged to try too ! At the table was the Barnard, this time a thin pock-marked man with a virtuous, unctuous voice who cried : ' Come, friends all, and try your fortune. As honest as the lady moon ! See, this worthy gentleman is to venture. Why ! You are fortunate at the first choice, sir, and have doubled your money ! '

Nicholas was watching, with amused indifference, their simple trickery that was as old as Ptolemy, when Fate suddenly had him by his heart and liver, as in fact it was accustomed to do a dozen times a day. A girl, who had been standing in the little crowd, seemed to decide that she would try her fortune. She pushed her way forward and, in a voice that had a slight foreign accent, said softly : ' I've a fancy to venture.' That would in the ordinary way have been nothing to Nicholas, but here there *was* something ! She was like a boy in build, with a boy's straight gaze from blue eyes, her flaxen hair coiled about her head ; she was laughing. She was as clean and strong and healthy as a young tree in the sun. Her hair shone, her eyes were full of light, her cheeks were rosy, her gown was of thick common stuff but blue like the Lake. She seemed to him a radiant, flaming, joyful splendour, and her splendour passed through him and set him on fire.

So, quite simply, he put one hand on the neck of the stout Verser and the other on the bony throttle of the seated Barnard and lifted them both in the air, kicking over the table with his foot.

The fat Verser he threw into the crowd, the Barnard he carried for a way, the little man screaming like a chicken and kicking his thin legs in their miserable hose. Then contemptuously he flung him into a huddle of sheep that were bleating up the street.

The crowd laughed and shouted, for anyone could do to a vagabond what he was able. They were anyone's game. Nicholas turned and, leading the bewildered girl behind the puppet-show, bowed, kissed her on the forehead quite reverently and asked her her name.

' Catherine Hodstetter.'

' Well, Catherine, trust no one in future but myself. I am the only honest man in this hoodman company. My name is Nicholas Herries. Repeat it after me.'

' Nicholas Herries.'

' Good. Remember it. I will return. I'll kiss you again that you may remember it the better.'

He kissed her again, this time not so reverently.

She watched him, her hand up against the sun, striding off. He seemed to her doubtless a god among men, come down for a brief visit from heaven.

An hour later, Nicholas and Robin were riding at the Lake side, along into Borrowdale towards the hamlet of Rosthwaite where their uncle's house was.

They had started none too early, for the winter day was all too short and the sun was already sinking behind the hills that rested, like couched animals, on the farther side of the Lake. The Lake's waters were molten gold, but already there sighed the trembling foreboding of the grey evening. The reeds and rushes at the water's edge shuddered and a flight of wild duck slowly winged towards the snow-darkening hills.

Peace was supreme, and, after the jolly noise of the town, the world was consecrated to some deeper interest, revealing a business that was not mortal.

Even Nicholas felt it.

' I shall ride this way again,' he said, ' and others of our line after me. Even they are riding beside me now. I have never felt that before in any other place. In these last two days I have met a man I failed, a man I hate and a girl I love.'

He looked longingly at the wild duck that were now like flecks of dust in the last blaze of the sunlight. He would have liked dearly to have had a try at them.

If this evening's peace so wrought upon Nicholas, how much more then upon Robin ! It was this very peace that he loved when, without disturbance from the outer world, he could let his mind dig into what was the *real* world, the world of the intellect and spirit. The gentleness, purity, sweetness, of his nature came largely from the fact that the life of the bustling, material sort was for him a kind of pageant, a play performed on a stage by actors who were none of them what they seemed. He was not himself what he seemed and it appeared to him that it was a kind of law to play a game with the rest ; to eat, drink, love, fight, wear clothes, sleep, so that, through all this, the *real* life might pursue its secret, destined way unchecked. Like all thinking young men of his time he was fascinated by the new learning, the Humanists, the discoverers and explorers, the scientists and doctors. The world was expanding under his very nose. He could not keep pace with it.

At this moment Robin was only thirty years before Edward Wright's great map, the first ever to be drawn on Mercator's principles of projection. Fifty years before this December evening, Magellan had sailed from Spain into the ' South Sea of Discovery ' and the Philippines. Off Patagonia he had seen great men clad in llama-skins and heard them bellow like bulls. Fifty years were gone since Spaniards or Portuguese had discovered all that part of America lying south of the latitude of Europe, and the west coasts of Africa and India. In 1497 Cabot had discovered Newfoundland and the neighbouring American continent. Less than twenty years before this December, Chancellor, in the *Bonaventure*, had been near to where Archangel now is and had travelled overland to Moscow, and the Muscovy Company had been formed in 1555. The English merchants had trafficked to the Canaries, Morocco and the Guinea Coast beyond Cape Verde. John Hawkins in 1562 had made West Africa half-way house to the West Indies. The battle for sea dominion was now ocean-wide. English captains plundered and Spanish officials tortured, burnt and made galley-slaves. Young men like Robin Herries were hearing, every day of their lives, of wonders, horrors, deeds of stupendous courage and sacrifice. No wonder that their hearts were fired within them !

In the Sciences too there were new wonders at every hour. In 1543 Copernicus had sent out to the world from his deathbed his great work *De revolutionibus orbium coelestium* and so laid the basis for ever of the new system of astronomy. There were the alchemists struggling to turn base metal into gold ; there were the doctors for ever experimenting on the human body for the better comfort of poor mankind.

But, best of all for Robin, there was the world of letters. He was, like most of his friends, a sufficient Latin and Greek scholar, but it was in his own dear tongue that the new learning was breeding and fostering a fresh and wonderful life. Sir Thomas More's *Utopia* was his own darling book and he was for ever dreaming, as did that splendid creator, of how the filth and disease and close darkness of his own towns and poor houses might be transformed into the light and space and clarity of another world. He had Tottel's *Miscellany of Songs and Sonnets*, that had first appeared twelve years ago, by heart. Wyatt and Henry Howard and Nicholas Grimald were his constant dear companions. He was, but secretly, a poet himself! All this life of discovery and science and letters was there chiefly to feed his inner, truer life.

Ever since his babyhood he had been interested in religion. As a mewling and puking infant he had looked up into the stout and worldly features of Mr. Hogben, the family Protestant chaplain, and wondered why he pinched up his nose and talked in that sing-song voice. Robin had been born in the winter of 1549, the very year in which Cranmer drew up the first English Prayer Book. Tyndale had been executed by the Spaniards in 1536, but before then had published in full the English New Testament. Coverdale followed him, and the Great Bible was officially adopted in 1539 and placed in all English churches by order of Henry VIII. Robin Herries was familiar with it from his earliest days — old Mr. Hogben was for ever reading from it, and as soon as Robin could speak he was reciting, in a shrill treble, passages out of it. He soon knew, too, Cranmer's *First Book of Homilies* and, later, most loved of all, until he found the *Utopia*, were Latimer's magnificent Sermons.

Beneath and beyond this reading, however, was his own eager and questioning mind. Mr. Hogben was soon little but a wheezing joke to both boys, but whereas Nicholas behaved as though the old chaplain did not exist, Robin would wonder why Tyndale and Cranmer and Latimer had suffered with such endurance and splendour for something that, in the hands of the Reverend William Hogben, was an empty farce. Was there something real here or was there not?

Soon, from listening to the talk of his elders, he began to wonder the more. Then, himself being some six or seven years of age, he realized that his father and mother were in great trouble. There came a night when they were all hurried away on horseback to an old, dark house beside silent water, and there for nearly a week were hidden in a small cupboard of a chamber.

Later again, men in armour came to their home and asked them questions and his mother wept. Finally came a day when Robin heard the bells ringing and on enquiry found that it was for ' the new Queen, God bless her '— and the Herries' troubles were over.

He discovered now that all these difficulties and distresses were caused by religion, and that indeed religion was the great divider of mankind, and that, because of religion, men burnt and hanged one another and tore out one another's bowels and cut off the privy members the one of the other.

This seemed to him very strange, for, as he understood it, ' God is Love ' and Christ Himself cared for all mankind, even the wine-bibbers and the Magdalenes. The state of the world was a great mystery to him until, some years before the present, he met an emaciated, star-eyed, fanatical priest, Stephen Rodney, who had quickly won control over him. Robin had visited Rodney in various odd places — inns and barns and London hostelries. Rodney had the habit of suddenly appearing in most unexpected quarters. Sir Michael Herries himself, being a stout and determined Lutheran, would not have tolerated him, but the active hunting of priests had not yet begun and Elizabeth's own tactics of compromise and toleration were still very generally practised.

Robin therefore had no difficulty in meeting Rodney, and his young idealistic soul was soon won by the fiery intensity and ruthless intelligence of this man. One thing Rodney soon made clear to Robin. That the one and only Church burnt, disembowelled, tortured, heretics only out of loving-kindness and solely for the heretics' own good. The actual sentences of death and torture were indeed never passed by the Church. Those were the business of the State. But, for the Church, the heretic's soul was the question. In one way or another he must be saved from the punishment of eternal fire. What was a little momentary disembowelling compared with everlasting flames and the eternal wrath of God ?

Then, following on this, it became clear that politics and religion were inextricably mixed, for how could the one and only Church rest while there was a Protestant ruler on the throne of England ? Elizabeth had not married, in spite of a succession of world-public flirtations, and Mary of Scotland — a Catholic, body and soul — was her legal successor. Was it not right to wish for a Queen of the true religion, even though she *had* married her husband's murderer ?

It happened then that, before Robin had taken this expedition northwards, he was beginning to pass very completely beneath the influence of Stephen Rodney. One thing only prevented his entire surrender, and that was Rodney's fierce and intolerant fanaticism. There was no strain of cruelty in Robin Herries. He was a thought too gentle for the age in which he lived. Rodney's wild exultations over the torturings and burnings in Mary Tudor's time found no echo in Robin's heart.

His mind loved to dwell on a loving, kindly, all-mankind-embracing Jesus. He was sure in his heart that Jesus would have spurned the burnings and quarterings with furious anger. He longed for the coming of Christ as he longed for More's Utopia. At this present time he was given up greatly to dreams and imaginations of a perfect world.

He was dreaming of this now as he rode beside his brother through the evening grey, pushing aside the branches that struck against his eyes, and, once and again, catching sight through a clearing of a hill range against an ice-cold, faint-green sky ; a hill, moth-soft, the snow mantle faintly silver, as a moon, riding boat-wise, sailed up into still and cloudless space. An owl called. Nicholas was singing.

> I can believe it shall you grieve,
>   And somewhat you distrain ;
> But afterward, your painës hard
>   Within a day or twain
> Shall soon aslake ; and ye shall take
>   Comfort to you again.
> Why should ye ought ? for, to make thought,
>   Your labour were in vain,

And thus I do ; and pray you to,
    As heartily as I can ;
For I must to the greenwood go,
    Alone, a banished man.

Dear Nicholas ! Here was the root of all Robin's human passion, and (it would have astonished Nicholas greatly had he known it) his burning love for his brother was protective quite as much as grateful. Nicholas had, physically, all their lives together, been his protector, and with that protection was a loving and quite unconscious patronage. Nevertheless, Robin knew all Nicholas' faults and weaknesses : how he spoke before he thought ; how, in the ardour of the moment, he would say more than he meant ; how he was generous but careless ; how he forgot a girl as soon as he had kissed her ; how he lived on the surface of life and was intellectually lazy ; how he often seemed boastful and arrogant to those who did not know him ; how he could sulk like a woman ; how he was often selfish and indulgent : all these weaknesses Robin knew and it was these weaknesses that he protected. It was even partly for these weaknesses that he loved him, and it was now as he saw his great dark bulk in the thin tissue light of the little moon that his heart went out to him and knew, with a sudden piercing dart of illumination, that if Stephen Rodney sentenced Nicholas Herries to the torture, he, Robin Herries, would hang Stephen Rodney scaffold-high on the nearest tree !

' Here is the turn ! ' Nicholas cried. ' Before the church, over the bridge and up the hill.'

To their left, ahead of them, they could see the bare ruined walls of a destroyed church or chapel. A river ran beside them and across this was a bridge. A few rough cottages stood in the now strengthening moonlight. Over the bridge and up the hill they clattered.

' There ! There ! ' Nicholas cried, whooping. ' Our uncle's strong castle ! '

To the right, nestled comfortably into the hollow of the hill, was the prettiest miniature manor-house you ever did find.

Seen, even thus, at the first sight in the moonshine, it was the naïvest, most romantic of little dwelling-places. It was built in imitation of the grand houses of the time. It had a gateway with an arch of entrance, a small walled forecourt. The house itself was in the shape of the letter H, the hall occupying the cross-stroke of the H and the other apartments in the vertical strokes of the H. The trim hedges of the garden, cut into the likeness of peacocks, dogs and monkeys, were darkly outlined against the night sky. The walls in the pale light had the colour of faint lemon-skin. The windows shone their welcome, and there, standing in the porch, was old Sir Martin Herries, waiting to greet his dear nephews. The two boys had not seen their uncle for some years and it was difficult not to smile at the quaint figure that he presented. He was an exceedingly thin old man. Down from his head to his shoulders hung long, yellow, lank locks and within this enclosure was an old bony face, the forehead seamed with a thousand wrinkles. On his head he was wearing a steeple-shaped high black hat. In spite of his age, his hair was still a pallid yellow. On his meagre chest was a heavy gold chain.

So soon as the brothers jumped from their horses a great barking of dogs broke out and the old man was in the strongest agitation, crying out: 'John! Peter! William! . . . Peter! William! John! Where are you, you rascals? Can't you mind the horses? Where are you, you malt-houses? Come out, you moon-calves! . . .' He was stamping with his feet and waving his arms. An elegant major-domo, carrying a staff and having a face with a great solemn mouth, appeared and behind him a servitor. Two hostlers bustled forward. The dogs ceased their clamour.

Sir Martin was at a moment quiet, caught both his nephews with his hands, kissed them on both cheeks and led them trippingly into the hall.

'Wait, Uncle. I must look to Juno,' Nicholas said, and went incontinently with the hostler to the stable.

Sir Martin stood staring after him.

'What a size! What a bull of a young man! What sinews! Why, Robin, he's like a giant at the fair.'

And when Nicholas returned, he must feel the muscles of his arms and his calves and finger him in the chest. But now he was all delight and happiness as he led the young men up the dark staircase to their bedroom.

' And how's all with you, lads ? How's my dear brother and sister ? How were the roses this summer at Mallory and the new Italian fountain ? Dear lads ! Dear lads . . . this is but a little house to my own fancy, but all that is in it is yours ! '

Later, washed and scented, Nicholas in his silver-grey doublet, Robin in black and rose, the two young men came down the stairs into the hall where they were to dine. An amusing sight met them, for instead of one old man to greet them there were three !

Sir Martin, his lank yellow hair now brushed and sleek, had on one side of him a stout old gentleman with a very red face and a bulbous nose, and on the other a sweet, precious old boy with silver-white hair and a face as pure and un-ravaged as a baby's. Sir Martin introduced them.

' Mr. Forster of Henditch — Mr. Michael Armstrong of Donnerthwaite. Friends of mine. . . .' Then he turned to a square-set, extremely pleasant-faced, rosy young man behind him, gravely dressed in black with a white ruff, and said : ' Mr. Anthony Pierson.'

The two old gentlemen were so greatly astonished at Nicholas that they stood with their mouths open, and there was something exceedingly comic in these three old men, side by side, motionless like images.

There were chairs, still great rarities, for Sir Martin who presided and Nicholas and Robin. Mr. Forster, Mr. Armstrong and young Mr. Pierson sat on stools. The hall itself was as clean and beautiful a little place as the boys had ever seen. Although the stone floor was strewn with rushes they were sweet-smelling and fresh. On one wall was a tapestry in colours of dark gold and vivid green and carnation showing Diana bathing. The hall was lit by candles in iron coronas suspended from the ceiling. Against the further wall was a splendid inlaid buffet of ebony mounted in silver. There was a cabinet inlaid with ivory and tortoiseshell. The oak panels of the walls were painted red with a handsome design in green. All this colour under the subdued musky light of the candles, springing into vividness on occasion with the leaping of the fire, gave a beauty and a poetry to this house that moved Robin most deeply. It seemed to him that, after riding through the sunset glow beside the still softly murmuring water, the hills gathering their evening shadow, he had passed into some good place, as it might be in his own loved Utopia, of another world. The charming faces of the three old men also delighted him. While he was feeling this, with a deep sense of happiness in his heart, he raised his eyes and met the steady gaze of young Mr. Pierson. They exchanged a long look, as though they were seeing into one another's very souls. Robin felt that some great event occurred to him at that moment.

After they had been eating for a while, four men quietly entered and, seating themselves at the end of the hall, began to play on their instruments and then to sing very softly. They sang ' Winter wakeneth all my care,' ' I sing of a maiden,' ' And wilt thou leave me thus ? ' and others. So gentle were their voices that they seemed like the melody of running water. Indeed Robin, when he had stood by his horse in the courtyard before being welcomed by his uncle, had heard the stream running on the hill most melodiously through the evening. The voices now seemed to carry on that harmony.

Nicholas, meanwhile, was more disturbed. He had begun his meal vigorously, as usual, with his hearty appetite, but when he had tasted his eel-pie, pullets and grease-gammon and pease before going on to further things, he looked about him and considered. He discovered that the three old gentlemen were talking, with quivering excitement, of the Northern Rebellion and that he, because he nodded with his mouth full, was apparently in agreement with them. This was the last thing that he wanted, for, by listening a little, his big ears pricked up over his food, he discovered that what the old gentlemen were talking, over the soft gentle melody of the madrigals, was treason of the most dangerous kind.

His Uncle Martin, waving his arms with a half-picked capon bone between his fingers, was lamenting, tears in his eyes, groans in his voice, that so many noble gentlemen had come to disaster and must chase their heels into Scotland. And why had they come to disaster ? Because the beautiful Queen, the rightful ruler of England, had been snatched out of their care and protection and hurried into a new bondage by those who had sworn to cherish purely her trust in them !

'But this is crazy treason,' thought Nicholas, looking anxiously about him. There seemed no cause for alarm. The long, bony major-domo with the large mouth was motioning with his staff to the two men-servants and the pretty maid who were carrying the dishes. The four men at the room's end were quietly playing on their viols and softly singing. Three dogs lay snoring in front of the great log fire. On the tapestry the naked Diana, in her golden-coloured skin, moved chastely to the purple stream, and as the tapestry rose ever so gently in the air her knee and thigh stirred as though in real truth she lived. No cause for alarm here ! The old red-faced boy was talking ardently of Westmorland and Cumberland, of their sympathies with the rebels, how they would have risen as one man had they but been given time. . . .

'They take it for surety,' Nicholas thought, 'that we are of their own political party.'

Then with a flash of revelation he saw it all. His uncle was a Catholic and so were these old men too. This was a Catholic house. This square-shouldered, smiling, round-faced young man Pierson was, in all probability, a Catholic priest. It had not been so five years ago. Martin Herries had not been a Catholic then. Or had he been so and kept it from his brother ?

In any case, whatever it had been then there was no doubt now. Nicholas looked anxiously across the table at young Robin. This was the last thing that he would have wished, to bring young Robin into a Catholic house, a nest of rebels against the Queen, his own very uncle too. He thought of rising and saying something in protest. But he stayed quiet. Unlike his customary habit he did nothing. A great unease seized him. An apprehension that had been with him, it seemed to him now, ever since the man on the moor had looked up at him with those pleading eyes. The candles seemed to shiver in their iron sockets, the fire to dim. He was afraid.

Meanwhile the meal had joyfully proceeded, all three old gentlemen were drunk, and Robin Herries was standing close to Anthony Pierson in the window embrasure beyond the stairs. Robin was aware now of the dark depth in Anthony Pierson's eyes. At first sight you would say ' This is a stout, commonplace, cheerful young man.' At a closer view you would deny all those adjectives. Although his cheeks were round, his limbs were hard ; although his smile was amiable, his eyes were stern and penetrating ; although outwardly he smiled, behind his smile was a passionate purpose.

Robin, at first sight of him, had loved him. This was the second love of his life, his brother being the first. There was to be a third.

Pierson's voice was soft and melodious.

' Mr. Rodney sent me a message that you would be here, Mr. Herries. I came especially to meet you. I am a Jesuit priest from Douai, a foundation recently instituted by Mr. Allen. I wish to be of service to you.'

Their eyes met once again in a concentrated gaze.

' I feel that already we are friends,' Robin said. Then he went on in a low voice : ' But I must tell you that I am not a Catholic. My parents are Lutheran and my brother here is of violent anti-Catholic opinions. He would say that he has no political or religious opinions at all, but he is ardently for the Queen and counts anyone his enemy who is against her. We were neither of us aware that our uncle had become a Catholic. We would not have come had we been aware. We have not seen our uncle for five years — and no rumour of this had reached our father.'

' And yourself ? What are *your* opinions, Mr. Herries ? ' Pierson asked him.

' I ? Oh, I am very young. I am interested in the humanities. I am, I hope, a loyal servant of Her Majesty.'

' Have you given any thought to religion ? '

' Of course I have thought of religion. I have had many talks with Stephen Rodney. I am altogether at odds with him in his eagerness for the persecution and burning of those who are not of his faith. I believe that Christ Himself would have forbidden these burnings and quarterings. . . .' Robin stopped. His voice was shaking with his emotion.

Anthony Pierson laid his broad, square hand on his arm.

' I too,' he said, ' am for gentleness and love. We will

discuss these matters again. I feel that already we are friends.
And also, if you will not think it impertinent, I am aware
that you see even now the bright pavilions on the horizon
and have begun your journey thither.'

' The bright pavilions ? ' asked Robin.

' The bright pavilions of God, the only resting-place for the
bodies and souls of blundering, weary travellers.'

He held out his hand. Robin took it.

' I need a friend,' Pierson said.

' I also,' Robin answered.

SYLVIA MASKED

IT was nearly a year before Nicholas met Philip Irvine again. In February 1570 he was fortunate enough to be a member of the *entourage* of old Lord Rottingham of Seeby on a visit to Paris. Old Rottingham was an ancient friend of Sir Michael's and, seeing Nicholas tilting with his young grandson on a frosty January morning, was so greatly pleased with his size and strength that he asked for the young man to accompany him. He went to Paris on no ordinary mission. The fact is that he was an alchemist in a private amateur way and, hearing about some very extraordinary experiments in Paris, determined to see for himself. What there happened to him, the charlatans, cutpurses and fortune-hunters who tried to inveigle him, the clever fashion in which, old as he was, he escaped the plunderers (with the exception of his one crazy fancy he was a shrewd old man), the strange back-quarters of Paris into which he ventured, the smells and obscenities, witches' Sabbaths, orgies and fairy-tales in which he was involved without any personal surrender whatever, all this would make a grand story of itself and may be told one day. There is a Journal still extant, kept by one of his secretaries, Peter Curling, filled with most interesting and unusual matter. Finally he stayed there for more than six months and Nicholas stayed there with him, receiving full board and lodging plus a number of delightful love affairs, four duels, and plenty of admirable exercise.

Of the necromancy he saw nothing; he took not the slightest interest therein. He was introduced to the French King and thought little of him. He kissed the hand of the Queen Mother and likened her, in his mind, to a queen of the Moon-Men he had seen in a fair at Edmonton. He admired her and fancied her capable of murder on a really handsome scale, which, two years later, was to prove a true prophecy.

41

He enjoyed Paris to the full, but thought poorly of Frenchmen. He, as was his rule, avoided politics, which was as well, for he was a Protestant, and Protestants, whatever the outward seeming might be, were none too popular at the French Court.

So he returned home in the autumn of the year, joyfully, healthily and eager for the English food again. When he saw his mother he squeezed her in his arms until she screamed aloud : he kissed all the maids of the household, exclaimed that Juno had proved herself better than any mare in France, and made old Hogben, the chaplain, drunk on the very first evening.

His first thought, however, as always, was for his brother. It was a grand moment when they met again after that long separation. When he had embraced him, Nicholas held Robin away from him and looked at him. He was pleased at what he saw. The boy was always a miracle to Nicholas, who was often tired of his own hulking health and size. Robin's beauty was of heaven. Here, for Nicholas, if he ever considered it, which he seldom did, was evidence of another, more spiritual world. For a swift passing instant he was ashamed of his Paris love-making, duelling and wine-bibbing.

In any case the boy was in splendid state ; his cheeks clear with health, his eyes shining with a great brightness, and love for his brother beaming from them. What had he to tell ? Not very much beyond the news of his letters. He had been quietly at home, he had visited at Sir Henry Sidney's, he had been to Court and kissed the Queen's hand. . . .

Only one thing that he said disturbed Nicholas. Robin mentioned Anthony Pierson.

' Anthony Pierson ? '

' Last Christmas. Don't you remember ? At our uncle's in Cumberland.'

' Oh yes, a stout, red-faced young man. He was a priest ? '

' Yes. A Jesuit from Douai.'

' And so ? '

' We were friends at that first meeting. He has been in England on several occasions.'

At sight of Nicholas' thundering brow Robin burst out laughing.

'I'm not a Catholic yet, Nick.'

'Priests are not liked and soon will be less so.'

'He is only my friend — not my religious adviser.'

'He would like to be, though. I know them. I hate all priests.'

'You should meet him,' Robin said.

Now it happened that Sir Michael had a brother Henry, a year younger than himself. This Henry was as unlike Michael as a brother may be and still have the same father and mother. He represented, however, from babyhood, a persistent element in the Herries' character, for, so soon as he could toddle, he was out to make all the material profit he might from his fellow human beings. Michael was always a gay, singing, merry kind of fellow, like his son Nicholas-to-be, and an easy prey to brother Henry's commercial mind. He bought from Henry toys of no value at all at inordinate prices ; entered, mildly and innocently, into little commercial arrangements always to his own disadvantage ; and was involved in small usuries that, being no mathematician, he never properly understood.

Henry grew up into a world ripe and ready for active minds like his. After the dissolution of the monasteries, there was plenty of land to be bought, by men in the right favour, for a song. Henry was always in the right favour where anyone important was concerned, and balanced himself marvellously during the difficult reigns of Edward and Mary : lending for handsome return, buying sharply at exactly the right moment and achieving the name everywhere of an excellent, trustworthy man of business. In the early years of Elizabeth he might, had he wished, have risen to a high place at Court — Cecil had his eye upon him — but, like so many Herries before and after him, he failed at the highest flights, wishing always for safety. He was twice married, first to Mary Trowneer, who brought him an excellent dowry, two fair sons, and a daughter, Barbara ; and, secondly, after an interval, to Grace Clyde, who bore him, when he was forty-four years of age, a daughter, Sylvia.

He had a fine country place at Chelsea and a town house

close to the Temple Gardens, where a little later, in 1576, he was to be greatly annoyed at the easy lease by Sir Christopher Hatton of the garden and orchard for the rent of a red rose, ten loads of hay and ten pounds per annum. To miss a simple thing like this was really an agony to him.

By now he was sixty years of age but still burly, rosy-faced and vigorous. He was outwardly a cheerful, welcoming companion, but the habit of taking advantage of others had withered his impulses and made him suspicious of even his own family. His wife had suffered for many years from stomach disorders, and any and every quack was at her service. His elder daughter, Barbara, now the wife of Tobias Garland, he saw but seldom. Of the boys, Edward was now thirty-four and Sidney thirty. Edward was as sharp and thrifty as his father, but Sidney had an unfortunate liking for low company, with whom he was jolly in a rather nervous and irritable fashion.

Of Sylvia, Nicholas and Robin knew little. They had not seen her for four years and then she had been but twelve years of age and quite uninteresting to growing young men.

For, sad to say, there had been a quarrel between the two families. Money meaning so much to Henry, he quite naturally patronized a brother who had managed to secure so little of it. But Michael was not an easy man to patronize, and one evening at the Chelsea manor there had been so unfortunate a quarrel and such hard words had been spoken that Michael had incontinently ordered his horses and ridden, there and then, to London. The quarrel between the brothers had not been healed, largely because neither party wished for the healing. Henry was always afraid that Michael would ask money of him, a thing that Michael never considered doing, and Michael was weary of the chaffing, superior joking of his self-satisfied brother. Nor had the ladies cared for one another since Nicholas' mother had told her sister-in-law to give up her quacks and nostrums and see whether her health was not therefore the better.

To Nicholas, his uncle, aunt and cousins were simply one great joke. He knew that Edward and Sidney were physically terrified of him and he would have enjoyed terrifying them

further. He had not the time to bother his head about
them.

It happened, however, that after his return from Paris he
heard, on a number of occasions, of the beauty of his cousin
Sylvia, now a girl of sixteen. He hoped that he might see her
somewhere in town or country, but his curiosity was not
satisfied and grew therefore the greater. Then, early in
December, he learned that his uncle was giving a masked ball
in his town house. Nicholas decided to go and he persuaded
Robin to go with him. They slept the night at the ' White
Hart ' in Southwark, and the next evening, cloaked and
shrouded, their masks close to hand, started on their adventure.

Distrusting their waterman's ability to shoot London
Bridge, which was dangerous not only from the breadth of
the piers and narrowness of the arches but also because of the
corn-mills that had been built in some of the openings, they
insisted on being landed above the bridge at the Old Swan
stairs.

Many and many a time had Robin crossed the river at
night and always there was something miraculous in that
journey. The swift flowing of the river, the clever handling
of the boat by the waterman, the craft that shot so gallantly
past them, the freshness of the breeze, the sense that he was
now at the very heart of the city that was surely the greatest
in the whole world — all these things elated and delighted
him. But on this night some spirit stirred in him of wonder,
of anticipation, that he had never known before. He did not
especially care for this adventure. He had thought it, from the
first, a foolish one and was sure that some family crisis would
come from it, for how could Nicholas, with his great size,
hope that his mask would disguise him ? He disliked his uncle
and two cousins as strongly as it was in his power to dislike
anybody and had no desire to be in communication with them
again. Nevertheless, as he sat there, his cloak lightly about
him against the cold, he was aware of an exulting happiness.

The night sky was thick with stars and against this radiance
the towers and roofs of the buildings on the other bank rose
in a delicacy of moth-silver chastity. The icy air, the swift
current of the water that caught the stars and the path of a

gold-plated moon in its ripples, brought his beloved Utopian world straight into his heart. Here was purity, a world of silver sharpness, space, and only the sounds that liberate stillness.

But there was more than that. He seemed to be on the eve of a great event. He wished to say something to his brother who now, like a little boy, was asking the waterman a lot of foolish questions. (' Aye, for a pin and a web there's nothing but cutting. A friend of my mother's had it and was in darkness a twelvemonth.' 'The tide's high. How deep is the water here ? I'd swim you to the bank for a silver sixpence. And your sixpences will be debased, I warrant. . . . Nay, not married ? You know a fine girl with the naked Indians in Fleet Street ? How fine ? . . . If that's a whitlow it must be cut. . . . I can tell you a surgeon — he'll do it for you for a passage or two across the river. . . .')

All men of their hands — watermen, draymen, farmers, hostlers, wrestlers and bear-wardens — loved Nicholas. First they were flattered by his size, to think they were allowed to converse with so prodigious a young man, and secondly Nicholas, although careful enough of his dignity if it were improperly challenged, was friend to all the world.

And so Robin did not disturb him but wondered why he had the sense of excitement and whether he might not sail down the river, out to the open seas, and discover for himself some of these countries of gold trees and spices and miraculous birds of which everyone was always talking.

They landed at the steps and Nicholas, by the light of the boat's lantern, examined the young waterman's whitlow very seriously, paid him the due and started up the dark miry pathway.

They were now at once in another world. The thick overhanging buildings almost touched above their heads. There was no lighting of any kind and both men had their hands on their rapiers, ready for cut-throats and vagabond soldiers and any lazy fellow who, by a sudden snatch, might obtain the price of a night's lodging. They had been going but a pace or two when an eerie cry broke the night's silence. It was a cry of agony but did not disturb them in the slightest, for it might be a murder, or a man in his sleep, or someone dying from the plague.

The plague indeed was never far away, nor was it difficult to understand the reason, for the stinks and waves of recurrent nastiness would have made them vomit were they not so used to the conditions as never to give them a thought. Proclamations were for ever being issued by magistrates — ' Where the infection is entered to cause fires to be made in the streets every morning and evening, wherein should be burnt frank-incense, pitch or some other sweet thing ' or ' to command that all excrements and filthy things voided from the infected places be not cast into streets or into sewers that are daily used to make drink or dress meat ' or ' No surgeons or barbers that use to let blood should cast it into the street or rivers. Nor should vaults nor privies be emptied therein, for it is a most dangerous thing.'

But no proclamations made the slightest difference, especially as the plague was the Act of God and it was not for the human soul to work against God's will. So they splashed with their leather boots through squash and squeak of filth and ordure, came on a dead dog under a lantern, swollen to three times his size, and found an old man in a doorway on the point of death from starvation.

Very heartily and in the most excellent spirits they pushed through the gates into the forecourt of their uncle's house, which was the scene of handsome bustle and confusion. The music could be heard coming from within the lighted house, horses were neighing, figures laughing and chattering passed up the torch-illuminated steps.

' There is something strange with me to-night,' Robin thought. ' I have known many scenes like this before, and yet the light and the dark, the sound of the music, the soothing sound of the falling fountain, these things are striking me newly as though I had been born but an hour ago.'

The figures, passing up and down the steps, were like ghosts as though they rose from the stone slabs of the court ; the lighted windows of the house were unsubstantial, as though made from air. For a moment he stood and looked back. The water of the fountain hung suspended in glittering drops against the torchlight. Then he put on his mask and entered.

In a small withdrawing-room they pulled off their leather boots, laid down their cloaks and appeared in their full splendour, Nicholas with a ruff larger than the immediate fashion, a doublet of rose and silver and silver hose, Robin in dark purple slashed with white which marvellously suited his slim body. A moment later they were in the great hall that was hung with tapestries. In the gallery the musicians were already playing. Henry Herries and his wife stood on the dais below the gallery, and the guests, as they arrived, moved to the dais, bowed low and then mingled with the crowd that was already dancing. The hall was lit by immense candelabra that glittered with a thousand facets. Servants crowded, looking over the gallery's balustrade at the scene and pointing out to one another the guests they recognised under the masks. Close beside Henry Herries was a long, lean, dough-faced man with lank hair and unmasked. This was Mr. Phineas Thatcher, Henry's confidential secretary. His long nose had once been pulled by Nicholas, who scornfully detested him. He belonged to the extreme sect of Puritans whose party was fast growing in the country. He was extremely able and, like his master, balanced nicely both his politics and his religion. It was said, however, that he was secretly an ardent fanatic.

When Nicholas and Robin advanced to the dais Nicholas was certain that Thatcher at once recognized him. He made no movement and spoke no word. The volte was in progress, a very difficult dance at which Nicholas prided himself. It consisted of a turn of the body with two steps, a high spring, and a pause with feet close together. Nicholas, in spite of his big body, was an excellent dancer, and as the French Court preferred, at this time, the volte to any other dance, he had but just known six months of constant practice in the most excellent company. He prided himself especially on his ' spring,' holding himself rigidly and alighting ' like a little bird,' as he said, ' delicately with no sound,' his two feet rigidly together.

So now, facing a beautiful lady with hair so flaxen as to

be almost white, he gazed into her eyes so intently that her bosom heaved and her hands fluttered.

'Sir, I am sure that I know you.'

He sprang magnificently, alighted delicately, then in the pause that followed said :

'You are right. I have come for what you promised me.'

'You have grown in the month since we met.'

'It is my doublet.' They turned together, did their two steps, leapt and once more faced one another. 'My new doublet,' he repeated. 'I was not wearing it on the last time.'

She giggled a little.

'No. Indeed you were not. You were wearing . . .'

He smiled. 'Exactly. These are clothes of courtesy. Those . . .'

'You were not dancing.'

'I was at your feet.'

She smiled.

'Your chin was not so round.'

'You saw it from a different angle.'

The dance was over. She took his arm. They vanished into the crowd. He knew that he had never seen her before and wondered how, without her mask, she would be. Now, close to her, he was afraid that her bosom was too massive.

Robin was not dancing. He had gone quietly to a pillar at the end of the hall and, leaning against it, in comparative obscurity, watched the scene. He could not rid himself of the sense that he was taking part in a fantasy, a masque. He was well-accustomed to that experience of the soul when the material world seems only a thin covering for the more real world beneath it. This sense would come upon him suddenly and he would even touch the stuff of his clothes to be certain of his own bodily existence. Music had especially this spiritual power over him, and now the viols seemed more human than the human voices and the sudden cry of the flute had had a ghostly urgency. The masked figures seemed to him so unsubstantial that he felt that, if he cried out, they would vanish, like trailing shimmering silk, into the air : the purple of shadows, the bright green like a parrot's wing, the rich rose brocade like a cloud of evening. One cry and they would be gone.

With this unreality was still this real sense of urgent, expectant happiness. Something was about to happen to him : something of an utter transcendent reality.

He moved, he eased his mask, raised his head, and saw, close to him, almost touching him, a girl.

She stood, all by herself, watching the dancers. She was no more than a child. She seemed indeed a baby behind her white silk mask, her slim immature neck inside the enormous ruff.

She was magnificently dressed — over-dressed, Robin at once saw. The first thing he felt about her — he was afterwards to smile tenderly at his accurate perception — was a certain pathos. She was over-dressed and a sort of symbol of all the over-grandeur of this ball. Robin had realized this at once, even in the courtyard. His uncle, the New Rich, flaunting splendour without taste. The musicians, for example, wore a crimson slashed with gold that hurt the eye. The candelabra were too vast. The colours of the tapestries, blue and orange and violet, were too crude.

So was this child. In the front of her lovely dark brown hair was a jewelled ship. The ship was of emerald and the sails of clear sapphires. Her farthingale was in a most extravagant style, fantastically enlarged at the hips. Her little breasts were squeezed into the stiff-pointed bodice. Her sleeves were cut and slashed and crossed with small puffings. The colour of the brocaded farthingale was a faint, very lovely rose, studded with pearls. The bodice was silver and the slashings of the sleeves were silver. In this elaborate exaggerated dress the child stood, staring at the dancers, her mouth open, as still as a little image. Under the white silk mask her childish excited mouth was a living protest against her anonymity. Robin felt that if, at another time, she were veiled from head to foot, and still he saw that mouth he would know her. The lips were beautiful, natural, healthy red, her cheeks, too, rosy with health. There was no sign on her of paint and powder, becoming very popular with ladies. Her emerald ship, her ruff, the cut of her farthingale and sleeves, the lavish scattering of the pearls about the rose brocade, these were exaggerations, but within them she was radiant, untouched, Nature herself.

She said aloud : ' After all the lessons he dances more oafishly than ever.'

She was speaking to herself. She made an effort over the word ' oafishly ' and even stammered very slightly. She saw Robin staring at her and raised her head with a great assumption of haughtiness. It was clear that she hated to have been heard speaking to herself. She began to move away, her head so erect that it surely must have hurt her.

Robin said : ' Please don't go away.'

' Why should I not ? ' she asked, and her voice was enchanting, a child's voice assuming maturity, very clear and bell-like.

She looked at him and smiled, and Robin loved her for that smile. It was quite clear that she considered him something worth staring at. In fact the two of them stood gazing at one another.

' So we meet again,' Robin said tenderly. It was the official, recognized opening at all masked balls.

' No.' She shook her head very decisively. ' We have never met before.' She smiled once more. ' And that is not curious, for this is my first ball.'

' It will, after to-night, be my first ball also,' Robin answered.

She came closer to him. She was utterly sincere in her honest gaze.

' I *have* seen you before, I think. And I know your voice. But not at a ball. A long time ago.'

Robin himself thought that, in some way, she was familiar to him. But not like this — and, yes, as she said, a long time ago. But it could not be so very long, for even now she was only a child.

' Why are you not dancing ? ' he asked her.

' The volte,' she answered very grandly, ' is not my sort of dancing. I prefer the pavane.'

' Will you dance the pavane with me ? '

' Yes,' she said, suddenly quite shy. ' If it is soon,' she added. ' I am not to stay very late.'

They continued to stare at one another.

' Will you not take your mask off for one moment ? '

His hand, moving as it seemed of its own volition, touched her sleeve.

'Perhaps we *do* know one another.'

She laughed and shook her head until the ship rocked as though on a stormy sea.

'No. Not before the general unmasking. They say it is unlucky.'

'You need not fear,' Robin said. 'Bad luck is not for you.'

She gave a sharp cry.

'Oh, you must not say that!' She was shaking her head. The little ship, loosened, fell to the floor. A tiny sapphire rolled to Robin's feet.

He picked the ship up and gave it her. She held it in her hand, looking at it.

'It was my father's Christmas gift. I don't know why. I never liked it. It's gaudy. I shall find Boniface to take it and put it away.'

He had the tiny sapphire in his hand.

'Then I may keep this?'

'If you care to. It's nothing.' She turned twice round on her high heels. 'Now — am I not better without the ship?'

'Very much better.'

The dancers were moving forward. The musicians struck up. It was a pavane.

The whole company was now formed in a great procession and in this Robin and the child took their places. He watched her now, delighting in her solemnity and gravity. He saw that she was widely recognized and was treated with ceremony. Who could she be? Why was it that he knew her and yet did not know her? She could not be the daughter of any high person at Court. No one accustomed to Court practices would so overdress her. And yet what a little lady she was! How criminal to emphasize her childishness with that exaggerated ruff! Nevertheless, how she carried her head with its lovely hair, so far lovelier now without the bejewelled ship. And with what a child's motion she sometimes raised her little hand to ease the mask that pinched her nose! With what perfect grace, too, she moved, two simple steps and a double one forward, the same number backwards. Again he had the sense that this was a dream and these dream-figures, the waves of mingled colours rising and falling while the musicians blared with their hautboys and trumpets. How exquisite that pause, when the wave is frozen into stillness, every figure carved from a jewelled form ; a great dignity and power seems to sweep through the air. ' We are the kings and queens of this world, transmuted into power by our terrible immobility ! ' Then, quite suddenly, the last movement, the galliard, come from the French Court to make the pavane less dull, all lively briskness, although not as yet allowing that frivolous kicking of the heels in the air, the capriole.

The music sang, the lights poured down, Robin had her hand in his.

' Soon, soon you shall unmask,' he whispered.

Two trumpets rang out. The dancers stayed. They moved back into a serried rank. The doors to the right of the dais opened and the masquers entered.

First came four blackamoors in silver, then the ' pageant,' or stage on wheels, moving with much clumsy creaking, and on it the captive Queen of the Moon, a lovely lady in scales of silver, weeping because she was captive. Four giants held dominion over her. The ' pageant ' stayed in front of the dais and one of the giants spouted verse, declaring his great powers, and summoning his men who presently appeared, a band of wild men naked to the waist and painted in horrible reds and greens. After this a distant trumpet sounded, a knight clad from head to feet in gold armour stated that he would rescue the Lady of the Moon, was defied by the giants, summoned his men who were likewise in gold armour. The knight challenged one of the giants to single combat, and a great battle followed in which the giant was worsted, whereupon the giant's men rushed upon the knight's men and there was a fine comic battle. The giants were slain, the knight mounted the ' pageant ' and claimed the Queen of the Moon.

He stood forward and cried : ' We command you all — our true and liege subjects — unmask ! '

At that, with a common gesture, the whole company unmasked. Trumpets blew a peal, the ' pageant,' rocking the Queen and knight on its path, moved away, a small blackamoor, alone now in the scene, stepped forward, declared that

C

love, as always it must, had won, that only one Queen in the
known world might command such devotion, and that now,
to please her, they would drink and feast in Her Honour!

The trumpets blared. The company shouted.

At the unmasking Robin turned to his child.

'Sylvia!'

'Cousin Robin!'

'It is four years. . . . You must forgive me.'

She looked at him with considering gravity.   'I know.
You have been very wrong not to have visited us.'

'Nicholas and I . . .'

'I don't care for Nicholas. He laughs at us. Mr. Thatcher
hates him because once he pulled his nose. But you, Robin,
are quite another thing. You were always kind. You read
to me once out of a book. Do you remember? Sir Thomas
More's *Utopia*. I can recall it exactly. It was in the Chelsea
garden and we could hear the apples fall on the grass. You
said you would read often and I believed you. I know now
that men are always false. . . .'

She walked, her hand quite confidently in his, chattering as
a little bird sings. They moved up the high staircase towards
the gallery where they were to eat. Robin knew that he had
been right in his expectation of happiness.

Nicholas, on his side, had plenty to think about. He had
recognized, immediately, that the knight in gold armour was
Philip Irvine. His mind flew instantly back to their last
meeting. In a sense, through the whole year, through all the
gaieties and adventures of Paris, his mind had never left it.
He was tied to the event with a conviction of implacable hatred.
To see him now, flaunting his beauty in his gold armour
before this admiring world, roused in Nicholas, who was not,
by nature, at all jealous or grudging, a sort of savage anger.
Irvine was in truth superb with his perfect shape, his dark
scorning face under the gold helmet. His voice too was
beautiful, low and ringing, understanding the rhythm and
colour of the poetry that he spoke, as Nicholas would never
understand them. Nicholas felt his own clumsiness, the

uncouth size and height of his limbs. He was always uncomfortable in grand clothes such as he was wearing now.
Irvine wore his glories to perfection. Nicholas was best in
shirt and hose, wrestling or digging or fighting with his fists,
or, in the country at home, carrying a child on his shoulder,
walking in from the harvest, or shooting in the long garden
between the clipped hedges at a toy pigeon, or lifting the garden-
barrel filled with weeds and emptying it on to the bonfire that
blazed in orange-gold to the pigeon-cote beyond the lawn.

It was the old antithesis. But *why* should he hate him so ?
It was, perhaps, because Irvine had made him, for the only
time in his life, betray a helpless man's trust. The shame of
that would never leave him as long as he lived. He had
asked himself again and again what he should have done for
that blue-eyed man ? Should he have jumped from his horse
at the first and defied Irvine ? The ignominy of it was that
Irvine had only been doing his duty. For months after, such
scenes, and worse scenes, had been repeated again and again
all over the North. It was perhaps the only occasion when
Elizabeth showed what was not truly in her cautious, considering, often generous character, real vindictive vengeance.
It left its mark for ever on those parts of England, that
Northern Rebellion !

Yes, but no matter the general case. What should *he*,
Nicholas Herries, have done ? He could see the dog leap now
on Gascoigne's back — and he was looking now into the
handsome, vain eyes of Irvine. There was not a shadow of
a space between them ! It was early morning. The candles
guttered on the long table of the small picture gallery where
some of the young men had gathered for a last joke and drink
before going home. There were perhaps a dozen of them in
silver and crimson and jade green, swinging their beautiful legs
from the table, most of them very drunk, all proclaiming their
pride in their Queen, their country, their future, themselves.

For, behind the noise and the drunkenness and the singing
of ribald songs and the heat and the long mirrors swaying
as the servant-men jogged them, carrying the liquor, and the
pictures of past and present Herries that Henry had had
painted (most of them very bad), and the splendid clock, with

the silver moon and gold stars and old man grinning in mother-
of pearl, that chimed tunes, and the bawdy picture in needlework of Susanna and the Elders ; behind all the trash and
traffic of the current world, there was a great fiery spirit of
new-born patriotism in the bosoms of these young men.
There were many, many thousands like them. For their
country had, in the years before Elizabeth came to its throne,
reached its lowest ignominy. There was little army, less navy.
Calais had been lost. A king of a foreign country, hated and
hating, had pushed his long nose contemptuously down the
London streets. There had been burnings and quarterings
at the order of foreign priests and Englishmen sold to Spain.
Shame, shame on a conquered, mocked country that had once
been great !

And then God had sent a Jael, a Princess who redeemed
them. From the moment that that red-haired, lantern-
jawed, cold-lipped girl had taken the government into her
hand, her people had hoped again. And now, within so short
a while, again there was a navy, the beginning of an army,
money was being saved, debased coin was called in — and
more than that, Englishmen were going out once more into
the world taking all that they were strong enough to take.
Never mind if what they took belonged to someone else !
He who is strongest seizes what he may. The power of the
mailed fist ! These young men sat there, stood there, shouted
there, crying their Queen's name, with a great joy once more
in their hearts, because the future belonged to them. God
was with them, their leader was God's servant, the world was
at their feet for the capture.

So, three hundred and fifty years later, a great body of
young patriots of another country would once again feel the
same exultations !

Although there were not more than twenty there, they were
representative. Edward Herries, very drunk, but his sharp
little eyes on the watch for an advantage. A strange fellow,
Falk Herries, son of a small squire in Wiltshire, a thin man with
a slight hump of one shoulder ; sardonic, able, believing in
nothing and nobody. Kennet Herries, a big, stout young man,
crimson-faced, noisy and boastful. Charles Lacey, a young

elegant poet and dandy. Tristram Cornwallis, a splendid
young soldier, a great favourite at Court ; Robert Rockage,
a serious young man and said to be a Catholic, a recent friend
of Robin's ; and Philip Irvine himself.

Nicholas, drunk enough to be noisily gay, was so close to
him that the stiff edgings of their doublets touched.

' Mr. Irvine — after a year we meet again.'

Irvine, very handsome in black and silver, was cordial.

' Why, Mr. Herries, I was hoping for a meeting. But you
have been in France, I hear.'

Nicholas nodded.

' Yes. You have not been North ? '

' No. That was but a temporary duty.'

' Your arm is recovered ? '

' It was but a scratch. We must have another meeting.
Of course a friendly one. I bear no grudge.'

Nicholas smiled. ' At any time. In any place I am at
your service.'

After that, for a while, he knew very little clearly. His
uncle had spoken to him with an almost over-eager kindness,
saying that he was glad that his nephews had honoured his
little entertainment, that he hoped that now again he would
see them constantly, that relations in these difficult days must
hold together. Nicholas had solemnly agreed to all these
courtesies. He was exceedingly popular with the young men.
They made him perform feats of strength ; he stripped to his
shirt and lifted a table. He raised young Rockage in one
hand and Charles Lacey in the other. He drank, he sang
choruses, he shouted again and again the health of their
Mistress. . . . And then the scene was confused. The candles
rushed like the wind across the table and burnt in one glorious
conflagration from which a spire of light ran rocking to the
naked cherubs painted on the ceiling. But the most disturbing thing was the mirrors that swayed backwards and
forwards, redoubled themselves so that heads of hair, noses
and mouths, ruffs and slashed doublets, multiplied, were connected and disconnected. He moved to a mirror to steady it
and stood there, rocking on his feet, seeing his own face,
flushed and wavering. He raised a hand, and, stepping aside,

saw the long, dark figure of Irvine, quite still in the mirror watching him. From Irvine's body all that queer conglomeration of arms and thighs and heads ran in a stream of colour into the candlelight, but Irvine himself was complete and immaculate in the snowy ruff, his thin brown hand resting on the gold hilt of his rapier.

A mad impulse to challenge him seized Nicholas. He jerked round to face the room, and then saw that Irvine was not there. He stumbled forward searching the room. Irvine was gone.

He was sober enough to realise that something else was doing. There had mounted on to the table, that was slippery with spilt wine, two men, both stripped to the waist. One was a big hulking fellow, with heavy breasts, a thick neck, black hair on his chest, that Nicholas recognized — a servant of Kennet Herries. The other he had never seen before : fair-haired, white-skinned, blue-eyed. They were to wrestle, there on the table. Bets were being laid. The young men crowded about the table. Nicholas, eagerly pushing forward, wagered on the fair young man. Then he held his breath. The lights steadied and hung in a circle above the two men, who advanced, hugged, strained, almost slipped, steadied themselves again, stayed, tight in one another's arms. Then the young man, his head raised, jerked with his leg ; the other staggered, tried to hold himself, then crashed over the table-edge, falling into Nicholas' arms.

He held the fellow for a moment, set him on his feet, where he stood, shamefacedly apologizing to his irate master.

The young man jumped lightly from the table.

' You did that well,' Nicholas said.

' Of course. There are two parts of England where they can wrestle — Cornwall and Cumberland. I come from one of them ? '

' From Cornwall ? '

' No. From Cumberland, sir.'

Someone had thrown the young man his shirt and he was now quickly and deftly buttoning it.

' From Cumberland,' Nicholas said eagerly.

' Yes, Mr. Herries.'

' You know me then ? '

The young man grinned.

' I come from a place Rosthwaite, near Keswick. I know your uncle.'

' My uncle ? I was there a year ago.'

' Yes, sir. I saw you.'

' You saw me ? '

' Riding away in the morning from your uncle's house. It was nine of the morning — a frosty, clear day.'

' You remember that ? '

' You are not lightly forgotten, sir.'

' What is your name ? '

' Gilbert Armstrong.'

' What are you doing in London ? '

' Your uncle is interested in the Newlands mines. I came down a week ago with letters. I return to-morrow. I am in service with Mr. Cowperthwaite in Keswick. Mr. Cowperthwaite knows your uncle well.'

Nicholas caught his arm.

' Do you know a girl — a German girl — in Keswick, called Catherine Hodstetter ? '

' No, sir.'

' Do you ride alone to-morrow ? '

' Yes, sir.'

' I will go with you. I will ride with you.'

He was sober now, longing with a passionate desire for that freshness instead of this wine-stink ; the moon rising above the moth-grey hills rather than this candlelight. . . .

There was more than that. Soon, in a month or so, he was to take over the charge of his father's property. His free young manhood would be ended. This should be his last gesture of freedom.

' By Jesu, I'll go with you. When do you start ? '

' I have some business with Mr. Herries in the morning. I should be ready by eleven forenoon.'

' I will meet you by Durham House, in the Strand.'

He clapped the man heartily on the shoulder and, now exceedingly happy, his head quite clear, he turned away to find Robin.

He found him standing in the doorway. The brothers smiled.

'Where were you, Robin ? I looked for you.'

'I was in Paradise,' Robin said, 'for a little. And, having discovered it, I mean shortly to return.'

THE MINERS

NICHOLAS HERRIES soon saw that, in this young Gilbert
Armstrong, he had found a companion after his own heart
and mind. During the ride up North they had many op-
portunities of mutual discovery. Now Nicholas was a man
who must see and feel a thing truly to believe in it. No
good to tell him that something existed because someone else
had seen it. True probably that men with three heads and
two fundaments lived on the other side of the sea, that pearls
were as common there as potatoes, and naked girls shining
like brown leather were your humble servants, but he must
see first for himself. He would in fact have been off on a
voyage of discovery with Drake or Hawkins or Grenville long
ago had it not been that his father depended on him to take
over the property and become head man of the house.

And so with everything. It was of no use talking to him of
the next world or a lump of coal that *might* become a lump
of gold or poems that told you about King Arthur or the Queen
of the Amazons. He must have reality. So it was apparently
with Armstrong, who was as sensible a young man as you
would find in England. He showed his common sense in the
first place by an instant worship of Nicholas. When they had
to share a bed at an inn, Gilbert was never tired of admiration
of Nicholas' thews and sinews. He had never before seen a
man so great physically who at the same time was so adroit,
lithe in his movements, delicate in his footwork. He taught
Nicholas all that he knew of wrestling, and this was to be
useful later. But it was not only, not chiefly, physical prowess
that began to bind the two men together. In all incidents and
crises they seemed to think alike ; Nicholas the master, Gilbert
the servant, but beneath that social difference the beginning of
a firm friendship.

61

Nothing very epochal occurred in their travels : there was a pedlar who was surely a Roman priest and carried in his buttock-pocket a Bull against the Queen, there were the vagrant soldiers who broke a window in the hostelry at Newbury and were put in the stocks, there was the thief hanging on the gibbet at the cross-roads by Doncaster whose nose was being pecked by gigantic crows as they passed, there were the two witches ducked to their death at the little village on the moor towards York city, and, best of all, there was the landlord of the scurvy inn below the Pennines who crept into Nicholas' room at night to steal from his bag, was caught by him, stripped as bare as the day he was born and tied to the pump in his courtyard for the rest of the night until he was found there by the maids in the morning purple with cold.

In these and all else Gilbert Armstrong showed admirable common sense, anticipating Nicholas in his own ideas about everything. He thought, as all true Englishmen thought, that no foreigner was worth a plate of pease, that everything the Queen did was right. What pleased him about the Queen was that she took her people into her confidence, that she talked to them as though she were their own brother or sister. He liked the way that she boxed the ears and pulled the noses of her courtiers and bishops. He liked her for her tempers and meannesses and flirtations and sudden generosities. He liked her because she was always a Queen and yet she was a common human being as well. He neither knew nor cared whether she was truly a virgin or no, whether she had been to bed with Robert Dudley or no. That always seemed to him a woman's own business. He asked Nicholas why it was that he and his brother had not sought service at Court. Surely no one in the realm would make so splendid a Queen's Pensioner as Nicholas ! Gilbert always asked questions directly, with no apologies for possible impertinences. He spoke as man to man.

'The Court ? ' asked Nicholas. 'What would I do with the Court ? My brother possibly. Can you see *me* twiddling my thumbs and bending my buttocks, and remembering my Latin tags and telling the Queen, with her black teeth and the rest, that I sigh my heart out to go to bed with her ? God forgive me, I mean nothing against Her Majesty, at whose nod I'd fight the whole of Spain if need be — but I'm no courtier, Gilbert. Fine clothes sit ill on my big body, my tongue's too clumsy for compliments. It's a game you must play, the Court game, with smiles for your enemy, and down on your hams to those you despise, and waiting in corridors and whispering for advancement.

'What I like, Gilbert, is an adventure like this — riding Juno on a fair road with all the world around you, three days and nights in that strange little town where you live and then back home again. I *must* be on the move, exercising my body and speaking to men I can trust and being friendly with women.'

'What do you think of the Roman religion?' Gilbert asked.

'Why, I think very evilly of it because it conspires against the Queen.'

'Do you think, Mr. Herries, there's another world besides this one?'

'I don't bother my head about it. Time enough when we get there.' But he sighed. He was thinking, as he always was, of Robin.

Gilbert interested Nicholas greatly with all that he had to say about the country life as he had found it. He spoke strongly and rather scornfully of the ' new gentlemen ' who were rising everywhere. Almost anyone now, by a little usury and cheating, could bear the charges of a gentleman, could have a coat of arms, and then be called ' master ' with the title ' esquire.' And with them were the new ' yeomen ' who were farmers of their own holdings but also farmed the squire's land, kept servants and grew rich. ' The new rich ' were in fact the subject of Gilbert's strong disgust. Nicholas thought of his Uncle Henry. He mentioned him.

'You had come to town on his business?'

'Yes, he has purchased some interest in the Newlands mine. Under the Queen of course. But then he's of a fine family. That's another matter.'

'There's none of our family ever been wealthy before,' Nicholas said.

'I have no belief in money,' Gilbert said, 'nor in great possessions. I will have a little house and a good horse, and my sons shall make their own way.'

'You will be married then?' Nicholas asked him.

'When the day comes. But I will have my freedom first.'

He complained that everywhere in England now they must be building, so that all the trees were cut down and the beautiful forests and wild life disappearing. He had no liking either for those new-fangled chimneys that everyone must be putting up, and thought that they gave men colds and rheumatism. Smoke hardened both timbers and men, keeping colds away.

But his principal and most vehement complaint was against the bodgers and loaders. The bodgers bought up all the stocks of corn and then raised the price so that the poor man could not buy his weekly needs. Already the land was taken from the poor man who had once, under the monasteries, in the good old days, enjoyed free use of it. And the bodgers were terrible men, he said, practising every kind of deceit. They kept the corn until it was musty, and then the poor man was forced to buy it and died of the plague. There were altogether too many dealers, and as there were no standard weights and measures, these dealers bought by the larger measure and sold by the smaller one.

In fact Gilbert did not like this new world that was springing up about him. England would soon be covered with houses and the middleman would make all the profit and country life would be spoilt. These carriages and coaches that were just coming in would make it so that you would have no peace any more and could not keep yourself safe from strangers. It was a noisy, cheap, common new world, and money was the only thing that mattered.

As to himself, he told Nicholas that he was the only son of his mother, a widow. His father had been a Cumbrian farmer who had been killed resisting Scottish raiders near Carlisle. His mother was of better birth, coming from a good Devon family — not that he was ashamed of his father's family. He was prouder of it than anything. His mother, an old lady of over sixty years, lived in a little house outside Keswick.

Nicholas felt once again the strange elation that he had known before as they rode over from Penrith. It was midway through the winter afternoon and the hills in the distance had a faint haze of sun upon their tops. Below them it was dark and the sky above them was black. Only this line of sunlight caught the heads of the hills, which were without snow, but seemed to tremble between the two darknesses as though showing their pleasure at the unexpected light.

They pulled in their horses for the moment and looked down at the Lake that was more faintly dark than the surrounding valley. The silence was so intense that they did not themselves speak. Any sound seemed like a desecration.

Nicholas slept at the inn, where he was greeted like an old friend. He was determined not, on this occasion, to visit his uncle. He had but three days to spend and they should be all his own.

In the morning of the following day they rode over to Newlands. When they had come down the little path and turned into the valley they were almost surrounded by hills. A thin rain was falling, a caressing rather than an unpleasant rain. With a breeze behind it the texture of the rain was like a curtain, and the clouds seemed to move with it so that there was constant stirring in the sky, and the hills seemed to shift with the sky. The bleating of sheep, the running of a stream, filled this little enclosed world with sound and with freshness. Life was everywhere, and an important life. Feeling that, you lost the strained insistence of your own personality. You were part of something larger than yourself.

As they rode slowly up the valley Nicholas saw that in the sky, through the rain, a circumference of pale gold was forming. Across this, sweeps of vaporous grey cloud were driving, but the gold grew ever more tensely powerful, and phantom sheets of light, as though thrown by a sun infinitely distant, spread affectionately upon the shoulders of the hills. The rain still sheeted the air, but in the valley there was a reflected glow as though from a conflagration many miles away. It was against this rain-driven iridescence that he saw men standing, buildings behind them and a mountain peaked like a horn (or so in that light it seemed) above them.

By some trick of light these men appeared gigantic : they were inhuman guardians of some protected sacred territory. Then, closely approached, they diminished, and, at that same moment, the sun broke through in the sky, a round disc of pale glowing white, and on the fell-side there sprang forward a stretch of crying green brighter than glass.

Nicholas stayed Juno, jumped off, let her nuzzle against his chest and waited.

Two of the men started forward and Gilbert Armstrong went to meet them. They shook hands, and then stood, apparently gazing at Nicholas. They told him afterwards that he also appeared to them a gigantic figure and, because of the rain and the shifting light, seemed to move in the air.

They met and Armstrong introduced them. One of them was called Christian Beck ; the other, Hans Opperer. Beck was a tall wiry man with a rugged skin and large rough hands. He looked like the branch of a tree. Opperer was stout and jolly, very German in appearance, with a heavy black beard. They both spoke English but with a strong accent.

They all stood there as though they were never going to move again. There was something exceedingly solid about the two Germans, their feet were planted deep into the soil. They knew Armstrong well, but Nicholas felt that they were suspicious of himself ; they must make quite sure of him before they moved back to the mine. What they seemed to be asking was : why was he there ? what purpose had he ?

' I will wait here if you wish,' he said, ' until my friend has done his business with you.'

' Nein, nein,' Opperer answered in a deep guttural voice. But after that he stood grinning, without, it seemed, any intention of moving.

' My uncle in London,' Nicholas said, ' has some new business in the mines here, but I myself am no man of business. I came from London with my friend here because I wanted fresh air and to be away from London for some days.'

' That is a beautiful horse,' Beck said solemnly.

Nicholas was delighted. He beamed like a boy. ' Come and see her. She is the finest mare in England.'

Beck came to Juno and felt her quarters and looked at her

mouth and stroked her back in the way of a man who knew
about horses, while Juno submitted patiently, turning her
beautiful eyes to her master, as much as to say : ' You are
here so this is permitted, but I would prefer that too many do
not touch me.'

Beck looked at Nicholas and smiled. His voice had now
quite a different tone.

' Come,' he said simply.

When they reached the mines they were in a world of
bustle and noise. Men were everywhere, moving like ghosts
in the wet mist. There was one long, stoutly-built house of
one storey ; there were a number of smaller buildings. A
load of wood was being dragged on a wheeled stretcher.
Everywhere there was the noise of creaking ropes and pulleys.
Near by was a smelt-house and there was a rhythmic, strong
beat from a smithy at the brow of the hill. Two men, in a
superior dress, were standing a little way off trying the ' streak '
on the touchstone ; a cart moved past them loaded with lime,
and in the further distance men were busy piling slate.

Everywhere movement and intense energy, as though this
were a little world all of its own, altogether unconscious of the
outer world, superior to it.

' Come in out of the rain, sir,' the stout Opperer said, and
Nicholas followed him into one of the smaller houses.

When he entered he was surprised by its comfort. The roof
was lined with netting, and this, Opperer explained, was to
keep out the bats who could be a trouble at night-time. The
room was smoky and close, but that was what Nicholas was
accustomed to. There was a broad, strong table, a handsome
carved settle, two chairs and some stools. On to one wall was
pinned a highly coloured picture of some foreign town.

Opperer motioned Nicholas to the chair and sat down with
Armstrong on the settle while Beck went to bring the wine.
They were silent for a time. Beck returned with Malvoisie,
Muscatel and Rhenish and a large half-consumed cold pie.

They drank one another's health. Two other men came in
and were introduced ; one, a little mousy man, was Hans
Dieneck. The other was a big-chested rather self-important
fellow in a rich brown fustian suit with a thin gold chain round

his neck. This was the foreman, Hans Häring.

Nicholas, who was intensely interested, asked innumerable questions.

' Are you making a good thing of this ? '

' A very good thing, Mr. Herries — or we shall do if we are given our rights.'

The Queen's personality hung above them all ; she interpenetrated their daily lives as she interpenetrated the lives of every man, woman and child in England. You saw her standing in the doorway of that room — her carroty hair, her pale bony face with the sharp eyes, the intense, severe, but human mouth, the high ruff, the jewels, the thin active fingers.

' If too many gentlemen in London haven't their fingers in out pie.'

' How long have you been here ? '

' It started in '64. A contract was made then between the Queen, Thomas Thurland, and our master Daniel Hochstetter. The Queen is to have one-tenth of the gold and silver and a royalty on the other metals.'

' Gold and silver ? ' Nicholas leaned forward eagerly. ' Have you found much of it ? '

' No, sir.' Opperer grinned through his beard. ' Very little. Copper's the thing.'

' Under what system do you work it ? Is this a good mine here in Newlands ? '

' Gottesgab ? The best. The best of them all. There are three sorts of miners — the Arbeiter, the day labourers, and the Geding, bargain or contract workers, and the Lehrenschaften, men who choose their own place, hew at their own pleasure and are paid a percentage on the ore's value.'

' Have the people of the place been friendly ? '

Opperer grinned again.

' There was some trouble at the beginning. Not much though. We are peaceful folk and the Keswick men soon found that we meant no harm. More than half of us have married Keswick women and they make good wives.'

The foreman spoke for the first time. He was a pompous man with much humming and hawing.

' They see now that these mines mean much profit for them.

The life of the whole district is changed. They have more money to spend than ever before.'

Beck broke in excitedly :

' And we have bought an island — Vicar's Island on the Lake. It was a ruin when we purchased it, one little tumbled house and the land covered with growth. We are clearing it now and we will build there and settle. There is to be a wind-mill and a brewery and we shall make a garden. We bought it for sixty pounds.'

Beck spoke of the island as though it were his own ; his eyes shone and his hands trembled.

' Do your wives and families not live with you ? '

' Of course, sir. We have our homes in and around Keswick. Sometimes when there is much work at Gottesgab they come out to us for the night. This evening some of them are coming.'

Opperer, who seemed to have taken a liking to Nicholas, said :

' You should stay with us here to-night, Mr. Herries, and see how it is. We have music and dancing as we have at home.'

Nicholas slapped his knee. ' Indeed I will, if you wish me to. I like it here. I could be a miner myself.'

The wine had warmed all their hearts and they soon began to talk very sentimentally of their own homes in Germany, the bright houses with the painted eaves, the running rivers, broad and strong, the meadows in the winter flooded for skating, the festivals and, above all, the music. They were hungry here for music and for sun.

' Your English climate is good, but the sun never shines. It comes for a moment and then hides its head as though ashamed.'

But they liked the North of England people. They had much in common with themselves. They were slow and cautious and waited to see how a man was before they trusted him. But they could themselves be trusted. They made good friends when you knew them.

Finally, first and last, there was the Queen. They were eager to know whether Nicholas had met and spoken with her, and when he said that he had, and that he had seen her smack the cheek of a courtier so that her rings cut his flesh, and seen her with tears in her eyes because some old man had bent to kiss her hand and fainted with the emotion of it, and seen her smile at the crowd as she left her barge and take a child by the hand and stroke its hair, all this delighted them. She was the greatest woman in the world and, ' Almaynes ' though they were, it was for her they were working always. Would she but send them a message one day ! Ah ! that would be something ! Perhaps Mr. Herries, when he returned to London, could have a suggestion conveyed to her that she should write them a letter.

Even the pompous Mr. Häring drank her health in the excellent Rhenish. They all stood up with him and shouted :

' Her Majesty the Queen ! '

Later Opperer said : ' See where we sleep.' He took Nicholas' arm and they went into the long low building. The early afternoon had brought a pale thin wash of sun to all the valley. The sunlight was cold but tender. Inside the building was a kind of dormitory with some thirty stuffed couches and a deep-red figured curtain drawn across one end.

' It's behind this the women sleep when they come.'

Some dozen naked men were sprawled asleep — night workers.

' Now I must go on my business,' Opperer said. ' I have much to do. Soon if you watch you will see the women coming up the valley. To-night we will have songs and we'll dance.'

He looked at Nicholas, pulling his black beard, his eyes twinkling. He laid his hand against Nicholas' neck. His eyes were filled with friendly kindliness.

' You are as proper a young man as I have ever seen. Yes, even in my own country.' He held out his hand. ' If I am familiar, Mr. Herries, tell me so. I am not a man of fine manners. But I am a true Bavarian and such are worthy of any good man's friendship.'

Nicholas gripped his hand.

' Friends we are, Hans Opperer.'

Nicholas stood looking out across the valley. Gilbert Armstrong came to say farewell. He must stay the night with his old mother or there would be trouble. He suggested that, on the following morning, he should take Nicholas to see the island. At a distance he turned on his horse and waved his hand.

Nicholas standing, his legs straddling, thought : ' I've made two friends.' He was greatly pleased. Friendship to men of his time was as important as love and had in it often a romantic emotional quality, something perhaps of the old Greek spirit of mutual love and care growing up through common hardship and sacrifice. Nicholas was young and liked definite relationships, as again was the manner of his time. Friends or enemies — there was some hot stirring of the blood in all his doings : love, friendship, play, work ; love of women, love of friends, love of home and relations, love of country, love of danger, love of new experience — it was all ardour and fire for life. He must live : every minute of the day he must live. He swallowed new experience as a dog swallows meat.

Now, once more, he felt this consciousness that new life was pouring into his veins. Something unusual was occurring to him so that already this dying year seemed to him the most important he had known.

' What is it ? ' he thought. ' What was it I felt first a year ago, when I saw the man on the moor, and only now, the other night, in my uncle's house, when I saw Irvine's face in the mirror ? What is it ? Am I in love ? If so, with whom ? Am I sickening for the plague perhaps ? Are spirits warning me of some great event ? '

But he was never introspective. He could never think a thing out. He shook his great head and swung his great legs and knew that he was happy with a fine fiery sense of living. He knew that he loved this North country, this valley, these miners ; soon there would be girls and women dancing. But these men were real men, living a hard life, their muscles taut, their arms straining ; sleeping, when the moment came, as he had seen them in there, drunk with weariness, abandoning their strong bodies to the luxury of full absolute emotions, as he abandoned his.

He stretched his arms, grunted, and found a man at his

side. This man was perhaps thirty years of age, bare-headed, his hair very flaxen, strong, thick-set, short. He had a handsome, square, strong-jawed face but his expression was surly. They talked a little and the man was as though he were challenging Nicholas for his right to be there. He sniffed at Nicholas as one dog sniffs at another. Nicholas explained how and why he was there. The man told him his name — Joris Fisher. He was an Englishman working at Gottesgab. His work was finished for the day and he was now clean and in a good dark green doublet and hose. He was waiting, he explained, for the women coming in from Keswick.

'It's not often,' he said at last, 'we have strangers around here.'

'Nor do you like them,' Nicholas said, laughing, 'when they do come, Mr. Fisher.'

'That's as may be. But you'll be returning to London?'

'Who knows?' Nicholas went on teasing him. 'I shall see how these girls may be.'

Joris Fisher's face flushed.

'A gentleman from London has an advantage.'

'Do you think so? We shall see.'

And the time was not to be long, for now up the cool dusky valley (the sun having sunk into a bank of watery cloud) horses could be seen with women on them, and presently the women could be heard laughing and one of them singing.

When they were near, two or three of them waved their hands and several men ran towards them. When they were close Nicholas saw that one of them was the girl he had kissed a year ago in Keswick, Catherine Hodstetter.

She was sitting on a little horse, her back straight, her yellow hair coiled on top of her hatless head. Her dress was the gold-yellow of her hair, the stuff printed with little red and brown and white flowers. She saw Nicholas and of course at once recognized him. Who, having seen him, would ever forget him? She gave him one straight look with her bright blue eyes.

He saw then that Joris Fisher was already at her horse's head. She did not allow him to assist her but sprang to the ground.

'Ah, so that's the way it is,' Nicholas thought. Now

Opperer and Beck had joined the party. Their wives had
come and were introduced to Nicholas. Catherine Hodstetter
was introduced to him. He bowed and took her hand for an
instant. He was introduced to Mistress Hodstetter, Catherine's
mother. Here was a strange woman indeed ! She might have
been Catherine's elder sister ; she was slim and tall with hair
so pale as to be almost white. She wore a grey silk gown
with a little cloak of red. All this was ordinary enough.
What was there then that was strange ? Her face was long,
thin, sharply pointed and very pale. Her eyes were grey and
deep. They looked into you, through you, beyond you. She
was remote as though she were thinking of other things. For
a moment the four were in a group together : Nicholas, Fisher,
Catherine and her mother. Nicholas had an unpleasant feeling
about Mistress Hodstetter. She made him wish to be safe
and comfortable within doors.

The table was laden with food and drink. A great fire
burnt on the level hearth at the room end and the grey smoke
went curling in woolly curves about the room. It was stifling
and hot, but no one cared because they were accustomed to
it. The table was cleared away and they began to dance to
the music of an old scruffy man, hairy like a monkey, who
played well on the violin, and a young man with a flute. There
were perhaps thirty men and women. They sang as they
danced in and out, round and round, stamping with their feet.
They moved in a circle changing partners, and when the music
altered its tune they stopped and every man kissed the woman
he was with.

Nicholas danced with everyone except Catherine. He liked
Mistress Beck, a jolly, apple-dumpling woman who kissed him
with a great smack of the lips. She had a coarse and merry
tongue and said that any woman in his arms would be lost,
not know where she was, he was so large.

'I'd be her guide,' said Nicholas.

'Fancy a great London gentleman like you honouring us
poor folks.'

'Mine's the honour,' said Nicholas. 'Hasn't it been
strange to marry a German ? ' he asked.

' Germans are made just like other men,' she said, laughing.

' Have you children ? '

' One at present — a daughter, Urwyn — born last year.'

' And what will *she* be — a little German or a little Cumbrian ? '

' I'm a Bewley,' she said, as though she'd said ' I'm a Howard ' — ' And Bewleys are always Bewleys.'

' And are not Becks always Becks ? '

' He is half a Bewley already.'

And at last Nicholas had the information he was seeking. He sat with Hans Opperer drinking on the settle near the fire and watched the dancing.

' Now that's a fine girl,' he said to Opperer carelessly.

' Which girl ? '

' The one with the yellow hair and the broad back — with the flowers on her clothes.'

' Yes,' said Opperer, his beard deep in his drinking-mug. He looked up and wiped his black beard. ' That is Catherine — Catherine Hodstetter.'

' Her father works in the mines ? '

' She has no father.'

' That was her mother who came with her — standing now alone by the door ? '

Opperer grinned. ' Yes. You seem to take notice of her, Mr. Herries.'

Nicholas said : ' I notice every woman — and so do you, I wager.'

Opperer's gaze into the room was suddenly serious.

' Her situation is a sad one. She came with her father and mother here three years back. Six months later, Hodstetter was found drowned in the Lake by Portinskill — a little place outside Keswick.'

' That was a misfortune, but——'

' Yes. They say that her mother is a witch.'

' A witch ? ' Nicholas, horrified, repeated.

' They say so. They say Mistress Hodstetter contrived her man's death. You know what country people are. And I am not myself certain. Catherine's mother is not as other women. She is learned and goes into the country gathering herbs. They say she can heal any sickness.' He dropped his voice. ' They say she has been seen naked at night dancing at the Druids' Circle. There is a great fear because of her. This makes it a lonely life for Catherine, who is a good girl.'

Nicholas said nothing. He believed in witches and spells. His very soul trembled and, with that, he wished to rise and put his arm around Catherine and protect her. He watched her. She appeared happy enough. She danced with a grace and lightness that was remarkable in anyone of her strong vigorous frame, and when the dancers paused and all together sang a chorus, she lifted up her face, her eyes shining in a happy pleasure, and sang like a bird on a tree.

Joris Fisher was clearly her courtier; he danced with her a number of times and always his set, sulky face commanded hers. He spoke not at all, but when his arm was about her waist he held her as though he possessed her against the world.

In a pause while everyone was drinking and cracking chicken bones with their fingers and throwing marchpane into open grinning mouths, and the old monkey-man dreamily fondling the strings of his violin and the smoke turning faces into a ribald mist, Nicholas saw that she stood alone by the door. Then she slipped out.

He crossed the floor unnoticed and slipped out after her. She was alone, with the valley seethed in mist below her while a moon, gold, on its back, lay in a sky of frosted milk : soft, white, with only this shred of gold, but the crisp of frost curling the breath, stiffening the rough ragged soil at their feet.

It seemed that she had expected him, for she turned at sight of the great shadow that he flung from the lighted door behind him and said :

' I knew that one day you would come back.'

He did not touch her.

' You remembered it then ? '

Her hands were folded behind her lifted head. She was gazing at the gold moon-slip.

' Oh, I remember many things. You are larger than most men.'

He came nearer to her so that the stiff shoulder of his doublet touched her sleeve.

' It's very cold. Is there nowhere we can go ? '

She gave him her hand, smiling.

' Of course.'

She led him a little way up the hill until the first brow where there was the smithy. They went in and closed the door behind them. Stumbling, he found some straw, very friendly with the smell of horses. He lay down in it and at once she was folded on to him, in his arms. There was a thick frothy moonlight from the window. They kissed many times. Her cheek lay against his. Her hand on his heart felt a tumultuous deep beating. He laid his hand gently on her breast and then began, with great delicacy, to undo the buttons of her dress.

Herself as gently as he, she stayed his hand.

' I loved you from the first moment I saw you in Keswick. But we shall never be lovers — never, never, never.'

She said these last words with an infinity of sadness and, to his great surprise, he found that she was crying. Tears fell upon his palm. This roused him to a violent passion. He would have betrayed himself and her had it not been that she offered neither resistance nor response. His hand stayed on her uncovered breast. He allowed her to rise and arrange herself, coiling up the hair that had come uncoiled, fastening the buttons. He saw her as a dim aureoled shadow in the moonlight.

He sat up on the straw, staring at her.

' It is for longer then,' he said at last, ' than a moment.'

' For me it is for so long that it will never end. But for you, I am sure, only one girl more.'

She suddenly knelt down, catching his hand in hers.

' We must not stay here. They will already wonder where you are.'

She put up her hand to his cheek.

' You must understand that I am separate from everyone. My mother and I are outside all happiness, all real friendliness, and I think that our end will be very unfortunate. You are a gentleman and to-morrow you will go and never think of me again. But you have kissed me and held me in your arms, and that is as much good fortune, I expect, as I shall ever have in my life.'

' How is this then ? ' Nicholas said quickly. ' How many hundreds of girls I have kissed I don't know — kissed and forgotten. A year ago I kissed you for one moment and rode out of Keswick. A year later in a room with mirrors and candles I see a man of your country and the first thing I ask him is, " Do you know Catherine Hodstetter ? " And the next day I ride North to find you.'

She caught him up. ' A long room with mirrors and candles and two men are wrestling on a table. You look in the mirrors for someone's face—' She seemed ashamed. ' I saw it all. My mother showed me . . . she has a power . . . she knew you would be here.'

' Then,' he cried eagerly, holding her once again tightly in his arms, ' we are bound. In some way we are bound. Listen, I am here to-morrow. We will ride into the hills——'

She struggled a little and, once more to his own surprise, he released her.

She kneeled towards him, placed her hand on his heart inside the doublet. With her other hand drew his head down, and kissed his forehead, his eyes, his mouth. Then she slipped out of the door. When he followed her he saw only the mist stirring like water in the valley and the thin moon like a boat in the sky.

When he went into the shouting, smoking, drunken room she was not there, nor her mother.

Nor did he see her on the following day.

IN A HOUSE OF LIGHT AND DANGER

ROBIN HERRIES closed the heavy door behind him and knew, with intense relief, that he had made no sound. From the scented lawn he could hear the boy's voice singing :

> Ah ! my heart, ah ! What aileth thee
> To set so light my liberty,
> Making me bond when I was free ?
> Ah ! my heart, ah ! What aileth thee ?
>
> When thou wert rid from all distress,
> Void of all pain and pensiveness,
> To choose again a new mistress,
> Ah ! my heart, ah ! What aileth thee ?
>
> When thou wert well, thou could not hold ;
> To turn again, that were too bold.
> There's to renew my sorrows old,
> Ah ! my heart, ah ! What aileth thee ?

The voice was like a thin rapier of sharp and margined light cutting across the green lower sky. He could see this lower sky through the open mullioned window that looked out from the passage where he was standing.

They were all seated out there on the lawn to watch the sun sink above the formal clipped hedges. In his mind's eye he could see it all, so close to him and so dangerous : the oak table with the wine and fruit and comfits, his mother in the high carved chair, the others standing or seated on cushions on the grass — Sir Michael and Henry Herries, their old quarrel now composed, Nicholas, his aunt, Philip Irvine, the scornful Falk, Charles Lacey, Robert Rockage, Edward and Sidney Herries, the unpleasant Phineas, and — Sylvia.

The boy's voice came again, as though it had some personal message for him :

I hoped full well all had been done,
But now my hope is ta'en and won,
To my torment to yield so soon,
Ah! my heart, ah! What aileth thee?

The voice ceased. There was applause, hand-clapping, laughter.

Robin moved softly to the outer door. He was in the narrow rough-stoned passage that led from the main hall to the buttery. He knew that the servants were busied in the dining-hall preparing for the dancing that would follow when they were weary of sitting on the lawn. Nevertheless at any moment a servant might appear. What was he to do?

Ten minutes ago he had been standing a little back from the table near one of the box-hedges, watching Sylvia Herries, amused by the self-importance of his Uncle Henry, absorbing delightedly the scents from the neighbouring hayfield and the stocks and the pinks, hearing the plash from the fountain falling through the summer air, itself a song, never for an instant losing the sight and movement of his beloved child who sat, with so grave and dignified an air, watching the singer — all this as though a moment of his life had crystallized like a globe of diamond lustre hanging against that perfect sunny evening sky — when he felt his arm touched.

He turned, and there, behind the box-hedge, was a yokel, his clothes soiled, his face grimed with dust and sweat, in a yokel's large country hat. This man had the countenance of Anthony Pierson. Robin whispered his name. The other nodded and huskily answered : ' We are in peril. Open the back door for us — by the yard.'

He had glanced at the group preoccupied by the singing, heard, as though it were a farewell, the thin lute and the clear voice, skirted the lawn, entered the house and slipped to the stone passage.

Even then, before he opened the door into the yard, his hand paused. This was the first time ever that Anthony had asked his help. Anthony was his friend for whom he cared more than anyone in the world save Sylvia and Nicholas. But this was his own home, the home of his father and mother, sacred soil. To conceal Catholic priests there would engage

them all in the gravest of dangers. They would be liable to
the law as he would be. The penalties were fearful. Nor was
he himself a Catholic.

They could not have chosen a worse time for their coming.
The house was filled with guests. Irvine hated him and his
brother; Phineas Thatcher, a Puritan and his uncle's man, was
as mean and spying a creature as you could find. And yet
. . . And yet . . . Anthony was his friend and as noble a
man as Robin had ever known.

Very, very softly he unlatched the door. Two figures were
standing there.

'Come in,' Robin whispered. 'Quickly. Quickly.' They
slipped inside.

He had spent the better part of that afternoon away from
the others, not out of sight, ready for any duty, most agreeable
and friendly with his eager, rather shy smile, if anyone wanted
him — but yet apart.

He had found in himself, ever since that meeting with
Sylvia at the masked ball, an increased preoccupation with his
own lovely world, the world of Utopia, of the golden-sanded
shore beyond the sea, the world of the bright pavilions of God.
' They acknowledge God to be the author and governor of the
world, and the fountain of all the good that they receive : for
which they offer up their thanksgivings to Him, and, in particular, they bless Him for His goodness in ordering it so that
they are born under a Government that is the happiest in the
world and are of a religion that they hope is the truest of all
others ; but, if they are mistaken, and if there is either a better
government or a religion more acceptable to God, they implore
His goodness to let them know it, vowing that they resolve to
follow Him whithersoever He leads them. . . .'

So wrote his beloved Sir Thomas More of the Utopians
. . . ' if there is either a better government or a religion more
acceptable to God . . .' Somewhere, Robin knew, there
were both a better government and a better religion — but
where ? Could Anthony Pierson show it him ? Or his young
child friend Philip Sidney ? Did his uncle and aunt with their
complacent common-sense business air know of it ? Did his

father and mother know of it ? Did his beloved Nicholas ?

And he realized, as have so many of his kind, before him and after him, that the majority of his fellow-men cared for none of these things — but had enough to do to follow their daily business of work, food and drink, copulation and fighting.

Of the minority who *did* so care, the most were fanatics, demanding the rack, the thumbscrew, the fire, for all who did not bow to the altar, turn last or not, swear by transubstantiation as they themselves did.

Robin was most certainly not as these. He was a Middleman, a Facing-both-ways in that he wanted a Utopia of friendly happy people, free to worship God as they would, free of speech, free of habit, tolerant and tolerating.

Yet this did not altogether go with the mystical spirit that would never let him quiet. When Anthony Pierson spoke to him with such confidence and certainty, his eyes burning with delight that he could surrender himself so completely to the rules of his Order and be ready to be racked and burned if so commanded, then something stirred in Robin, something fiercer than his longing for any gentle, sweet Utopia. There *was* a better world just beyond sight and, when he found it, it might order him to a sterner, more violent sacrifice. He did not know. He was increasingly at war with himself.

To all this tapestry his sudden love for Sylvia Herries had only added fresh blazing strands of colour. He had seen her some half-dozen times since that first meeting. Although at seventeen girls were mature and ready for marriage Sylvia was not. She had been kept quietly at home so that, when she did at last make her appearance, all the world might wonder. And so, in this year 1571, all the world *did* wonder ! It was the fashion to admire tall women and Sylvia Herries was not tall. Women must be learned and be able to make fine Latin speeches like their Queen. Sylvia was not clever at books and had a very poor knowledge of Latin and Greek. Young women of fashion must have conceits at their finger-ends, be able to cap verses, at an instant's notice, with young men like Rockage or Lacey. Sylvia had no power at all for capping verses and did not understand them when capped. Young women of that day to be popular must be coquettish, know everything about men, how to capture them, how to tease them when captured, how to let them go, how to call them back again. Sylvia could not coquette, could not tease, could not dissemble. There was something childish and tender and honest about her that would perhaps never be eradicated.

It was this very simplicity and childlikeness that won her favour. It seemed so queer and unlikely a thing to come out of that money-making sharp advantage-eyed family. It appeared scarcely possible that she was the child of Henry Herries and the half-sister of Edward and Sidney.

'Mercury,' Charles Lacey said, 'having one day nothing better to do picked a daisy to give, on his return to Olympus, to the wife of Jupiter. She is weary of ropes of pearls, thick bars of amethyst and diamonds like hen's eggs. But, seeing a swan in flight, Mercury pursued it and dropped the daisy, which did not wither and die, as nature intended, but took new life from the tender grasses and the morning dew — so Sylvia was born.'

Very pretty. He told it to Sylvia, who did not understand a word of it. She understood very quickly, however, that her cousin Robin was in love with her.

She had understood it on that first night.

He did not know what she herself felt. She was still such a child that it seemed a wicked thing to press her to any acknowledgment. He felt a perfect happy comradeship when he was with her and he thought that she felt that too when she was with him.

He did not wish to touch her or even to speak to her. There was something in his nature that found things a little more perfect while they were still a way off. He was quite happy, as now, to be lying his length on the grass, listening to the nonsense that Arabella Lacey, Charles' sister, was saying to Rockage, to watch amusedly Nicholas' extreme solemnity as the head gardener, a long lanky creature with tow hair (but a marvellous gardener), came and spoke to him (for was not Nicholas bull in his own paddock now?), to listen to the reapers singing from the meadow, to stare, bemusedly, as

though all his life he had stared at the shapes of the hedges,
the ship, the peacocks, the old man with the beard, the crowing
cock.

Then Nicholas came and threw his gigantic bulk on the
grass beside him.

' Well, old lad, of what are you thinking this lovely day ? '

' I was listening to Arabella's nonsense ' (her shrill clear
voice broke across the air : ' But that is not enough. If Leda
preferred a swan to all other fowl and Ganymede cried for a
pricked finger, why, I'll wager my shoes with the black pearls
against your gold chain, Robert, that Jupiter was so vexed
at his negligence, that, wearying of Leda, he baked comfits
for Ganymede and . . .'), ' to the pleasant reapers and
admiring your own self-importance——'

' Nothing else ? ' Nicholas smiled. ' It's pleasant here, but
— heigh-ho ! — shall I endure it while Grenville is finding
pearls like grain in a cornfield and bags of gold under every
Spaniard's bed and——'

Robin broke in — to his own surprise quite hotly. ' Something is happening to this country. We are growing greedy
for money. All these tales of treasure snatched from the
Spaniards and cities in America built of gold — our thoughts
bite on nothing but these and how much we can take that
doesn't belong to us. Why, the Queen herself——'

Nicholas laid his big brown hand on his brother's thigh.

' Hist ! Take care of the creeping Thatcher. He has a
thousand ears and he hates us.' He drew nearer to his brother,
laying his arm about his neck.

' There is another thing, Robin. I am in love.'

' Yes,' Robin said. ' Not for the first time.'

' But this is different. It is a girl I have seen twice, kissed
twice, been with but a quarter of an hour in all.'

' Had you been with her longer,' Robin said, ' you would
not now be in love with her.'

' Maybe,' Nicholas said.

In all these months he had told his brother nothing of his
Northern adventure. He had spoken to no living soul of it.
He told Robin now, his face almost in the grass, biting the
cold blades between his lips. He did not know what had

caught him. He had known a thousand girls. He had ridden south, determining to put it altogether from his mind. She was only one like another. And yet he could not forget her. Something within him was always urging him to ride north and see her again. Perhaps she had bewitched him. Her mother was a witch. Or perhaps the North had bewitched him. There was something there that he could find nowhere else, the stinging air, the moving clouds, the bare fells. . . . He sighed again.

' I can't rid my mind of her.'

Robin looked at him with concern. This was unlike Nicholas, who gave no thought to anything save what was happening at the moment.

Nicholas sat up. ' How I hate him ! ' he said. ' Oh, how I hate him ! '

They both looked at Philip Irvine, who was bending over Sylvia and teasing her with a wine-coloured carnation.

Robin considered. ' It is his vanity,' he said at last. ' I have never known any man so vain. His vanity is so deep that it is seated in his spleen. He does verily believe that for wisdom he exceeds Burghley ; for charm, our Philip Sidney ; for bravery, Hawkins ; for audacity, Drake. Touch his vanity and he stings like a snake. And you must touch it if you touch *him*, for he is all vanity.'

' He is the only creature in all the world I hate,' Nicholas said, ' for he caused me to betray a naked man. But it is earlier than that. It goes back and it stretches forward. It stretches forward, Robin. Bad work will come of it one day.'

Robin smiled. ' You twist your old head too fiercely. He is not worth your hate, for he is not evil but only vain — and vanity is so easily pricked.'

It was a little after this, when Nicholas left him, that he stood by the hedge and the boy sang and Pierson touched his shoulder.

The two men slipped in. The summer evening light was everywhere, so Robin took them up three steps of the crooked round staircase that they might stand in the shadow of the bend. They stood close to the wall. The man with Pierson was a thin, burning-eyed man, with a jutting, dirty chin. They spoke in whispers.

'Mr. Anstey,' Pierson said. Robin bowed. Mr. Anstey raised a bony, grimy hand in blessing.

'We are in peril of our lives for a bag that Burghley's men have taken at Salisbury. I have no time for the story now, but can you keep us here till morning, Robin? We rode hoping to be in London by nightfall, but my horse stumbled and fell in the West Road and at last we must take to our legs. We have been disguised from Salisbury and in the early morning we can get to a safe house in Southwark. We were frightened two miles from here at an alehouse where Anstey recognized one of the Government men.'

He drew Robin for a moment close to him. 'I have always vowed not to bring you into this, Robin, but we dare not go forward for several hours.'

Robin said : 'What did they find?'

'Letters from France. Since the Queen's excommunication everything has been much harder . . .' He broke off. It seemed that he saw in Robin's eyes some doubt. He moved a step down.

'I understand, Robin. You dare not——'

Robin pulled him up the stair again.

'No, no. It is only that you could not have found a more unhappy moment. The house is filled with people and——'

He drew himself in close against the stone, pushing back Anthony Pierson's stout body with his hand against the wall. Mr. Anstey silently climbed two more steps and stood above them in the shadow.

Someone was in the stone passage. Robin heard the voice of Mellon, the major-domo, an old, trusted and impertinent servant.

'Knaves! Knaves and rascals, the lot of them. As though the rats had been at the mulberries. . . .' With that mystical sentence he began, to Robin's extreme horror, to climb the stair. Faithful servant he was and devoted to Robin in his own fashion, having swaddled and bathed and slapped him, in the proper time, but he was a chatterer and a gossip and, on his weak day, a wine-bibber. He was old now, a

D

skeleton of a man with bent and cracking knees. So now he began to climb the stairs, singing *sotto voce* to himself in a strangely whispering, whining, tuneless utterance :

> ' Sometimes he would gasp
> When he saw a wasp ;
> A fly or a gnat,
> He would fly at that ;
> And prettily he would pant
> When he saw an ant ;
> Lord, how he would pry
> After the butterfly ! . . .'

He passed them and then, two steps above Mr. Anstey, paused, blowing.

' The knaves — the careless bastardy knaves — and my poor knees and all the company after sunset. Ah, Crissy, Crissy, 'tis not here at all but in the buttery. . . . I put it there myself at noon. . . .' He started down again, breaking once more into his funny croaking wail :

> ' And when I said " Phip ! Phip ! "
> Then he would leap and skip,
> And take me by the lip——'

Then, most lugubriously :

> ' When I saw my sparrow die ! '

He stopped for a pause exactly opposite Robin, murmuring : ' Aye, the buttery. Right-hand second shelf in the buttery,' and so went down to the stone passage, repeating as he went through the door :

> ' When I saw my sparrow die ! '

' Quick ! Follow me ! ' Robin whispered and dashed up to the stair-head followed by the two priests.

He had the very place, although it increased his own personal responsibility. Off his own bedroom there was in the wall a small closet, larger than a priest's hole, concealed by the wall-painting of Troilus and Cressida that had hung there ever since he could remember. A bare little place and uncomfortable, but for the occasion it would do.

At the top of the stair a long, narrow passage led to his room, and inside this, at once he lifted the canvas wall-painting, slid the panel and showed them the empty place. Nothing was in it save a large spider-web hanging from the door to the ceiling.

In a drawer he found some bedding. ' This must do. And here is a candle. It is the most now I can find.'

Pierson kissed him on both cheeks. Suddenly Anstey clutched the door with his hand.

' Food,' Pierson whispered. ' If you could manage something. We have had nothing since last night. We could not stay in the alehouse.'

Robin slid back the panel, dropped the canvas and hurried from the room.

They were coming into the house as Robin entered the buttery. He could see through the window how they formed a sort of procession. They were singing :

> ' Pastime with good company
> I love, and shall, until I die.'

They made a canon of it, Arabella Lacey and Sylvia leading ; Charles Lacey, Rockage and Irvine following ; Nicholas lumbering along, carrying a spade in his hand, and occasionally joining in. The old people, his mother, father, uncle and aunt, walked more soberly at a little distance. They made a beautiful picture, for the sun's clear evening rays stroked gently the lawn ; green light with motes dancing in the gold-washed ladders between the hedges. The colours of the clothes shone as though freshly minted : Irvine's doublet of mulberry purple slashed with silver, Rockage in flaming orange, Arabella in stiff seeded gold and a high white ruff. Even yet the reapers could be heard singing, like the murmurs of a stream, from a distant field.

Very pretty, but he had not time for prettiness. And indeed he had not. For, even as he had in his hands a jug of beer, half a venison pie, a bread loaf, old Mellon with his wand and chain of office was standing in the doorway, staring at him.

' Why, Master Robin——'

led.

, it is for an old man and woman over by the
came on them but now and the old woman has a
she shakes till her head rolls — and the old man
hand. . . . I'll bring them some money from my

. . .'

e brushed past Mellon and ran up the stone staircase,
le the old man looked about him muttering : ' But the
nison — the parsley venison.'

It could not be helped, and it was, on the moment, a
stupid answer, for the old man might send to the stables to
see where the vagrants had got to — the old fool was a garrulous talker and there was always the long-eared, thin, bitter
shadow of Phineas Thatcher around the corner. Still, he had
not the time to consider. He slid the panel and looked in to
find Anthony standing against the wall and the priest Anstey
lying on the bedding soaked in sleep.

Anthony eagerly took the food and drink from him, had
a draught of the beer, tore a hunch off the pie and the loaf,
greedily ate and drank. While he did so he dragged Robin
down on to the end of the bedding and, his mouth full, put
his arms round Robin's neck, holding him tightly to him.
Then, clasping his hand, he began in a hurried, excited whisper :

' Oh, forgive me, forgive me. I had no right to come here
nor to bring him with me. . . . Hist ! What was that ?
Down ! Close — against me ! ' They stayed pressed together,
scarcely breathing. Someone had come into the room, steps
moved, hesitated. Then the whining voice of old Mellon was
heard : ' Master Robin ! Master Robin ! . . .' Then the
steps died away.

' Tiresome old fool ! '

' Yes,' Anthony whispered. ' I must not keep you or
they'll be up here after you, all of them. Only this, Robin.
I've longed for you for months. You are the only human thing
I love any more. Do you understand that ? And you, even
you, are against our Orders. No human love, no tenderness,
no longing for bodily contact — no love, no love, no love —
save of God, and He is our general not our lover. Do you
understand that, Robin ? That you are a weakness to me, a

cause of surrender, something I'm afraid to confess.'

His hand was hot and damp, his eyes restless with some ardent longing.

' I have gone far since our last meeting. I have cast every-thing and everyone away save you. That I love you is a sin, but love you I must, and one day you also will see as I see and we will be martyred together. You will see that your Queen is no Queen, for she has been rejected by God and it is the duty of all who serve God to work her destruction . . . There is another Queen, unfortunate, betrayed, imprisoned, God's servant . . .'

Robin nodded. The rest of Anthony's talk had been mad and wild, for he was hungry and crazy for lack of sleep. But in this there was something that Robin felt with all the passion of his longing for the beautiful, the unattainable. That lovely, betrayed prisoner who had trusted in friend, brother, lover, sister-queen, and been betrayed by them all. There was something in this picture that moved him to trembling.

' Yes, yes,' he said. ' Later in the night, when all are in bed. I must go down, Tony. And you must sleep. Wait. Lie down — I'll make it comfortable for you.'

Anthony's eyes were haggard for want of sleep : they had that sightless searching stare of the sleepless man. He lay down beside Anstey, who through this time had not stirred. Robin folded a cloak around him and went.

In the hall they were eating and drinking. The candles had not yet been lit and the late sun was streaming through the deep crimsons and dark blues of the high window opposite the gallery.

They all greeted Robin with a shout. ' Where have you been ? What doing ? Traitor ! Deserter ! ' He went over to his mother and, leaning on the arm of her chair, bent forward and kissed her.

' There were two old vagrants near the stable, mother. I took them some food.'

His mother was a little woman with snow-white hair and a back as straight as a board. She had been born Cicely Goring and her father had been a small impecunious Somerset squire. One of those squires with a few fields, two dogs, a horse, and the Bible in the window-seat. She was not yet sixty, but her hair had been white at forty. She was not beautiful, but her figure was so fine, her skin so delicate that she resembled one of those glass coloured ornaments just then so fashionable everywhere. Her sons and husband adored her. She could always have anything she wanted, but she wanted very little except her family, her garden, her needlework, and a little visiting. Robin thought as, leaning over, his cheek almost touched hers, how royal she seemed, her head crowned with its white hair set so regally in the stiff ruff, beside his blowzy aunt who was covered with jewels. ' All women,' he thought, ' when they marry Herries men become themselves Herries — Herries of the one sort or the other. For we are of two sorts, spirit and flesh — and this conflict in our blood is never resolved.'

He kissed his mother's cheek and then went to sit down beside Arabella Lacey. Everyone was in tremendous spirits : old Mellon came in, followed by two servants, all bearing the silver candlesticks which they set along the table. The new crisping sparkling flame gave an added lustre to the scene. The wine was passing. Voices were rising, everyone was talking at once.

Robin's heart was beating with fright. He thought that he had never been truly frightened before. At any moment the officers, in pursuit of the priests, might arrive at the house and demand a search. He might himself at once be under suspicion, for it had long been known that he was a friend of Pierson. He would keep them as long as he could from his own room, but his very effort to hinder them would make them suspect him. Old Mellon had seen him with the food. There might be somebody who, under interrogation, would admit to having seen the priests in the yard. His mind flew then to the discovery — Pierson and Anstey dragged from their hiding, the family exposed and charged. . . . At that he looked at his mother, his father with his white stiff beard, the kindly lines about his eyes, the cordial hospitable smile, and then at Nicholas, whom he loved so dearly, who at the moment was fixing an apple with the end of his rapier and handing it, with a deep bow, to Sylvia, Nicholas who hated the Catholics, who

perhaps would never forgive his brother. . . . Oh, if there
was a discovery this would be ruin for all whom he loved.
How Uncle Henry would hate him for thus injuring his social
prospects, and if his uncle hated him what of Sylvia ?

Behind all these things lay a terror of physical pain. Robin
was not of the unimaginative confident courage of Nicholas.
His more spiritual visionary nature showed him horrors and
distresses long before they arrived. He was very young and,
as with every young man of his day, the rack and thumbscrew
and, worst of all, the ' peine forte et dure ' were so close to
everyday life as to be part of it. He saw everything : the
capture, the cell, the grim interrogation, the stripping, the
ropes, the first turn of the engine. . . .

' Robin,' Arabella was crying, ' you heard nothing of what
I was saying. I shall punish you. You are condemned'—
she bent a little closer, whispering —' to spend an evening
alone with Mr. Thatcher a hundred miles from anywhere.'

But there was the other side. Anthony had spoken of
Mary of Scots and, at that, a wild unreasoned longing had
leapt within him. She was imprisoned, desolate, cut off from
her baby, her friends. She was brave, still royal, a woman,
he was sure, whom he could serve to any bitter end.

Why did he feel this about her ? What connection had he
with her ? Why was she mixed in his mind with everything
that was to him holy, worshipful, beautiful ?

He had risen : the servants were clearing the tables : they
were going to dance. Should he slip up to his room and make
sure that all was safe ? It had been madly risky to leave them
there, so that any servant could push aside the panel and find
them there. Anthony would be sleeping now. . . . But no
one had slid that panel for years and years. The servants for
the most part did not know that there was a room at all.

Then he saw that Thatcher, standing alone in the window
embrasure, was watching him. That man was for ever watching something. It was his penalty that, because he was Henry
Herries' man, he must be always doing things that he loathed :
attending dancing that he disliked, plays that he abhorred,
chambering and wantoning at which even his very soul was

sick. But is it *me* that he is watching, Robin wondered. He hates Nicholas, but myself he has always flattered. Does he suspect anything? Has he had private information? Is he one of Burghley's men?

To his enchanted delight he heard Sylvia speaking to him.

' Cousin Robin, I have something to say to you.'

He heard his aunt close to him talking with that mysterious, wheezing, frog-like croaking that was so especially hers, about her fear of the plague and a wonderful remedy that she had, something to do with snake's spittle and the urine of a goat. Something you drank apparently. ' I'd rather have the plague,' he thought.

But he was walking down the pleached alley with Sylvia. The sun had sunk — there was no moon — and so over the garden there lay that warm star-shine shadow of the summer evening. So drowsy was the air that when in the faint breeze the flowers wavered ever so slightly it seemed that they nodded their heads in sleep. From the very heart of the splashing fountain — Neptune riding a whale — came the carnation-thyme-dark corn scent as of crushed flowers drenched with sun. She leant over and stirred her hand in the fountain. Then they moved on to where, between the posts of the hedges, they could see the broad cornfield and the snakeskin-shadowed hill beyond.

' You have paid me very little attention this evening,' Sylvia said.

The one thing he had determined was that he would not be drawn away from the house. What was happening while he was away? Who knew but that Phineas Thatcher was not that moment quietly opening the door of his room? Tony Pierson or Anstey might well be snoring. . . . Or, impatient of confinement or for some natural reason, might slide the panel, slip into his room and find Thatcher there waiting for them. . . . Or, worst of all, they might think it his step they heard and call out his name! A thousand alarms fired his blood while the carnation scent was in his nostril and a late bird called in a broken drunken whirl across the corn. So, terrified, excited, loving, a child, a man, he drew Sylvia into his arms and kissed her.

' Sylvia — Sylvia — I love you.'

' And I love you, Robin.'

' Oh, Sylvia ! '

' Oh, Robin ! '

' Don't move — don't speak.'

The bird called again and again. The lights blazed from the house. An owl hooted. A little bird gave its death-cry.

' I will ask Uncle Henry this very night——'

She drew back and he saw that she was frightened.

' Oh no — no. You must not say a word, Robin.'

She looked now a discovered nervous child who was to be punished for some sin.

' But why——? '

' They want me to make a fine marriage. My father says that everything for him hangs on it. Edward and Sidney are always pressing me. They say it must be someone fine and wealthy.'

' But I—— '

' You are not wealthy, Robin, and you are just our cousin. My father wants something finer than our family.'

He felt a disgust. If his uncle had been there he would have told him . . .

' And you——? '

She stopped suddenly in the path and, with the sweetest, most childlike gesture, stood on the toes of her silver shoes, put her hands on his breast and kissed him.

' I loved you from that first night in our house — the moment I saw you. I always will. But you must say nothing to anyone as yet. Promise me.'

' Oh, I promise you.' She was wearing the ridiculous little ship in her hair. He felt in his doublet and produced the tiny jewel that had fallen from the ship on the night of the ball.

' I carry this always next to my heart.'

She started away from him. Her eyes stared with fear.

' There is Mr. Thatcher,' she said.

He was standing in the doorway, the lights flaring behind him.

' Your mother is looking for you.'

She walked past him, her head in the air. Mr. Thatcher
said nothing to Robin at all.

But now he felt bold enough to face all the Thatchers, the
Queen's officers, the secret judges in the world. He showed
himself for a moment and watched the dancing. He looked up
at the gallery and saw the second gardener, his father's man-
servant, and a young man, Mellon's son, playing for their life
on two fiddles and a flute, and excellently they played. He
smiled because they were dressed in green velvet and gilt
buttons with the Herries crest on their sleeve — the only little
attempt at false grandeur his father ever made.

Then he quietly left the hall and started for his room. As
he reached the top of the winding staircase, someone mounted
behind him and caught his arm. It was Philip Irvine.

Robin stopped at the stair-head and turned smiling with
his charming nervous boyish friendliness.

' Well — good night.'

Irvine looked at him, also smiling.

' You are early.'

' Yes. I am gruesomely weary.'

He started towards his room, thinking to shake Irvine off,
but down the passage they went.

Robin, terrified, baffled, opened his door. Irvine entered
with him. Did he know, suspect ? Was he playing with him ?
Irvine's eyes went at once to the painted cloth of Troilus and
Cressida.

' Cressida is no beauty there,' he said, pointing and laughing.
' Her nose is crooked.'

' That has been there ever since I can remember.'

' Does it conceal a door ? '

Robin had taken off his doublet and unfastened his points.
He stretched his arms now, yawning. Irvine stood there,
swaying a little on his legs. He was carrying in his hand a
spice-ball at which he sniffed once and again. Round his neck
hung a superb chain of garnets. His vanity was apparent in
every breath and movement, but there was something charming, even innocent as well. Robin, sitting on the bed-edge,
listening for every sound, trying not to stare at Troilus and his

fat golden-painted hound, with desperation tried to catch
Irvine's words, for they reached over a kind of murmuring
water-music that played in his ears.

'Your brother hates me. He is quite foolish about it, for
I bear him no malice. It was about some wretched fellow
whom my dogs destroyed in the Northern Rebellion. I did
but my duty. . . . But I do not like your brother. He is a
blundering oafish fellow. I say that to annoy you because I
like to see you start and a flush come from your heart. Were
I like Paulton or Havering, I would make love to you, but I
am not of that kind. Woman was made for me, arranged and
perfected for proper intercourse. Boys are clumsy, sweating,
ill-fashioned. But I like you, Robin. May I call you so?
You are both gentle and intelligent — not at all like your big
clumsy brother, whom I will kill one day if he is not careful. . . .'

Then he went into a long, extremely egotistic discourse
about his ambitions, disappointments, friends and enemies. He
sought for no reply. He saw only his own figure, as though
repeated in mirror after mirror into infinite distance.

'I am no madman. I have no expectation beyond my
deserts, but I fancy that there is no injustice in my supposing
that I am of better birth, better mind, handsomer appearance
than many. I would not say this to any, save an old friend
like yourself.' (His egotism swallowed acquaintance and dis-
gorged it as friendship within a minute or two.) 'I flatter
myself that I have a just view of myself. I am no Narcissus,
although Narcissus himself had no more reason to fear Echo
than I have. I am exactly the man of my time and position
for a place at Court. I have asked Sir Francis Etheredge——'

Then began a long detailed summary of all the intrigues
and plottings to keep him out of Court circles. You would
fancy, to listen, that the London world of fashion had no
business in life except to keep Philip Irvine from Court. And
yet, if you listened and were fair, you must admit to a certain
pathos of ingenuous youth in Irvine's own picture of himself.
He would always be one of those egotists who can see no one
right but themselves ; who, in later years, will slip behind the
times and make themselves fools because they do not know

that time, weather, habit, philosophy and religion have all changed while they were blustering. For Irvine, as with all vain men, had cruelty born of fear, and despotism born of self-insecurity, in his nature. He explained that he must marry, and marry money. He had already someone in his eye. And then with money, his position at Court . . .

He broke off.

' I swear that you have not listened to a syllable.'

' Of course. Of course,' Robin said.

Irvine came over and tapped his cheek. ' Yes, if I were of another mind I could make love to you,' he said affably.

Robin, mad, poor boy, with apprehension, yet a native resentment rising in him, drew back.

' Have no fear,' Irvine said, laughing. ' Only when all women are eliminated with the plague perhaps——'

He followed Robin's eyes.

' How you gaze at the picture ! I swear Cressida is your love, with her swollen pink nose and a lip that a wasp must have stung.' He went over to it.

' You have some girl hidden behind it, I daresay.' He raised it. Robin did not speak.

' No. . . . There is nothing.' He came back and stood staring almost sullenly into Robin's face.

' Why is it that I feel a kind of horror of you ? As though we are mixed in some dreadful misfortune. . . . And yet I like you.'

Robin stared up at him. And, as the two men looked into one another's face, to both of them came a choking almost suffocating beating of the heart, as though a vial had been unstoppered and an acrid grey smoke plugged their nostrils.

' Well '— Irvine swaggered to the door —' Robin, my pretty Adonis, I shall be innocent at least of *your* raping. But your large, swaggering brother — bid him beware. Let him scowl once too often and his liver shall be split. Good night.'

Robin waited until the steps had quite died away. Now he could hear, only as the singing of a distant humming-top, the playing of the music from the great hall. He must not undress — yet he must seem natural if by any chance someone should knock on his door. Above all, he must not sleep. He was infinitely weary. The agitations of the evening, Anthony Pierson and his love for him, his far greater love for Sylvia (it was this, above all, that had exhausted him. She stood on her toes, reached up to him, placed her hands on his breast . . .), and through all this, behind it and belonging to it, the picture of the imprisoned Queen that Pierson had stirred in his imagination. Ah, what a tangle life was ! These strands, so different, meeting to form his history, and influencing through that history the lives of so many yet unborn ! It was as though, in his own slender inexperienced being, he had the fates of all the Herries yet to come. And Irvine ? Why, as he looked into his face, had he been aware of that sick foreboding ? And why had he liked him better than he could ever have supposed ?

His head was flaming. He went to the window and threw it back and looked over the dark garden to the quiet eternal line of the gentle Downs ! How brief was man's life in comparison with that steady permanence ! His sons would look on them, and his sons' sons when he was long forgotten, as though he had never been. Where then were God's Bright Pavilions, and dare he, so insignificant and brief a creature, ever hope to find them ? And yet there was no passion, not even his love for Sylvia, that lay so deep within him.

He put on his bed-gown and lay down on his bed. For a while perhaps he slept. At least he was in another world, travelling with Anthony over mountains, and Anthony pointed, crying : ' They are there ! I see them ! At last ! At last ! '

He opened his eyes to find Pierson and the silent Anstey beside his bed. He realized, at the same moment, that the house was quiet, there was no music.

' We must be on our way,' Anthony whispered. He went with them to the stair-head and listened. In the dark yard Anthony kissed him. Then, without a word, the two shadows slipped into the shadow.

Robin softly re-entered the house. He stood listening, for he had fancied that there was a step on the stair. He moved forward and listened again. There was no one there. The house was as silent as death.

BARTHOLOMEW

EVERYTHING moves but Time, and Nicholas Herries, not given to imaginative speculation, nevertheless felt himself one of those horned animals moving frantically in a glass bottle that the Indians showed in the Strand and offered to sell for a silver sixpence.

Not that Nicholas himself was not free, but he had not known, before he undertook it, the work that the overlordship of Mallory would entail. He had not expected for one thing that his father would abandon his duties so utterly ; but, from the instant that the household was called together, addressed solemnly by Sir Michael and then handed over, body and soul, to Nicholas, the old man sank gleefully to his pleasant laziness.

He busied himself, it is true, with all kinds of excitements about his house and garden. With a gentle but eager smile behind his stiff white beard, he would walk up and down the shady pleached alleys ; turn on the device of the fountain whereby Neptune would, most unexpectedly, discharge water and damp the onlooker ; admire the topiary work of yews and privet (topiary work is a fine art) ; study the herbs in the herb-garden, and the artichokes, cucumbers and pompions in the vegetable garden. In the house too, he would constantly admire his Flemish tapestry, the carved chimney-overmantels, the straw mattings and even rugs, now supplanting filthy rushes, the gilt and silver plate set out on the oak cupboard, especially a solid gold Spanish spice-dish. He would wander into the bedrooms and see that in the beds the straw was well laid under the canvas and that the ermine rug was properly unrolled ; then he would sit on one after another of the gilded Spanish-leather chairs and investigate the works of the great Herries clock in which, through doors of graven copper, the sea ebbed and flowed. In the gallery he would study the family portraits and flick the dust off them with his lace kerchief and would go and play, clumsily and out of tune, on the little organ, the virginals and the viol.

He took, in fact, an entirely new interest in his house and property now that he no longer had to work for it. Mallory was a small house as country houses went. Henry Herries' place in Chelsea was already twice the size of it, but it was very lovely with its white plaster and black beams, herb and flower gardens and the Downs beyond protecting it. These Herries loved every stone and sod of it.

Nicholas did indeed, and was exceedingly happy. This was the right work for him, and his jokes and laughter with the men and women on the place could be heard sometimes up the village street or away in the centre of the cornfields. They all loved him, yes, far more than they had loved his father, who had been a little apart from them, singing out of tune to himself as though they were not there, and suddenly out of temper with them for no reason at all. Nicholas would lose his temper and roar like a bull and pick a carter up by the wide seat of his breeches and shake him like a mouse. Nicholas would be out of sorts and sulk like a child, and sometimes he would kiss one of the house or farm girls more than was safe or seemly, but always they could understand him. They knew *why* he did the things he did, and he would sing with them while they were carting the hay, or dance with them or drink with them. And yet he was always a gentleman. They never forgot it and they never resented it.

So he, Nicholas, was very happy and the Mallory property flourished. Only, as the months went on, one thing distressed him — his brother Robin.

Robin, whom he loved more than anyone alive, was not happy. Ever since the summer night when Uncle Henry, his children and his friends had come, Robin had been unhappy. Nicholas knew that it dated from that day. He suspected that it had to do with Sylvia Herries.

So one evening he came into Robin's room and found him on his bed, reading ; so he pushed him to the wall, lay down beside him, taking most of the bed, put his arm around him, drew him close and asked him what the matter was.

Robin told him at once. He was in a fiery passion for Sylvia Herries and she too loved him. But they could scarcely ever meet and if they *did* meet, someone was always there. Worst of all Sylvia herself was so strange, appearing to love him and at the same time to be desperately afraid of her father. Robin wished to have it all clear and open, but she implored him to tell her father nothing. Why was this? He had no idea.

And, thirdly, Philip Irvine was always about the place. ' The queer thing, Nick, is that I don't dislike him as you do — but we both of us have a sort of dim fear about us as though we saw into the future.'

Seeing into the future was a joke to Nicholas, who found the present quite enough for him, so, sucking a straw that he had brought in from the stable, he pulled Robin's hair, told him not to worry and that he should have his Sylvia.

Then, by himself, he puzzled much over this matter. He knew that Robin's nature was shy and delicate, that he never cared to push his own interests, and that, when he felt deeply, he was the more silent. Nicholas loved his brother so dearly that he could not bear that he should not have anything that he wanted.

And why should he not have Sylvia? Theirs was the older branch of the house and Robin was one of the finest, noblest and handsomest young men in England. So at least Nicholas considered.

At last Nicholas decided that he would go himself and speak to his uncle on this very important matter. Sylvia urged Robin to silence only because she was a child and did not know what men were like. Nicholas knew that his uncle, outwardly at least, flattered him. He was always inviting him. They should have a friendly talk together and he would say nothing to Robin because Robin would certainly try to dissuade him. Nicholas was not in general good at keeping secrets, but this time he spoke to nobody.

Before his visit there arrived dreadful news from France. About one o'clock on Sunday morning, August 24th, of this year 1572 there began in Paris a most terrible bloody massacre of Huguenots. It was the more horrible because Paris was at that time filled with thousands of gay unsuspecting Huguenots celebrating the marriage of Henry of Navarre with Marguerite of Valois. This wedding had been intended to mark the end of the French religious troubles.

News came through but slowly. It was known that the great Coligny was brutally murdered and that Queen Elizabeth and the English Court were horrified and revolted. Every kind of story was circulating through London, a collection of verified and unverified horrors that angered even the hard-headed Englishman of the city, who was well used to hangings and quarterings and burnings at the stake.

However, on the morning Nicholas selected to visit his uncle London seemed to have given her soul over to gaiety, noise and industry. It was an early hour, for Nicholas had decided that he would join in the general family meal that would begin about eleven o'clock. He, attended by Jack Oates, who walked behind him, his nose in the air and a despising expression on his countenance, had crossed the river, and now took his time down the Strand, missing nothing that was amusing, and attracting, because of his size and the independent confidence of his carriage, a great deal of attention.

This was one of those mornings early in September when, even though you may be in the heart of the city, a glittering frost seems but just to have been dissipated by the sun, and the air is, you fancy, filled with the whispers of golden-russet, wafer-thin leaves.

As a fact it was a glorious morning of sun, and hot. The first thing noticed by any stranger, new to that world, would have been the multitude of stenches — stench of unwashed and sweating bodies, lousy coats and jerkins, spilled filth from the windows, ordure of beast and man, decaying fish in the gutters, animals' blood from the butchers', dead cats, dead dogs, dead rats, dead pigeons, dead babies now and again, and a murdered man with his throat cut, lying two days now without discovery in the side lane running from Durham House to the river.

No one cared for the smells, although one or two of the

grander kind carried spice-balls at which occasionally they sniffed. And after the smells the noise !

The whole street, from end to end, was one yell, scream and whistle. At the upper end of the Strand were the nobler houses with their gardens and trees sloping to the river, but from Uncle Henry's house to St. Paul's and beyond was the Fair of all Vanity Fairs. Nicholas had it in mind to buy for his mother one of those French caps that had but newly come to town.

As he stepped across the road down the hill to Ludgate, the splendid walls and tower of St. Paul's Church rising like a blessed miracle on the hill in front of him, he was forced for a moment to stop and gaze — even though he knew London so well.

It was a day of especial shining glitter and blaze of colour. The little clouds raced along the blue sky, but no one regarded them, the waters ran, from one of the main conduits, gallantly, leapingly in the gutters. The bells of churches gambolled in the air. Somewhere a cannon was firing and trumpets playing.

And human voices ! What a babble !

On the small cobbled street itself there were carts with creaking, screaming wheels, horses with jangling harness, a grand coach lumbering, jolting over mud and stone, hawkers' barrows, pedlars' trays on wheels. And everywhere human beings, most of whom seemed to be shouting about one thing or another.

There were many soldiers, for it was only in the former June that the Duke of Norfolk had been executed for his share in the Ridolfi plot, soldiers just back from the foreign wars in cassocks of pale blue Yorkshire cloth, a buckskin jerkin and a red cap ; then there were old disbanded soldiers, much shabbier than these, and after them bands of the downright beggars. Nicholas himself was jostled against now by a company of as veritable rogues as could be found in the city. In rags of shreds and patches, one of them with a black shade over one eye, one of them with his nostrils slit, and one huge fat fellow winking at him indecently as much as to say : ' We're two fine big-built rascals together, we are.'

Even as he stood about looking around for a haberdasher's where he might buy his French cap, a thin peak-bearded man bound on a hurdle was being dragged along, accompanied by a whole company of merry jesting-like boys, to be hanged and dismembered while still alive at Tyburn, whose bar was already loaded with grinning bird-pecked heads whitened with bird-droppings until they looked like speckled cheeses. From the shops that lined the street came the yells and cries of the prentices who, on a fine morning like this, enjoyed the sun, the gaiety and the general movement to the very full. In this part of the Strand they were hopefully on the look-out for a fight, because the students of the Inns of Court were not far away and might attempt a raid as quick as a bell's ringing. Old people remembered the Evil May Day of 1517 when the military had to be called out to quiet them.

Thieves were everywhere in spite of the fact that death was the penalty for the theft of goods worth more than two shillings. It was Jack Oates' principal office to walk behind Nicholas with his eyes active to see that no one approached near enough to his master to rob him.

And so, in the midst of all this babel of carts, and men shouting for passage, and prentices crying out their masters' wares, and beggars whining for gifts, and bells ringing and dogs barking and wheels creaking, Nicholas stood looking about him under the lovely sun seeking for a haberdasher's.

A moment later he had seen one and strode his way across. This shop was, as most shops still were, a single room on the street's level, with a large unglazed window whose shutter let down to form a counter. In the doorway, sunning herself, the wife of the proprietor sat, the prentice near by was bawling at the top of his voice, while on the counter lay a selection of very pretty things imported from France. Nicholas, whose thighs and chest were greatly admired by the proprietor's wife, who whispered in his ear that she lived over the shop and her husband was often in Norwich, soon found the prettiest cap of purple velvet and seed pearls, dignified, handsome and very foreign.

As he turned away, bowing with elaborate irony to the smiling lady, he was stopped by a crowd who were watching some soldiers on the march and fancied that there was a whisper in his ear, ' Beware the Catholics near at home. You are in danger.' He turned sharply, his hand on his dagger, but saw no one watching him. He asked Oates : ' Did anyone speak to me ? '

' Why, no, master.'

Entering his uncle's house, he felt, as he often did on an ordinary day, that it was more of a business place than a home. On a night of entertainment it would be all candlelight and music, but that was not its true life. Here was the very soul of the merchandising, business, profit-making Herries inhabiting. Across the hall clerks with pens behind their ears were hurrying. Through an open door he could see a room with a long table covered with papers, and small tables at which dully-clad men were sitting.

Running up the grand staircase, two steps at a time, he found them already seated at their meal in the room with the mirrors where Gilbert Armstrong had wrestled. He stood in the doorway grinning and, while they were greeting him, perceived several things : one that the food was mean and poor, as it always was, another that his aunt had her physician beside her, a little pursy man with a wart on his nose, another that Phineas Thatcher was yellow in the face as though with jaundice, another that Sylvia was the only member of the family glad to see him.

After he had sat down with them he quickly perceived that there was something truly the matter and then learnt that Sidney Herries had returned but the night before from France, that he had been in Paris during the Bartholomew Massacre and was deeply wrought by his experience as though he were altogether another creature.

Mistress Herries waved her hands, mopped her eyes and could not be silent for an instant. Queerly enough, Nicholas found himself, for the first time in his life, sympathizing with his poor aunt. He might lack imagination, but his heart responded always and instantly to any real distress. This *was* real, the one real thing in Grace Herries' nature, her love for, and adoration of, her stepsons. She forgot now even her ailments, pushing the physician aside with an impatient blow in the stomach.

' You know, nephew, that it pleases us all to have you here

and that you are ever welcome in this house, but when you
see the poor boy you will not know him. The physician has
given him a draught and he is sleeping, but he has not until
now slept for a whole fortnight. When he entered this room
last night I lifted my hands and screamed. It was a ghost and
yet our own son——'

She snatched a little glass bottle from the physician's hands
and sniffed at it.

' I hope,' Nicholas said, ' that no bodily harm——'

' No,' his uncle answered. ' He has no bodily hurt, but
he is haunted by what he has seen. You shall yourself hear
later. It is a fearful story.'

' And your uncle would not suffer me to hear his story.
As though I could bear not to know what it was that had
changed him so ! He was always so merry, a joke and a song
with anyone — and last night he stood there by the lighted
candles, his face drawn and his eyes astare and his poor throat
moving but no word coming——'

She broke off and began to sob. Uncle Henry stuttered
impatiently :

' There . . . there . . . sweetheart ! Mompsen, see to her.
That draught you had for my son may serve for her. There !
There ! Go with her to her room, Mompsen. Go with
Mompsen, sweetheart.'

So Aunt Grace wandered out with a kind of dog-whimper
and giving Nicholas a watery smile as she passed him.

' It is her heart,' Uncle Henry explained. ' Any agitation
is bad for it. When she lies on her side at night her heart
leaps within her like a dog on a chain.'

' Too much fat about her heart,' Nicholas said laconically.
He rose, pushing back his chair. ' I want some conversation
with you, Uncle Henry — and alone, to ourselves.' As he said
this he turned and grinned at the lank-haired, yellow-faced
Phineas. When he looked at him he could never forget the
occasion when he had caught Phineas mumbling round the
bosom of one of the kitchen-maids at Mallory — she a little
country girl and screaming her life out at him. It was then that
he had pulled Phineas' long, cold nose and, after that, raised
him and sat him up on the edge of the big water-butt, where

he had stayed, with his bony legs hanging over the edge, until rescued with pompous surprise by old Mellon. ' Fie ! Fie ! Trying to rape a poor country girl, and you a Puritan, Mr. Thatcher,' Nicholas had remarked.

Phineas hated him, of course, from that moment, with a dangerous hatred. Dangerous because Phineas *was* dangerous. The world is filled, not with good and bad people, but with the builders and the destroyers, and the battle between them is eternal. Phineas Thatcher was a destroyer only because he wanted to build later on. But the practice of destroying, denying, sneering at the builders and generally having a good lachrymose time leads to self-flattery. It is hard not to believe yourself a fine fellow when you are nobly and loudly against the government. So Phineas thought Nicholas a ribald, lecherous, bullying lout and bided his revenge.

Nicholas and his uncle went to the leather-walled room where the head of the house conducted his business. Henry Herries had bought the Spanish leather at a bargain, and very handsome it looked fastened with big round brass nails. Over the stone fireplace was a coloured map of Europe, the seas liberal with dolphins, barques, naked Neptunes and spouting whales. On the table were papers in neatly bound packets, a handsome gold inkhorn and huge red-leather account-books. Nicholas and his uncle had scarcely sat down when young Sidney Herries came in.

Then indeed was Nicholas startled. Sidney Herries was a changed young man. Unlike his elder brother Edward he had a round, stupid but not unfriendly face and a sturdy body. He had been always a good deal of a fool and fond of low company. He had given his father a great deal of worry, especially since a low girl of an inn near St. Paul's had come to him accusing Sidney of the paternity of her child.

The man who stood now in the doorway, looking at them with a kind of remote sternness, was no lecherous young fool. His face was drawn and pale ; his hand was on his dagger-hilt as though he were on his guard. He came forward and shook Nicholas' hand. ' Good day, Cousin Nicholas.'

He has been through something, Nicholas thought, that has shaken his very soul, and he put his hand on Sidney's shoulder and felt him lean, for a moment, against him. He fancied even that Sidney was delighted to see him, as though he would find new courage in his great size and strength.

Uncle Henry, who as a rule had no understanding of anything save business feelings, drew out a chair.

' Sit you down, Sidney. I cannot say of course whether you would care to tell Nicholas something——'

' I would ! I would ! ' Sidney said with a strange eagerness, and he turned on his chair towards Nicholas ; from beginning to end after that he scarcely once looked away from Nicholas' face. The only sound in the room besides Sidney's voice was the heavy solemn rhythm of the clock on the wall.

' I should wish to tell you, Cousin Nicholas,' Sidney said, ' because I cannot lose the thing from my brain. Perhaps if I release it, it will stay with me less. I will tell you everything. It must go ; it must leave me or I shall be out of my wits.

' My father sent me to Paris to stay with M. de Roux, a banker friend of his, and most fortunately, as it happened, a Catholic. My father thought too that I should enjoy this special time in Paris with the Navarre marriage and the festivities.

' He had a lodging in the Rue Quincampoix, which is not very distant from the Rue St. Honoré, as you are probably aware, Nicholas. I am sure that M. de Roux had no knowledge whatever of the coming event. He had been like a father to me during the earlier weeks. He is a bachelor of some sixty years, jolly, stout, fond of company, but thinking, I found, little of women, having a great deal of business to consider. He had many friends both Catholic and Protestant. On the Saturday afternoon he went to pay a visit at Coligny's hôtel. Coligny, as you know, had been wounded by an assassin, a little while before. I believe that many gentlemen were present to express their regrets. M. de Roux was one of the last to leave and he heard Coligny's son-in-law, Téligny, enquire of the Admiral whether he would like any of them to keep watch in his house during the night, and the Admiral said it was more labour than needed and thanked them with loving words.'

Sidney now drew his chair nearer to Nicholas, almost as though he were seeking for protection.

' I'll tell you everything, cousin ! I'll leave nothing out ! Do you see ? Nothing ! Nothing ! '

Nicholas put out his broad hand and rested it on Sidney's shoulder.

' Well, then, M. de Roux returned — about six o'clock I think it was. We were to spend a quiet evening together. His old housekeeper had prepared supper for us. He had made a very famous collection of missals, French and Italian, and for an hour or two we looked at these together. During these last weeks, Nicholas, he had won much influence over me. I had come to love him, for he is a good and true man and he had shown me doctrines of life and ways of conduct that no one had ever shown me before. At last we embraced and I went to my bed. It was a warm parched night and I lay naked, unable to sleep. I fancy now that M. de Roux was himself made uneasy by something he had heard at the Admiral's. I remember that I pushed the window open and looked out over the Paris roofs. There was not a breath stirring and every sound came clearly, and soon I was interested by the noise of men marching, and it seemed to me that there was an unusual light of torches reflected in the sky. All the same I thought little of it and went back to my bed, leaving the window open, and even slept a little.'

Sidney stopped. He looked wildly about the room. Drawing still closer to Nicholas he went on, the words coming faster and faster :

' I was wakened by a bell. I can hear it in my ears now, a heavy booming bell that went on and on. At once through my open window it was as though the roof of Paris had come off — bells were ringing, shots were firing, the rushing of steps, cries and shouts. I did not know what to do. I stood there, naked, looking about me. A moment later M. de Roux entered. He was fully dressed with rapier and dagger. He seemed frantic. He cried again and again, seizing my bare shoulder and shaking me : " Dress ! Dress ! For Christ's sake, your clothes ! " and himself helped me, kneeling down and tying my points, never ceasing to cry out in a sort of horrified whisper, " Nay ! Nay ! Christ help us ! Christ and Our Lady ! " When I was clothed he tied a white sleeve on my arm, caught up my hat that was on a chair and fastened a white linen cross in the band. I saw then that he also had a white sleeve and a white cross in his hat that he had thrown on the bed. Oh, Nicholas, what should I have done ? Did I deny my religion ? Did I show myself a coward ? But I was bewildered, you understand, and stared at him and continued asking, " But what is it ? What is it ? " for the noise increased with every moment and there were frightful cries, screams that turned my blood to water. M. de Roux himself seemed out of his mind, for his speech was all broken. He said, " Remember you are a Catholic — everywhere you are a Catholic. I did not know that this was what they intended. You are a Catholic, a Catholic. . . ."

' He told me afterwards that had he been calm and thought wisely he would never have stirred from that house, for he was safe where he was and known to everyone for a sober and honest Catholic. I remember, father, you yourself told me that you would not have sent me to him had he not been so good a man that his religion could harm no one. But in the sudden horror of the moment he thought it safer that he and the housekeeper and myself should go but a few streets away to the hôtel of a great Catholic friend of his, M. de Vrillac. It seemed to him, I suppose, a little distance and he feared that they might fire the building where we were. So we hastened down the staircase and into the street. . . .

' The street . . . the street ! . . .' he repeated to himself, his eyes staring into a horrible distance.

Nicholas put his arm around him. Then he went on :

' The street ! . . . Oh, Christ, the street ! ' He caught Nicholas' doublet with his hand and pushed with his knuckles into Nicholas' chest. ' The tumult ! It was fearful. At once, you must understand, I was in a mad world, just stepping from that house into the street. Bells were clanging, doors crashing, musket-shots firing, and worst of all a great yell, like animals — bears, wolves, what you will — or, no, better, like the insane ; a noise on one note, as though it came from a crack in the sky. . . . I was knocked on to my knees by a rush of armed men and when I got to my feet I was nearly knocked down again — by a butcher — by a butcher — by a butcher. . . .'

He began to repeat this in a sort of sing-song as though he did not know what he was saying. Nicholas took him, then, between his thighs and held him against his chest and stroked his hair as though he were a little child, saying :

' There ! Wait. Rest awhile. Tell us another day. . . .' And very tenderly he kissed his cheek.

Sidney looked into his broad boyish face with the short nose and wide calm forehead, looked at him wonderingly as though he had never seen him before, and then at his great body. His own face smoothed, his eyes lost their wildness ; he turned, leaning against Nicholas' thigh, and seemed to see his father for the first time. He spoke in a normal steady voice and caught Nicholas' hand, going back to his chair.

' No. . . . It takes me at times as though I were there again. All will be well now. I had best finish it. This big man in a smock with blood drying on his cheek, he was dragging a naked girl — but upside-down, bumping her head on the stones. She was quite naked and screamed like a door creak-ing. As he pushed past me he drove his knife into her breast. Her blood hit me like a whip. And then, Nicholas, I was mad too. I walked steadily forward. I had forgotten M. de Roux and all else. I saw things as though they were things in a theatre. I felt no pity, no horror, no sorrow. Only I retched in my stomach as though I would be sick and could not. I heard myself making those retching noises. I picked up a head, Nicholas, by the long black hair and I threw it into the gutter as you would a pompion. My face and my hands were covered with blood and I walked on in all that noise. A house was burning and crackling, muskets firing right in my ear, and that scream always, a scream out of all tune. But however fearful the noise was I heard myself retching. Tick-tick-tick — like a clock. And there was a smell — blood dry and blood wet and blood falling in your eyes. You have heard of some of the dreadful things : the worst was when Henry of Navarre rose meaning to go to the King's levee and demand justice for the Admiral. At the foot of the stairs he was

arrested. A list of his gentlemen had been prepared. As each
man answered to his name he stepped into the courtyard, and
had to make his way through a double line of Swiss mer-
cenaries. Sword, spear, halberd soon finished them. They
say that two hundred of the best blood of France lay there in a
heap under the Palace wall while the King looked down from
the window.

'The Swiss plundered them and they say that many ladies
of Queen Catherine came later to laugh at them and especially
to examine M. Soubise because his wife had sought divorce
on grounds of nullity of marriage. . . .' Sidney turned, with
grave, controlled seriousness, to Nicholas. 'I tell you, Cousin
Nicholas — because you must remember. Because it was the
Catholics who did these things. The Catholics! Never forget.
It will be like that here, too, one day if we are not careful.
For myself I do not know where I was for the rest of that
morning. But I know some of the things I saw. I saw the
river water running with thick iridescent stinking blood. I
saw the living, tied hand and foot, thrown off the bridges. I
saw a man with two little children — pitifully crying for their
mother — in a creel, and he stood on the Louvre bank and
threw them into the river as you would blind kittens. I saw a
baby, scarcely able to walk, dragged with a cord round its
neck, falling on its little knees, bleeding but too frightened to
cry, and children of nine and ten years were dragging it. I
saw a woman clinging with her hands to the wooden piles of
the bridge, and men, laughing, stoning her, and at last the
body floating away and then her long hair being entangled with
the woodwork. I stood and watched that, Nicholas. I saw a
big man with a beard carrying a child, and the child smiled
and played with his beard. And the man turned and grinned
at me and said, " He loves me, no ? " and he stabbed the child
in the neck and threw it into the Seine. There was one house,
they say, where all the inhabitants were murdered save a little
girl who was dipped in the blood of her father and mother.
The famous Protestant bookseller, Niquet, was burnt over a
slow fire made of his own books. . . .

'And I wandered on, wandered on, and at last I was by
the river and a man and a woman were on the bank, leant

against the wall, dead in one another's arms, and I snuggled into them and slept, the sun on my face. . . .'

He stopped. Not a word was spoken. Nicholas felt in himself a sick disgust, and with it, what was unusual for him, a speculation about life. This then was what life was : a filthiness, a stink, a bestiality. He had seen it in terms of sun, rain, crops, laughing battle, love, bodily pleasures, love of his brother — and, with that, through the brass nails in the leather, he saw, what was so seldom out of his mind, the girl turning, looking down at him on the straw, slipping through the door. . . . Yes, he wanted to live, however bestial life might be. But the filthy Catholics. He had always distrusted them, against the Queen as they were, but now he saw that they wanted watching. They would bring in these bastard foreigners and be tearing at good English throats. . . . He had been staring at the wall : he turned round and saw that Sidney was gone.

He raised his broad good-natured face, wrinkled now with a twisting puzzle, to his uncle, who sat nervously tapping papers on the table with his fingers.

' A bad affair, Uncle Henry. Poor Sidney has had a hurt over it.'

Henry Herries smoothed his beard with his hand, and at once his features that had been quite honestly paternal were business again. He got on his feet.

' Well, well. . . . The boy will recover. But the laws against the Catholics must be strengthened. No doubt at all. They must be strengthened.' He moved towards the door and Nicholas stopped him.

' Wait, Uncle Henry. There's something I want to say.'

' Well, my boy ? '

He turned round, beaming. When he looked at his big nephew he always imagined six thieves breaking through into his strong-room and Nicholas cracking all their heads at one blow. He put his hand on Nicholas' arm. It gave him pleasure to feel his muscle.

' It is this, uncle. It is my brother Robin.'

His uncle said nothing, so Nicholas, smiling, continued: 'He loves Sylvia. Has done for a year. She loves him also, I believe.'

Still Uncle Henry said nothing, but he had dropped his friendly hand.

' He has a notion that he must not speak to you of this. Sylvia has begged him to be silent. I love my brother more than anything or anyone on this earth. I think it a charming notion that they should marry — and I have the fancy that you would not disapprove.'

He ceased because he was aware that he was being given no sort of encouragement. There was silence in the room save for the steady solemn ticking of the clock.

Nicholas began again more truculently. His temper was always easily roused.

' It is surely a good plan, Uncle Henry. Robin is a sweet lad, noble-hearted, a poet, a wit, and loved by all the world.'

Henry Herries at last said slowly : ' No. It is impossible — now or ever.'

Nicholas, keeping his temper down for dear Robin's sake, said : ' Impossible ! But how ? Why ? '

His uncle went to the door.

' I will tell you why.'

Nicholas, standing there bewildered and ready to be in a furious temper of pride and disappointment for his dear Robin, heard his uncle open the door of the next room and say something. He returned with Mr. Phineas Thatcher, who stood just inside the door as though ready to escape.

' Mr. Thatcher. I beg you. Tell my nephew why his brother cannot marry my daughter.'

Phineas said : ' Because he is a Catholic.'

Nicholas sprang forward. ' That is a lie. A foul bastard lie ! '

' Tell him further, Mr. Thatcher.'

Phineas, as though he were reciting a love poem, so unctuous was his voice, went on : ' Summer last year Mr. Robin Herries concealed two priests a night in Mallory.'

Nicholas with a strangle of rage was at his throat, but Uncle Henry quietly held his arm and remarked : ' You must be fair, Nicholas. Mr. Thatcher has his proof.'

Nicholas stayed where he was. With a flash of certainty he knew that this was true.

Phineas, who now was flat against the door, his hand on the bolt, said : 'I myself saw him. It was the summer night when we all — Mr. Herries, Mistress Herries, Mr. Irvine and others were at Mallory. We stayed on the lawn until evening. I first saw your brother, Mr. Nicholas, speak to a common fellow behind the hedge. That aroused my interest. Afterwards your house-man, Mellon, told me that he had interrupted your brother carrying food from the buttery. Finally at two in the morning I saw them depart, your brother guiding them into the court. I knew who they were. Pierson and Anstey were their names, but I said nothing to the authorities because of the honour of the family.'

Nicholas caught his throat this time. 'You damnable, cursed spy ! You filthy, loitering, creeping spy !'

He threw Thatcher on to his knees.

Then he went from the house without another word.

SATAN IN WATENDLATH

AT Rosthwaite Nicholas Herries stood in the hall looking
about him. There was everything just as it had been when he
had seen it last. There was the beautiful tapestry, in carnation
and green and gold, of Diana bathing. There, the inlaid
buffet of ebony mounted in silver, the red and green panels.
He could see them all seated at the table : the three old men,
the young priest, Robin. He could hear the voices of the men
singing. He could taste on his tongue the tart seasoned flavour
of the eel-pie. And nevertheless how different it all now was !

He stood there towering over little Mr. Forster of Henditch,
the old man with the silver hair and the baby face. The old
man in his black suit with the white ruff, his pink unlined
forehead and cheek, his mild rather rheumy blue eyes that
he raised, with pleasant and courteous attention, to Nicholas'
giant form — this little old man seemed the only thing alive in
the house. Outside in the courtyard Gilbert Armstrong was
waiting. There was no sound but the crooning of pigeons in
the pigeon-cote. Through the open window the thin warm
spring sun poured in, striking lovely lights in the tapestry.
But it was the house of the dead.

Nicholas had been nearly a week too late. His uncle had
in reality been dead before he started from London. Robin,
to whom the house, everything in it, the piece of land, had
been left, was in the Netherlands, travelling with Charles
Lacey. It had been Robin who had been wanted, not Nicholas.

He knew, as he stood there, smiling at the gentle little
man, that he represented the enemy, and his sense of Robin's
danger that had been passionately active ever since he had
listened to the Bartholomew horrors in his uncle's house was
vividly increased. His uncle had left all that he had to Robin:
his uncle had died a Catholic and been buried in the vault at
Henditch, Mr. Forster's place, as a Catholic.

Since that French massacre of August '72 — now nine months old — the hostility to the Catholics, that had been quiet since Elizabeth's accession, had flamed into life. Nicholas felt it in himself. He hated the Catholics, as murderers of innocent women and children, as enemies of the Queen. And his own brother . . .

He had said no word to Robin of his visit to Uncle Henry. His attitude to Robin had been the same as before except that it had been watchful and more tender. He had said once :

' The Bartholomew massacre. I can't get it out of my head, Robin. If that Catholic horror should be repeated here.'

And Robin, steadily regarding him, had answered, ' I also hate that cruelty.'

But the authorities ? They must have known that his uncle here was a Catholic, they must have noted well that this house had been left to Robin. Even now, on this sunny spring morning, there must be spies about the house. . . .

So, loudly and without pause, he said to Mr. Forster :

' I am sorry, Mr. Forster, that I did not see my uncle. I am more sorry still that he has left this place to my brother.'

' Why ? ' asked Mr. Forster.

' I am a Protestant, as is also my brother. The authorities may regard it strangely that my brother should inherit a Catholic property. It may place him under suspicion.'

Mr. Forster regarded him with mild surprise.

' Why, no, Mr. Herries. The Catholics who plot against Her Majesty *may* be under suspicion. But everyone in this district loved your uncle and knows that he was most loyal.'

' I have no doubt of his loyalty nor of yours, Mr. Forster, but since the Bartholomew night things are changed.' To his own surprise he shuddered. ' There is a fear abroad that such things might be attempted in England.'

Mr. Forster put his thin purple-veined hand on Nicholas' riding-coat.

' Have no fears,' he said, as though he were speaking to a child. ' I am an old man and so it is perhaps little to say, but to-night if it were necessary I would die for the Queen. And so would your uncle have done.'

Nicholas laughed.

'There is no question of dying, Mr. Forster. I may remain here a night or two ? There are some papers I must see, a little business . . .'

'Why, of course ! ' He bustled about, calling servants, sending for the stable-man.

Nicholas joined Gilbert.

'I'll see to Juno.' He looked about him. 'It's peaceful enough, Gilbert,'— dropping his voice he said —' but I don't like it. There's danger here.'

They stood close together, side by side ; Gilbert with the ruddy-brown complexion, the thick sturdiness of limb belonging to a man who was always in the open air, Nicholas with that boyish sense of springing vitality that went so remarkably with his great size. Nevertheless Gilbert, who had not seen him for more than a year, who, unknown even to himself, had longed for his return, realized in Nicholas a new maturity. Something had happened to him. He was no longer the young man of two years back. It might be perhaps the authority he had now in his father's place.

Thinking of that made Gilbert, on a quick impulse, determine to speak, and even as he determined he realized what an odd relationship there was between them — one of master and servant and at the same time of equals, of friend and friend.

As Gilbert Armstrong spoke the words that were to alter his whole life he took in, with his quick country eyes, the scene. He would never forget it again but carry it always with him as one does a key, a knife, a little brass box. Up the fell, the hills above Watendlath were dead grey and a line of wood to the left was a dull unstirring brown but lit by larch green and budding birch. The house itself was pearl-rose in the sunlight. The sky was as pale as a blue shadow on white water. A great many birds were singing, and from every side came the sound of the water of the swollen becks. The thin stretches of snow on the higher hills were now lit with sun and truly were radiant with a blazing glow — but a thin covering it was, so thin that it might lift at any instant and curl into the blue baseless air like smoke. He stood seeing and hearing, with an extra intentness, as though he knew that this was the most important moment of his life.

E

He stood shoulder to shoulder with Nicholas Herries, not as serving-man but as comrade and faithful helper for the remainder of their two lives.

' I want to say something to you.' His words had the rough warm rhythm of the Cumbrian tongue, an accent that is made of honesty, freedom and pigheadedness.

Nicholas, who had been lost in his own thoughts, turned and looked at the stolid Gilbert and felt, like a touch on the arm, a reassurance.

' What is it ? '

' I have had a year to think of it. I have thought of it very often.'

' Thought ? . . . of what ? '

' Of yourself, Mr. Herries. I wish to know whether I may come to you and bide with you—' He added deeply, firmly, as though he were swearing an oath, ' Always.'

Nicholas stared at him. This was a proper man and he loved him.

' Always ? That is a word without a tail——'

' I mean it every whit. I think I belonged to you from the day when I first saw you riding in the morning from this house.'

' Belong ? ' Nicholas shook his head. ' That is not a word to use. No man has any service save to the Queen.'

' To the Queen ? Yes, I pay that service. But it is impersonal. I belong to the sky, this earth, and in especial this mile or two of country—' He stopped. He raised his hand as though in a gesture of farewell. ' I had not time to tell you yet. My mother died six weeks back.'

Nicholas put his hand on his shoulder.

' I am now a free man,' Gilbert said.

' And at once you would go into servitude again ? '

' Not into servitude. We are man to man. But I have known no one in my life yet whom I would follow as I would follow you. When I am not with you something is lacking. I can do many things.'

Nicholas' hand tightened on his shoulder.

' You would leave this country you love so ? '

' I would go anywhere with you.'

' And what about women ? '

Gilbert laughed.

' I am like any other man about women. But there are
women in the South as well as the North.'

' Jack Oates will hate you and maybe poison your porridge.'

' No one shall harm either of us while the two of us are one
man.'

Nicholas laughed. He was cheered again. His regular
mood had returned — the sun was shining on the violet-grey
of the pigeon's wing and the larches burnt on the hill.

' That is a password that I will have written above my
chimney-piece. No one shall harm either of us while the two
of us are one man.'

He took off his riding-glove and held out his hand.

' Very well then. It is an oath.'

And they clasped hands while old Mr. Forster, looking
from a window, wondered what these two big men were
pledging.

' Always . . . Always . . . Always . . .'

Gilbert had said it. The pigeon, disturbed by a stamping
of Juno's hoof, had whirred in a tumbling symmetry to the
air, echoing ' Always.' The young larch trees burning on the
hill had echoed it.

And now, two days later, Nicholas repeated it. ' Always.
Always,' looking down at the swirling, kitten-like, fierce little
eddies of the Lake flooding-water. ' Always. . . . Always . . .'
but now it was of a far greater seriousness, for he was saying
it to a woman. Men were good as companions, to jest with,
to fight with, to trust and defend and laugh with — but no
man who ever lived could place Nicholas in this strange turmoil
under whose disturbing confusion he now suffered.

He was on the Germans' island and a great curtain of dark
velvet cloud hung behind the hills on the Lake's farther side.
Straight down through the heart of this curtain from an eye-
dazzling, knife-blade band of light, shafts of sun struck fan-
shaped and shadowed as though with dancing motes. So on
the grey-winged Lake, pools of deep daffodil broke, and on the
surface of these pools whirls of water, because the Lake was
flooded, curled like black snakes.

He was on the island that the German miners had now

made their home. Hans Opperer and Beck had encountered
him in Keswick. Oh, but how delighted they had been !
Opperer had at first been shy and then, suddenly losing all
restraint, had hugged and kissed him.

So the next day Nicholas must go and see what a wonderful
place they had made of the island. As indeed they had !
Derwent Island was near to the shore and a path ran down
from the town to a little rough landing-stage. In the eleventh
century it had been called Horse Island and belonged to
Fountains Abbey. Then it was called Vicar's Island and was
thick with trees. But now most of the trees were gone ; everything was trim and tidy with a proper German tidiness.
Nicholas marvelled at the beauty and neatness of it. There was
a brewery with living-rooms adjoining it. There was a pigeon-
house painted a bright green ; a windmill painted crimson,
and this could be seen, with its wings beautifully turning, from
all parts of the Lake ; there were pigsties with fine handsome
pigs ; but best of all, an enchanting garden that had a smooth
lawn running to the Lake edge, box hedges and flowers —
now all the flowers of the spring — in lines and pools of colour
under the open sky.

Before this magical island swung and heaved, on this spring
day, the Lake of Derwent. Dark shadows in the sky made
dark shadows in the Lake, but it was the spring rains that had
caused the rise, so that the Lake was like a cup filled to its very
brim. A breath on the surface, and a shudder heaved the
water to a running race so that in ripples of pale silver and
glassy heaving shoulders of water the edge was over-topped,
and up on to the thin grasses and shining pebbles and satin-
mackerel roots of the silver birch it welled and sucked and
clung.

From end to end of the Lake ran the ripples and sudden
whips of dark water and little mad scrambles of fret and
foam like the playing of puppies or children. Then, after
these, the long calm parental roll, making all smooth again.
Beneath the frets and eddies, constantly broken by them, lay
the dead-brown reflected hills with their slender caps of
snow.

Nicholas, leaving Opperer at the brewery, had turned from

the lawn to the thicket at the Lake edge, and it had been no
surprise at all to see Catherine Hodstetter there, on her knees
on the pebbly strand, washing clothes.

Since he came this time to Rosthwaite her name had not
passed his lips. He had not, in fact, spoken her name to any
living soul since he had last seen her in Newlands. He never
prayed at all, either to God or man, but if he had made a
prayer it would be that he never might see her again. Not
one single day since the Newlands visit had passed without
his thinking of her. He was sure that if she had been his
mistress he would, after a week of it, have never thought of
her again. Or would that physical intimacy have bound them
together irrevocably ? What madness was it in his brain ?

Some six months ago, lying with a lady of the Court, a
light friend of Charles Lacey's, at an inn on the river near
Twickenham, early in the morning, as the faint glow stirred
behind the window, turning on his side and seeing her with
her mouth open asleep, his body had been of a sudden so
passionately possessed with a longing for this German girl
that he had almost cried out aloud. It was then, at that early
hour, when such thin vaporous fancies possess us, that he
had been suddenly certain that the girl, the daughter of a
witch, had bewitched him. It could only be a spell. He had
smacked his chest, crying out aloud, ' A witch ! A witch !
By Jesu, a witch ! '— and the Court lady had awakened and
buried her head in his arm-pit, and his boredom had been like
a sickness.

' A witch ! A witch ! ' and there she was before the swirling
water, on her knees, washing the clothes.

She heard his step and turned her body towards him. As
in the instance of their other meetings, so now. It was an
event so natural and, for them both, so joyous that there was
little to say. She stood up, moving her strong arms to her
yellow braided hair. The little pebbled hollow where they
met was bounded by the trees : in front of them was the Lake.
He took her in his arms and they stayed strained, body to
body, mouth to mouth, while the water whirled on to the
grasses and the shafts of light from the dark bands of cloud
spread into a wide sweep of sun across the flanks of the hills.

Then they stood, hand in hand, side by side, looking out to the sun-stirred Lake.

'I intended to go without seeing you,' Nicholas said.

'I knew you were here. I know when you are within distance of me.'

'What is to be done?' Nicholas asked. 'We must talk. Sit here on this stone. I must resolve this for myself as well as for you.'

'What is there to resolve?' She was so happy and her eyes shone with so deep a look that he turned his head away from her.

'This must be resolved, Catherine. It is three years since our first meeting. I have never been rid of you from then until now.'

'Nor I of you.'

'Well, what is it to be? Will you come away with me? We will ride into Scotland, live in the hills for a time, know one another body and soul. Then I will go back to my father's house. That way our longing will be satisfied. Then we will be friends the rest of our days. We stop now on the edge of satisfaction.' He put his arm round her. 'Feel my heart beating against your hand. I am a man like any other and it is getting so now that when another woman is in my arms I think only of you. Until that week when first I failed to help a man who needed me and I kissed you in the Keswick Square everything had been as it was. I ate, I slept, I fought, I loved, and all was as it seemed to be. But since that day what is not there has more power over me than what is. A man's life, I should imagine, is set on the ground, and there is a door to go out from and a bed for him to sleep on and the sky is constant for him and these are the things that he must do : fear no man, honour the Queen, have his bodily needs and find every day sufficient for itself. But now '— he looked round to her, bewildered, his eyes puckered —'there is nothing simple any more, loving is not a simple loving and my enemy is seen in a mirror.' He said, his hand touching her breast, 'Have you bewitched me, Catherine?'

She shook her head.

'No, I have not bewitched you. But let me tell you, once

and for ever. When, a long time ago in Germany, I knew what my mother was and that her blood ran through my own body, I swore on the altar of our little church in Devingen that I would give that body to no man, would bear no child, would die as I must live — alone. Until I saw you it was not difficult. I had my longings like any other girl, and when a man kissed me, sometimes my blood would beat in my ears, but it became a habit, even a pride, to know that I was apart, and it grew in my mind that I was meant for some great work like the Maid in France. When I stood alone in my room and looked through the window at the trees standing so strongly by the river and the clouds driving so fiercely across the sky, I thought I was like them. . . . After I loved you I knew that it was not so. . . .'

He gazed into her face, his hand held hers as though he would break it.

' Tell me the truth, Catherine. Your mother — what is she ? '

' My mother is a very strange woman. She is not evil, but — but — oh, how can I tell you ? If you could have been with me ! Sometimes at night when we two are alone in the house my mother is not my mother. She is possessed by a power that if she were not herself good would lead her into terrible places. In my room, alone, above stairs, I can feel cold come into the house, and I have been to the stair-head and looked down, and in the room there is light and no light, and my mother sits straight in her chair and perhaps there is something at her feet and perhaps there is not. I have seen the flames leap in the fire and a wind has shaken the hangings and something has passed out through the door. I have seen my mother, naked, crouching on the floor, her hands cupped as though holding a vessel——'

' There is nothing in this,' Nicholas said, whispering.

' But there is. One day they will come and take her and burn her. She loves me and has a great heart and much wisdom. But she has told me. She cannot go back now. Knowing so much, she must know more. There is a great bat flies in front of the moon. I have seen it often and it hangs by its feet to the tree, and the fire inside the house leaps. . . .'

She came very close to him and cupped his face in her hands.

' Listen. I believe now that perhaps we will never be separated. And I know that we can never be together. You must try, with all the strength you have, to forget me. You must be not only passive as you have been, but you must fight. You must cry when you pray : " Mary, Mother of Jesus, deliver me ! Mary, Mother of Jesus, deliver me ! " Perhaps there is a Mary, Mother of Jesus. It may be that there was never one on this earth, but if she is there as they say, listening, she will hear and will save us both. Because for me there is one thing more terrible than my mother's end, which can be only the one end : that worse thing is that I should ever harm you.'

She moved away from him.

' If there is a God, may He keep us apart — always.'

But he made a pledge ; he was alone, for she had gone with the basket of washed clothes while he stared beyond her into the water.

He said out aloud : ' I swear fidelity.'

To what would he be faithful ? He did not know as yet. He was only a young man growing. He sat there a long time, wanting only her body. All this talk about witches, bats, the moon, was nonsense. He had a wild idea of riding to her cottage and, with Gilbert's aid, snatching her away, and, whether she liked it or no, carrying her off to the Border country and loving her there until he was tired. Then he would let her return to her mother. And he would have a fight or two to keep his hand in, and some drinking spells. After that he would return to Mallory and do his work like a good young man. He stood doubtfully. He shook his big head and, with his dagger, cut slices of bark off a tree. What was happening to his life that had formerly been so simple? There was Robin nearly a Catholic, and hatred of Irvine and love of a girl who was never there. . . . If it were not for his home duty he would go off with Drake or Hawkins. . . . That might be after all the best thing. There was simple fighting there and comrades and gold. . . . But he shook his head again. In some way that would be disloyal to everything that he loved. He had some task to perform. But what ?

' I swear fidelity.' But to what ? To whom ?

At least he was hungry and thirsty now. *There* was a problem easily resolved.

When he was back in the Rosthwaite house it was a delightful pleasure to find Gilbert Armstrong settled in there. Gilbert had brought a leather bag with all his property in it : a suit of clothes, shirts and hose, a sword with a carved hilt, a decorated saddle, his mother's gold wedding ring, an illuminated Psalm book, a volume of bawdy songs, and an ivory jack-in-the-box phallus that a pedlar had sold him, and thirty pounds in gold — all his worldly goods. He moved a truckle-bed into an attic room and would abide there for life if Nicholas wished him. He had that gift, possessed by simple, untroubled, unsubtle men, of settling anywhere, at an instant's notice, with the greatest comfort and for ever if need be.

Nicholas was surprised in himself to find what great pleasure, comfort, reassurance, Gilbert's company gave him. That alone proved how greatly he, Nicholas, was changing. A year or two back he needed nobody ; he could meet every trouble that came. But now there were some troubles that were not so simple.

On that very first night he fell into the habit that was to last for ever afterwards. In his furred crimson bed-gown he went up to Gilbert's attic, found him in his naked bed snoring like a drunken trumpeter with his mouth wide open. Remorselessly he shook him wide awake. Sitting on the pallet which he bore down to the rush floor with his weight, he told Gilbert everything about Catherine, every single thing.

' If I could have her, Gilbert, there'd be an end — or would there ? But I cannot have her. She says something and slips away. Why cannot I get her out of my mind ? Has she bewitched me, do you think ? And, Gilbert, how much do I pay you now for your services ? We said nothing about it.'

Gilbert sat up, rubbed his bare chest, yawned, blinked his eyes.

' I was dreaming of a goat being milked by a girl with red hair.' He grinned and drew the pelted covering up to his chin with a sort of bashfulness.

' It's plaguy cold. Pay me what you will. You must buy

me a horse and I must have my own room.'

Nicholas went on telling him about Catherine. ' I should be afraid of her. She speaks with a foreign accent and I have never had traffic with German girls. She says her mother is a witch, or at least she says that she sits on the floor and the fire leaps and things pass in and out of the room and a big bat hangs with its feet to a tree. What do you think, Gilbert ? Does the Devil walk abroad like a minister of the Church or fly like a bat ? Can old women, as they say, fly through the window at night-time and suck your blood ? '

' I only believe what I see, Mr. Herries,' Gilbert said firmly. ' But to-morrow night there is a moon and if the sky's clear and you will come with me to Watendlath——'

' What is Watendlath ? ' Nicholas asked.

' It is a little piece of dark water just above here, sunk in the hills. If we go up after midnight we may see a thing or two. I have been myself only once and I saw — I can't say what I saw — this is a strange place——'

' How do you mean — this is a strange place ? '

' It is like none other in England. It has been so shut away for so long that old deeds and old people — long, long forgotten things — have remained shut up in it. I am a Cumbrian man and am proud to be one, and I know that Cumbrian men and women are the most sturdy and the most heart-and-bone men and women in the world, believing only what they see and saying naught — but they are double-world also and have lived for so long so close to the same earth without moving that things past are the same as things present, and they can see the future if they care to bother their heads about it. Mostly they bother their heads about nothing but the sheep and the cows——'

Nicholas drew his bed-gown closer about him.

' There is more in this world than ever I thought when I was younger. Now tell me, Gilbert — what is said about this girl and her mother by the people here ? '

' The Keswick people know little about her, and her mother lives to herself. But the miners like the girl. On all hands she is known to be a strong woman of her word, honest and kindly, asking nothing of anybody. There are several who would marry her in spite of the mother. Of *her* they are afraid, but she is splendid with herbs, they say, and can cure a man of anything.'

' What do you yourself think of it ? '

' I think, Mr. Herries, that what she told you is right — that is, never to see her again nor think of her if you can help it. One day they will take her mother and burn her. You come with me to-morrow night over the hill, and maybe it will cure you.'

Nicholas got up.

' I think there is someone listening at the door,' he said.

He stole across the floor, flashed open the door. There was no one there, but they both fancied that they heard a creak on the stair.

When they started out on their adventure Nicholas felt as pleased as a schoolboy and as agreeably frightened as one.

He did not believe in God, or at least had never seriously considered Him, but he did believe in the Devil, who was an adversary walking about the earth, seeking whom he might devour. If a Devil there were, then witches, his servants, must also be allowed. He did not know quite what he was going to see, but climbing the hill above Rosthwaite, he had his hand on his dagger-hilt, and his face wore that open schoolboy expression of one who is ' ready for anything ' and hopes to have a tale to tell when he ' gets back to the other boys.'

This strange country, too, that seemed to have ' caught him by the tail,' to be forcing him into those mysterious boundaries again and again, was showing him an aspect that he had not seen before. Washed in moonlight, these little hills were as gigantic as the mountains of the world. The sky was covered with a network of soft fleecy clouds and through these the pale lambent moon seemed to move as though sleep-walking. The only sound was the rough breaking of dry twigs by the two men, the relentless beautiful monotony of the running streams, the owls' cry.

Nicholas was no poet, but when they reached the hill's ridge and he looked back over Borrowdale valley he cried out. Scafell and Gavel hung black over the silver bowl that the moonlight made.   But it was the stillness of the valley that brought tears to his eyes.   It had a deep pathos as of something helpless, innocent and fated.   He thought again, he did not know why, of his words, ' I swear fidelity.'   Something good and true in him commanded for the moment all his carelessness, his material triviality, his lasciviousness, his lightmindedness. It was as though, on his way to meet the Devil, he said : ' I believe in God.'

' You are right,' he said to Gilbert.   ' This is like no other place.   And myself and my sons and my sons' sons belong here.'

But Armstrong motioned him to be silent.

' We may meet one or two,' he said, in a voice as soft as the misty light around them.

For a while they walked on the level top, their feet sinking into squashy bog.   They could see, across the valley, Scafell and Gavel ; at the far end beyond the Lake, Skiddaw ; at their side, Glaramara ; and the stream running madly at their right down to Rosthwaite had in its voice both scorn and strength. There were patches of snow, like grey moss in the moonlight in their path.

Five minutes later and Watendlath appeared.   It was a tarn, a small lake, now quite black because the moonlight lay on the flank of the farther bank and on the tower and broken walls of a small ruined house.   The hill and the house were so white as leprosy and the water jet.   Nothing, no bird or sheep, was visible in this forlorn place.   There were some trees close to where they stood, gaunt haggard trees with no leaves as yet.   As they had come over the ridge and down a little way the sound of the stream was cut off.   This place was so still that Nicholas was afraid to move forward.   He did not know what cowardice meant but was well experienced in fear.   This was the worst fear, the fear of the other world, for he believed, as did all of his fellows, that any man had unfair odds to face when Satan was in question.

So he crossed himself and repeated the Lord's Prayer rather as he would take a bolus against the plague.

Gilbert started down the hill and he followed.   At the hill-foot there was a group of trees and then a stretch of bog and reeds leading to the tarn.

'Here,' Gilbert said. 'We will wait here.' So they stood behind the trees, close pressed together.

Silence and the passing of time can do much, most especially when you are waiting for the Devil, and it seemed to Nicholas that, after a while, the tarn's breast shuddered and the reeds began to stir although there was no wind. Also the fleecy fragments of cloud passed into a spider-web thinness, veiling the sky ; behind this there was a cold light but now no visible moon. To his strained attention the tower and ruined house seemed to come nearer so that he could see rafters and at the top of the tower a bell. He was viciously cold. Gilbert caught his arm, pinching it.

'Look, Mr. Herries !' he whispered.

He looked. From the door of the ruined house a little crowd of men and women emerged. They were soundless, stood in a group, then began to run scattering and spreading towards the tarn. As they ran they screeched.

The effect of that sound breaking on to the silence was very eerie. The screeching was animal, not quite bird-like, not quite human.

Four women ran along the meadow on the other side of the tarn. They were dressed, it seemed, in some grey material that flew above their heads. Nicholas could see that they were picking their skirts up above their knees and kicking their legs. One of them ran round and round in circles screeching like a throat-cut pig.

Gilbert muttered : 'Oh Lord ! Mr. Herries, I can tell that one. She is the wife of Abraham Schaaf, the Jew in Keswick who buys lead from the miners.'

There was nothing in all this performance so far but silliness. The women now joined hands, yelling and screaming, and as they grew ever more excited they tore at their clothes. Nicholas could see quite clearly that one of them was almost naked, a girl with her hair tumbling about her bare shoulders. A horrid fear seized him lest this should be Catherine. He saw that the girl, followed by an old woman, who was prancing about, now bending down on all fours, now giving little leaps into the air, moved forward into the tarn. As she came striding through the cold dark water he saw that she was stark, with big firm breasts and broad white shoulders. She was not Catherine. She tossed her head as though she were a horse.

How cold it must be! he thought. How fearfully cold! She stood in the water up to the chin.

She began to chant, waving her arms, and the women in a group on the bank caught up the chant — all dreadfully out of tune and broken with laughter and yells and cries like birds.

On the left of the black tarn there was a rock with a pointed erected head. The two groups joined and all moved towards the stone. Nicholas could see them very clearly now: three old women; the girl, who was wearing a cloak over her shoulders and bound about her waist; one tall commanding woman who stood apart from the others; two men — one thin, young and dark; the other bent, old, with a grey beard.

They gathered now about the stone, all bending inwards towards the centre. The silence was as deep and unstirred as it had been before their arrival. A thin column of smoke rose from the stone and then a bright darting flame. They began to chant again, one male voice strong and resolute, the others cracked and uncertain.

A cry rose from inside the circle; a cry — piercing, agonizing, high.

Gilbert caught Nicholas by the shoulders. 'It is a goat. It's nothing. I've slit the throat of many a one.'

Nicholas said: 'I thought it was a child. This is devilish. . . .'

'Foolish,' Gilbert answered. 'Don't move. Stay where you are. A pack of old women. The young man is the son of the baker, Morley. They've said for a long time——'

He stopped. Both men stayed, rigid, staring. For Nicholas was never to know if he saw anything or what he saw. A pack of old women, a column of smoke, the dark, unmoved water . . .

But the sky had thickened, the light dimmed. The smoke rose above the stone like a snake and, although there was no wind, it blew, in tuggy gusts, leftwards to the Lake. Did the sky break and the clouds, thick like smoke, drive across the tarn? What shadow of cloud floated against the snow-flank of the hill? And did he see, or did he not see, figures flying through the air, the high reeds blowing although there was no wind, and hear the bell in the ruined house sounding a shrill note like a pencil scratching on a slate? He strained his eyes upwards and saw a sickly moon, the colour of yellow soap, break the mist, and something — was it a bird, a bat, a cloud? — cross the moon's face. One, and now another, and now a third . . .

He looked down again. No figure broke the landscape's silence. Only, above the erected stone, a thin little waver of smoke.

He caught Gilbert's arm.

' What did I see ? '

' Nothing,' Gilbert answered. ' Some old mad women who will be burnt one day for their nonsense.' Then, after a moment's hesitation, he added : ' Mr. Herries — the tall woman — apart from the others — that was Catherine Hodstetter's mother.'

ROBIN HERRIES *LOQUITUR :* HE LOSES HIS LADY

. . . And so, although you may hate him from your heart's very core and therefore acknowledge in yourself a most unworthy prejudice, the man may yet be of no kind of merit. I will acknowledge that to myself, for I have studied him these three years, and I think that he has, for no very plain reason, put his best foot forward with me, and I have seen any best there may be in him. But there *is* no best.

I will consider you, Philip Irvine, fairly. You are deeply, bottomlessly proud and, although of fine family, appear always as though you were newly great and were one of the new young men. That salt of commonness I may detect all through your breeding. With every gesture you proclaim your self-greatness, and if one does not grasp it sufficiently you tell me and insist, by word of mouth, that I shall know it. When you come into fresh company, or any company where you are uncertain, you look about you angrily, and if you are not at once reassured by some sycophancy, your proud anger increases, and you try to force it on your company that it is by some rudeness of theirs (of which of course they are altogether ignorant) that you are offended. And so you hope to win the first trick of the game before they are ready. If you have an insult easy to hand you will use it, as in forgetting someone's name although you know it well enough. And then by cold politeness assuming a condescension and even a suffering patience with them for intruding on you.

If you use a man, whether to take his money or receive an introduction that you need, or any service, you will be short with him if you dare and receive the favour as only part of what is always due to you. You have a charm which is true, but you are so inordinately proud of it, and use it so openly to your advantage that the trick of it is seen very quickly.

You are handsome but are so inordinately vain of this that many men laugh at you for it. But the most of women oddly prefer that you should have this vanity and praise you for it. Ambitious vulgar men like Uncle Henry who have, since childhood, practised to be all things to all men, admire you for your scornful haughtiness. It is to them a feat of arms that you should challenge so many poor horsemen without being unseated. Your courage, which is a true courage, places the cowards, of whom there are many, cringing at your shoes, but they give you no pleasure, for you are vain enough to recognize them for the poor creatures they are.

Within your brain, a place of small and congested compass, there is a constant wonder that you are not further in the world than you are. To be among the highest at Court, to have your ears pinched by Majesty and Burghley's beard confidentially in your chin, seems to you to be but your barest right, and yet you are not even within the Court's outer boundaries. Nor ever will be, whatever your old savage of a mother may do for you. And, when once more the intrigue has failed, you post down to that grim Essex country, and in that chill mansion of yours, with the rain beating the windows, you crouch with her over the poor, starved fire, plotting anew.

Therefore, poor defeated creature, you have turned in your anger and done this hateful thing. . . . Oh God, God, God ! . . . Have pity on me, have pity on her . . . save us both. . . . Out of this shame pluck for us some merit. Out of this shame . . .

I am quiet again and can assemble every detail to trap this madness and hold it bound in its dark corner with its long scratch-bearded moping face turned to the plastered wall.

I am Robin Francis Herries, younger son of Sir Michael Herries of Court Mallory in Sussex. I am twenty-four years of age in this Year of Grace 1573. I returned but a month ago from travelling in the Netherlands with my friend, Mr. Charles Lacey.

It is now by my clock twenty-seven minutes after three of the morning of April the Fourth. I am well in body but sick in mind. I am at the sign of the Grapes in Southwark.

My hair is brushed, my face is clean. I am in my bed-gown of
furred purple velvet. The hangings of my bed are in green,
yellow and red, figuring a hawking match. My taper burns
steadily. There is no wind.

Thus it was Philip Sidney's advice to pour my heart out
and let it break on paper, for that is the first prelude, he says,
to mending it again. And so, my mouth grave and my mind
set on the purpose, I recover the event.

I had a foreboding before ever I set out for my cousin,
Jennifer Herries. She lives — and I lay it on to the paper like a
sort of bitter offering, the name of the very heart of our meeting with its small close garden of herbs, the lute of ivory, the
stool that the good Queen Katherine of Aragon embroidered,
the white dog with the clipped tail, and the two parrots of
crimson and grass-green that call, one, ' Marjorie . . .
Marjorie . . .' and the other, ' Come for your hair to be
washed ! '— she lives, with her sister Celia, these two, beyond
Chelsea, not distant from my Uncle Henry.

My dear Uncle Henry, my beloved Uncle Henry . . . who
will spend his sixpence with a great deal of flourishing and no
man makes more of a pint of wine than he ! So record it,
my white paper and darkened room, for the taper slides, head
sideways, into a lethargy. There, I have spunked it again and
the hawking of the bed-tester is all flourishing in the new light
with birds and the red king on the white roan.

So my cousins, on the Northumberland side, Jennifer and
Celia have been — for two years now — our rendezvous-
makers.

Ah, Sylvia, Sylvia, Sylvia, Sylvia, Sylvia. . . . Now the
page is filled with your name, black-scrawled with it, and yet
the word ' faithless ' is not written.

How many a time have you kissed me there while the
herbs scent the air in the little garden and the dog with the
clipped tail, his legs spread, waits till the flea shall slumber.
You have kissed me, as you did the first time, standing on your
toes, your small hand on my breast. On my very heart —
my heart naked like a pear under the velvet. While your
nurse swills the ale in the buttery, tickling, I don't doubt,
Jennifer Herries' long lean serving-man in his most tender

places, for she is a bawdy heart and generous.   My fair
cousins, one with the heavy moustache, the other with the
three chins, bend in the herb-garden, seeking the eternal good
of others ; for they, having no hopes of a lover and dis-
believing a God, turn most marvellously to the curing of their
neighbours' aches and mortalities.   The scent of their herbs
goes God-wards although they are blind to that destination,
while you, Sylvia, leaning upon me, your child-face stretched
up to mine, my hand cupping your neck, you repeat : ' I love
you !   I love you !   I love you ! ' the clock of your infidelities
recording its eternally forsworn oaths.

But forgive me, child.   Child, child, forgive me.

At this last meeting but the last one, when the snow was on
the ground, the herbs in silver burial, the logs leaping into
such amber glory that I caught you and lifted you and pressed
my lips against your little breasts and cried, ' When ?   When ?
When ? . . . Why may I not speak ? '

And you said, your right breast against my cheek, ' Put
me down, Robin,' and I put you down and you said, terror in
your eyes, ' I have but now learnt.   Twice you have concealed
priests at Mallory.   You are spied upon and watched.   You
are a Catholic.'

I stood, staring at the grass-green of the parrot, silent.
They knew, then !   I might have guessed it long, long ago.

' Your father . . .'

She nodded.   Her eyes were as wide as saucers.

' Phineas Thatcher ? '

She nodded again.   ' The first time he saw you — at
Mallory.'

I saw that she was quivering, so I took her in my arms and
she huddled in them, closer and closer, like any child.   She went
on again : ' My father told Nicholas many many months ago.'

' Nicholas ! '   (My dear beloved Nick who would die for
me — and I for him.)

' He came to ask my father to permit our marriage.   It
was then that father told him.   But *I* didn't know at that time.
I have only now learnt — from my mother.'

(So Nick has known all these months and has said no word.
So, too, one day I will serve him, God willing.)

'Your mother told you — she has other plans for you then?'

I felt her detach herself, as a bird from its shell. It was an unfolding, a withdrawal of the soul as well as of the body. But this was not the first withdrawal. It had been coming for many months. During this last year she has been growing fast — and towards gaiety.

She has been wanting pleasure, the lights and colours and senses of the world. Aye, the senses! There have been hours of this rendezvous when I have known that she was child no longer, stirrings of the body, murmurings, placings of the hands — I think with another her virginity would not have been safe, and it has been hard, by the witness of Christ's own body, to be myself withdrawn. Loving her so, mouth to mouth, breast to breast . . . and she has known the danger well and I have been ever graver with the burden of it, and she, the fountain of Cupid's bare body splashing its water above the herb-garden, has murmured to me : 'Closer, dear Robin. Hold me, dear Robin — your hand, dear Robin.' Her eyes have shone and her wet mouth smiled — but always, hiding, frightened, unknowing, the child lost in this house of pleasure, and I, knowing it was so, have not harmed her. And she, loving me, has turned even more from me because she has been bruised with ignorant longing.

It was not unexpected when she said : 'And so, Robin, my dear, my dear, we can never, never be married.'

'I am not a Catholic,' I said.

But she kissed me on my eyes and then, for a lifetime, on my lips, and went away with her nurse. And I knew well enough that they were making some plans for her.

My little clock of silver and ebony strikes four and plays its tune of 'Dorcas is willing' with the little hesitation on the last note but two that gives it a personal familiarity with myself, as though it said 'I am yours, Master. Though all else may fail you.'

. . . And so, after she was gone, using, as I well knew, this rendezvous never again, I kept silence. For a long month I kept it.

Will Nick ever know how dearly now I loved him ? Did he feel in the touch of my hand my gratitude ? I know not, for Nicholas, my big brother, is not given to these niceties although he too is made by the years something other, I fancy, from what he was, and thought steals like a stranger into his brain, wondering at the empty room and, in a while, bringing her own furniture.

I kept silence until that Eighth of May that is now only to-day. I fancy that we cheat ourselves over Time, which is assuredly not as the clocks mark it ; for by the clock, six of the evening is just nine hours from three of this morning, but for myself, who am only an item in Time, it is the gulf of experience from one life to another. And yet not altogether, for in the little goldsmith's shop by West Cheap one Robin Herries was half out of the door and another entering.

For a month then I heard nothing. I bided at home and worked at my translation of Suetonius, his *History of the Twelve Caesars*. Ye blind Caesars, without eyes or mouths, that, cheating me once by your ghostly presence, promised me fame — and now another will be before me to give Suetonius' history to the English world, for Sylvia has slain your Twelve Emperors. I threw Suetonius against the wall and rode to London.

For a wild month, crowded with sun and rain and yet empty as Uncle Henry's charity, I had waited. No word. No sign. So I must know. I must speak with her.

What mad fantasies I had in my brain as I rode over the bridge and into the street. I would carry her from them all, ride madly North to Scotland, or to Southampton and take boat . . . but she herself did not wish it and God does not wish it. The very skies do not wish it, for above my head the heavens lay like a lid on a pan. Set in that grey heaviness was a dead sun, dead for May, when there should be light and brightness. You might, an you were Hercules, stand on the roofs of this little stinking town and, raising your great arm, lift that heavy lid. Push with your hand against the sky, brave fellow. Thrust away, my hearty ! The sweat will run down your beard and your eyes be blinded, your great heart hammer your ribs, your throat be dry as matchwood, but strain and you will have your reward. For the sky will lift backwards like a chest-cover. All the men of the street and the fields will look up, thinking that at last, after so many cheated chances, they will see God. And what will they see, O my Hercules?

Dead sun and dead sun and dead sun. Thousands upon thousands like maggoty cheeses spread on a dish-clout. These suns will not stir nor will they twinkle. The light in them is sulphurous. They burn with the dying fires of cheated hopes and false love and abandoned worship. And so, my Hercules, drop the lid again. You have strained your muscle to no purpose. You are once more among men who have lost desire now for the unrevealed and hope for the promised land, and, their daily business over, will lie down there where they are and flicker no eyelid as old man Death, so humble in his monotonous duty, approaches.

I entered the goldsmith's in West Cheap to purchase a treasure for my beloved. I had given her my heart, but that she must not wear, and my more sensual parts are dangerous, so a gold chain or buttons of diamonds, rubies and orient pearl. The shop was dark and I was an old customer of his: an Italian, Annibale Zanti. The shop was dark and Zanti's brown fingers laid out his treasures, while in front of the shop the apprentice's shrill cry for customers was interrupted by his howlings, for his duties were interrupted by baitings from two other apprentices. On Zanti's shelf was a bowl of rose-coloured Italian design. As I looked at it my old self went out of the door, my new self — a stern lean-chapped stranger — stared in. Can a snake not slough its skin? Why, young Prince, your lady has left you, and you, stripping in your agony everything from you, the purple doublet with buttons of pearl, the cambric shirt, the crucifix against your warm flesh, and then the flesh itself, as the Indians do when they catch Hawkins' men, hanging their fleshly vestiture on the upas tree for the monkeys to water, and so to the very bone. Take it between your thumbs, for it must be broken ere it is mended again. Why, it is broken already! Snapped in a neat sequence of quarters. Who has done this! Why, the Fool himself — all because his lady turned him out of doors. Well, then, mend the bone again. See how quickly and neatly it fits together again ! The rib ! The rib ! But on this occasion man is fashioned from it, not woman. We will fashion no more women. We will have women no more in this fair city but only the eunuchs and the pretty boys, the first for their wisdom and gratifying impotency, the last for the excellent ways they have for the pleasing of old men. And so, in a generation or two, man will be at an end. No propagation from eunuchs and pretty boys, howsoever earnestly you work at it !

The rib is productive. The bones mend and Mr. Herries stands up again, the skin falls gently on the bones and the velvet falls on the skin, and the birds' droppings on the velvet. And so, bird-snouted but firm rejecter of women, he peers in through Zanti's shop, while the old body, slain by false women, and so a ghost in the city, passes out like the wind and is blown like a leaf across the roof-tops.

There is a new Herries staring at the rose-coloured bowl and he has asked Zanti the price of it, but when he drags it forward the rose is out of the colour. It is drab — glass only.

I left Zanti's shop, with my buttons of pearl and gold for my little love. And I was met by the Beggars.

There they came down West Cheap, a mass of them, some without ears, some without lips, some without a nose, many blind, many without a leg or so, some naked of all but a clout for decency, some in ragged finery of faded velvet, soldiers wandering the country, sailors rebellious from the fleet. Women drunken and screaming, some pushing a cart, others ringing bells, some carrying children on their shoulders, women pregnant and limping — and the fierce beggars, the audacious, cracking their whips, shouting abuse, others snivelling for bread, whining for a coin, some mountebanking, leaping from back to back, somersaulting as they would at a fair, then, with many improper gestures tempting the maids, one, crowned with a paper hat, mocking the Pope of Rome, some wrestling and fighting as they walk — all huddling, thumping, shouting, screaming, making water, tearing at rotten bread with their black teeth, spitting and mewing like cats, laughing, singing, hugging and embracing, falling and jumping — the Beggars, once more, have come to Town.

They come thus, like rats from the sewer, up into the air when the plague is stealing upon them. So it must be. I could feel, as I stood there, outside Zanti's shop, that faint, half-sweet, half-rotten odour. I could fancy — for my fancy now is sharp, having with my new bones a new perception — that with my eyes I could see curling around the cobble-stones faint blue wisps of mist that are the skirts of the plague. The Beggars are come. The plague is come. A fine new world for the new Robin !

So, under the eaves and the close-hanging boards and plaster, the Beggars go. The air is filled with their cries and their stench and the pushing whack and thud of their sweating bodies. But overhead it is little better. The dead sun still lies like a cheese on the heavy table of the sky. The Beggars gaze not skywards, but an they did they would get no benefit of it. For God has closed the lid down on his earth and turned aside to more profitable ventures. Like lice on a corpse, the Beggars swarm and curl and feed.

I was happy to see the blue vapours of the plague curl between the stones. For man has made of God's world a filthy sewer and the end is better than the continuing.

And so I came to my uncle's house. Here is sanity. The songs of the Beggars are cut off by the high gates. The fountain plays in the courtyard. In the offices in my uncle's house men are busy counting the gold. You can hear the bags rustle and the coins chink and the dog snuffle, in contented sleep, before the fire as the cooks prepare for the feast and the musicians practise on the lute and tabor. As I mount the great staircase to greet my aunt, who is ' better to-day, thank you,' there is the scent of spring flowers in my nostrils. ' You will see Sylvia. I know that you have come to see Sylvia, nephew Robin.'

But first I see Irvine.

He stood at the top of the stairs, handsome in black and silver and very friendly. He greeted me as he might his own child — very damnably condescending. I had it in mind to

say to him : ' I am twenty-four years of age,' and my hand
was on my dagger.

' Young Robin. . . . Young Robin.'

He put his hand through my arm, drew me close to him
and looked into my eyes.

' Two years too late,' he said, kissed my left cheek and
left me.

There was the room with the mirrors. Uncle Henry and
Sylvia stood together, infinitely repeated, while through the
open window (how sultry the air was !) I heard a drum beat
from the street.

Sylvia — she had on her breast a diamond that turned and
flashed against the white velvet ; I had not seen the diamond
before this — looked past me. In all the mirrors her face was
turned away from me.

Sylvia . . . Sylvia . . . Sylvia . . .

My uncle said, very grandly, as though he were announcing
his new governorship of Paradise : ' You have come on a
good day. Sylvia's betrothal . . .'

I broke in, stiffly, ' He is very fortunate,' and then, most
foolishly, ' I am twenty-four years of age. Tell him that.
Philip Irvine is only twenty-nine, I think.'

I kissed Sylvia on the cheek. For a moment she clung to
me with both hands but said nothing. I felt the jewelled
buttons in my pocket against my thigh.

I walked out and down the stairs, as though I would walk
down for ever into the rottenness that lies under the stones. . . .

O our father which art in heaven, hallowed be thy name.
Let thy kingdom come. Thy will be fulfilled. . . .

END OF PART I

PART II

THE LOVERS AGAINST GOD

JOURNEY TO THE DARK TOWER

DUSK crept upon them very early. Sylvia (now Sylvia Irvine, a staid married woman of twenty years) drew her heavy blue cloak more tightly about her and strengthened her clasp on her husband's waist. She was riding pillion and enjoyed the sensation of physical closeness, so that if she raised her hand she could feel, beneath the thin netted armour, the beating of his heart.

She liked this physical proximity, but last night at the inn where they had slept she had been frightened of it. She had claimed (as so many young brides before and after her !) a nervous headache, and he, giving her an intense look, without kissing her, had bowed and withdrawn.

Only yesterday morning they had been married, and she, standing beside him, had thought, ' To-night, dear God, I shall be naked in his arms ! ' and had smiled with pleasure at the thought. And then, when it had come to it, terror had seized her — one more night . . . only one more night. Better that it should be, the first time, in their own place, the wonderful Castle that was now to be Sylvia's home. Safe in her own home, allowed to lie abed of the morning, allowed to lie there while he bent over her and kissed her ere he went off about his morning duties.

Her dear Philip ! How truly she loved him — and how little she knew him ! She had loved poor Robin Herries too, and had known him, after all, far better than she now knew Philip. Yes, she had loved him. Her heart beat faster, her hand tightened at Philip's waist as she thought of him. How desperate he had been that last time in the London house ! With what a set face he had walked from the room ! How dearly he had loved her in that place where was Queen Katherine's stool ; she could hear the sharp shrill bark of the white dog with the clipped tail, and her own voice, 'Hold me closer, dear Robin . . . your hand, dear Robin . . .'; and last night she had turned her husband from her room.

Poor Robin ! Pity that they thought him a Catholic, for he was so sweet, so young and so ardent : he could be so learned and so merry and so kind. So kind, so kind. . . . Her gloved fingers pressed against Philip's thigh. And Philip was in every way a better one to marry. He was a man, fierce, unafraid, someone who would defend a wife against the world : while Robin was a brother, close to one, dear to one, but subject to the same fears and perils as oneself. No protection. She had been often more frightened with him than away from him.

But she was going to be frightened no more. She had been a child. Now she was a woman. She had escaped from home where there had been many things to frighten her. Her father storming, her mother crying, that loathsome Mr. Thatcher feeling her leg beneath her clothes, Puritan though he was, Sidney drunken, and Edward lying and hypocritical.

Throughout the wedding she had been thinking : 'I am going to escape all this. No more Nurse smacking my buttocks and Phineas Thatcher eyeing me evilly, and my father whipping my shoulder-blades, and being denied money, and made to sit straight on a chair for silly Town visitors. . . . No more. No more.' She thought of the wedding, the trumpeters, the circle of rosebuds against her forehead, her mother kissing her as she had never before, the bells ringing, the old nurse crying, the two cousins who had given shelter so often to Robin and herself regarding her with puzzled dim eyes . . . but always, always Philip : Philip so splendid in his rose-red dress, holding himself like a king, haughty, as she wished him to be.

Philip, now her husband for ever and ever, her protector, her lover. . . . She was so happy that, pressed against him, she broke into a torrent of words : 'And your mother . . . oh, I know how I shall love her ! for my own mother has not been easy to love. Always with spasms or the megrim and the doctor examining her water far too often, for, in my opinion, it makes one only think of maladies one hasn't got to be for ever calling the doctor.

' But I will help your mother with the bed-things and the herbs and seeing that the rushes are fresh, and I can cook, too, Philip — some cakes straight from the Court in Paris that Mr. Lacey brought back in a book that had them. I will make your mother love me even though I take you from her.'

She paused. She thought that he would say something. But he said nothing. She was too happy, too simply delighted at being married and the sole care of her beloved, admired, so-handsome Philip, to cease. She continued, asking questions about the Castle, the village where the Castle was, the villagers whom she would befriend, when they would have her father and mother and brothers to stay. She stopped at last : Philip had not spoken.

The silence that followed was knit together by a little wailing wind that, blowing across the long flats, seemed personally to persuade them that a dreary evening was closing down on them. Sylvia had never seen this kind of country before. Her life had been divided between the London house and the country house ; in both of these there had been constant activity. For the first time she was aware now of her surroundings, and this early afternoon was not a happy choice for her first view of the Essex flats. A space of yellow in the darkening sky seemed to be reflected in the dreary expanse, giving the effect here and there of dirty stagnant water. Against the sky, clumps of reeds stood up like thin hungry fingers. Once or twice they passed through villages where the houses were hovels and life was dead ; once, at a cross-road, a hanged man creaked in the gibbet-chains. Once an old bearded man, nearly naked, ran beside them for a while crying for bread, and would have persisted had not one of Irvine's men slashed at him with his whip. Sylvia saw the old man fall and then rise, stand, looking after them, raising his bleeding arm.

Two men on horses carried their luggage : one of these Sylvia already knew, a fat smiling fellow with a cast in one eye and always grinning ; the other was a slim young man, haughty in feature and absolutely silent. The first was called Simon ; the second, Luke. Philip called them his two Apostles.

At last she could not endure the silence and so again she asked questions.

' Is it far now ? '

' We are almost there.'

' I am tired and cold. Is Essex always cold ? '

She asked this last as a little joke and laughed, but Philip
answered her rather sternly : ' It will be a poor thing if you
dislike your home before you have seen it.' Then he added
more pleasantly : ' It is always raining in England.'

She asked : ' Do you think your mother will like me ? '

' My mother is a just woman about everyone.'

' Well, I shall make her like me.'

She fancied that it was because she had said that she had a
headache last night that he was stern with her, so now she
whispered softly : ' I will show you to-night that I love you,
Philip.'

He made no answer.

She reflected upon all that she had heard about husbands
from her friends. She knew that they must be humoured,
must be allowed their sports and warlike pursuits as they
professed them, that no wife, if she is wise, expresses amazement at anything a husband may say or do. She was too
happy now at her new freedom and dignity as a married woman,
at her love for Philip, at her excitement because soon she would
see her mother-in-law and her splendid new home, to be distressed because Philip was not more talkative. She recalled
the times during his courtship of her when he had been so
charming, had kissed her so tenderly, had been so careful of
her comfort. She had all her plans made, and the chief of
them was that she would praise him for everything that he
did, for she had already learnt that he was vain. But it was
proper for a man to be vain ; Robin had not been vain
enough.

The dark was really now descending and the wind, blowing
across from the sea, cried about them and was bitterly cold.
It was a new cold to Sylvia, for it had a salt tang in it and a
hint of the fields of ice many hundreds of miles away. As it
tweaked her nose and her cheeks and her chin, she bent her
head against Philip's warm back. There was nothing to be
heard now but the clop-clop of the horses' hooves and the cry
of the wind.

They came to a village, and a man ran out from a door, holding a rough torch that blew coarsely in the wind. When he saw them he bowed low. Sylvia's heart beat swiftly. ' This is *our* village. We are arrived.' She could see little of it in the dark : only the tower of a church, and she heard water running. But she thought : ' Here will be *my* people and I will be so very good to them. They shall have everything I can give them.'

Then she saw a pile of buildings, black and strong. There was a gate which slowly opened for them. They rode in over cobbles. At last they were at Drunning Place.

Philip dismounted and then helped Sylvia down. As they stood there in the driving wind the house seemed gigantic above them ; part of it she could see was like a fortress with a square tower, narrow windows, and she fancied there was a moat. On her right the building was more recent and apparently of wood. There were no lights in the windows, and Philip, who had made the bell ring again and again, now impatiently struck on the great door with his fist. Suddenly the door opened and an old bent man stood, holding a light.

Philip strode in. The old man seemed all of a maze.

' We expected you to-morrow, Master Philip. The mistress said to-morrow. It was to-morrow. . . .'

Philip did not answer him ; there appeared at the end of the vast hall a tall thin man in black and yellow, carrying a staff.

' Where is my mother ? ' Philip asked.

The man bowed as though he were moved by strings. He spoke in a shrill, rather absurd voice as though he were repeating words he had learned by heart.

' The mistress is in her room.'

Philip strode forward and Sylvia followed. As she went she had time to notice that everything was of stone, and bare. They went through folding doors and into a long room so cold that it struck Sylvia like a blow of the hand.

The room was Gothic with pointed stone windows. There were Flemish hangings on the walls, but they were faded and tattered. In the huge stone fireplace a little cold flame struggled, and close to this, in an embroidered chair, her feet on a stool,

F

sat an elderly woman. Beside her, on another stool, sat a plain woman reading aloud. The woman in the chair turned when she saw them and at once rose, kicking the stool away with her foot. Sylvia had never seen such a woman. She was some sixty years old and perfectly square in build, set and sturdy like a rock. She wore a great and not over-cleanly ruff and a dress of shabby black. Her face was as square as her body, and in the light of the candles seemed yellow in colour. An expanse of yellow face, the eyes close together, and a snub short nose. She had an expression of tremendous dignity : her body carried itself as though the mass of it were held together by one single thought — that it was a precious, wonderful and immovable body.

She was, however, delighted to see her son. The little eyes sparkled, the thick mouth smiled ; she held out both her hands.

Philip moved to her with a wonderful dignity, and it was very splendid to see their greeting, as of a king and queen encountering before their subjects. Philip kissed his mother on both cheeks.

' But we had not expected you until to-morrow.' She had a deep voice like a man's.

' The wedding was yesterday. You were missed by everyone.'

' You know, Philip, that my heart prevents me . . .'

' You are well, mother ? '

' As well as may be. I never complain.'

It was now that she considered Sylvia. She stood regarding her. Sylvia came forward.

' This is my wife, mother.'

' Humph ! She is very small. Come here, child.'

Sylvia came to her. She had not yet taken off her blue cloak.

The old lady shook her head impatiently.

' Take off your travelling things and let me see you.'

Sylvia did so. Perhaps she should embrace this block of immobility. She could not.

' Yes, you are small-boned, but you look healthy enough. What can you do ? Can you cook ? '

' Yes — a little.'

' A little ? That is a poor answer. Are you a housewife ?
Can you sew and mend ?'

Sylvia thought that she would show spirit, so, smiling, she
answered :

' I will do my best to help in everything — to please Philip.'

' You will please Philip best,' the old lady answered, ' by
giving him a son. The sooner you start about it the better.'
She uttered a coarse rollicking laugh, like a countryman or
sailor who had made a bawdy joke. Her eyes never left
Sylvia, examining her in every detail. ' You are weary, I
suppose,' she said, rather scornfully. ' Food will be found for
you, although it was to-morrow we were expecting you.' She
looked as though she blamed Sylvia for this.

' Oh no, I am not weary. Philip's horse is a fine one and
the journey was new to me. I have been little away from
London. . . .'

Philip cut this chatter short, motioning her to the door
and following her. Before they were out of the room the
serving-woman had begun reading again.

They climbed a narrow stone stair, crossed a dark passage
and came into their room, the man-servant, in black and yellow,
walking in front of them carrying his staff in one hand and
a high silver candlestick in the other and moving with great
ceremony.

He placed the candlestick on a table and lit other candles.
He turned and in his ridiculous voice called to someone to
bring logs for the fire. A girl entered, curtsied and knelt
down to lay the fire. A wind, as sharp as the one on the road,
blew across the floor and stirred the not over-clean rushes.
As with everything else here, the room was vast but furnished
meagrely, with a great four-poster bed, a black oak chest, a
large table, another smaller one with a silver ewer and basin,
and some stools. The stone walls were bare.

When the man and girl were gone, Philip said brusquely :

' You have no time to change your clothes. I am as
hungry as a Dane. Wash your face and we will go down.'

She would have liked to kiss him, for he looked so very
splendid and commanding, but she did not dare.

He stood watching her with a dumb stare.

'Come. Hurry. My mother hates to be kept.'

What a child! he thought. I have married a baby! She came, then, impulsively, stood on her toes, as she had been used to do with Robin Herries, and kissed him.

'I am your wife, Philip. At last, after all the waiting. Are you not glad?'

'You were not my wife last night.'

'No. I was weary with the excitement. And it was an inn, and the men teasing the bear in the courtyard. . . . But now . . .'

'Yes — and now!' His voice was suddenly shrill and excited with a note of almost agony in it. 'Now — now . . .! Are you not watching everything and wondering at everything, and saying to yourself — "Is not this poor? Is not this mean? What a bare empty place! I had not thought it would be like this. How the rushes stink and the hangings on the walls are tattered! At my father's it is not like this. And how ugly his mother is and her gown is faded!" Are you not thinking this and other things to yourself? You are! You are! You are!'

He held her with his hands at arms' length and was shaking her.

She cried out: 'No. No, Philip. No!'

'Yes — and you thought me so fine in London. You did not know that we live like rats down here and always shall live. Because we have enemies — do you hear? You are married to a man who is persecuted for no fault and harried with injustice.

'Let them do their worst, then, and keep my mother and myself at bare-bones. Let them pretend to grant us something and then bait us. Let them try to get our good name into their clutches. The rareness of this custom shall make us pitiless when at last it comes. And so I tell them. And you can tell your big fat cousin Nicholas the same — that I hate him and will one day have his guts — and so for the lot of them. . . .'

He paused as if for breath, and stared about him as though distracted. Then he caught the look of her eyes, exactly those of a frightened child, and he paused, was quite quickly once again the proud, reserved, handsome young man.

With a little stammer Sylvia said : ' I want you to know, Philip, that I love you and would never mock you and would defend you always before the world.'

' Defend me ? '   He stared at her fiercely. ' Who dares attack me ?   They had better not.   Defend me ?   What do you say — defend me ? '

She tried to still her trembling, and then did a marvellously courageous thing. She put her hand in his.

' Let us go down.'

They supped in the great hall, which was a vast empty place with swords and rapiers hanging on the wall, two tattered flags and a gallery with the woodwork broken. Besides Sylvia, Philip and his mother there were two others at table. One was Mr. Honey, the Protestant parson, a meek sancti- monious man who had a snuffle in his nose that reminded Sylvia of Phineas Thatcher when he was at his prayers. Mr. Honey was a dirty little man with traces of food on his parson's bands, and finger-nails as black as mourning. He looked starved and eyed the food quite wolfishly.

The other was altogether his opposite — a big, broad, coarse fellow, Captain Winterset by name. Captain Winterset was of the sort that Sylvia had seen at times in company with her brother Sidney ; rough, loud-oathed, obscene, drunken, roystering, interfering, noisy.   She had always instantly avoided such a type and it frightened her that now she would be forced, it seemed, to live under the same roof with this man. He wore tattered finery, soiled lace, dirty gold, a jewelled button half off its fastening, and his face was of the colour of raw beef.   He was firmly built with great square shoulders and the chest of a Hercules.   She noticed that he had beautiful slender hands.   He had also an impudent eye that was already undressing her as she sat there opposite him.

It was not a pleasant meal ; the cold was bitter, winds playing like puppies about the stone floor.   The major-domo with the silly voice marched about with his stick of office and ordered the two men-servants, one of whom was Luke, Philip's bodyguard.   The food was very wretched : a lukewarm pease soup, mutton half cooked, an ill-smelling rabbit pie, and a dish of unripe apples and pears. There was ale to drink; otherwise water.

Mistress Irvine sat rock-like without speaking. Her broad face was so utterly impassive that you could not believe it made of flesh and blood. For the first part conversation was a monologue from Captain Winterset, who ate and drank like a famished animal and talked all at the same time.

He had been with Sir Thomas Stukeley to Spain, one of the adventurers who sailed with him from Waterford. That in itself had been a disgraceful affair, for Stukeley had broken his parole to Henry Sidney to achieve it. However, words of honour were nothing to the worthy Captain, and he described, with much coarse humour and vividness, how they had embarked as if for London, but made for the open sea and finally landed in Galicia. The King of Spain was told of their arrival and sent for them to Madrid. There Stukeley, vouched for by the Duke of Feria, was received at Court, knighted, and even given a palace to live in.

With a fierce and hearty derision Winterset described how cleverly Stukeley filled King Philip's ears with tales of his great influence in England, and persuaded him that there was no one better in the world for helping a rising in Ireland against the Queen.

Winterset was going on to an eloquent description of his lively amours with the ladies in Madrid and a fearful account of the horrors of the Inquisition, when the old lady stopped him.

' I seem to have heard all this before, Captain.'

The Captain smirked at Sylvia.

' We must entertain the young lady,' he said. He bowed : ' At your service any time.'

The cold angry voice of Philip cut the draughty air.

' That's sufficient, Carey. I have told you before. You go too much on, hap what may.'

But Winterset had no fear of him. His face flushed a deeper red.

' Come, Philip,' he said. ' I scorn no man so much as a surly threatener.' Then he smiled, his rugged face broadening most villainously. ' We understand one another, lad — and I'll have some more of the pie.'

Then they began to talk of Margaret, Countess of Lennox, mother of the murdered Darnley, and how she had repudiated Mary of Scots ; but lately, believing that Elizabeth would soon die, had sent Mary a paper acquitting her of all complicity in Darnley's murder, and then secretly married her other son, Charles Stuart, Earl of Lennox, to Elizabeth Cavendish, Lady Shrewsbury's daughter. How furious the Queen had been at this, sending Margaret Lennox to the Tower and nearly executing Lady Shrewsbury.

But what interested them all, so that their heads came together and, almost, food was forgotten, was the possibility of Elizabeth's death and Mary's triumph. In spite of their Protestantism, the old lady and her son had a frantic, almost insane grudge at the Court for its denying Philip preferment. At the same time they detested the Scottish woman and had many a gross and horrible tale to tell of her, even affirming that she had seduced her guardian, old Shrewsbury, and describing in detail the manner of it. When the parson left the table, which he did with many sighs and bowings and wiping the grease off his chin with the back of his hand, they set to with a vengeance, and, forgetting altogether the girl at the table, the old lady and the Captain were as common and filthy as scullions in the kitchen.

Sylvia's home had been, in many ways, stupid, tyrannous and mean, but no one had ever before spoken like this in front of her. Some of it she did not understand, but she gathered enough to feel rising in her a new fear and terror.

Quite suddenly it seemed to her that she was in a world of witches and devils. The cold walls down which were streaks of damp glittering in the candlelight like snails' tracks, the vastness of the hall so that it stretched away into a darkness indeterminate, peopled, it might be, with mocking listeners, the loneliness so that, for the first time, there was no one at all to whom she might turn. And then, over, through, part of all this, the two voices, both deep and chuckling, spilling this filth, describing these stew-affairs in crawling detail. . . .

Beneath the table she dug her nails into her hands. She looked and saw that Philip was, most curiously, watching her.

His gaze was fixed on her as though he would not omit a moment of this experience of hers. As soon as she knew this her own pride rose. For she was a Herries — not a very important family perhaps, but scattered about England and Scotland, through centuries doing its part and paying its way, having a certain spiritual history, preferring its own birth and begetting to any other : she was a Herries and she would stand her ground.

This place was altogether different from her expectation of it. Philip himself was utterly changed from the man she had married — was it only yesterday ? She must not, if she were to keep her spirit, even begin to envisage this new world into which she had travelled and where now she must stay : but on this first night at least she would show no surrender.

So she smiled at Philip, and in a voice that trembled a very little she asked for a small green apple as though it were the very fruit of Heaven.

Afterwards, huddling for warmth near to the fire-place, his nose purple, Mr. Honey read from Lydgate's *Falls of Princes*, an odd contrast with the table-talk. Philip and Winterset sat in a corner and played with ' a pair of cards ' at Primero. Philip wore his great-coat with the high fur collar. Madame Irvine sat straight up in her chair picking at her sallow teeth with a gold toothpick, the only costly thing Sylvia had yet seen about her.

Sylvia sat, turning round and round her wedding-ring, her gimmal, two hoops joined and each set with a turquoise. A costly ring it had been and it was remarkable that Philip had afforded it. It made Sylvia, for some deep ungrasped reason, think of the little jewelled ship she had worn in her hair at the ball when Robin had first seen her. She sighed. Poor Robin !

Poor Mr. Honey too, because, in spite of the fire, he could not keep his eyes open. He started and shook his head and blinked his eyes and at last the book fell with a crash to the floor.

The old lady would have scolded him severely, but she was herself fast asleep, snoring with her mouth open. She tottered off like a drunken woman to her bed.

At their door Philip said : ' Go and get to bed. I will be with you shortly.'

Standing close to the little fire, Sylvia, sleepily, let her clothes drop to her feet, found a clean silk shift from the luggage that lay about the room, and climbed into the great four-poster. For the first time she had undressed without a maid, or rather it had been her old nurse that had fussed about her, now coddling her, now scolding her, chattering, telling tales, putting all to rights. Well, doubtless there would be a maid in the morning, some country maid who would tell her the gossip of the village.

She sat upright in the bed, feeling dreadfully alone. It had come at last — this knowing a man. Her friends told her that it was a marvel, but now she was not so sure. Were Philip kind to her . . . but to-night he had been most ungracious. It would have been wiser to have submitted in the inn. Her refusal had provoked him. But once he were beside her and her arms around him all would be well. With love all these things necessary to marriage were handsome ; without love . . . In spite of herself she began to shiver and shake. It was pitilessly cold. But it was not the cold that made her tremble. *Did* she love Philip ? Of a certain she loved the grand fearless figure who had kissed her eyes and laid her hand against his cheek. But did she love this other Philip who had stared at her during supper, watching her take the bawdy talk of his mother ? *That* Philip was a stranger. To lie in *his* arms would be a fearful, cruel thing.

Her body shook and in spite of herself she began to cry. She was a child and terribly frightened. She did not want to be married nor to lie in the arms of any man. This great room frightened her, and the silly flickering candles. Holding her hands together she tried to pray : ' O Jesu, Son of God . . .' But the words would not come.

The door opened and closed with a jesting creak and Philip stood there, in his high-furred bed-gown, naked underneath it. He had heard her crying.

' Why are you crying ? '

' I don't — don't know.'

' Get out of bed and come to me.'

She climbed down and went over to him, looking a very child in her long hair and silk shift.

' Why are you crying ?   Are you afraid ? '

' Yes, I am.'   His breast, as smooth as the silk of her shift, was bare and waxen-white between the thick dark fur of his gown.   He looked to her gigantic.

' Were you afraid last night ? '

' I was weary.'

' Are you weary now ? '

' No.'

' Listen then.   Here you are and here you stay.   You do my bidding in all things.   We may be poor, my mother and I, but we are proud.   Do you love me ? '

' Yes, Philip.'

' Will you do in all things as I tell you ? '

' Yes, Philip.'

' Nor laugh at our poverty or the bareness of this place ? '

' No, Philip.'

' Come to me then.'

He caught her so fiercely and held her against him so roughly that she cried out.   He picked her off the floor and crushed her to him, fixing back her head, kissing her breasts.

She cried out, screaming with fear and terror.   Laughing, and stuffing her mouth with the folds of her shift, he carried her to the bed.

THE CHILD INTO THE WOMAN

EARLY in February 1575, four months after Sylvia's grand wedding, Sidney Herries went down to Essex to see what had happened to her. Not father nor mother nor brothers had set an eye on her since the wedding day. No one of them had received an invitation, as had naturally been expected, to Drunning Place. Philip Irvine had not, it appeared, slipped into London, and, if he had, most certainly he had paid no visit to his father-in-law.

At Christmas-time Sylvia had written them a letter wishing them all the happiness of the season ; a strangely stiff unnatural letter they had thought it, almost as though it had been dictated to her by her awful old mother-in-law. In fact, from the moment of reading that letter, Sylvia's mother had known no peace and given her family no peace. She might be hypochondriacal and set upon her own misfortunes, but she was a mother after all. In truth, all the family discovered that they had loved Sylvia very dearly. She had been the baby of them all, and they remembered her gaiety and sweetness and discovered in her a uniqueness of personality that they had not sufficiently realized when she was with them.

Henry took his great mind for a moment off his business and wrote to Philip, asking him whether he would not soon be in London. Sylvia's mother wrote her passionate letters, telling her how grievously they missed her and that her own maladies were grievously increased by her constant anxiety. Philip replied to Henry with a brief letter saying that he was busied about the place and that Sylvia was well and sent her love ; he said nothing at all about visiting London.

Edward and Sidney had always detested Philip, for he had patronized and mocked them continually. They had at the same time admired and feared him. But Edward had little heart and was busy in the work of following his father, whose decease would be certainly a pity but also an advantage.

Sidney was quite another. He was now thirty-five years of age and had wasted all his youth in riotous living and bad companions. His experiences of Bartholomew, however, had done something to him. Following that experience he had developed an interest in scientific discovery which had altogether steadied him, and although he still had his moments of wildness and excited passions for women (not easy to gratify this last, for he was a stout, pasty-faced man with a certain nervous awkwardness), yet he was a serious and decent member of society. Other emotions that Bartholomew had left with him were an almost insane hatred of Catholics and a love and admiration for his big cousin Nicholas. At the last resort it was he rather than any other member of the family who cared in truth for his step-sister. He loved her and hated Philip.

So, in the early days of February, he determined to go down to Essex and see for himself what was happening. In good fortune this visit was not difficult, for a bare twelve miles from Drunning Place lived some Herries — Guy and Rosemary Herries.

Guy Herries was related to Henry distantly, both of them having the same great-grandfather — old Roger Herries of very ill fame, who, in the fifteenth century, had been a sort of freebooter in Norfolk. Guy Herries was, of all peculiar things, a painter and as poor as a wandering monk. He painted portraits and landscapes, passionately influenced by the Italian masters, having spent his youth with ardour in Rome and Florence. This was not the kind of man, of course, that Henry Herries could at all respect, all the more that Guy, a large, loose, blond man, was perfectly happy and despised wealth, Courts, preferment, cities — all the properties that make this life so truly worth living. Guy and Henry in fact represented those opposites in the Herries character that, again and again, gave their family history a dramatic piquancy. Guy and Rosemary had one daughter — Rosamund — the darling of their lives.

So Sidney rode down into Essex and towards evening found himself on the edge of a wood and, at the end of a path, saw a cottage of white plaster and heavy oak beams, and, in the doorway of the passage, the whole family — Guy, Rosemary and their daughter Rosamund. Guy was a broad, tall, loose-limbed fellow with curly hair as faintly yellow as a young duckling's. He had the Herries long nose which had unfortunately been broken in some fight or other, the Herries high cheekbones, and eyes as light blue as early sun water. He was a merry, careless, godless, lecherous kind of fellow who anticipated, by a number of centuries, a descendant of his to be called Benjamin, but in spite of his occasional tumblings with pretty girls and drinking bouts at the ' Veiled Lady ' in Dogget village, he loved his wife dearly and she loved him.

She loved him because Rosemary Herries was a plump, full-breasted, rosy, happy woman who never expected men to be other than they were, who preferred life to be simple and straightforward, who loved her husband and thought him a genius.

The only child of these two, Rosamund, was, Sidney thought before his first evening was over, a very queer girl. She was not quite nine years of age at this time and Sidney had never seen her before. She was plain almost to ugliness, so long and stringy was she and, apparently, none too easy in the command of her limbs. She had good grey eyes that looked you full in the face, but her complexion was sallow and freckled, her nose snub and her hair lank and tow-coloured.

Sidney couldn't pretend that he liked her, for she had so very sarcastic and rude a manner of speaking, saying just what she thought and caring nothing for hurting other people's feelings. This was natural perhaps, for she had lived very much alone with her parents and they treated her as though she were a grown person like themselves. She moved about the cottage quite wildly, suddenly jumping and skipping, laughing apparently without reason, singing snatches of song and behaving absurdly with a sort of mongrel spaniel whom she called the Earl of Leicester or, for short, ' Mumps.'

She would be rude to Sidney at a moment, contradicting him quite flatly, and then she would smile at him with a brightening sweetness and her voice would be soft instead of harsh and critical. She had plenty of brains, and Sidney noticed that her father enquired her opinion and considered seriously her answers.

During the evening poor Sidney was exceedingly happy — *poor* Sidney because, in his daily life, he was happy so seldom, being driven by gusts of lecheries, desires, suspicions that he was mocked, longing for more erudition. For he knew that he was a plain unattractive man whose youth had been evil. No one cared for him — save his step-mother. And he himself cared for no one very much but Nicholas, who had been so kind and tender to him over Bartholomew.

Here for the first time, in this very simple family, he was with people who seemed honestly to like him, who looked into his pale pasty face as though they accepted it without dismay, who listened to his clumsy enthusiasms for the new science, his stumbling account of John Field's confirmation of Copernicus or the injustice of Burghley's sending the alchemist de Lannoy to the Tower in '67 for ' attempting to convert metal into gold.' Why should not metal be converted into gold ? The man's sallow face began to flush and his dull eyes to sparkle, while the child, her thin hands pressed between her bare knees, watched him with absorption.

But also, on the other side, Sidney studied Guy's painting with the greatest attention. Knowing little about picture-making but deeply admiring it, he thought Guy a genius, which Guy was not.

But Guy had learnt a good deal, had a passionate industry and a lively fancy. He fascinated Sidney with his account of his visit to the Castle at Mantua to see the series of paintings of the Trojan War there, made by the famous Giulio Romano. He had himself copied some of them, and as Sidney looked at their colours and the boldness of their execution, his fingers trembled and his breath came short.

Guy himself, it seemed, could do almost anything, executing portraits in the favourite manner, that is, making a rather hasty sketch of features and then elaborating in the greatest detail stuffs and jewels and ornaments. He also painted pictures of the mythological school after the Italians, having an especially daring and brilliant exposition of Venus and

Adonis. He had executed miniatures of his wife and daughter, and had also shown his skill in some fantastic 'perspectives' very much in the fashion of the time.

With all this he showed not an atom of vanity, saying that creators were the happiest of all men even though they failed in their aim, and that it mattered little what happened to the work after you had made it : the making of it was all.

It was late that evening before Sidney revealed to them what was the real purpose of his visit. He began rather nervously, his hands gripping his stout knees. The low, heavy-beamed chamber seemed to him to sail on wave after wave of bright puce colour. The wall-hangings had the freshness of new corn, or a wave as it turns, or a star suddenly brilliant after a sunfall. There were pictures of Troy Town inspired by Giulio Romano. There were rugs on the floor, still a rarity in many houses. There was a large unfinished landscape on an easel, painted in brilliant purples, olives and orange. Alone on a stand by the fire was a sculpture of a man throwing the discus, that Guy had brought with him from Rome.

The air smelt sweet and flowers scented the room although it was February. Sidney in his heavy stuffed doublet of dark crimson, his stiff crinkling ruff, his silk hose that pricked his too-white, too-sensitive legs, felt town-encumbered. Looking back to the stinking London streets, the darkness of his father's house, seeing himself move, as he always moved in London, furtively as though someone might stick a dagger between his shoulder-blades (this after Bartholomew), he felt here that he was in a new-created world.

He pulled awkwardly at the heavy gold chain round his neck and said with unusual impulse : 'I feel that I could take everything off.'

'Well, why not ? ' said Guy. 'No one would mind. We go without clothes here day after day in the summer.'

Sidney looked about him. 'It is this — the fresh colours, the smell of flowers, that naked statue — everything, as it were, for the first time. I feel as though I had never breathed before.' He smiled with the customary suspicion out of his eyes. 'Metal made into gold,' he said, as though to himself. 'It can be.'

He cleared his throat and went on, modestly, as though he would ask their advice.

' You are but twelve miles or so from Drunning Place.'

' It is a comfortable morning's walk — two hours' ride.'

' You have seen my sister ? '

This was a question it was clear they had been expecting.

Guy, his blue eyes as bright as though with fire, answered : ' No. We have wished to. But, to be honest, Cousin Sidney, the old lady is no pleasant customer. She is seen about in her own neighbourhood in an old half-coach half-cart drawn by two old horses, their halters tied with straw, an old man bent double in an aged green coat driving them. That is the only time she is seen. Until his marriage to your sister, Irvine, as you know, has been in most part in London.'

' What have you heard of my sister ? '

' We have heard nothing.'

There was a pause ; then Rosemary Herries said softly :

' We have been to blame. We have told one another again and again to pay our visit, but Guy has a deep dislike of interference either of himself with others, or of others here. Then the old lady is arrogant and can curse like a cast-off Low Countries soldier. And then we were afraid of suffering some impertinence.'

Sidney began to speak eagerly.

' You see, Sylvia was more of a child than is usual at her years. We had kept her at home and she was as bright and merry as a little bird. But in the last years she formed some attachment to our cousin, Robin Herries. He is, it is said, a Catholic and has sheltered priests at Mallory, and this made any question of him impossible. So when Philip Irvine loved her my father thought him a good match, although my brother and I had never trusted him ; he has always beaten us off to a distance as though he thought us altogether unworthy of him. But it seemed that he loved our little sister and she him and the match was made.

' When she departed with him after the wedding she was crowned with happiness and we thought all was well. But from that moment of her departure until now, with the exception of one letter written by her at Christmas-tide, we have seen and heard nothing. I must see her for myself, Philip Irvine or no Philip Irvine. I love her very dearly. She was like a bird,' he repeated, ' always singing. Her silence. . . . Her silence . . .' His eyes were filled with tears and he beat with his white hands on his knees.

The child Rosamund had been listening as though she were personally engaged in the affair.

Guy Herries said : ' You would ride over and see for yourself ? '

' Yes. And without warning. I must see things as they are.' He hesitated. ' Perhaps — you would come with me ? '

Guy laughed. ' Yes. All three of us. We will pull the old lady's beard. They say there is a bird's-nest in every window-sill.'

Sidney got up and shook Guy's hand.

' You are kin-brother to my cousin Nicholas, who can lift two men with one hand.'

As they pulled their horses up in front of the iron gateway, the snow began to fall ; fluttering moth-wing fragments, floating down from a faintly orange sky. Against this snow-mist the towers and walls of Drunning were gigantic, the bare branches to the side of it cutting the sky like spears. The rough fellow who opened the gate allowed their horses into the cobbled courtyard, and there they stood before the black heavy door while the serving-man went to find somebody.

At last the black door was pulled back and they were in the vast hall with the broken minstrel gallery and the torn flags. The domo in black and yellow marched off to find his mistress.

' By Jesu, it's cold,' Guy muttered.

They saw the streaks of damp staining the walls. From somewhere a dog howled. The thin man and his stick of office appeared in a far distance.

' Will you please to follow me ? '— piping like a eunuch and bowing like a China model.

Guy strode forward as though he were taking the place by storm. The others followed.

And there they all were, drawn up as though for their

picture. By the snivelling fire the serving-maid was on the stool, a book on her lap. In the high-backed chair was the lady mother, her shoulders as broad as a militiaman's and her black silk with a rent in it. Behind her, his head and peaked beard raised to neck-breaking point, was the domo. Standing in the middle of the floor, quite by herself, in a dress of canary and silver, was Sylvia Irvine. Beside the leaded window were Philip and Carey Winterset. It was exactly as though they had set themselves for their picture on hearing the bell sound, and a picture it made Guy at once conceive — a grim one, with that fat yellow-faced woman in the high chair, her broad bosom bound in by the shabby silk and her thick knees set like rocks against the flood; the tattered Flemish wall-hangings with legs of horses and trumpeters slanting in mid-air and the flames of a burning village torn with white patches; the ceremony, the poverty, the neglect, the silence . . . and in the middle of the huge, windy, cold room the woman he had never seen before, in canary-silver, with a little pale face with the set lifelessness of wax, turning the ring on her finger.

The Guy Herries branch of that English tribe was un-accustomed to any abashment, so Rosemary Herries came forward and curtsied, while old Madame Irvine stood up and nodded her head.

'I should have paid my visit a long time before this, but it will be our excuse maybe if I say that it is the very first visit we have ever paid.'

Her rich hearty laugh rang out as she turned and introduced her long-legged coltish child, her robust husband and pasty-faced Sidney.

The real drama was in Sidney's eyes because he could not take them off his little sister. There she stood in the middle of the floor, staring and turning her ring. Why, within six months it had been that she would have run to him with a glad cry, been caught in his arms, stood on her toes and kissed his mouth. Now she did not stir. He fancied that at the moment his eyes met hers there was a flash of communication, but, if there was, it was gone as soon as arrived.

When, after his introduction to the old woman, he turned

to her again she was coming towards him. She held out her hand : he took it and kissed her cheek, which was cold as a shell.

' Sidney — I had never expected this ! '

He drew her a little apart.

' Nor I this. Quickly, while we have time, tell me, Sis — you have not written since Christmas. We have none of us had a sign. Why is it ? Why have you not written ? '

He was gazing into her face so intently that he was able to see her lips tremble. He saw too that there was a second's movement of the head as though she were looking to see who was listening.

' I am married, Sidney.'

' I know. I know.' His own hands were trembling. ' But we did not think that you would cut yourself off from us. . . .' He saw terror in her eyes so he broke his sentence and said, with low urgency : ' Tell me — for your mother's sake — only this thing — you are happy ? — you are content ? '

She stiffened ; her eyes went beyond her brother to the wall. Philip Irvine was at Sidney's elbow.

' How fares everyone in London, brother Sidney ? '

' You have not been to enquire ? '

' No. I am a bucolic. I am become a plain country fellow. My conversation is entirely amongst beasts.'

Sidney felt his fear which, since Bartholomew, oppressed him without warning and often, it seemed, without cause. This time it was not without cause, for his fear of Philip was an old matter ; moreover, he hated this ruined and tumbling house and, with every moment in it, he wished the more strongly (and, as he knew, the more vainly) to take his sister away from it. But how was he to have some private word with her, to reassure her that they all at home loved her and were determined that she should come to no ill ?

Philip went on, mocking Sidney :

' My habitation is a poor roof with loop-holes that let out the smoke ; it must seem wretched to you, brother, after your own town house. It is a wonder that Sylvia stays with me. It can only be love that makes her.'

Both men waited for her answer ; there was an astonishing

hurt impertinence in Philip's voice as though inwardly he were raging with some acute annoyance.

'His pride is hurt,' Sidney thought, and to his own surprise felt a sudden almost tender pity for him.

Sylvia said quietly : 'Wives must be wives. I am a married woman now, Sidney.'

He realized with a start, which Philip's keen scornful glance caught, that it was true. In these months she had changed from a child to a woman. Before this she had never known control. What she felt, whether it were love or anger or desire, she must out with. In so short a time she had learnt control. And what had taught her ? Unhappiness. Extreme, agonizing unhappiness. There had been some shock that, in a moment, had changed her. He himself knew how that could be. She was in the house of her enemies. He looked about him. Philip, his mother, the red-faced bully over there. At that instant the red-faced bully joined them. Philip introduced them.

'Captain Carey Winterset — my wife's brother, Mr. Sidney Herries.'

Both men bowed. This was a very other matter from Philip — a decayed gentleman, professional bully, in tarnished gold and lace, his hand always on his rapier. Philip went on :

'Captain Winterset is shortly leaving for Cumberland. He has business there that is also mine. Have you not, Carey ? '

Winterset grinned. 'Yes, boy. Proper business.'

Philip continued : 'Cousin Robin has a place there now, I believe — left to him by an old Catholic uncle.'

He waited for Sidney's confirmation.

'And his stout brother, my dear friend Nicholas, stays there, I believe. Carey, you may meet with him.'

'I should like nothing better,' Winterset said.

'I would go with you, but to me now the only vice is ill-husbandry. If the land is cared for, nothing troubles me. So I must stay and leave bolder adventures to my friends.'

There was something behind all this. Sidney felt the danger as though the great bare room were at a secret pass, instantly filled with armed figures. And the centre of the danger was Sylvia. But she had neither moved nor spoken.

'What do you think?' Philip asked his wife. 'Will Cousin Robin and Carey here be good friends?'

She looked at both men. Then she smiled.

'That is for Robin to say,' she answered. She looked at Winterset with a scorn and disgust that she did not attempt to conceal : ' I have heard,' she said, ' that the North Country is dangerous — it is keen and the wind whips the throat.'

Winterset began to bluster, but they were interrupted, for they were all to be shown the house. To be shown it, as soon became clear, to get rid of them. Never were visitors less wanted. No food or drink had been offered them, and Madame Irvine, with a dislike unhidden, begged that they would see the house and excuse her accompanying them for her rheumatics and a cold that she had.

They set off under Philip's scornful guidance. Sidney, angry, distressed, not knowing what he must do, found himself following at the end with the long-legged child.

'That is your sister?' she asked, with a broken girlish attempt at a whisper.

'Of course.'

'Cousin Sidney, do you know what you must do?'

'What must I do?'

'When we are at the door by the horses you must fling your cloak about her head, tumble her on to your horse and ride as though the Devil were behind you.'

'The Devil?' he stammered, looking at her miserably, for he was a most unhappy man.

'At present,' she continued, 'he is in front of you. I will catch him about the leg — while you seize your sister.'

'Seize my sister? But she is a married woman — this is her home.'

'If, without knowing it, I have married the Devil my friends must aid me.' She looked at him with extreme irritation. ' But no — you are not, I can see, that kind of man ! '

How queer a girl ! He disliked her extremely. But he scarcely heard her, for he was straining all his wits as to how he could have a private word with Sylvia.

Very peculiar was Philip's fashion of conducting them. He walked with his head in air as though he were a Prince of the

Blood, and all the time he spoke fiercely as though they had insulted him.

'Here you may see how bare it is! This room has only crumbling furniture. See how these chairs are falling — worms — worms. And yet they are but from the Seventh Henry's time. . . . These stairs are irregular. There are holes. Be careful. The rats have been at them. This was once a fine tapestry piece —" The Battle of Agincourt "— but it is threadbare and will soon, I doubt not, fall to dust. . . . A noble room once. Note the windows. Now it has a ghost for its company. An erring Irvine lady strangled by her loving husband. Listen! You can hear her thin dress sweep the floor.'

It seemed that they *could* hear something. The domo was holding high the two silver candlesticks. It was the snow brushing the windows.

'And now you must see the dungeon. Through this narrow door and down the stone steps. It is a fine dungeon and many have died there. An inch of water lies in it.'

It was now that Sidney was able to exchange a few words with Sylvia. She had waited at the top of the narrow winding staircase. Sidney, seeing his opportunity, came back. There was something touching in the tenderness of his anxious heavy face. She felt it. She had her farthingale in one hand as though she were play-acting in a dress too long for her, and for a moment she behaved like a child, catching his arm.

'Oh, Sidney, you should not have come!'

She dropped his arm again immediately.

'Why not?' he said fiercely.

'They do not care for unexpected visitors. They hate that strangers should see this place. They are ashamed of it and proud of it too.'

They were in the grey dusk of the falling snow.

She added with a catch of the breath: 'Philip will never forgive me for this!'

'Philip! Are you on those terms then?'

'Those terms! Any terms!' She began to speak wildly. 'Tell my mother. . . . Tell her . . .'

'Yes,' Sidney said, putting his arm about her.

' We have only a moment.   They will be coming back.'

' You are trembling.'

She steadied herself.

' Tell her that all is well with me.   I cannot come to London at present, I have my duties here.   But all is well with me.'

' All is *not* well,' he broke indignantly upon her.   ' Something terrible has happened.'

' Nothing terrible.   Only marriage. . . .   I did not know. No one advised . . .'

They were coming back.   Their voices climbed the stair.

' Tell them all — I am happy.   I love them.'   Then she caught his arm, whispering : ' If you have the lucky chance — Robin.   Tell him to be careful — in Cumberland — and Nicholas.'

Only one thing more occurred.   As they said farewell in the great hall Rosamund Herries' eyes met Sylvia's.   They exchanged a long glance.   This was only a gawky child, but there was something in her serious, anxious, friendly gaze that warmed Sylvia's heart.   They both smiled.

Sylvia came to her, holding out her hand.

' I am glad you came,' she said.

Rosamund answered, staring into Sylvia's face : ' I will do anything, anywhere.   Only tell me.'

There had been three Herries' vows, not lovers' vows, until now in this chain of events.   Robin Herries to Anthony Pierson, Nicholas Herries to Gilbert Armstrong, Rosamund Herries to Sylvia Irvine.   All these vows were kept.

They mounted their horses and rode away through the snow which now was falling fast.

THE FIGHT BY HAWKSHEAD

THAT winter of 1574–5 and the long spring of 1575 was the happiest period in Nicholas' happy life that he had yet known.

From October 1574 until 1575 he never left, for a single night, his father's house. He never on a single occasion visited London. He worked from early morning until dark fell ; on the farm, in the garden, about the house. As he worked he sang. In the evenings he played chess with his father, talked to his mother, yawned, stretched his legs, fenced with any friend who happened there, wrestled with Gilbert Armstrong and joined in part-song when part-song was going. At times he ' stained his gentility with droppings of ale.' He tumbled into his bed and slept, his head on his hand, like a baby.

His happiness came from two great things — his love of the right work for the right man, and his pleasure in perfect company. He told his father that he had never begot him. He accused his mother of no sin, but his had been a miraculous birth, he begotten out of the summer air when the sun shone hot on a cornfield. For he was no gentleman, he declared, but belonged to the English soil so deeply that he could never pull his thick legs out of it. He was at the prime of his young manhood, although at thirty many of his contemporaries were wise and learned men about the Court. But he had no desire for wisdom beyond the wisdom of husbandry and all things of the open air.

But he was aware at this time, as many hundreds of thousands of young men were also at this time aware, of a new pride in England. He was no politician, and it mattered nothing to him that Quiroga was, at the moment, warning his King Philip against Elizabeth's mission in Spain, or that Alva was in a furious rage about the Low Countries, or that his

Queen was pursuing her usual policy of facing both ways to the infinite ultimate profit of her country.

But it *did* matter to him most deeply that he should find an eyrie of hawks in his own ground or that a mare of a good strain should successfully foal, or that he should himself invent a new mixing of dung and white marl better than any he had tried before, or that his oxen should be larger, taller, heavier than the oxen of his neighbours. The farms belonging to Mallory had during his father's time fallen to comfortable sloth. They were now paying handsomely and a beautiful sight to behold for anyone who knew about farms. And this was English soil. As he helped with the ploughing, tended with his own hands the sheep and cows, walked, shouting and cursing and laughing, about his fields, it seemed to him that he was King of England, or as good as any king. He realized, although he would never put it into words, that because of the wisdom and hardihood of his great and glorious sovereign a new England *was* growing there beneath his feet. Her ships were abroad plundering the bastard foreigner, her great captains were seizing lands that didn't belong to them. Everywhere the world was waking to a fearful awareness of a new power that only thirty years back had scarcely breathed. There *could* be no place in the Universe (of which he had but a scanty notion) as sweet as England, breathing such delicious airs, growing such trees and flowers, sheltering such noble animals.

As he lay on his broad back, in that last moment of dim consciousness before sleep, he saw the whole expanse of England covered with vast armies of lowing kine, white myriads of sheep, woods with their ancient giant trees (although these, alas ! were being ignobly slaughtered), the blue sea running to the golden sand, and the horizon crowded with the gleaming sails of English ships. When it rained it was a lovely English rain, and when the mists gathered from the river they were kindly, protective, grass and fruit producing. His contempt for all foreigners and their foreign snotty breeding-places was profound. He knew no humility about England or the Englishman. Only if an Englishman were a Catholic he sniffed him as he would a foreigner. Everywhere this pride in England was going up in songs and poems. When he wrestled with Gilbert Armstrong and was thrown by him, as his back bumped the earth he felt that he was coming home. He was part with the grass that he lay upon, the streams that he bathed in, the rich dung that he spread upon his fields.

And his second source of happiness was the loving, fatherly, motherly care he felt for the men and women who worked with him.

Here, too, he was aware there was the rising of a new force in England, although he could not of course see that this force would, in a hundred years or two, govern and control his dear country. Susan Hackett, whose posterior he pinched ; James Forceaway, whose giant shoulders bent down to lift the new posts for the new gates on the Western Drive ; Hob Greening, the cunning little bastard who sang from the top of the haycart in his lovely sweet tenor Surrey's ' O Happy Dames that may embrace the fruit of your delight '— it was more than he could ever imagine that Sue and James and Hob should ever have power above their masters.

But they *were* new people. The Eighth Henry, with his destruction of the monasteries, had thrown these Susans and Hobs out into the world of their own hopes and imaginations. They were thinking for themselves at last, and their Queen, by her glorious deeds, was giving them a new ambition and a fresh, personal, individual pride. He loved them all both as friend and master. He would laugh with them, sing with them, be at times drunk and lecherous with them : but through it all they never forgot that he was Master. Say what he would, behave as he would, *he* was Master, they were Man. But he grew, during that winter, to become a kind of legend in the district. His size and strength and good-nature they could not exaggerate, but in the alehouses and cottages and on the village greens, they attributed to him almost miraculous powers and spoke as though he were of another flesh from ordinary man. And they said that a hundred urchins or more tumbling about goose-ponds or chasing the cat were of his creation. And in this last they were altogether slanderous.

Finally, with all his comradeship in the field, when, dressed in his finery, he walked with his father and mother to the little church at the end of the Park on a Sunday, they stood and doffed their hats and said that he was noble enough to be King of England and that Leicester was nothing to him.

So all went very happily until a certain April night and a dream he had.

He dreamt of Catherine Hodstetter as he had often dreamt before. Catherine was a constant undercurrent flowing beneath his daily happy life, and not Catherine only but the North Country to which he belonged. He thought of the North Country partly because of Gilbert Armstrong. Gilbert was now part of himself and, he often thought, the better part, because Gilbert never did the shameful things he did. Gilbert never tumbled girls, never was drunken, never lost his temper. And yet Gilbert was no paragon ; it was simply that his character was as pure and direct as the stone, the cloud, the running stream. Gilbert never analysed, never subtilized, never wondered at anything. He would argue because he loved arguing, but he would smile when Nicholas grew hot and angry, and say : ' I kiss my hand and cry " Madame." You have the last word.'

The strange thing about him was that he was not homesick for the North and yet carried it always about with him. This was partly because of a roughness in his accent but much more than that. He seemed to walk for ever on the springing turf of the Tops and in his voice there was an echo of the fresh-running streams. Whenever Gilbert was with him Nicholas thought, often without knowing it, of Catherine. He never moved, although this also he did not know, without carrying the North Country with him.

He dreamed of Catherine often and she was always, in these dreams, at one remove from him. The odd thing was that he did not expect this to be other. He had heard young Philip Sidney say once that every man must have in his life a passion beyond his reach, that the savours of this passion were sweeter than any other savours. So he felt, with a certain magnanimity and pride in himself, about Catherine.

She was the temptation that he had beaten — ' *Retro me, Sathanas.*' He did not acknowledge to himself that he had beaten it only because she wished it. He would have had her by now a hundred times had she been willing. But she was the ' strangeness ' in his life — she and the North Country. A kind of dream, a sort of vision, something like the Bright Pavilions of which Robin spoke.

But this night when he dreamt of her the dream was different from any other that he had had. There was a towering cloud of smoke and, when it cleared, the Tarn of Watendlath black and unruffled. Catherine was sinking in those cold dark waters, and as she sank witches flew through the smoke above her like bats mocking her. She did not cry out to him to help her, but her eyes were fixed on him. . . .

Waking in the early morning he decided that he would go North. Robin had been back in his house in Rosthwaite a month now. He, Nicholas, would go and see what was happening to the boy, concerning whom indeed he was none too easy. And he had been at home for a long spell.

So he rode North with Gilbert Armstrong.

It was a pale primrose evening of mid-April when he greeted his brother in the courtyard of the little Rosthwaite house, and he knew instantly that something most serious had occurred.

He did not quite know how he was aware of it. There was a hush about the place and the country around. The snow still lay in the evening sun like rose-grey cloud on the fell-tops. The spring was backward here in the North and there was the chill of new hidden primrose leaves and fresh water running over stones, but a bird sang bravely and thin snow soiled against the lee of the gate was pitted with the holes that the thaw had made.

Except for the bird there was not a sound to be heard when the brothers embraced ; only, Nicholas thought : ' I have ridden all these days several steps into Robin's trouble.'

So that night as they sat alone together in front of the open fire, Nicholas put his hand on Robin's arm and asked what the trouble was :

' Are you become a secret Catholic ? '

Vehemently Robin answered : ' No. No ! Never ! '

'Are they disturbing you because this is a Catholic house?'

'No one is disturbing me.'

'Have priests been here?'

Robin did not answer. After a silence — Nicholas never could endure silences — he thought he would unburden his mind.

'All our growing up,' he began, 'we were together so as to be one — one heart, one mind (although yours was even then so much the greater), one body (although there mine was the greater).' Here he chuckled. 'Was it not so?'

'Yes,' Robin said, smiling.

'And so it was, I think, until we were men. Our trust was so that we never needed to ask a question. You had the learning and I had the strength — not that you were not strong, nor that I could not boast of a certain knowledge — dogs, horses, the crops, and a pass with the rapier. We were together. We were one.' He sighed portentously and took a long draught from the jack beside him. 'Then there came a change. It began, I think, at the time of the Northern Rebellion when we met here at Keswick and I stuck Philip Irvine through the arm for not minding my word.' He chuckled and drank again. 'And so then. After that you fell in with the priest Pierson and loved our cousin Sylvia. Then came Bartholomew and now Sylvia has wed Irvine — and so — and so — we are no longer together. I know nothing of how you travel. About me there is nothing to know. About you, everything.'

He drew Robin towards him.

'From the day you were born I have loved you, and so I will till I die. I am not a subtle man like your Philip Sidneys and Peaches and Grevilles — but I am faithful. I ask for no confidence. I shall love you always whether or no. But it is true that we have grown apart and I am unhappy because of it. Moreover I feel that there is a great peril ahead of you. If you will tell me nothing I will ask nothing. But I would be more comfortable if I knew a little.'

Robin rested his head a little closer against his brother's arm. Then of a sudden he sat up and leant his elbows on his knees towards the fire, looking into it.

' I suppose there is something to tell,' he said at last.
' And yet I scarcely know what. Since I have become a man
two things have happened to me : the one, meeting Pierson ;
the other, loving Sylvia — whom I shall love until the end and
beyond,' he added in a whisper.

He turned and looked at his brother, his dark eyes burning
in his thin face, his high forehead white and strong in the
firelight, his body moved with a passionate energy.

' Oh, Nicholas, what can I tell you ? For to you these
things that possess me day and night are only straws to make
an idle controversy. It is the form and figure of Christ Himself that possesses me. Not Pierson's Catholic way nor your
Protestant way neither. No way but His own life and presence.
His presence that is always with me, not reproaching me nor
ordering me to another way of life nor saying that I do ill nor
insisting that I persecute my brother men, but only pleading
with me that He may come nearer to me, that I will entertain
Him as my guest and friend.

' The Catholics say that because He loves us we must
upset governments and bring on civil wars and suffer martyr-
dom. I think He wants no cruelty nor that men should suffer
more than they already do. But I hear His voice and see His
face. Not torn and bleeding, His body racked on the cross.
Not weak and like a woman as the painters have made Him.
But only as a friend, loving me — strong, laughing, wise,
tender — and urging me without cease to do something concerning this state of the world that is so crooked and perverse.
There is a hell here now on this earth — a destiny that must
be divine is warped at every turn by man's cruelty to man.
Men starve, women are tortured, children cry. There *is* a
way and He knows it — but it is to ourselves He leaves it to
straighten. He does us that honour and we are not worthy
of it. I love Him and would serve Him and cannot tell how.
There *are* the Bright Pavilions, as Pierson once said to me,
but I know not how to reach them. The Catholic way is not
my way. . . . I pray to Him and feel His hand on my shoulder,
but I cannot act. I am held in a bog of indecision.'

Nicholas waited. ' And then ? ' he said at last.

' Yes, there is something more.' He began to speak fiercely

and in a torrent of words as though he would defy his brother to interrupt him.

'You don't know, Nicholas, what constant company Pierson, Parsons, Cumberlege have been keeping with me. I have no notion why it is, but it seems that they would sooner make me a Catholic than any man in the country, work harder for it, I mean — I who am nobody, nothing. And it is not easy for me because of my love for Pierson. We were together from the first moment of our meeting here in this house. There is another thing too. The Queen of the Scots.'

'She is not Queen any longer,' Nicholas said.

'Ah, but she is! They cannot dethrone her! They may imprison her, torture her, break their word to her, but she is Queen — and rightfully of England too.'

('Here is treason,' Nicholas thought. 'And grave too. But I cannot be angry with him and I must not frighten him. But I have left him too long alone to the influence of these priests.')

'And then?' he said again.

'Why, then . . . why, then . . . how can everyone not see what is right, what is wrong — how that God is on one side and the Devil on the other? They who see it are the Catholics and the Catholics alone. Everything they believe is right save the dogmas of their religion. How can the Pope be God's voice when there have been so many wicked and vicious Popes? They say that it is God acting through man, that man is only the instrument — but would God then permit the instrument to be so vile? And there is Bartholomew — and even now Parsons and Cumberlege are crazy for persecution and the stake to be back again, and they ardently approve the Spanish Inquisition. But the Queen of the Scots is on another foot, and in some way, in some place I must serve her, Nicholas . . .'

He stopped for breath. He seemed almost at that moment a madman.

'You know, lad,' Nicholas said gently, 'this is treason. That you are speaking against your Queen, your country. That if those words were overheard there would be the torture-chamber, perhaps the stake, bitter disgrace for your father and mother who love you.'

Robin's eyes sought Nicholas' broad kindly face.

' God knows I love you and my mother, my father. But, Nicholas, if you could see Parsons and Cumberlege — their courage and steadfastness, their lack of all fear because they serve God. And if you could hear the truth about Queen Mary — how roughly she is treated, how she is sick, how she is denied her friends — and that after she was promised safe-conduct and protection by our Queen—'

Then, unexpectedly, his hand shot out and gripped his brother's knee.

' There is yet another thing — that I have told no man and *will* tell no man but you, Nicholas. I am a coward. I know the path I should follow and dare not, because I am afraid. I am afraid of pain, of the rack and the screw. I am afraid of the bloody drawing and quartering, so that they snatch you down before you are yet dead and cut open your belly and tumble out your entrails before your living eyes. . . . I am afraid, I am afraid. I have dreamed many times of a scene, myself hanging before a sea of faces, my body a fiery torture and the sun blazing like an oven : I wake crying, tears wet on my cheek.'

He hid his face in his hands.

Nicholas said sternly : ' Leave it, Robin. Leave it all. These priests will make you a priest and a Catholic. Leave it. Come home and become a poet like Sidney. They'll find you a place at Court easily enough. Be with us — your father, your mother, myself, who love you. These priests are false and will betray you.'

He caught Robin in his arms and held him as though against the world. Robin withdrew at last, stirred the fire, then rose, stretching his arms.

' There is yet one thing more,' he said, ' and then I am done. Sylvia——'

' Sylvia ? '

' I have been told that she is most desperately unhappy, that Irvine already mistreats her. Sidney Herries went to Essex to see for himself because they had had no word from her. He found her changed, aged, unhappy like something caught in a trap.'

Nicholas also rose, stretching his arms and legs.

' Irvine,' he said.

' Yes — Irvine.'

And on that the brothers clasped hands.

Nicholas could not be sober-serious for long. Robin's confession had wonderfully cleared the air and now the two of them were never apart, riding, fishing, visiting Newlands and Nicholas' old friends Hans Opperer and Beck. He asked also for Joris Fisher, Catherine's old suitor, but was told that he had vanished a year back and that no one knew where he was.

It was on a bright shining day when the little town sparkled like a jewel that Nicholas, sitting his horse in the main street, listened to the burly Opperer, also on *his* horse, complaining of his misfortunes. Things had not, in these last years, been going well for the ' Almaynes.' Nothing had been right for them since the trial, back in 1568, between the Queen and the Earl of Northumberland. He had complained that it was *his* property the miners were occupying, the Queen had answered haughtily, and then, when it came to a trial, the majority of the judges and barons of the Exchequer had decided that there was more gold and silver in these mines than copper and lead and that therefore the Queen was in her right.

' Saving Her Majesty,' said Opperer, ' a monstrous unfair decision, for of gold and silver there is simply none at all.' Then, after every kind of labour and expense, when they had put copper on the market there was no market to supply, not even a coinage. And the Queen, now she realized that her fairy gold was not to be found, had lost interest.

' As to the people here, after our early disputes, they were friendly enough when they found that there was something to be got from us ; and, for the last seven years, we have given a new life and prosperity to this town that, before we came, was dead for half the year. But now that we don't prosper as we did they care for us less, although our men have married their girls and have sought in everything to be decent citizens. But to the last we shall be Almaynes to them — they are the snottiest, narrowest, stupidest, most obstinate animals on the face of the known earth. A foreigner is to them a goblin or a fair-zany.'

G

Here Nicholas felt something guilty because of his own foreigner prejudice. Strange, when he thought of it, that these Germans were the only foreigners he ever had liked.

' See here now,' Opperer said, turning his head and looking up the street to where the town stocks were planted. There was a man in them now, a thick dirty fellow with a tousled head of hair and a broken nose that looked twice as crooked in the sunlight. He was drunk and shouting and striving to kick with his legs, while some boys and an old crazy man stood by teasing him.

' That's Hans Selzenstollen. It's his own blame that he's there. The town constable was right enough, for he threw a stone and broke a window in Crosthwaite Church. But he's married to a decent Keswick girl, Christina, and has two children by her. It does us no good for him to be exposed to the town. " Another Almayne," they say, and are encouraging his Christina to return to her mother.'

Opperer sighed a mighty sigh and was about to unload some more of his sorrows when Nicholas' attention was taken by a scattering of small boys, a farmer and two cows, before a gentleman on horseback who advanced up the street as though he commanded not only the little town but the whole of England. And yet he was a very shabby hero, greatly over-decorated with a headpiece that had a dent in it, a soiled doublet of tarnished gold and broken mesh, and a face much the worse for wind, weather and wine. He was attended by two followers on very sorry horses but in countenance as truculent as he.

' And who may this be ? ' Nicholas asked, laughing.

' I can tell you,' Opperer answered. ' He has been here a se'nnight or more and three days back he rode to Gottesgab and was for asking us a meddle of questions to which we gave short answers. He said he was a Captain Winterset, and while he has been here he has swaggered and pestered the women and is as haughty as Satan.'

Then a remarkable thing happened, for while Nicholas was set laughing, the horseman saw him, drew up his horse, stared as though his eyes would fall out of his head and rode on, looking back at Nicholas as he rode.

'And here is Catherine Hodstetter,' Opperer said. 'She is an old acquaintance of yours, I think, Mr. Herries.'

So it had happened as simply as that ! — as always when he did not search her out but let destiny settle the meeting. She stood there as straight as a tree, her flaxen hair in coils beneath the blue cap, her eyes shining with joy, one hand on her breast.

He moved on his horse a little away from Opperer, and she stood, one hand on the saddle, looking up at him, the sun like fire in her hair.

'I was not coming to you,' Nicholas said. 'I was determined not to come.'

'It matters nothing. We are always together.'

'Are you happy ? Is all well with you ?'

She laughed.

'With *me*, yes. Nothing can touch me. I run like the wind, smoke a fox, climb a hill, and when I sleep, dream about you riding down the lane on a hay-cart, singing while the rabbits run for their lives in the evening sun.'

'Can I see you this time ?' he asked, bending forward. He was aware that the whole town was watching. 'I ask you every time so I ask you now. Will you come away with me for a night and be alone with me in some place ?'

'No, I will not. Once we possess one another we lose one another. All the town is watching us so I can say it with safety. I love you with my soul first, with my body nearly as much. But my soul first — and I am a foreigner and the daughter of a forbidden woman. I have told you all this before.'

'Yes. We repeat the same words at every meeting and at every meeting we are bound more closely together. There never was anyone,' Nicholas said, sighing, never removing his gaze for one moment from her face, 'who took more simply what he wanted than I. Here I take something in a more difficult way.'

He knew that their meeting was almost over. There was no man in England less a mystic or given to belief in things he could not see nor hear nor touch, but at every meeting with Catherine Hodstetter it had been the same : the moment had stood still like the obedient sun with Joshua. These moments were eternal and Time was humbugged.

So now he saw the sun shining on the field and the line of hill like a fish's back, a clump of blossoms in the paved garden near the Guard House so hard and white that they were like petals of glittering ice. The man in the stocks had his tousled head forward, tumbled now in sleep, and the hair of his head was transmuted into crocodile-skin by the shadow of a near-by pent-house roof. The hilt of Gilbert Armstrong's rapier sparkled like a bunch of jewels. At the forge opposite, a horse was being shod and the sparks flew up like fiery midges dancing, a life's instant, in the air. Gipsies had camped their coloured cart on the meadow above the river and he could see the smoke rising in a grey-silver spiral from their fire. Doves, sunlight on their wings, flew, at some alarm, in a cloud of white and purple from a dove-cote half hidden by trees. A beggar walked and then at sight of the grand horse-men stood staring and scratching his chest. There was a purple feather waving in his torn cap.

All these fragments of light and colour stood still in Nicholas' heart and mind for ever. He would never forget the least of them until he died.

Then he turned to Catherine again. He absorbed into his very soul her blue cap, her yellow hair, her eyes and mouth and chin, her white neck and firm strong breasts, her waist, and the stiff blue stuff of her simple dress, her brown shoes with brass buckles. Then his eyes went back to her eyes again. They smiled in perfect confidence and trust and with no anxiety.

Her eyes left him. She stared up the street and his eyes followed hers. A tall woman of fine carriage in a grey hat and cloak was coming down the street. She looked neither to right nor left. As she came everyone parted to keep her path clear. A woman pulled two children roughly away ; a farmer shouted to his cow and whacked it over the street. The boys that had been about to rouse the man in the stocks took to their heels and ran. Women leaned out of windows staring without a word. The beggar hustled into a doorway.

Quite alone, the whole street clear for her, the woman

walked. Catherine, smiling, went to meet her and, joining her, put her hand through her arm. The two of them proceeded, mother and daughter. At the street end they turned towards the river and disappeared.

A week later Nicholas and Armstrong rode off for a two days' hunting or any other adventure that pleasant destiny might provide for them.

It was Nicholas' plan and for two reasons. One was that all day he suffered from an urge to find out Catherine Hodstetter. Well, why should he not ? She must yield to him at the last. She loved him. Where was the woman who loved a man did not yield at the last ? Then came the oddest part of it. That with all his soul he fought with himself that she should not yield. Yielding she was lost. She would be like just another who had yielded to him. And if she did not yield he would be angry and, angry, would say cruel things to her that, being said, would destroy the special quality of this strange non-tangible relationship. He must not see her save when he *must*.

His other reason was that there was something in Robin's house from which he wished to escape. Not dear Robin himself : something in the walls, the floors, the beams, something that had been placed there perhaps by his old uncle — the odours and subtleties of Catholics. It was as though he could smell the incense and hear the tinkling of the bell.

So he rode out with Gilbert Armstrong, and at once, as their horses felt their way through the tangled paths and over the thick mud to Keswick, he lifted his arms and shouted :
' Are you not happy now, Gilbert ? Is it not a grand thing to be out of any house ? '

' Yes, Mr. Herries.'

' I love my brother more than any man alive, but I think his house stinks. Tell me, Gilbert, how can you bear to be with me in the South when there is this great windy unmade country that belongs to you ? '

' Because I am your man, Mr. Herries — and because anyone who is born here carries it with him wherever he goes.'

' And some who are not born here, for I swear that now *I*

carry it with me and am never free of it : but that maybe is because I love a girl who will have none of me — the best way, Gilbert, because you love her for ever. What kind of girl do you love the best, Gilbert ? '

' The one that is most like a woman, Mr. Herries. The one that is soft of cheek and strong-breasted and melts away in your arms.'

' By Jesu, a poet's tongue — the poor country wench who melts like her own butter. But this is happiness, as I see it, Gilbert ! To be free, to owe no man anything, to be afraid of no man, to have a strong horse under you and a sword at your side, to feel the wind on your face and your heart steady in your breast, to love one or two faithfully and be ready to die at a moment without a grudge — but first of them all, to be a free man ! '

The first night they stayed at a meagre inn near Ambleside where the food was bacon and cabbage vilely cooked, where they slept together in their clothes because of the filthiness of the bedding. But they were as fresh as a day's dawning when next morning they rode into Hawkshead.

Here they did some sight-seeing, for it was as strange a little place as they had ever seen, built as though a tearing giant had thrown the houses together higgledy-piggledy, one house leaning on another, doors high in air where the windows should be, steps to an upper floor, gutters running sideways and sheep looking forth from the bed-rooms.

The grammar-school was still ten years abuilding so that they could not see it, but the Church was of interest because it was but newly built on an old Norman foundation, and indeed, as an old sexton, doubled with rheumatism and blind of one eye, informed them, much older than Norman.

Then they rode on again up on to the fells beyond, where they had a handsome view of Coniston Water and noticed for the first time that a storm was brewing and black clouds sulkily piling above the grey white-touched lake.

Here, on the fell, with nothing in sight but the sky and tufts of grass tugging at the ground, they discovered an old tower. It had been built on a time for defence against invaders, and was still in good repair, the lowest room piled with dank straw, a narrow little stone stair and the upper room with some of the rough stones that had fallen from the roofing lying about it.

Here they sat and munched some bread and cheese while their horses cropped at the turf. They were kings of the whole world, and Nicholas felt such a blessed content that he wondered why it was that he was not satisfied to be a simple farmer in this blessed country and let all the noisy world go by. He said so and Armstrong answered : ' We are not alone. There are horsemen on the horizon.'

So there were, five of them.

First they were little cloud-marks, then they were puppets pulled by strings, then they were dancing dolls.

' There are five of them,' Nicholas said.

' They are coming this way.'

The two men stood straining to see. Because the clouds had massed black, but the sun was set in the foreground, these five men sparkled quartz-like. Their horses surged and stopped. One rider was in front of the rest.

' They look as though they were hunting something,' Nicholas said.

' They are much in love with themselves,' Armstrong said, arguing from a kind of cock of the head the leader had. They moved forward once more.

' Why ! It is my battered Captain ! ' Nicholas cried. Then, turning to Armstrong and laughing : ' What was it they called him ? '

' Winterset. Captain Winterset.'

' He has been wenching in Keswick most villainously and swaggers like a Privy Councillor.'

The visitors arrived nearer ; in fact they were well within speaking distance. The Captain wore light mail and a yellow feather stuck in his helmet. There was a rapier against his thigh and a dagger at his hip. Over his meshed gloves he wore a ring with a ruby. His face was mottled and in decomposition. But he looked, in spite of all contrary efforts, a gentleman.

Winterset sat his horse, motionless, staring at Nicholas and Armstrong, and behind him in a huddle his four attendants.

Two were the men that Nicholas had seen follow him in Keswick. Of these two, one was long and thin with a ridiculous hook nose and large black eyes that were never still, squinting, staring, switching from side to side. You would have said that strings pulled them from within. The other was fat and small, his shabby armour enclosing him like a shell. He sat his horse as though he were asleep.

The other two were tall, broad, as like as two pins and with stupid country faces. They wore no armour, but leather jerkins and big jackboots. They carried swords.

This company, so motionless and staring and stupid, had about it something remarkably comic, and after a moment Nicholas began to laugh ; and he laughed and laughed, and the sudden faint thunder in the hills seemed to echo him.

His laughter did not embarrass Winterset, for he sat his horse, staring scornfully, and pulling occasionally at his rein, the only movement he made.

Nicholas came forward, thrusting down his laughter and looking with a smile into Winterset's little eyes.

' Have you lost your way, sir ? Or you are uneasy about the coming storm and seek shelter here ? There is room for all of us.'

Winterset stared at him with the greatest contempt, but the men, Armstrong saw, were interested. They had never before seen so gigantic a gentleman. Armstrong fancied that the tall thin fellow half turned his horse as though he would ride it away.

' I seek no shelter,' Winterset answered. ' It is yourself I am after, Mr. Nicholas Herries. I have been seeking you all morning.'

' Ah, you know me.'

' I know you most excellently — for a swollen boasting sot and a coward whom the apprehension of any danger loosens pitifully.'

Nicholas could not believe the evidence of his bodily senses. He opened wide his fine innocent eyes : his mouth also opened ever so slightly. He was not angry, but incredulous.

' *What* did you venture ? ' he enquired.

' I named you a sot and a coward ! '

The fellow had been sent, then, to insult him. By whom ? Who would use this broken-down shabby-suited gentleman ? But instinctively, in a second of trained perception, he noted several things : first, that this Winterset really *was* a gentleman ; secondly, that he greatly enjoyed the job (there was exultation in all his drink-damaged features) ; thirdly, that however drunken he might be now and again he was, at the moment, most perfectly sober ; fourthly, that a man of this sort would be, almost to certainty, a most excellent swordsman ; fifthly, that the numbers were five to two ; sixthly, that the sky was blackening, the light would be bad ; seventhly, that being outnumbered the tower would be the wisest background for them ; eighthly, that he did not know *how* accomplished a swordsman Armstrong might be ; ninthly and lastly, he was longing for a fight and would have the greatest pleasure in slicing a piece off Winterset's nose.

So he evinced no displeasure at all but grinned like a boy.

' Come, sir. Many things may be said against me as against any man. But sot am I not, and coward am I not. What is your quarrel ? '

Winterset leaned over his horse towards Nicholas and said quite confidentially : ' You are a braggart the world wishes to be rid of. And I have come to do the world that service.'

Now *what*, Nicholas was thinking, was the reason of this ? This thing was arranged and prepared. It was doubtless for this reason that Winterset was in Keswick. Sent by whom ? And in a flash Nicholas had it. Irvine of course. Irvine, Irvine, Irvine. Busy on his own affairs or for some reason important to himself wishing not just now to venture, he had sent a deputy. Irvine was no coward but also he took no risks. Winterset was his bravo, hired out for a sum. And Winterset liked it. Such an encounter as this was for Winterset as good as a debauch.

Yes, Winterset was pleased, and Nicholas, realizing this, looked around him to see exactly how the land lay. First he caught the eye of his dear horse Juno who, perfectly aware that events were toward, flashed a glance at her master which

said : ' I am here ready and prepared for an instant's command. I am delighted that there is to be some action again.
I have had a tame paddock-life long enough.'

Then he included Armstrong who, his body solid and set,
stood, his hand on his sword-hilt, square-footed and quiet-
eyed.

Then he surveyed the land and saw the hills trembling
under the weight of thunder and a pale light as of sword-play
striking the fell. Yes, five to two. The tower was their
vantage-ground.

So he walked a step to the empty yawning stone door, and
Gilbert Armstrong, as though he was physically part of him,
was at his side.

' Now, Captain Winterset, at your service or good-day as
you please.'

Winterset called the lean man to him and they palavered.
Nicholas, watching with an eye like his own sword, had already
given the four ruffians names. He had long learnt that if
there is a fight on, nothing is more useful than a flashing
summary of your adversary's circumstances. Nothing is unimportant. The lean man with the swivel eye he named
Hungry, the round fat man Bacchus, and of the two yokels
one, distinguished by a yellow-red forelock, was Matthew,
the other Mark. And he noted to himself that Hungry could
be caught at the ankles, Bacchus would be wheezy in the
stomach, Matthew had a thick stertorous neck, and Mark's
thighs were too heavy for quick movement. The other
thought in his head again and again was — how good is
Gilbert at this ? For he had never as yet seen Gilbert in a real
fight.

After the whispered discussion between Winterset and his
man Hungry they all dismounted. Winterset drew his rapier
with an over-dramatic flourish. Nicholas and Armstrong had
theirs out at the same instant.

' It is plain enough that you are a coward,' Winterset
remarked. ' The sight of a naked blade drives you to the
wall.'

' Not in the least,' Nicholas answered. ' I would have you
observe, Captain, that you are five to our two. I would that

you also noticed my size. My back is easily reached by those not too readily guardian of their honour. And you, Captain, although your soiled feather blows bravely, are by general reputation none too careful of that commodity.'

He was hitting in the dark but he went further :

' The very sort of Captain, in fact, whom Mr. Philip Irvine, always ready that others should carry his more filthy burdens, would select as deputy.'

(' Blackguardly on Irvine,' he thought, ' who is filthy indeed but brave with it.')

He saw that he had touched the shabby Captain, who was shabby no longer, for he was in so great a rage that he was transformed into some nobler category of men by it.

He advanced a pace or two, his head forward.

' This is no quarrel but my own.'

' Yours ! ' Nicholas cried. ' How can that be ? We have not met until to-day.'

' You insulted me in the town market-place.'

' Insulted ! Inconceivable ! '

' You commented on me coarsely to your companion. And for that,' Winterset said quietly, ' you shall surely die ! '

At the word all five were upon them, three at Armstrong, Winterset on Nicholas, and the yokel Mark seeking his chance to be in with his uncivilized and most villainous-faced dagger at Nicholas' back. The fight was set.

Nicholas realized, once more, a number of verities. First, that Winterset was as able a swordsman as he had hoped for ; secondly, that there was no sense of shame in this company and that no trick would be too vile for them ; thirdly, that Armstrong could not, in the light of day and with no aid from either man or nature, hope to deal with all three at one and the same time.

He beat Winterset's defence, slipped to one side, cried, ' In, Gilbert ! In ! ' and felt Armstrong slip past him into the tower. He lunged with a furious rage at Winterset, who, for a second, stepped back. Nicholas slipped his great bulk into the tower after Gilbert.

Now he was happy indeed, for he had what he loved —

tactics at his command. A fight as a fight was something, but a fight in which he could, because his brain in these things was quick, order events to his liking : *that* was bread and wine to his constitution !

So, now, turning his head left and right, he considered the conditions. There was a moment's pause. For one thing Winterset and his men did not know what was inside the tower. For all they could tell there might be an army ! Next, the light was very peculiar. The storm lay like a snake-skin shadow across the aperture that had been once a barred window, but the sun, before final defeat, flung a white shine on the walls, the straw and a broken bar of iron-nailed wood. Nicholas saw that on the wall there were three black rings. He stood in the room's centre, kicking the straw away from him. He bent down and, with the greatest ease, lifted the bar of wood high : then, knowing that it was strong and the nails jagged, he laid it down again. He whirled his rapier about his head, pawing impatiently with his foot.

' Quick, Gilbert ! At my side ! A little to the rear ! They're in ! '

Winterset stood in the doorway, bareheaded, his rapier moving in his hand like a snake. Bacchus and Mark were before him, Matthew and Hungry behind. As though the plan had been well concerted the two men behind him attacked Armstrong ; Winterset, Nicholas.

Now no man spoke ; the feet could be heard rustling in the straw, and there was a crack of thunder like a whip. No man heard the thunder.

There followed for Nicholas as exciting a bout as he could ever remember. He had, truly, to look to himself and could spare no glance for Gilbert. Winterset was of the Italian kind of swordsman, as were all the better fighters of the time — that is, he was like a cat on his feet and his arm had the motions of a snake, stiffening with a hiss, bending back like a bow, wriggling in a crawl and then flashing forward, up or down, as when a snake strikes. His blade played a tune, moving for a while in the rhythm of a dance, then quivering as a high singer might on a scaling note. His rapier was alive as water is alive, water that is its own master, that slides or falls or

rises by its own power and inner volition. And with his
rapier went his body. You would have thought to see him
that dissipation had won him, that he would be scant of
breath and too fat about the heart, that his legs were too
thick and his loins too stiff. But this was his life, the life for
which he had been born. Scandalous in everything, faithless
to man and woman, intemperate and despairing partaker of
filthy vices, always from hand to mouth, cruel in perfidy and,
at the last, true not even to himself, yet as soon as he
was fighting he was clear-brained, single-souled, an artist, a
master, living only for a grand end.

Nicholas had not lived in a fighting world so little but that
he knew an artist in this kind. His own heart rose greatly to
the challenge. He was happy now as he had been happy
singing home his father's corn. But this was another happiness, for he was an artist too, and this was the best fight his
life had yet known.

He saw at once that Winterset was quicker than he, but
finally, if the fight lasted, in less good condition. But Winterset's attack was now so buoyantly ferocious that, for the first
minute, it seemed to Nicholas that he was fighting a dozen
men. Winterset's rapier was not part of Winterset, but alive
by itself with a voice and a hot breath and a body of its own.
He was forced on the defence, and he cursed the straw behind
him lest he should stumble. Also, out of the corner of his
eye, he saw the other two not engaged with Armstrong creeping
to the rear. Armstrong could not last at this, with two men
in front of him, two men behind. Also, without Armstrong,
do what he would he could not, in that open room, alone be
the master of five.

He lunged. His rapier slid on Winterset's, the blades
kissing. He stepped back, making as though he stumbled.
With a cry of triumph, the first sound that he had made,
Winterset was after him, but Nicholas, moving his rapier in
front of him, ceaselessly restless, had slid sideways to the
stone stair.

' The stair ! The stair ! ' he cried.

Then Armstrong did a grand thing, for he lowered his
sword, took a step to the left and drove his fist full into little

Bacchus' face. Bacchus dropped. With a leap Armstrong was up the stair and Nicholas on the lowest step.

Slowly, his sword in circles, in lines, flashing in the dark yellow sombre shadow like a flame, Nicholas backed step by step.

The two men, panting, stood one behind the other at the stair-head.

Again there was a pause. Nicholas, looking down at the four men hesitating below him, felt an extraordinary exhilaration. He heard now for the first time the storm raging over his head, and noticed the yellow sulphurous half-light in which figures were illuminated but as unreal as ghosts.

He shouted to them, laughing : ' Come then ! You will not leave it like this — four of you ! Shoot up your necks to your fortunes ! Here is a sorry sight for true Englishmen ! You, Mr. Hungry, let me feed your stomach. Now then, Matthew, Mark, apostles of true valour, where are your country manners ? Having thrust yourselves into gentle company you must stay for it. You will expostulate, I don't doubt, with your oxen very understandingly. Well, then, let's have a word or two. On a piece of beef you are terrible fasteners. Here's a blade or two for you to fasten on.'

He must have seemed to them a devilish giant of a man, clothed in sulphur, with his vastness and the voice and laugh of a boy and good-humoured threatening terror, for his rapier, like the lightning of the storm, was never still.

Nevertheless some kind of rage maddened them, and three of them — Hungry, Matthew and Mark — flung themselves up the steps. Then things happened quickly, for Hungry met Nicholas' sword in the neck, gave a shrill scream like a wrung hen and fell, his arms flailing the air, backwards against the other two, rolled off them and smashed to the bottom. But before Nicholas had quite withdrawn his sword Matthew and Mark had flung themselves at him, butted him furiously in the stomach so that he fell backwards. Armstrong lugged his body back into the little room, and then, in the half dark, fought with sword and body, arms and legs, the two Apostles, who raged now in a frenzy, bellowing like bulls. The rain was coming down as from a broken-tin heaven and a flash of lightning showed Nicholas on his feet. Mark and Armstrong were at it, here, there, up and down, weapon against weapon, and Matthew was against the wall to get skilfully to the rear. But Nicholas was upon him. He had him in his arms, crushing him to him as he might love him to madness. He lifted him. Matthew's legs kicked. His neck was pressed by Nicholas' great thumb. His chest was bare, and the shoulder cracked. He screamed his last agony, and it came through the air like a child's whistle. Then, with a swing and his buttocks bare, he rushed through the window like thistledown and was caught by the thunder, dropped into silence.

The other Apostle, cut through the groin, fell at Armstrong's feet, and Winterset, waiting, stood in the doorway.

'And now,' he said, 'it is our affair again.'

'Stand aside, Gilbert,' Nicholas cried, laughing. 'There can be no foul play now.'

They bowed, they measured swords, stepped back. Beyond the window there was a broad tawny lion's mane of a gap between the black thunder, and the light from it was faint, sickly, while the fresh cold rain fell with the monotony of the beating of a giant hammer.

In this pale light they fought, but it was a good fight, although it was a fight that could have but one ending. After a passage of attack and retreat, of blade upon blade and a scratch on Nicholas' thigh, after a dreadful moment when Nicholas all but slipped in the Apostle's blood, Winterset's breath began to fail. His arm did not move with the quickness that it had done in the lower room. The muscles of his legs were weary. He backed to the wall, his eyes staring as though they saw a horror. The red veins on his swollen cheeks stood out like wounds. He lunged and missed. His sword flew into the air.

Nicholas picked it up.

'I keep this, Captain,' Nicholas said. 'And now ride away. You are the shadow of my enemy, not the substance. It had been better if you had not pressed these poor fellows to their death, but you obeyed the orders of a less honourable man. Good day, Captain.'

Winterset had stood against the wall, his hands at his side.

He said at last, hoarsely : 'You have spared my life, Mr. Herries. That is not easy to forgive.'

He looked for a moment at the dead staring face of his hired servant. He turned his back, without fear, and descended.

Then Nicholas heard the storm crashing on to his uplifted head.

THE THREE PRIESTS

ROBIN was quite alone in the house except for old Mounsey and his wife — Mounsey seventy-two and Henrietta sixty-eight, who cared for him with the carefulness, the stealthy quiet, the bright-eyed watchfulness of mice just out of the wainscot.

After Nicholas' departure he had felt a desperate unhappiness and this had endured for many weeks. There had been a day when Nicholas had had an adventure, for he had returned in the evening drenched with a thunderstorm and suffering from a flesh wound in the thigh. Robin had asked no questions. This was an occasion, he realized, when, to save *his* honesty before enquiring authorities, Nicholas preferred that he should be truly ignorant. All that he and Keswick knew was that, on the morning following, a farmer found three dead men laid out on the fell above Hawkshead, their bodies devoutly arranged, their hands crossed on their breasts : one had died from a sword-thrust in the neck, one from a sword-thrust in the belly, one had his head dashed in from a fall. The only other thing that Keswick knew was that the scandalous Captain Winterset was seen no more.

Robin found that, after this day, Nicholas was altogether at his sweetest and most charming. So gay and merry was he that even the mouse-Mounseys giggled and chuckled at his behaviour. His care for Robin was stronger, more watchful, more devoted than ever before. When he departed, after hugging him, he said : ' Come down to us, lad, Mallory's your home. We'll find you a place at Court or whatever your heart desires.' This made him think, perhaps, of Sylvia Irvine, for he added : ' I will get news . . . maybe visit her myself. Irvine will be wanting to hear my account . . .'

' Of what ? ' asked Robin, laughing.

' Of the new way to pay old debts.'

Nevertheless Robin stayed on through the summer. It was

as though he were waiting for a message. It came. A young farmer driving his sheep up the road dropped a piece of paper through the gate. He had seen Robin standing in the court-yard. The paper said that there would be a fine lot of pippins to be bought up at Green House in Skiddaw Forest on the evening of September 28th.

Robin knew that Green House in Skiddaw Forest. He had been there before. It was an empty, half-tumbled farm manor-house, slipping to ruin.

As he read the paper he had again that awesome sense of destiny moving behind the event, that came to him so often. This did not make him afraid, but strengthened his belief that he was travelling on so definite a path that all he had personally to bring was passivity. How he acted in the events prepared for him — whether well or ill, with cowardice or courage, ah, *that* was *his* affair ! — but not only he : Nicholas, Sylvia, Irvine ; nay, all men alive had the Tournament Ground waiting for them. The trumpets would sound, their names would be called. . . . He shivered although the September sun was warm. He crumpled the piece of paper in his hand and then went in and threw it in the kitchen fire.

Pierson would be there. He would see Pierson ! Pierson and Nicholas ! What opposites ! And yet how dearly he loved and admired them both ! But, intellectually, he was all on Pierson's side ! He hated Nicholas' boasting — not about himself, for there was never anyone more personally modest — but about England's greatness and her plundering and ravish-ing, and ordering everything by force. What right had England to take what wasn't hers, simply because she was the stronger ? What were Drake and Hawkins and the rest but pirates, and Elizabeth as big a pirate as any ? If force ruled the world, then farewell to all the beautiful qualities of man — loving-kindness, equity, tolerance for the weak, justice for the oppressed. And he thought again of Mary of Scotland, ever filling his mind and heart. Oh ! that this destiny of his would allow him in some way to serve her !

On the appointed day he rode off alone to Skiddaw Forest. He rode alone and when, under that darkening September sky, he turned toward Skiddaw, no other human being in sight, only the thick unhandsome Herdwick sheep cropping the turf, he felt with a fierce illuminating pang his own loneliness. He had, it seemed to him, no friend close to him in all the world. Nicholas, Pierson, they were absorbed in their own affairs. Sylvia was married to his enemy. All the men and women he knew held faiths or doctrines or rules of life that were not his. He could not believe other than he did ; he could not be false to himself. It seemed to him too that of late a new kind of shyness had crept over him, and that this held him back from all contacts. There was some secret in his heart that he could yield to no one — and he did not know what this secret was ! Yet, with this, his heart was aching with a love for all humanity. He longed to serve his fellow-men and help them in their unhappiness and misfortune. But he could not go to them and they would not come to him.

This sense of his loneliness was so awful that it was like a physical hurt, something that wounded his heart, and if he put his hand against his naked breast he could feel his heart turning, as though away from him. The figure of Christ was turned from him also, and he had, at that moment, a temptation to believe that there *was* no Christ. This was a myth, made by men for the cheating of men. Death would come, after a life of empty loneliness, and that would be the end. He saw Pierson and Campion and the others as fanatics who had persuaded themselves to believe in a faded old-fashioned story and to suffer for it in an apotheosis of self-cheating, worthless suffering.

That day when he had heard of Sylvia's betrothal had struck him so deep a blow that his whole nature had been changed by it. His longing to love and be loved moved in him now not as an active happiness, but as a frustrated, defeated ambition, never to be realized. His loneliness was a darkness that clouded his eyes and muffled his voice.

The late afternoon was warm. He could see the berries reddening on the rowans, smell the wild thyme and hear in the distance some little invisible waterfall tumbling. At one high point before he crossed into the breach between Skiddaw and Blencathra he caught a fragment of Derwentwater with the late sun shining on it, saw one of the wooded islands like a green cap floating ; the peaceful serenity of the gold water brought no peace to his heart, but rather the crags of Skiddaw, opposite him, a dark red with patches of gilded green, this roughness and indifference told the truth now : ' You are alone and life is a mask, one mask that gives place to another, all these masks concealing — nothing.'

As he rode his horse up the Blencathra slope and then turned it along the little wandering stony path under Skiddaw, the air was dusky and birds flew without sound above his head. A running stream and his horse's hooves striking against the stones were the only sounds.

The desolation of this place into which he was now entering made it the subject of many local tales and superstitions. No one, unless he had business that compelled him to pass through to Uldale or one of the hamlets in the valley beyond, would venture there after dusk. It was said that in the very old days, when the Northmen held Welsh and English as their servants, there was held here, in the Forest, a Thing or Assembly and that out of this a great quarrel grew, and there was a fearful massacre of men, women and children. Keswick men said that at night they had heard the screams of the children and seen wild figures outlined against the sky. There was a superstition, too, that under Skiddaw there was a vast chamber where the spirits of all the old heroes dwelt and feasted. Men swore that they had heard, coming from the caverns of the mountain, wassail songs, great choruses and the laughter of giants. It was most certainly true that no one who had ever tried to make a living in the Forest had succeeded. Now there remained only the ruins of this same house to which Robin was riding.

He was not himself afraid. Ghosts could not trouble him. And yet he started when he saw, standing to the right of the little stream, a woman wearing a grey cloak. As he came near to her he saw that she was no ghost but very mortal. A strong commanding woman with piercing eyes and a noble friendly gaze. He knew her. Frau Hodstetter of Keswick, reputed by most to be a witch.

He was not frightened by witches any more than by ghosts, so he stopped his horse and said kindly :

' Is there anything I can do for you, Frau Hodstetter ? '

' No, Mr. Herries, thank you.'

He saw that she was carrying an open basket, and that it was filled with small earthy green plants.

' You have been finding herbs ? '

' Yes. This is a good hour, before the sun falls behind the mountains.'

He looked and saw that the patch of sky between the two hills was a fiery rose, that thousands of tiny fragments of cloud were floating like the wings of birds, while the slopes of the hills grew smoky. The last calm light lay down the valley.

He let his horse drink in the stream while he leant over, speaking to her.

' Then you don't fear to be in this lonely place so late ? '

' Why, Mr. Herries ? Why should I fear ? '

' Someone might do you a hurt.'

' For lust ? I am too old. For hatred ? One alone would not dare. One day they will gather in numbers, and on that hillside '— she pointed to Blencathra — ' I shall burn.'

He looked at her with horror.

' You cannot tell . . .'

' I can tell.'

' Then if the future is settled . . .'

She knelt down and plucked a little green plant with its roots from the stream.

' We grow into the future by our own behaviour — but the future is there awaiting us.'

Robin stared at her. She seemed to be part of the gathering dusk.

' Then it *is* true. There are prophets and prophetesses. There are — witches.'

' As they call me. As they will call me when they burn me. Men are so ignorant and will be for many thousands of years to come. There are other worlds besides this one — many powers moving about this world that men cannot see. For a few the past, present and future move as one time. For a few the earth is a crust thinner. I see now, as I watch, men passing who are not yet born, and I see you, Mr. Herries . . .'

' Yes ? '

' There is a great hall and a sick woman with her wig awry. There is a silence and a little dog whimpers so that all hear him. I see you there . . .'

' Yes.'

' And I see you again. You suffer and you are happy. There is a man with his chest bare. He has a brown mole under his left breast.'

' I suffer . . .'

' Yes. You answer your question by suffering. The question you are always asking.

There was a silence that seemed to be blessed because of the great peace made by the sound of the little running river.

' Why,' Robin asked, ' if you know such dreadful things are going to happen to you here, do you not go away ? '

She placed her broad, firm, strong hand on his knee. The touch of it was comforting and reassuring.

' We cannot go away from the places where we are intended to be. If I went away I must come back. Besides, wherever I might be the end would be the same. So with you. Wherever you are, whatever you do, the end will be the same. You make your character but not the place where you are. Your friends and enemies are given to you. You are free in behaviour but not in circumstance.

' When I was a child in Germany watching the soldiers march to the wars, my hand in my mother's, I foresaw this meeting by the running stream. You are going to the Mass. That is well because God is in every honest prayer. You will suffer for them but never be one of them.'

' Whom do you mean ? '

' The men with whom you will speak to-night. Some of them will suffer before you. You have many years still.'

' How can you say that ? I may stab myself now with this dagger if I will. I have only to raise my hand.'

' No. You cannot. You will not.'

Smiling to show her that she was foolish he moved his hand towards his dagger. But he found that he did not wish to. His hand fell to his side.

'Why,' he suddenly cried out with passion, 'does God let this world be so evil?'

'God has given man power to do what he wishes. It is all in man's power.'

'God has not made man strong enough.'

'God has made man so that he must fight. Life would be nothing if everything were easy. The power of evil is a real power. I could show it you now if I wished. It is behind my back.'

The light was so indistinct that he could be sure of nothing, and his imagination was stirred and apprehensive. So that it was not true that he saw behind her the soiled, ribbed, ant-grey wings of a large bat with a snout and jagged teeth.

She held his hand for a moment.

'I wish you well, Mr. Herries. And it *will* be well.'

'For you also, Frau Hodstetter,' he said, and rode on his way.

Now as he rode it grew dark. There was no moon; there were no stars. But the path was clear or at least the horse seemed to find it so.

Robin bent his thoughts to his present adventure. For it *was* an adventure and a grave risk. Although the penalties at present imposed on the Catholics were light compared with those of two years later they were even now, so soon as religion became intermingled with politics, serious enough. Through all history religious persecution has been active because of political fear. After Norfolk's execution and the Ridolfi plot, fear was alive up and down the whole country. Despots — and the Tudors were still despots: it was not until James II threw the Great Seal into the Thames that despotism was finished in England — persecute religious sects because they are afraid for their own physical safety. Elizabeth herself might not be afraid, but her servants were afraid — for themselves as well as for her.

And in Robin it was this mixture of politics and religion that caught him. Had the Scottish Queen not been a prisoner in England his interest in the Catholics might have died. But indignation against injustice was a fire in his breast. Because the authorities were unjust therefore they were against God, and when they were against God they were against Christ.

As he rode on he prayed. If that woman's words were true, then one day he must suffer, and suffer most horribly. Physically! Physically! It was his body that cried out. Physical pain was something that his intense awareness of life and the power of his imagination made horrible to him as it was not horrible to the strong and insensitive men around him. Here, in this black place between the hills, imagination worked more readily. An old man whom he had met in London had been racked in Henry VIII's day, and he had described to Robin, then only a boy, the ghastly agony of that torture. The first wrench when iron pincers snatch at the muscles and flood them with molten lead. The second wrench, when the dagger strikes straight to the heart, as it seems, and your own torn ligaments cry out, like live things, to you for pity. The third wrench when, just before you fall, screaming, into a black pit of horror, at that last instant Pain himself, black-visaged, with iron nails sharp as needles, tears your flesh triumphantly into shreds and your sweating brow is soaked in the cold heat of blood. Robin had never forgotten a word of it. The old man had enjoyed telling his story.

Behind this fear was the deeper one that, because of the torture, he might commit some dreadful betrayal. A friend, Pierson. Even his dear brother Nicholas.

'Oh, God, be with me! Christ Jesu, Son of God, be at my side when the day comes. Take me in Thine arms, at the terrible moment, so that I may have no fear.'

He was glad when he reached the place. There was a strange silence. Men and women arrived with lanterns and only the lanterns seemed alive. Horses were tethered and cropping the grass.

The building was dark, but when Robin entered he found that sacking had been hung over the open spaces. A table had been dressed as an altar and some thirty persons, men and women, were kneeling on the stone floor. As they knelt and prayed, at the same time their eyes searched the company lest there should be any traitor there. They were of all classes and all were known to Robin, at least by sight. There was

Mr. Forster of Henditch with his wife and daughter, Mr. Charles Gunter of Morris Hall, Mr. Harris of Dunbone with his wife. There were farm men, farm girls, a few shopmen from Keswick.

He knelt down among them. The candles blew in the air and their waxy scent touched his nostrils. The bareness and coolness and simplicity of the room comforted him. He began to pray.

Three priests in their vestments entered. One was Pierson; one Cumberlege — a very thin tall man with a tortured face and fiery fanatical eyes. But the third caused him great surprise. He knew him at once from Pierson's description. Pierson had been with him at Douai and worshipped him. His name was Campion. Robin was surprised because, only in the preceding year, Campion had been sent to Prague as Professor, and Pierson had said that there could be no likelihood of his coming to England.

He was a man of no remarkable strength of body, but his mouth was grave and kind, and his eyes lovely in their saintly tenderness and illuminating power.

' Here truly,' Robin thought, ' is a man of God.'

The Mass followed.

Campion came forward to speak to them.

His voice was gentle but not weak. His tone had a courtesy that seemed to say : ' We are companions, guests, in a good house. Let us behave with gratitude and kindliness.' There was a fine culture, although his words were very simple. Most marked of all there was a deep underlying strength that gave a challenging authority to every sentence. This said : ' When you have discovered, as I have, what reality is, everything that is not real is unimportant. And when you know that certain things are true all other things are unimportant. If I have courage it is because I have no time to think whether I have courage or no. If I have patience it is because the goal for which I am striving is very far distant. If I am gentle it is because we are all going the same hard road. If I am tender it is because I love my fellow-men but God more. If I am happy it is because of the company my soul keeps.'

In his sermon he said among other things : ' My children,

do not despise yourselves because you feel fear. It is right to be afraid. When I think of the facts of the torture-chamber I also am afraid, but when I think of damage done to my immortal soul I am more afraid yet. One of the conditions of human life is fear, because God would not wish you to be too secure. But, more than that, these are times of great uncertainty because certain men value material power above spiritual, and would destroy spiritual things because they are dangerous to material things. They persecute us because we hold to God, and in the years that are coming they will persecute us more savagely because they will fear us more. So be afraid and through your fear lose yourselves in God who will uphold you, folding His arms about you, clasping you to His breast, keeping you safe.'

In another place he said about Love :

' I would not have you be too celibate. I myself love the things of this world — the books that I have read and written, the pictures I have seen painted, good food, all beauty that comes from God. And,' he added, a lovely half-roguish smile illuminating his face, ' I am myself writing a play at this very time concerning Saul and one day it may be played. And I know well what love of another human being is. In the watches of the night I have been tempted as all human beings are tempted, and I have loved my brother man with more than a brother's love. And I would say to you that no love is wrong if God comes first in it. For if God comes first He must purify all that is evil in it and turn it to Himself. Love suffereth and is kind. I have a dog,' he added, looking for a moment boy-like, ' in Prague, very lovable. And when I return he will almost burst his heart with joy. So he, in his own way, knoweth God.'

At the end of his sermon his voice took a sterner note :

' Laziness is of the Devil. For God never said : " Lay all this upon Me and I will see to it." God never said : " Put your trust in Me, for I can do it." Rather He said : " I have made you a man with the sinews of a man. On yourself the responsibility lies. I thought that you would prefer it so." And how it must grieve Him to see our confusion when the way is so clear, to behold our choice so evil when right and

wrong are so plainly distinguished, to discover our stupidities
so far beyond belief when He Himself had given us wisdom,
to perceive our lust as of the monkey, our filthy grovellings
as of the pariah-dog, our cruelty, our lechery, our lust of the
flesh. . . . Oh, Man ! Oh, Man ! What dost thou make
of thyself ? What ruin lies about thee, how fair are the
palaces thou hast destroyed, how loud is the sound of the
weeping of thy sons and thy daughters because of their own
feebleness ! '

He ended :

' I had no right to come to England. I stole away and
must at once return. But I shall think of you and pray God
for you and love you. And one day it may be God's will
that I return here and will see you again.'

After it was all over, Robin waited until the people had
gone out into the darkness. Then he climbed some crooked
stairs into what had once been a hayloft. This room, smelling
musty and timelessly of straw, apples, mice, was lit by three
candles. Pierson and Campion, stripped, were rubbing something on to their bodies. Father Cumberlege, dressed as a
cartman, in a country hat and a smock, was pacing about
muttering to himself. The two naked men made a contrast ;
for Pierson was now thick as a bull, hairy-chested, hairy-
legged ; while Campion was pink-fleshed with not a hair on
his chest, delicate, his hands and feet small as a woman's, his
pale shoulders a little rounded. Robin took a bottle from
Pierson's hand and began to rub his back.

' This is a marvellous ointment a lady at Canterbury gave
us.'

' Shall I rub your legs ? '

' Yes. Even though it is not seen it gives you confidence. . . .'

' You are very strong now.'

' Yes, I am. I am always on the move.'

' Your thighs are like iron.'

' I can walk thirty miles a day.'

Campion was pulling a rough country shirt over his head.
His eyes emerged from the top of it, innocent, wise, with fire,

but gentle. He stood, his bare legs under his shirt, like a little boy.

Cumberlege, looking little like a carter, was walking fiercely about.

'How long, O Lord, how long? Is this land never to be free? Are Thy Saints to be racked and burned eternally?'

'Not eternally, Henry,' Campion said, laughing. 'After the rack — Paradise.'

Cumberlege turned upon him.

'Prague has done something to you, Edmund. It is not perhaps good for your soul. They listen to your lectures and your wonderful prose and forget God.'

Campion, drawing on rough hose, shook his head, still smiling.

'You are too impatient, Henry. You would have God blow his trumpet and all His enemies be scattered. God does not work in that way — and He *wishes* us to laugh. Not every day perhaps. On a Tuesday and a Thursday.'

But Cumberlege answered: 'You are wrong, Edmund. You are wrong. How can we laugh when the sheep are ravened by the wolves, when a heretic is on the throne, when we must creep, as we do now, from hedge to hedge in a poor disguise . . .' He broke off, his thin body quivering. 'Hist! What was that?'

All four turned. Robin instinctively felt for his sword. It was the man in charge of the horses, who said that they must hasten. It was not safe. There had been a man in the congregation whom no one had known . . .

Pierson, clothed, and looking like a ruffian soldier on the tramp, took Robin over to Campion, who seemed now like an innocent simple country fellow.

'Father, this is my dearest friend, Mr. Robin Herries.'

Campion laid his hands on Robin's shoulders, looking into his face with great affection.

'I know. I have heard of you, Mr. Herries.'

'I am not a Catholic, Father.'

'There is time, my lad. There is time. God chooses His own time.'

'But I would serve God.'

Campion looked at him with great affection.

' And so you shall. And so you shall.'

They had drawn a little apart. Cumberlege was calling out that they must go.

' I wish that I could see you again, Father.'

' You must come to Prague. I live and work there.'

Robin hesitated. Some power that he had not expected drove him to speak :

' I am in trouble, Father. I am in danger of a great sin. I love a woman who is already married. I cannot destroy my desire. I loved her before she was married. I shall love her until I die. I hate her husband.'

' Kneel with me and we will pray to God.'

They knelt down close together and Campion said a prayer.

When they rose Cumberlege called again : ' We must be going.'

' Come to Prague,' Campion said again. ' Or in any case travel for awhile. Leave England. There must be work for you in some other country.'

Robin knelt and received his blessing.

He had a last word with Pierson ; the three priests vanished into the darkness.

Now he was quite alone. The candles were all blown out. It was as though no one had ever been there. Only his horse moved restlessly, and the wind blew the trees into a kind of night-charged tune.

PERIL IN ESSEX

ROBIN HERRIES took Campion's advice and travelled abroad.
He was travelling, studying, writing, observing, until the
middle of 1578. He visited Campion in Prague, the Pope in
Rome, William of Orange in the Low Countries (this last
Elizabeth was leaving at this time entirely alone to face his
enemies), the Medici in Paris, and by all these so different
persons was considered an elegant cultured gentleman, reserved, of charming manners, but, at the last, a little dull.
Campion did not think this last of him, and there was a week
in Prague when Robin was within a short step of being received
into the Catholic Church. Robin did not take that step.

In Paris he saw the Alençon marriage brewing. In company
with Alençon he could not believe that his own great Queen
would consider this monkey seriously for a single moment.
To take him to bed with her ! Incredible ! Nor would
Alençon himself care for it, as he was a notorious pervert,
and was followed by a convoy of pretty, twittering, painted
boys. He was hideously ugly, deformed, and of a mincing
effeminacy. But he was amusing and Elizabeth adored
amusing company, let the morals be what they might. He was,
in fact, amusing and agreeable, kind-hearted and generous,
unusually so for that cold and ferocious Court. Robin
became quite attached to him after he had made it perfectly
clear that he was not conceivably to be won into Alençon's
closer intimacies.

This meeting with Alençon had its effect on his developing
history, because it drove him yet further in the direction of his
destiny. What was he to think of a Queen who could consider,
even for political reasons, this deformed pervert as a husband ?
He seemed to see Elizabeth now as a monstrous horror —
painted, bewigged, stiff with jewels, her sharp fingers heavy

with rings, her peaked nose, her tempers and moods and lies and parsimonies, eaten with foolish vanity at which the whole world laughed, her intriguing soul empty of morality, truth, honour, affection.   And on the other side, languishing, year after year, in most unjust imprisonment, the good Scottish woman, so patient, regal, dignified under her persecutions ! The time would come when he would serve her and satisfy, at least in part, that constant longing in his soul for the accomplishment of some service for God's sake.

And not for Sylvia Irvine's sake ? Here was the question that, quite honestly (for he *was* honest with himself), he asked himself. He could not rid himself of her. Little things — a bejewelled glove, a portrait on ivory, a windy day with the leaves blowing into his face, a tune on the viol, the baying of a hound, the moon above a Paris street — anything, nothing, and she came back to him, sometimes as she had been when they walked as lovers in the secret garden, sometimes as she had been when he had seen her, so long ago, at her father's ball for the first time, or as Sidney Herries had seen her, miserable, imprisoned, alone.

Oh ! he could not rid himself of her. He tried lechery but loathed it. He thrust himself into reading and also wrote a long poem about the fairies which might have anticipated the ' Nymphidia ' had it not been so worthless that he destroyed it. He occupied himself with bodily exercises, made himself a most expert swordsman, quick and adept at fives and tennis. But he fought, he played with half a heart.

Courts disgusted him. The Medici seemed to him the wickedest old horror he had ever encountered even in night-mares. She was polite to him. She liked his ascetic face, his slender body. She pawed him with her yellow hands. He hung his head and prayed to God. But Sylvia Irvine persisted. He returned to England a haunted man.

They all perceived it. After the first delight at getting him back was over they all at Mallory perceived it — his father, now a man of sixty-nine, his mother, Nicholas, Gilbert Arm-strong, the servants. One change was that he was now a perfect, nay, a great man of the world. He was now someone to whom life at the Courts of Europe was an accustomed thing. He would speak of the Prince of Orange or Alençon or Mendoza as though these great men were accustomed to consider him of their company. Yet there was no arrogance or impatience in his manner, which was of an exquisite courtesy and kindness. He thought little enough of Courts, and when they pressed him to take some position at the English Court which could easily be found for him, he laughed and said he would rather be a galley-slave. ' Herries,' he said, ' were never intended for high positions. They lodge in the middle of things and that is where they will always be.'

It was a sad disappointment to his mother that she should have two such splendid sons and that neither should seek advancement. They were growing : Nicholas was now thirty-four, Robin twenty-nine. Of Nicholas she had now given up all hope. He was nothing but ' a great brown farmer ' and so would always be, but Robin, so handsome, so clever, so perfectly at ease with all men and all women, designed for a fine Court career, the very young man to capture the Queen's fancy, as other young men were doing — it was a tragedy. She did not know what he would be at. He would not have a career ; he would not marry. That ' child affair ' with Sylvia his cousin must now be over ; she, poor child, was unhappy enough by all she heard.

And so she wandered on to Nicholas and asked him whether she and his father were to pass away without the joy of holding a grandchild in their arms. To which Nicholas, putting his arm around her and laughing, answered that it was easy enough to make a child or two but not always so happy a business after the child was made.

The other change in Robin affected them all — his reserve. He had always been more secret than the rest of them, living in his own thoughts and the world of his imagination, but that had been an abstractedness of mind rather than — what it now was — a complete shutting of himself away.

What Nicholas had feared had now come to pass : their communion was, for the time at least, altogether broken. Robin loved him still, but would tell him nothing — nothing that mattered. Of what was he thinking ? Nicholas had no idea. Was he still preoccupied with his old life ? Nicholas did not know. Had he become, in this interval, a Catholic? Nicholas feared it might be so but had no knowledge. Nicholas had now a very considerable life in London and many friends there. But Robin, although he accompanied Nicholas to London and even, on two occasions, to Court, and was thought by everyone — by every lady at least — to be beautiful, sad and charming, shared in nothing.

Then, in the summer of this year he went, quite without warning, on a visit to his relations, Guy Herries and family. He had never seen them. He said that they had invited him.

Before he went he had a quick word with his brother.

'Robin, I know why you are going.'

'Dear Nicholas — I have acquired a deep interest in picture-painting.'

'No. It is not that. For Christ's true sake, Robin, have a care.'

'This is my business,' Robin said, growing a little pale.

'I know. I know. Since your return we have not been together — not truly as we used to be. I have asked no question and I will not. But Irvine. . . . He is not for your dealing. They say he has become most arrogant and quarrelsome. And that she——'

'And she?'

'Is proud and silent. Lady Herbert met her at some place on the Border, not far from Carlisle, where they were visiting — she and Irvine.'

'Yes?'

'She is changed, Robin — altogether changed. She is beautiful and haughty. Not a child any more. And——'

'Yes?'

'Oh, we are fools to be talking thus! We who have told one another everything since we were cradled! But I ask you nothing. Only give Irvine no cause for quarrel. He is mine — not yours, dear Robin.'

Robin smiled gravely.

'I am to stay with our cousins.'

'Yes. And they are but twelve miles from——'

'Be happy, Nicholas. I am not set on making old wounds bleed.'

H

He rode down with one servant on a long July day.

It was wonderful to feel really hot in England ; at midday he and his man stopped at a stream in a wood, stripped, bathed, and then ate pies and fruit at the stream's side. The man was called Cheveley and was a fat whey-faced man, frightened of the cold running water, and stood in it all huddled up like a pale mis-shapen piece of pastry, with his rough hands clasping his thighs, and he looked so ridiculous that Robin laughed heartily for the first time for months.

But Cheveley was not so bad a fellow, devoted to his master and very honest. His weakness was for women, especially stout ones. See a stout, smiling, big-bosomed woman come along and Cheveley flushed and all his fat body began to tremble. But he had been with Robin on his travels and picked up a thing or two. He could read and write and play the tabor and beat rhythmically a drum. Even more than stout women he loved animals, and was much mocked at for his indignation when they were tortured or killed. This tenderness was unusual in his time, but no amount of chaff turned him from this. Little birds would settle on his finger, dogs follow him, horses do anything for him. He had a scar now on the back of his hand that came from a scratch a bear had given him when he tried to rescue it from its baiting. And yet he was as soft and dough-faced a fellow as you could fancy running for his life on any occasion. But he did not. He had a stout heart.

So they sat now side by side while the light dappled the leaves and the stream laughed as it ran, and they ate venison pie and drank Rhenish. The deer came down, drank in the stream and were fed by them. Over the rough path a vast, lumbering, four-wheeled chariot drawn by six horses came plunging, lurching along, making a most terrible noise.

Robin read aloud from his poetry book :

' My galley, chargèd with forgetfulness,
    Thorough sharp seas in winter nights doth pass
    'Tween rock and rock ; and eke mine enemy, alas !
    That is my Lord steereth with cruelness ;
    And every oar a thought in readiness,
    As though that death were light in such a case.

An endless wind doth tear the sail apace
Of forcèd sighs, and trusty fearfulness ;
A rain of tears, a cloud of dark disdain,
Hath done the wearèd cords great hinderance,
Wreathèd with error and eke with ignorance.
The stars be hid that led me to this pain.
Drownèd is reason that should me comfort,
And I remain despairing of the port.'

'That is a melancholy poem,' Cheveley said, blinking his eyes, for he was sleepy after the bathe, the food and the hot sun.

Robin put his book down and looked at the flashing stream.

'What do you make of this life, Cheveley? When you were in that stream but now, a hideous forked thing out of any reasonable shape. Take no offence. We are all hideous in our natural bodies save when we are very young. And yet love can so cheat us. A high fleshy bosom is sufficient to make you think of all the wonders of God, the wheeling stars, the fires of the Borealis and the bitter Polish ice. And yet, once you have bedded her, instantly all the glories of God are shrunk to a cinder and there is a chill in your voice and you have a rheum. Is it not all a cheat ?'

Cheveley grinned.

'I think before it is a cheat it is a very passionate pleasure,' he said. 'And if, after it were finished, desire still lingered, life would be one long lechery, which would be bad for business.'

'Well argued,' said Robin. 'And so it would. Now we'll on.'

He was greatly pleased with this branch of the Herries family when, in the evening, he found them. Like all Herries always, he had a strong family feeling and it was pleasant to discover three relations so worthy of their blood as these were. He liked Guy instantly for his honesty, his yellow Saxon colouring, his love for his art, his unselfconscious enjoyment of life. And he liked Rosemary for her natural friendliness and passion for her husband and child, and healthy out-of-doorness. He found the child, Rosamund, now twelve years of age, strange indeed. She was not now so ugly as she had been three years before when Sidney Herries had first seen her, but she was still freckled and pasty-faced and tow-haired and long, coltish-like, in the legs. She was now, even more than then, no respecter of persons and said exactly what she pleased. She had no manners at all and no control of her limbs, for she still had the habit of dancing about, cracking her fingers, waving her arms, singing out of tune, laughing wildly. But Robin knew enough of human beings to know well that here was somebody real in the making.

At first he was shy of her. His mind was deeply set on other things. Guy painted a portrait of him and he would sit, motionless, looking out on to the sunlit wood, thinking, brooding, preparing . . .

On the third day he found himself alone with Rosamund. She said abruptly : ' We went only once to Drunning — years ago when I was nine. Cousin Sidney was here.'

He started. His grave eyes were fixed on her. She talked to him, standing stiffly in front of him, turning in her hands a small gilt Italian plate.

' They didn't care for us. The old lady hated us. But Sylvia at the last said we should be friends — she and I. I have never seen her again.'

Still he said nothing.

' She meant it then. She is not allowed to be free.'

' Why do you tell me this ? ' he asked at length, hoarsely.

' Because you must go and see her. You must help her.'

' Why ? '

She stamped her foot. ' No one does anything. Sidney has never come again. No one has come. When I am grown I shall not allow such unhappiness.'

She began to sway from the hips.

' Be still ! Be still ! ' he said angrily.

' Your brother Nicholas would have rescued her long ere this.'

She waited, but he was silent, looking at her with great distaste.

' I love Nicholas although I have never seen him. Soon we are going to London on a visit.'

A wonderful change came over her ugly face. Her eyes could be beautiful, he realized, and her mouth tender.

' I know nothing of the world as yet. You have been in Courts and are a man. Why do you do nothing ? '

She came forward and put her hand on his arm.

' What does it matter about danger ? My father says that we must not meddle with what is not our affair, but I think we must. In my room there is a looking-glass and I look at myself and see how ugly I am. But when I am a grown woman I shall be more free for that. Beautiful ladies have their beauty to consider and whether it lasts and what they will suffer when it is gone. But I shall have none of those things to consider and no one will observe me.'

She looked intently in his eyes.

' Cousin Robin, you have come here for that, have you not ? '

' For what ? '

' To see her and help her.'

He nodded.

' I knew it and if I can help you . . .'

' No, my dear. I must do it alone.'

She leaned up and kissed his cheek.

' Tell her when you see her that I have remembered what she said. That I am twelve years old now and shall shortly be a woman. That I am near and at hand.'

She ran off out of the room.

That funny little conversation decided him. Not that he had doubted. But he had wanted a sign.

On that same evening he told Guy that he would soon return and he rode off. It was a dusky evening with a dull gold light above the ground and in the higher air a dark sense of thunder. When he had ridden his twelve miles the sky was molten lead and the heat intense. Not a bird sang. Drunning Place was dark and clenched together like a closed hand. On the nearer side of the road that ran past the Place was a wood, and here Robin stayed with his horse. He was quite un-decided what he should do. He had a fantastic desire that she should walk past alone, and he thrust his wishes upon God, praying that she should be given to him so simply. But God does not satisfy man's weakness at the first trial. He gives a chance.

A few drops of rain fell like little bullets among the trees. He tied his horse to a tree in the heart of the wood and walked along the wood's barrier where he could see the road and the Place. Never was anything more dead. It was a corpse of a house. No human being was to be seen, not a breath moved in the trees. There was only the sound of the slow, sullen, hesitating rain.

He came out into the road. Defiance and a great hatred of Irvine was in his oppressed heart. He would like nothing better than for that man to step into the road. He might kill him, for he was now a most accomplished swordsman. But in his soul he knew that it was not to end thus. For how long now he had fought against this surrender. In what places, during these last years, he had prayed to be rid of this torment — in close rooms above crowded streets, watching sword-play, dancing in the French Palace, listening to Campion's lectures, on his pallet at night in some country inn, riding his horse furiously down the straight French road between the poplars. All, all had been in vain. As he had ridden his horse out of London six days back he was lost and he had known it. It was as though, with one quick gesture, he had turned his back upon God.

But now that he was near to her he cared for nothing else.

He walked down the road and at last saw a small green door in the wall, and against the door a spade and some faggots. This led him to guess that someone was soon returning and that the little door might be for the moment unlocked. He pushed it with his hand and it creaked wheezily back. He slipped inside and found himself in a walled garden of stunted fruit trees, vegetables and herbs. But what a neglected place ! It was as though the Curse of God lay upon it, for the cabbages were half eaten, the apple trees decayed, the herbs dried and withering. The ground was parched and there were spiders' webs on the brick walls. He hurried across. The door in the farther wall was open and showed the way into what had once been a fine ornamental garden. There was a broad green path scattered with statues. The statues of Jupiter, Mercury, Juno, and the rest of the mythology, suffered from broken noses, castration and chipped buttocks. Yew and privet had once been cut into fantastic shapes of dogs and monkeys, ships and lions. It must once have been remarkable topiary, but long ere this the poor things had grown unchecked and now showed an uncouth wildness. There was a fountain that did not play, turfed seats with daisies flaunting untidily on them, and a peaked garden-house with the roof in tatters.

A moment later Robin saw Irvine. Irvine, in a suit of crimson velvet, stood, staring, motionless at the house-end of the path, his hand on his rapier-hilt.

For a blind second Robin was certain that he himself had been seen. He was standing beside a clipped yew that had once been an open-mouthed roaring lion but was now overgrown into confusion. He could not tell, from where he stood, how far this yew covered him from Irvine's vision, or whether it covered him at all. So, his heart beating high, he waited for the challenge. He anticipated it with joy. A physical contact with his enemy would be a flood-gate for these years of repressed emotions. Were he killed — what mattered it? And if he killed Irvine — ah! what a release would be there! So eager was he that he had almost moved himself to challenge.

But Irvine had not seen him. The climax must wait, and again he felt in his soul that it was not here or now, but in another place and more distant.

He stayed behind the yew and watched Irvine walk down the path towards him. The rain had ceased, but the heat was damp and sweating. Irvine walked as though he had the world at his feet. It seemed as though something pleased him, for he was smiling to himself. He had aged into a mature man since Robin had last seen him, but his beauty was as great as ever — only it was now another beauty, thickened, stiffened, the lines hard on his face and contemptuous, his body lissom but broadened. He moved like an actor behaving for the benefit of one appreciative audience, himself. His darkness had a radiance in it as there is a handsome sombre light in black steel. His face was not evil, but of a haughtiness

so extreme that you might wonder that he would consent to
smile even for himself. A lightly-clipped black moustache
and a small neatly-pointed black beard accentuated the pale-
ness of his cheek and brow. His nostrils and mouth were
sharply cut. His crimson suit was in excellent fashion and
stamped with small carved gold buttons. His head was bare.

Robin marked every detail, for here was the new Philip
Irvine with whom, from now on, he must deal. For he too,
from the moment when he had taken that step out of London,
was a new Robin Herries.

Irvine walked so close by him as almost to fan Robin's
cheek with his breath. Yes, he was pleased. He was humming
to himself as he walked. He passed on to the left and Robin
heard the gate of the other garden close behind him.

So he was out of the way ! A miraculous piece of fortune.
Robin skirted the path, slipping from gelded Mercury to
noseless Jupiter, from Jupiter to one-breasted Minerva, for
it would be no climax but only a pitiful misfortune if a servant
now should see him. He was by the wall of the house, and
some broken stone steps led up to a stone walk. Here was an
archway and beyond the archway an open door. He was
inside the Place. He stood against the wall, holding his breath,
but there was no sound anywhere. He slipped up some stairs,
crossed a dark sad passage, pushed a door and was in a little
room lit with two candles and hung with faded tapestry.
The two candles in old gold unpolished candlesticks stood on a
table that looked like an altar but was not one. It was covered
with a Turkish cloth of purple and silver thread, and in the
centre was a stand with an illuminated Missal of the Hours
open on it. The old tapestry was moth-eaten and torn, but
it told a story from end to end of the room, the story of a man
murdered — for he lay on his bed naked and the blood pouring
from him, and men were riding furiously through the forest,
dogs chasing them, and there was a lady in a coif on a tower
wringing her hands and men feasting with a grisly bearded
head on a platter in front of them. The candles flickered and
made the murdered man rise up and down on his bed.

The little room was stinkingly hot, with an odour as of
some animal dead beyond the wainscot. The candlelight

filled the small space with shadows, and it was as though a hand advanced to turn a page of the missal and then retreated again.

At last, feeling stifled, Robin tried the further door and found that it opened. He stepped forward into a bedroom hung with painted cloths, water-staining on canvas of scenes from the life of Moses.

The bed in the centre of the room was a very fine one made of walnut, carved and inlaid with a panelled head. The curtains were of rose and grey needlework with magnificent basses interwoven with gold.

But it was not the bed at which Robin looked. Sylvia was kneeling against it, with her back to him, in prayer. He did not move; it seemed to him that he did not breathe. He saw her in her broad panniered dress of white and gold, her head bent between her hands; three candles on a table near her threw a light around her and a circle of light on the ceiling above her.

She rose, sighed and turned round. She said nothing when she saw him. She must have thought him a spirit, for she put out her hands to ward him off. Then, when he smiled, she ran to him and, just as she had done in the old days, stood on the toes of her gold shoes to kiss him.

They had no excuses to make, scarcely a question to ask, and for a time she had even no thought of his danger. They needed one another so desperately : the years of their separation and the circumstances of their lives had mounted their desires so lamentably that he held her in his arms and then laid her on the bed and sat with her head against his shoulder without any thought but that at last she was with him and that she was as glad as he. At this time any sensual feeling was lost in their souls' longing for one another.

The imagination of both of them had been in the main spiritual, although where the spiritual ends and the physical begins it is always hard to say ; if it had not been so, none of the later events would have been as they were.

Their association now was filled with their first need — that they should be together.

' I have waited five years.'

' I intended never to see you again. But it has been too strong for me.'

' Every night for five years when I have blown the candle I have said a prayer for you.'

' Sylvia.'

' Robin.'

' Sylvia . . . Sylvia . . . Sylvia.'

' Robin.'

She lay with her hand against his cheek.

' I have travelled twice to the North with Philip. I heard you had a house there. Once when we went hawking we rode as far as — as far as — I forget the name, but I heard that you lived near. Philip told me. He hates you and Nicholas more than any two men in the world.'

Even then she did not appear to think at all of his danger. She was lost altogether in the spiritual ecstasy of being with him again. It *was* an ecstasy. Her slight body trembled : as she touched him her fingers trembled. When she spoke her throat was caught and words came out half strangled. Her eyes stared into his face as though they would bring him inside her own body so that he would be with her for evermore. The sound of his voice was such a delight to her that she said :

' Say my name again.'

' Sylvia.'

' And again.'

' Sylvia.'

She fastened her hands about his throat, then undid the top buttons of his doublet and kissed the hollow of his neck.

' I cannot have another of these five years like this last.'

' No. My fight is finished. I will carry you off from this dungeon.'

' Not yet.' She caught her throat with her hand. ' I am going to bear a child. At last. His child. He has desired it with a frightful desire. Now he knows that it is to be he is like a man in a triumph. And also this very week he is to have the important place at Court he has wanted so long. We shall be in London and I shall see you.'

That woke her to present perils, for she caught him by the shoulders.

' If he meets you he will kill you.'

' He has gone down through the garden. I saw him go.'

' But he will return. Or the servants — or my old witch of a mother-in-law who has eyes in her yellow back.'

' I can die here and now. There could be nothing finer.'

' No. No.' She began to be agonized. She drew him from the bed and stood pushing him with her hands towards the door. ' He hates you so that he would have you racked in front of him if he could. And there is Winterset here too. Carey Winterset, whose men Nicholas killed in Cumberland. If they catch you they will. . . . Oh, what they will . . .'

Robin, so happy that he could not speak, carried her off her feet against his chest. He held her in his arms, kissing her hair.

' You are a woman now — yes, and I am a man. Love me. Love me. Love me. Sylvia, love me.'

But now her terror was too strong for her.

' Listen. We will not ruin everything now just when we have found one another again.' She struggled down to her feet. ' I can endure now. Nothing will be too long or too hard. I can send word to you through that child — she came here once.'

' Yes. She told me to tell you that she was, now as then, ready to do anything.'

At that moment they both saw the handle on the door turn. He slipped behind the bed. He saw the door open and, standing there, the most grotesque old woman, mountainous, with a broad fat yellow face, huge breasts, leaning on a stick.

' You have been long coming. And where is Philip ? Eh, these stairs and my legs.'

' You should have sent for me.'

The old woman's eyes went greedily round the room.

' You shall not take that bed with you to London.'

' I have no wish to.'

And I smell candles burning. Not here. Somewhere . . .'
She sniffed and her head sank into her neck and her little eyes shot about the room. She stumped across, opened the farther door, saw the two candles burning by the missal, blew

them out, then turned and stood, her thick legs widely planted, looking straight at the bed.

Sylvia made no movement.

' No. You shall not have the bed,' she repeated. ' Come down. Help me down the stairs.'

She went to the other door and into the passage. In a flare of the candle from the open door Robin had stepped across the room and into the dark one beyond. Sylvia went out. She gave her arm to her mother-in-law. They began to descend the stone stair. Robin stood in the candle-smelling dark. He was impressing upon himself every detail : the little room with the tapestry of the murdered man, the Turkish cloth, the old gold candlesticks and then the walnut bed, the cloth paintings, Sylvia's gold and white dress, her running to him and kissing him, her lying on the bed with her head on his breast — all, all that he might never, as long as he lived, forget. She was a woman. She loved him now as a woman. Until now he had no regrets, no thought of sin or mishap, only a great happiness flooded him as though the sun shone within him, irradiating all his body.

He could not move. He was in such a bliss of happiness that it was like a trance. She was coming to London. He would see her. Somehow they would be together. Neither death nor disgrace seemed, at that moment, anything to him.

At last, with a deep sigh, he went across the passage, on to the stone steps, down into the garden.

The storm had passed away. There was a twilight and like a ghost he passed through it. He had a panic that the little outer door might now be locked, but it was not. The road was deserted. Under the trees a lighter dark lay upon the dark. His horse was there and rubbed its nose against his sleeve.

THE SIN

In the middle of the afternoon the sun broke for a brief
while through the mist, and the line of the Cumbrian hills
stood out blazing in rosy gold like guardians of a longed-for
Paradise.

The village of Seascale consisted of a few cottages little
more than huts, ' The Huntsman's Horn ' a neglected hostelry,
the ruin of a church destroyed in Henry VIII's time, and a
long shining waste of beach bounded by a grey still sea. On
the horizon, facing this sudden flaunting of the sun, the Isle
of Man sat like a humped mole.

The sun shone also upon a flashing blade — old Captain
Gadchick practising with his rapier on the empty sands. His
head was bare and his white locks fell over his crimson collar
while his long thin shanks in their crimson tight covering,
and his long thin arms in their puffed crimson sleeves, moved
with a precision and agility very wonderful in so aged a gentleman. He and his insomnia figured in the Herries family
fortunes, although he would never know it. For his insomnia
made him on the following morning ride earlier than his
custom, towards Ravenglass, and, so riding, he saw two others
riding and observed them. And what he observed he narrated
in London by chance a month later to some gentlemen at the
' Golden Horn ' in the Strand. One of these gentlemen was
Philip Irvine. What the Captain had observed was a diamond
jewel in a lady's hat.

All that he was doing now was flashing his rapier on the
wide grey sands while a trio of gulls, crying desolately, hovered
and swooped above his head, hoping that this mechanical
figure might produce some refuse for their scavenging interest.
He was practising the Spanish attack — the *pasada* of twenty-
four inches, the *pasada simple* of thirty inches, the *pasada*

225

doble, composed of the first two and executed by the two feet alternately.

As he practised he hissed through his teeth like a hostler. It was a work of supererogation perhaps, for he was seventy-five years of age and was not likely to fight a duel again this side of Heaven. He had been a great duellist in his time, but now his fires had died down, he was at peace with all the world, lodged at the ' Huntsman's Horn,' rode his nag and paid a yearly visit to London, riding there by slow stages, and spending lavishly for a month or two before returning to his solitude. His rapier flashed in the rays of the sun, his body moved, the gulls screamed. Then he paused and looked about him. He turned back to the hills and observed, as he had often done before, that they were like giants resting, one leaning forward on his arms, another raising his head in a kind of impertinent stare, a third couched in sleep. He breathed the air and sniffed the sea-stillness.

The gulls had flown out to the sea. There was only the distant rhythm of the tide to break the silence. The sand was iridescent in the sun's glow ; then, as though a lantern were switched off, had the grey gnarled surface of a cat's paw. The sun was gone. It was very chill. The old man sighed, fastened his rapier to his side, picked up his velvet cap and walked, head up, back erect, towards the inn above the sand-dunes.

A short half-mile from the hamlet, perched on the cliff above them, was a stout little house of wood and stone. The mist was now driving in looping waves about the sand ; the sea was blotted out but sang, like a muffled kettle, at the mist's heart. From the sea-windows of the house you looked down beyond the world's end. The box hedge and the tiny garden showed myriads of drops of water : a garden of cobwebs on the edge of nothing.

The road that led to Drigg was swept with a mist that wetted Robin Herries through his cloak to his skin. Yet he was burning with a fire that dried his cheeks to parchment and burnt his throat.

He rode slowly, letting the horse take its way. He was going to the little stone house owned by Jacob Entwhistle and his wife Mary. Jacob was a cousin of Robin's housekeeper at Rosthwaite, blind and over seventy; his wife was, however, a vigorous sixty.

A week ago Philip and Sylvia Irvine had come, after a series of visits, to stay with Sir Roger and Lady Blennerhasset, some ten miles from Carlisle. Robin was at Rosthwaite. A few days back Philip Irvine had been called to Newcastle on urgent business. Alice Blennerhasset and Sylvia had ridden off to see something of the country. They had slept at Penrith and at Ravenglass. Lady Blennerhasset would stay yet one more night at Ravenglass. It was supposed that Sylvia Irvine was with her. She was not. She was riding at that moment towards Seascale. Sylvia and Robin would stay that night at the small stone house as Mr. Forrester and his wife. Yes — on their way to Carlisle. Thence to Edinburgh, where Mr. Forrester had business. . . .

So, the moment, after years of waiting, had arrived. Alice Blennerhasset, who detested Philip and had had in her time many lovers, was the only conspirator; Roger Blennerhasset, a stupid, complaisant, and passionately hunting gentleman was glad that the two ladies should, for a few days, amuse themselves away from him. He was a bachelor at heart.

Robin Herries was only a name to him. He was a man so greatly pleased with himself, his position and his belongings, that he never troubled himself with speculations. His fancy, like an old man's spectacles, made a great letter of a small print, and the book that he read from was written by himself. So that *he* was no danger.

There *was* no danger; Robin did not know that an old gentleman, in a crimson suit, had, an hour earlier, been flashing his sword on the sands while the sun was out. But even *had* he known, he was past, perhaps, all caring. Had Philip himself advanced towards him out of the mist, he might not have stayed him. The barrier had been spiritual, not physical. That barrier had been flung down and he was already committing the act.

He had stayed the night before at Morecambe, giving the name of Forrester at the inn. He had been alone at the inn and all day had ridden slowly through sun and mist by the sea, or with the sea at most a few fields distant. He had ridden really like a haunted man, as, indeed, we are all haunted when the barrier is at last flung down. Hooded ethereal figures had ridden at his side and not one had whispered ' Go back ! ' God, who for most of his life had been present with him, although always unseen, had been quite blotted out. This was a fiery, dim world, altogether filled with physical passion. He was *all* body, a flaming leaping heart, a tight constricted middle with a fierce pulse beating there, the rest of his body a cloud, save his brain which was furiously active, yet with only muddled thoughts.

If the Devil walks this world, then he was riding beside Robin now, but it was not the Devil of the story-book, horned and hoofed, but a gentle, friendly copy of Robin himself, whispering now and again, ' You will have your desire now. At last your longing is to be satisfied. How wise you are ! '

He found the house quite easily, for he had been given good directions and been told that there would be a ship's figure-head in the garden, a painted figure of a woman, leaning forward with a faded gilt crown. There she was, bedewed with a thousand drops of water. He knocked on the door, and a comfortable, full-breasted woman opened it to him.

There was a living-room with the beams painted with a thin gilt, an open fireplace, a long oak refectory table, a piece of a painted cloth with bright red and blue colours, hanging loosely to the plastered wall. There were two green birds in a gilded cage, and old blind Entwhistle beside the fire. The blind man was playing on a cithern, picking the wires with the quill. The instrument seemed alive in the firelight, for it had a grotesquely carved head of a man mocking with an open mouth. The old man did not stop his playing as Robin stood in the open door, but finished his piece. Then he looked up and, as though he saw with his pricked pointed ear from which tufts of white hair sprang, said : ' Who is it, Mary ? '

' It is Mr. Forrester, Dad. He is to bide the night with us. Your lady is not with you, sir ? '

' She will be here presently. May I see our room ? '

' Of course, sir. It is very simple. We are only accustomed

to our own family, but our cousins asked us. They are servants to Mr. Robin Herries of Rosthwaite, and we have wished many a time to visit there, but it is a far journey and Mr. Herries is a Catholic, they say, and in these times—' She stopped, putting her fingers to her mouth. ' But there, I talk on and on — and this is the room, sir. There is a closet for the lady and on a fine day a handsome view over the sea.'

It was simple enough, having a bed with faded canary hangings, a broken mirror and a clay jug and basin. There were rushes on the floor. There was a small closet in which a man could stand upright, and on the wall opposite the door a bright blue figure of a ship crudely painted.

Robin took off his cloak, pulled off his riding-boots and, from the bag that he had brought with him, found silver brushes and comb, a fresh ruff, a scent for his face and hands, and a ring with a diamond and two pearls. He had also in an ebony box a rose of gold with its heart a single ruby, and this he fastened on the breast of his black velvet suit. He was in black from foot to head save for the diamond buckles on the shoes that he now wore, silver bands to his sleeves, and his fresh ruff.

He sat on the bed, straining his ears to listen. He went to the door and held it a little ajar so that he should know of her arrival. The thin, picked strain of the cithern came to his ears, and the plod-plod of the woman as she moved about her cooking.

He went back to the bed. He was wildly excited and, at the same time, pervaded by an extraordinary hot weariness. He touched his cheek with his hand. It was flaming.

Intolerably restless, he called down the stairs to the woman, asking whether she had any ale. When she brought it he asked her a number of foolish, useless questions as to whether it rained here often, he had heard that it did . . . how far was the Isle of Man ? Did they catch fish here ? Did the Scottish soldiers harass them here ? He had heard that they had been as far as Morecambe. What would they have for their dinner ?

They would have a lentil soup, a capon, a neat's tongue broiled, a marchpane pudding. The marchpane a sister had sent her from Newcastle. They would have the room to themselves to eat in, for the old man went to his bed early because his limbs were always aching — it was a kind of ague he had, which was why they had not been over to visit their cousins at Rosthwaite, because the old man could not sit a horse any longer, but they would willingly go and they had heard that Mr. Herries was a good man and an honest.

Listening to this praise of himself but dimly, for he was straining his ears for another sound, he heard, through the creeping cithern, a knock on the outer door. Or was it not so?

' I think I heard—' He paused. He fancied he heard it again. ' There — a second time.'

The woman regarded him owlishly.

' I heard nothing.'

He jumped up and shook her fat shoulder.

' She is at the door, I tell you. She is waiting — waiting.'

A third time a knock came, this time clearly.

He stood, his feet planted in the centre of the room, a roaring in his ears. It was as though the sea, but hot now like molten lead, had invaded the room. Through the roar he heard a woman's voice and Mrs. Entwhistle answering her.

' Mr. Forrester is upstairs,' he heard Mrs. Entwhistle say.

Someone mounted. The stairs creaked. The cithern continued. His gaze at the door was a lunatic's.

As Sylvia stepped in she took off her round black velvet cap with the diamond in the front of it. She closed the door behind her. She was in his arms.

He was startled, even at that first moment of meeting, by the ferocity with which she encountered him. With the whole strength of her little body she pressed herself against him, making him — strong as he was — rock on his feet. Her hands held his cheeks, then his neck. Their embrace was long and soundless and, when at last he made a movement, her hands clung to his doublet, unfastened it, flew to his breast and clung to his flesh as though they were part of it.

He caught her arms, and she, swaying a little in his grasp, was carried to the bed. He sat down, gently detaching her hands, held her tightly with his right arm, pressing her to his side, kissing her hair and her eyes.

' I have been in a torment of fear that you would not come.'

' There was no difficulty. Nothing — no man — nothing '
— she caught her breath, her hand at her throat — ' could have
stopped me.'

' You met no one on the way ? '

' No one. There was a sea-mist all the day.'

She sat a little apart from him and considered him. He
was now a true man, spare, excellently handsome in the dark
quiet eyes, the moulding of cheek and nose and mouth, with a
royal carriage of the head and straight, proud balance of the
shoulders. His body was to her, in every part of it, shining
with a special light, as though there had never been any other
physical presence like it. Their fugitive snatched meetings
over several years, and the denial of absolute final contact,
gave it that preciousness.

After that contact the human body is so often ridiculous
or pitiful or deformed that great wisdom and deep tenderness
are demanded of any lover. But she saw now only an almost
blinding radiance.

For neither of them just now was any world real but the
fiery enchanting one whose only inhabitants they were, as
though, caught together, they breathed inside a crystal globe
filled with light and heat : beyond the globe a dead world,
grey, cold, ashen.

They spoke together, scarcely waiting for one another's
answers. They clung together and parted and clung again.
Then, abruptly, he rose from the bed and moved to the window.

' Sylvia, we must be for a little quite ordinary staid persons.
As though we had been married fifty years. I am Mr. Forrester,
an English gentleman, passing on to Edinburgh for business.
You are my wife, bravely accompanying me.'

She went across the room to pick up her hat. The diamond
was in the shape of a star. It flashed as she turned the star
in her hands. He looked at it.

' Was that wise ? Philip knows it so well. If someone
saw . . .'

She laughed. She was so happy that you could feel the
movements of her spirits dancing in her body.

' I will pluck it out. Throw it into the sea. But my father gave it me once, when he had made a good profit with a Spaniard.'

' No. The sea-mist, God be thanked, hides everything. Everything. Only within it we are bound to one another. . . .'

He went downstairs and fetched what she had brought with her, then left her to arrange herself. He went out to the shed at the back of the house and saw that the two horses were fed and comfortable. When he returned the meal was ready, the table lit with candles in old pewter candlesticks.

The old man, he supposed, was gone to bed, but he fancied, all through the meal, that he heard the thin watery strain of the cithern. They were neither of them hungry, but Mrs. Entwhistle, who waited on them most friendlily, was proud of her cooking, and so they did what they could.

She broke in at times with questions and interjections as : ' What do they say in London ? That the Queen will make this French marriage ? . . . I do not believe myself in foreigners or Catholics. The country is better without them. . . . My man is a good old man. Some things are follies to him now that were wisdom to him when he was young and could see, but blindness made the world a new country for him.'

After the meal, while she cleared the table and put apples and oranges on it, the two sat side by side on stools in front of the open fire, not speaking. They heard the birds move and twitter beneath the green cloth that had been put over the cage ; at times they could hear the sea, for the tide was now in.

At last, with a curtsied good-night, she was gone. Slowly, as though they would charge every moment with a fuller richness, they moved upstairs.

Inside the room Sylvia flung her clothes off, almost tearing them from her, letting them lie in a heap on the rushes. Then she went across to him, and, standing on her toes, kissed him.

In the canopied bed they lay, as it seemed for an eternity, lip upon lip, but without moving.

Behind the physical rapture Robin had a deeper consciousness with eyes that saw and ears that heard. He was outside his preoccupied body, or rather above it, and he whispered

to his other self : ' This is perfection. Make this moment
your eternity, for by *my* reckoning, which has not yet begun,
this eternity is but a moment.'

The love ecstasy followed. His head in the hollow of her
shoulder, his hand cupped around her little breast, he found
himself crying. He had not cried since he was a child. She
thought the tears on her shoulder were sweat from his body.

He had raised his knees and she was folded between his
knees and his breast, curled up as the child is curled in the
womb. She was curled on her side, her arm around his neck,
her hair against his chin. She was very heavy but he felt no
pain or weariness, and they talked softly, like very old friends,
which indeed they were.

' We shall meet now often in London — every week if we
care to.'

' I know a place, near the village of Chelsea . . . a woman
keeps a house . . .'

' Or, for an hour, in Westminster. The old sempstress my
father had . . .'

She shivered a little, against his skin : his hand was damp
against her dry flesh.

' Why do you tremble — my love, my darling, my sweetness, my darling ? ' He shifted her weight, slipping her thigh
from his, so that it rested on the bed. His other self, now more
active, whispered : ' And this flesh — bones, muscle, veins.
Cut, like a butcher, a slab of it. Beauty, tenderness, the
ecstasy of completion lie not in this. . . . Oh God, oh God,
where is Thy Temple ? . . . not here . . . not here. . . .'

She answered : ' Philip has spies. I am not sure that we
were not seen meeting in Essex.'

He raised her in his arms, laid her gently on the pillow
and began, rhythmically, to stroke her strands of soft thick
hair. He asked her the foolish question that has never any
true answer.

' Do you love me for ever ? For ever and ever ? '

She replied at once with passionate confidence.

' For ever and ever.'

He saw, with a blinding flash of prevision, that that was
true. It *could* be true of a woman, an unmixed devotion,

but never of a man, whose fidelity might indeed be true but never unmixed. His could not be unmixed because God would not let it be. ' The Bright Pavilions . . . the Bright Pavilions '— but Sylvia never gave a thought to God, had never done. *Her* bright pavilions were here and now, with their planting in Robin's body, even now as her lips sought his again and her body twisted into his and once more they were lost in a crying, shouting defiance — as the many-starred rocket explodes against the true stars, that are fixed and unchanged long after the dry stick has hurtled to the ground.

After a while they slept, her cheek against his side, his hand against her breast. But it was not of her that he dreamt. At first his dreams were wild and unconnected — his youth, his mother and father, the rooms at home, figures flying through the trim hedges, Anthony Pierson, the hideous grin of Phineas Thatcher, figures whose faces he could not discern, a tempest roaring through the trees, a fountain blowing wildly against the rain, above and through everything the thin wail of the cithern . . .

The wind fell, the waters of the fountain stiffened to ice. He was struggling to hide his face from icy cold. To the horizon stretched a vast ribbed plain of snow. Immediately in front of him was a deep black tarn, bounded by ice-sloped hills, and in the tarn struggled a magnificent white horse. He watched, longing to help, unable to move. The great horse, with a tossing white mane, fought to escape from the tarn. Its hooves struck the ice but could not hold ; with a great heave, as it seemed in his dream, of all the strength there was in the world, it struck and struck again, almost fell back, but caught firmer hold and was up and away, white against white, lost in the snow.

Robin cried out and woke to find himself sitting up, his body stung with an agony of anxiety. ' He is out ! He is out ! He is away ! He is away ! '

He turned to find Sylvia also wakened. He caught her in his arms, kissing her pitifully, half lost still in his dreams.

' Never fear. Never fear. We will escape. No one shall find us. We will run, we will outspeed them. Keep by me. There, there ! There is no cause for terror. . . . We have done wrong but they shall not know. It is only ourselves we have harmed, and that is God's business. The horse is safe — God saw to it. . . .'

He did not know what he was murmuring. He slept again and she lay in his arms, not sleeping, fearing Philip.

Very early, in a grey drizzle, they rode next morning away. They were silent and absorbed in their own thoughts. They never saw an old man in a faded red jerkin ride past them.

LONDON GLORY

A GREAT wave of joy and brightness swept over England.

The failure of the Catholic rebellions in Ireland and Scotland (the former connected with most frightful atrocities), the increasing Protestantism throughout the country and the enlarged alarm felt at the movements of Jesuit priests led in January '81 to an ' Act to Restrain Her Majesty's subjects in their due Allegiance ' and this Act made it ' High Treason to reconcile any to the Church of Rome, or to aid or conceal those who were so doing.'

This Act greatly pleased the majority of people, because the English were as they always had been and always will be, slow to make their minds up, lazy and muddled in their thinking, but all for action at a moment which seems to observers far too late but, in the nick of time, wins the occasion.

Queen Elizabeth was now forty-eight years of age, and her presence, her spirit, her person dominated not only her own country from end to end but a large portion of the habitable globe as well.

When she had come to the throne England had neither army nor navy ; its coffers were empty ; religious quarrel divided it from one end to the other.

Whatever her weaknesses, cruelties, indecisions, she had bred in her people a great pride and a new defiance. The tragic results of the dissolution of the monasteries were already settling into some kind of order. There was still much discontent, much hardship, dire perils threatened from abroad. Mary of Scots was a constant danger at home. The Queen was often incalculable, as in the question of the French marriage. Both army and navy were still far from what they ought to be. Both Ireland and Scotland might grow into dangers again at any sudden flick of Time's finger. There

236

were dirt and poverty and plague and misery as always. But the Queen would see that they came to no harm ; the Queen was the match of any proud ambitious foreigner ; the Queen knew what she was about even though her ministers did not ; the Queen might be miserly, but that was because the resources of the country must be treasured and strengthened ; the Queen would spend money, though, when she came among her people ; the Queen enjoyed dancing and singing and music even as they did ; the Queen covered her person with jewels not for her own vanity (or but a little for that), rather because she would have them all splendid and arrayed as a great people should be ; the Queen had a temper like any man, and could curse and swear like a common soldier ; the Queen was alive and variable, so that her favourites could not guess whether it would be a kiss or a blow ; the Queen was learned and could recite Latin like a Professor ; the Queen, whether herself a virgin or no, believed in the pleasure of the physical senses and wished a propagating people ; the Queen loved herself as every woman should, but more than herself she loved her country and would sacrifice herself to it ; the Queen thought always that an Englishman came first of all men, as all good Englishmen should think ; the Queen believed in God but was not afraid of Him.

This wave of patriotic pride and joy expressed itself everywhere in dances and games and masques and festivals. Life was hard, food difficult to get, Death always round the corner, but meanwhile this threatened existence was illuminated with the happiness of the moment. The new consciousness of patriotism, this fresh reanimated pride in England warmed the very soil on which the thousands of feet were dancing.

And nowhere more than in London. And in no family more than in the Herries family.

It was, in sober fact, somewhere about this time that the Herries family first found itself as a definite entity. This happened partly because of the new patriotism that was drawing all Englishmen together, partly because, in 1579, old Sir Michael Herries died and Nicholas Herries became recognized family head, partly because trade and commerce were advancing, and these Herries, as distinct from their grander Norfolk cousins or their proud Scottish relations, were always good English middle-class, sometimes a little above trade ; ultimately, as later Family Chronicles show, squires, owners of land, country landed gentry, but never higher than that, and never wishing to be.

They had had a poor sense of belonging to one another before this time. It was undoubtedly Nicholas who gave them a better one. Old Geoffrey Herries, born at the end of the fourteenth century, had been the first notable member of this branch, and notorious is a better word for him perhaps. It is of him the story is told of his building two of his daughters into his castle wall (he had a stronghold near the Welsh border), to die of suffocation because they refused to marry two of his favourite ruffians. After him his son Roger was no better, and then quite suddenly, at the end of the fifteenth century, the family became very respectable. One of Roger's sons, Gilbert, married Alice Walpole, also related to the Howards, and she had all the Walpole traits of English obstinacy, self-satisfaction and lack of imagination. So she, on her side, helped the strain of British middle-class attention to the practical things that really matter, while, at the other end, another of Roger's sons, Humphrey, married Margaret Wade, an admirable woman who made two pennies spring from where one had been before. Humphrey himself was a ' freak '— one of those freaks for ever appearing in the Herries family. He liked illuminating on parchment and believed in witches and kept white mice in a cage and taught them to speak like humans.

It is from his loins all the same (and Margaret's practical common-sense womb) that the true centre of this Herries family sprang. Humphrey — the grandfather of Nicholas and Robin — had three sons whom already we know, Henry, Michael and Martin. Henry was the commercial man ; Michael, the gentleman ; Martin, something of the recluse, and away a little in the distance was the Gilbert branch with its Walpole mingling of sense and arrogance and good sturdy independence. The present representatives were Thomas, rather an oaf of a man who, just about this time, bought a place in the North near Kirkby Lonsdale, and Lucy, a handsome ambitious woman who married Sir James Courthope. Between these branches came the descendant of old Roger's second son — Guy the artist, father of young, freckle-faced Rosamund.

See then the confused and distant strains that an ordinary English family can bring into its body politic within a generation or two ! The sub-savage brutalities of a robber chief, old Geoffrey, the business ambitions of Gilbert, the magic and necromancy of Humphrey, the steady bourgeoisie of Alice Walpole, the snobbery of Lucy Courthope, the artistic soul of Guy, the strength and vitality of Nicholas, the dreams and longings of Robin. . . .

Nicholas, who was now, in '81, thirty-seven years of age, became, at his father's death, king of the family. He had, in the last ten years, developed a very passion for the Herries stock. First, when he took office from his father, it had been the immediate ground of Mallory that he had loved. It had been as though he had said to himself, ' I have here a square of English soil to do with as I wish. I love everything concerning it. I will make it as fruitful, as rich, as perfect as is in my power.' His very soul got embedded in the place. Every blade of corn, every foal born on the farm, every trim cut hedge, every deep-red rose, even the worms that crawled, after rain, their lengths across the lawn — all these had a dedicated life, because they were Herries, because they were English.

But after the good old man his father nodded in his chair one evening over a game of chess and passed away, a new sense came to Nicholas. He was already the father of his house. He would now be the friend and brother of all his family.

He invited the Courthopes to visit him at Mallory, and a royal time they had there. He flattered Lucy's snobberies and listened to Sir James, who was a bore, on military tactics. He sent a letter to Guy inviting him also, with *his* family, but Guy friendlily refused, saying he was no good in grand places. Edward now was married to a pinch-faced woman with money named Agatha, and he had two little girls, Janet and Martha. They also came to Mallory, and there was Thomas, Lucy Courthope's brother, a fine stout old bachelor of sixty or so who rode over from Dulwich, where he sometimes lived and went drunken to bed many nights, time and time again, and loved Nicholas like a brother.

With all this Nicholas, now in his middle years, had become a man of real importance and wisdom. Not important in his own estimate, for there was never a creature more modest, nor wise in book-learning, but important because he was influencing the world in honesty and valour, and wise because he was learning much about life that was true and understanding and far-seeing. He was in no sort of way a perfect man. He could be choleric, was at times lecherous, was — about very many things — ignorant, and too often obstinate in the things he did not know, but he had a warm, loving heart, gave his word and kept it, and loved to be alive with all his active soul.

He had only one grief in the world, but this was persistent and not to be healed — his separation from Robin. That separation had begun long ago. Time kaleidoscoped things and it seemed to him, looking back through the years, that it had begun on that day in the North of his first meeting with Irvine. It had not in fact been so. It had begun perhaps on that day in his Uncle Henry's house when he had been told that Robin was a Catholic. Or it had begun . . . nay, how could one tell ? These divisions of spirit from spirit were subtle mysteries, a mesh of tiny links.

There had come, however, a worse day. He recalled it exactly. He was washing his hands, grimy from the garden, in a basin. He thought that he would wash more thoroughly and pulled his shirt over his head. He stood, staring into a little silver mirror that hung over the basin, rubbing his chest, feeling health and vigour pour over him. He saw Robin's face in the mirror. He had thought he was in the North, was madly delighted at his unexpected return, would have turned wildly to greet him, but he saw the mirrored face again.

It was a mask, not a face. From that moment he had never seen Robin's living face.

Something had happened in the North. Robin had now a desperate, a mortal secret. Nicholas was not the kind of man to penetrate anyone's secret. Give him a confidence and he would respect it until his death, but he was clumsy at inviting one. He had a feminine delicacy about a direct demand. He was not subtle about another's nature ; he could not understand fine shades. So, for the time at least, he lost Robin and suffered accordingly. He suffered horribly because he did not know what danger he might be in. He tried to watch over him, but Robin was now constantly in London. Most odd of all he was, it seemed, a friend of Irvine's, and when Nicholas thought of that he had again his old sense that he was playing his part blindly in some drama that had opened on that day in the North.

His love for his brother only deepened. He was a fantastically faithful man. When he loved, as he did his mother, Robin, Armstrong, the girl in the North whom he never saw, would never possess, but carried inside his skin, he loved really for evermore. He was too simple-minded to admit all the mouse-like creepings of doubts and suspicions that beset cleverer lovers.

The London gaiety of that summer of 1581 had a kind of madness in it. Certainly the French, who were just now very numerous in the town, gave an additional spirit to it. They, above all other people, knew how to deck the passing moment with ingenuity, colour, malice and an amoral wisdom.

In July of this year the Duchess of Newbury gave a great ball in the new banqueting-house in Westminster for the French Ambassador. These banqueting-houses were a fresh fashion, temporary houses set up to give ampler room for the needs of the more elaborate masques and dances that were now in vogue. The finest as yet ever seen was this one in Westminster, and Holinshed's very words are the best description of it.

' *A banketting house was begun at Westminster, on the south-west side of her majestie's palace of White hall, made in maner and forme of a long square, three hundred thirtie and two feet in measure about ; thirtie principals made of great masts, being fortie foot in length a peece, standing upright ; betweene every one of these masts ten foot asunder and more. The walles of this house were closed with canvas, and painted all the outsides of the same most artificiallie with a work called rustike, much like to stone. This house had two hundred and ninetie and two lights of glasse. The sides within the same house was made with ten heights of degrees for people to stand upon ; and in the top of this house was wrought most cunninglie upon canvas, works of ivie and hollie, with pendents made of wicker rods, and garnished with baie, rue and all maner of strange flowers garnished with spangles of gold, as also beautified with hanging toseaus made of hollie and ivie, with all maner of strange fruits, as pomegranate, orenges, pompions, cucumbers, grapes, carnets, with such other like, spangled with gold, and most richlie hanged. Betwixt these works of baies and ivie, were great spaces of canvas, which was most cunninglie painted, the clouds with starres, the sunne and sunne beams, with divers other cotes of sundrie sorts belonging to the queen's majestie, most richlie garnished with gold. There were all manner of persons working on this house, to the number of three hundred seventie and five ; two men had mischances, the one brakeing his leg, and so did the other. This house was made in three weeks and three daies, and was ended the eighteenth daie of Aprill ; and cost one thousand seven hundred fortie and four pounds, nineteene shillings and od monie ; as I was crediblie informed by the worshipfull master Thomas Grave surveyor unto her majestie's workers, who served and gave orders for the same, as appeareth by record.'*

This ' house,' constructed though it was of such flimsy materials, lasted ' with much propping ' until 1607, and was then replaced by King James with one of brick and stone. The Queen herself most graciously gave permission to the Duchess to hold her ball there ; it was the first great ball there since its building, and the Queen herself was to be present at it. On the very day before the ball the Queen had a malady of the stomach and was forced to her bed.

Now it happened by a curious chance that this great ball, for which invitations were like golden gifts from heaven, was the sign and seal of the first true coming together of the Herries family in England. None of the guests at the ball were aware of this, of course, or would have cared if they *had* known ; no Herries was actively aware of it.

It happened, however, that the Duchess of Newbury had an exceptional liking for Nicholas. Their common interest was of all things farming, for the Duchess, an Amazonian kind of woman, had estates not far distant from Mallory. She was at this time about forty years of age and made friends with Nicholas, the first time, in a haycart. That they made afterwards an even closer friendship in bed together was locally gossiped. No one knew or would ever know.

They were excellent friends and Nicholas taught the Duchess one or two wrestling falls and some excellent passes with the rapier. The Duke, who was a scholar, a friend of young Gabriel Harvey, whom he had helped towards a Fellowship at Pembroke, had assisted John Sadler of Corpus Christi to translate a treatise on the art of war by Vegetius. This was published in 1572 and the Duke was as proud as though he had begot a boy of the Duchess, which alas he was never able to do.

So the Duchess was very fond indeed of Nicholas and was always pressing him to come to Court. She told the Queen of him, and the Queen, hearing of his size and sinews, expressed an interest in him, but Nicholas would not budge. He could have married, it was thought, the Duchess' daughter Penthesilea, but she was a ' wambley ' kind of girl, and in any case Nicholas, having known the mother so well, could scarcely in decency marry the daughter.

So Nicholas was not only himself invited to the ball, but bidden to bring any of his relations with him. So Robin and Nicholas, Edward and Agatha, Sidney, Guy and Rosemary and Rosamund, Thomas Herries the old bachelor from Kirkby Lonsdale, Lucy Courthope and her husband, were all at this memorable, famous ball — the first ball in the Herries chronicles, and certainly not the last.

Nicholas, not given to raptures about beauty, was blinded by the splendour of the scene when he entered the banqueting-house. He stood there, his legs straddled, gazing. The dress that he wore that night is still in the records : [1] ' Doublet and trunk of vertical bands of dark green velvet embroidered

---

[1] J. Congreve, *Notes from the Daily Life of an Elizabethan Gentleman.* Bucks and Winter, 1896.

in scarlet, white and gold. Sleeves of embroidered white satin. A small plain circular ruff, black velvet belts, white silk hosen, and golden satin shoes with gold lace roses.'

Beside it on the margin is written : ' Newbury Masque, July 20, 1581 — washing and starching of ruff, one shilling.' And there is a very crude drawing of a donkey's head and a meaningless entry : ' Truss of hay. Two moons.'

Nicholas had started out from Mallory obsessed with his own clothes. He had never in his life seen anything so fine as he was, nor had his mother, who, old lady though she was, clapped her hands and danced at the sight. He was in love with his golden satin shoes, with the gold lace roses, especially as he was always afraid of his big clumsy feet. But now he forgot himself and just stared with his mouth open. First he could think of nothing but the illumination, ' the two hundred and ninetie and two lights of glasse.' These were in the form of vase candelabra with glass drops concealing candles. The light radiated in a great sheen of mingled glass and colour. As the candles, guarded though they were, blew a little in the breeze, a trembling passed through the hall almost as though there had been a whispered blowing of trumpets.

This great sea of sparkling starry light illuminated the marvellous, never-before-equalled, unsurpassable ceiling. It was at this that Nicholas especially stared, his head back, his huge body in its coloured splendours scarcely balanced as he gazed.

A very great artist must have designed this ceiling, for so many incongruous matters met in so perfect a harmony. The ivy, holly and other branches painted on the canvas dropped pendants of leaves and flowers illuminated with ' spangles of gold,' and these pendants swung a little so that the gold, the crimsons, the bright marbled greens, the pigeon-violet of the grapes, seemed alive and active in some high heavenly garden. The fruits — the pompions and oranges and pomegranates — were in thick clusters and the colour of them so skilfully arranged that purple led to purple and saffron to amber and icy white to pearl grey. All these colours, moving very gently in the glittering blaze, were so actual that you could all but smell the flowers and taste the fruits. And all was just enough

carried into heaven to make it an unattainable dream of
Paradise.

When he turned his eyes to survey the general scene his
gaze was yet more dazzled. The imitation stone walls had
ranged against them on either side ten tiers of steps and these
tiers were painted a dull gold. It was on these that, during the
Masque, the gathering would sit. At the far end long buffets
were arranged and these were piled with food of every sort,
great vases of gold and innumerable gold plates and goblets of
crystal.

At the time of his arrival the guests were passing before
the Duke and Duchess, the French Ambassador and numerous
Court officials ; this long procession was a river of brilliant
colours, and above the river rose a shrill hubbub of voices.
The musicians, who were placed in a gallery at the hall-end,
played soft music.

Nicholas saw at once many persons whom he knew, but
joined himself to old Tom Herries, for whom he had a real
affection. This old boy, stout and red-faced, with white hair
and beard, had dressed himself in an elaborate affair of crimson
and gold, but was most uncomfortable in it, as he quickly
confided to Nicholas. He had, however, held, some ten years
earlier, a position at Court — only for some six months,
because he could not endure town life, but he was happy
pointing out Court officials from the Lord Chamberlain the
Earl of Sussex, Sir Christopher Hatton Vice-Chamberlain,
the Earl of Leicester Master of the Horse, the Treasurer of the
Household, Grooms of the Outer Chamber, Maids of Honour,
down to various small fry who had been fortunate to secure
invitations.

Nicholas knew many of these people personally, although
few of them intimately, and it was amusing to old Tom,
whose business was entirely with their private vices and none
too agreeable habits : how this fair lady ' stank ' so strongly
that all her lovers complained publicly of it ; how Sussex's
men had played privately a very coarse drama concerning
Leicester's men, accusing them of various foul diseases ; how
a certain French nobleman betrayed most publicly that he
possessed the same odd tastes as his master Alençon, and so on.

I

But the old man, with all his scandal, was a good old man. His mind was constantly occupied with his place at Kirkby Lonsdale, where he was looked on as a common father. He preferred, as was natural, the old times to the present, and the country above all else. Here he had common ground with Nicholas, and even as they were moving slowly to make their obeisance he was talking of his oxen as though they were humans and of what makes a fat pasture, and a long story about the burning of a stack of corn.

When they arrived and made a bow, the Duchess, magnificent in cloth of gold, gave Nicholas a sign of recognition. And that is all he saw of *that* ceremony.

The order of the night would be the dancing, the Masque, the supper. Hundreds of the guests were gathering in front of the supper-tables to wait for the Duchess and the French Ambassador to start the dancing — and here, moving into the thick of the crowd, Nicholas of a sudden was body to body with Philip Irvine, Sylvia and Robin.

So here was his enemy! Since the fight with Winterset six years back, Nicholas had not once set eyes on Irvine. Irvine, he heard, was busy with his new position at Court and was now a member of the Board of Green Cloth : Nicholas had heard that he was not popular at Court and this partly for his own pride, partly that his wife was considered cold and unfriendly (it was said that Irvine was much chagrined by this), and partly that he had not enough means to carry his position properly.

To-night he was one of the most handsome men in the hall. His body had slimmed and tautened until he had the air of a blade-sheath, and his dark complexion, the proud, insolent, but beautiful eyes, the sharp hard curve of his lip, these properties, as brilliant and perfected as steel, gave him attention everywhere. To-night he was dressed in his favourite black and silver, and Nicholas at once felt, as he always did beside him, clumsy and gaudy and bucolic.

All those years had passed since their fight on the moor, but time was nothing to Irvine. Nicholas was instantly aware of it. The duel between them had scarcely begun.

Robin was at one arm of Irvine's and Nicholas at the other,

and Nicholas had the instant's thought, as though someone
had whispered it : ' If Robin and I, now, on this minute, take
this fellow and stick a dagger in his guts, here on this shining
floor under the lights and gold, before the whole Court, we
will have done an excellent deed and saved great future unhappiness.'

It was so exactly as though someone had whispered this
in his ear that he half turned. But no one had spoken to him.

Only Irvine gave him a most friendly greeting. He pressed
his hand so that the heavy rings dug Nicholas' flesh, and
Nicholas returned the pressure with his own great fist, and
Irvine's eyes darkened and a little crooked frown appeared
for a moment above the eyebrows. Nicholas had not seen
his brother for a week and, as he kissed him on the cheek,
Robin's eyes caught Nicholas' as though they said : ' There
is no change. We are as we have always been. Believe in my
love and help me.'

There *was* an appeal, but how was Nicholas to help him
when he knew nothing ? and why had he, who was not given
to impressions, nevertheless this sense that Irvine was drawing
them both in, pursuing some old slowly maturing plan that
would involve both of them in disaster ?

It was not like him to think of disaster, especially on such
a night as this, and who was Irvine but a proud, poor-purse
fool ? But he thought : ' He has tried the duelling way ; he
sent men to murder me. Such simple plans are ended. We
have moved into a new stage, darker, more difficult, longer to
develop. . . .'

And he thought too : ' Why do I hate this man so bitterly ?
Yes, every inch of him from the black hairs on his head to the
silver roses on his shoes ? It is not my fashion to hate. I
hate the very principle of Irvine. I hate all men like him
who care nothing for the good of other men, nor want the
happiness of other men, who have no wish to make this world
more free and more fair.'

All the time that he was thinking these things he was
garrulously chattering to the three of them, about Mallory
and the crops and the new aviary that had been made for his
mother's pleasure and a stream that he had formed to run

beside the lawns . . . his great shoulders shaking with merriment and Robin saying : ' Why, Nick, those are the handsomest shoes in the whole company ! ' Even, in his fellowship,
his hand rested for a moment on Irvine's slim silver shoulder,
while within himself he was saying : ' This man is my enemy
until one of us is dead, and perhaps after that.'

He also, in his own simple way, considered Sylvia. He
discerned no signs between herself and Robin. She was
wearing a plain white satin dress with long pointed stomacher
over the bolster farthingale. The front of the skirt was
decorated with red and gold enamel ornaments. Nicholas
was not given to noticing what ladies wore, but he noticed
this one because it did not suit Sylvia's small pale stiff face
and her child's body. It was as though she had been made to
wear it by somebody's order. She was unhappy, he decided,
and like Robin wore a mask.

The Duchess and the French Ambassador came forward
and the dancing began. It was of course a pavane and the
Duchess danced it magnificently, her tall handsome body as
straight as a tree, her dark colouring contrasting finely with
her gold dress. Everyone now joined in, the dancers facing
one another and forming a kind of wheel, the arm rounded
beneath the cape, the hand resting on the sword-hilt and so
causing the point to raise the cloak like a peacock's tail.
Nicholas took out Edward's wife, Agatha — not because he
wished but because he thought it his duty as head of the
family to invite the least favoured member of it. For poor
Agatha was as plain as a distaff and sought to cover her
plainness by an over-eagerness in her dancing. ' What a
pair ! ' Nicholas thought ; contrasting in his mind Edward's
rounded fat body and face, and this scarecrow who was wearing crimson, the last colour in the world to suit her yellow,
ill-favoured face.

And then he forgot his partner and the Herries family and
everything except the exquisite pleasure of the dance itself.
Like many big heavy men, Nicholas danced with great lightness
and rhythm. Year by year the lively galliard was creeping in
on the stately formal pavane, and the contrast of the two gave
an added lustre to both.

At the beginning the world was a dream — a dream of *another* world now lost, a world where movement was so rigidly ordered that death was postponed eternally and life nearly slumbered. In such a world the colours of this pattern were constantly on the edge of a resolved form — *almost* the planet stayed its course. These figures of gold, purple and white hung as though gravely meditating on the pattern that was to be. Then a thin cry from the viols and the wheel was broken and the lights glittered down on to a slow-moving stream of new colours — orange and jet and the most brilliant rose. But when the galliard broke in on this, with its kick in front and its kick behind, it was as though the secret places of the world, so still and sacred, were broken in upon by a rout of revellers. Those innumerable faces that had been carven in thin alabaster were, at a moment, transformed with all the hearty sensualities of daily living. Faces broke into smiles, blood coursed through a thousand veins, hands were hotly pressed. The dance now was intricate, for there were the tourdion, the ruade, and even, at the last, the capriole.

Many were seated on the tiers watching, not wishing to expose their ignorance of the steps, and long before the dance was over Nicholas was wishing that he had chosen any partner but Agatha, who, flushed and her eyes screwed up in agonized bewilderment, bounded about and kicked and clapped her heels together like a donkey frisking in a paddock.

The moment the dance was ended Nicholas said : ' Who is that child standing there with Edward ? '

' Why ! You don't know ! ' Agatha cried in that shrill whistly voice especially given by God to foolish women.

' Had I known I wouldn't have asked,' Nicholas said, wishing to smack her.

' Of course . . . indeed . . . that is Guy's child, Rosamund.'

' Is Guy actually here then ? '

' No, indeed. Rosamund is staying with ourselves at Bucking. It is the child's first grand party.'

It clearly was, for Nicholas thought that he had never seen such a brightness of eye and such an ecstasy of enjoyment. The child was plain and badly dressed. Her nose was snub, her forehead freckled, but she was as alive as a parakeet.

'I must know her,' Nicholas said, and he went with Agatha to join them.

He took her little hand in his big one and smiled at her kindly. Rosamund stared at him with eyes of absolute adoration.

'You are Nicholas,' she said. She drew a deep breath. 'At last !'

'Why at last ?' he asked her.

'Because I have loved you all my life, although I have never seen you before.'

They all laughed, but Agatha corrected her. 'A pretty thing . . . I am for ever telling you to think first . . .'

Rosamund paid her no attention. Her eyes were fixed on Nicholas' face.

'All my life !' he said mockingly. 'That is not very long.'

'I am over fifteen years of age and that is something.'

'This is your first ball.'

'And this is the best moment of it.'

There was some great quality about the child ; he knew what it was. It was her honesty. He was himself very honest and so at once they had a bond.

Robin danced in the first pavane with Sylvia. Irvine, with a smile and a friendly pressure on Robin's arm, urged them to make part of the middle group next to the Court group. He would not dance now, but later if he had a mind.

They had not met for a month and, as was now always the case, so soon as they were together they were possessed with one another and yet must pay one another no more than ordinary attention.

During the last year, driven by the impossibility of their being ever alone, they had resorted, on several occasions, to a desperate expedient, meeting at the house of a Mary Rolles in Southwark. This woman, a widow, had been once maid to Sylvia's mother and, so far as they knew, was devoted and trustworthy. They practised this only when Philip was for certain away from London. He had, for some time past, been entrusted with business concerning Mary of Scots, visiting her confinement to make reports. He was away for a week or more at one time.

But the risk, as they knew, was a fearful one. Worse than this was the effect on them both of the plotting, the secrecy, the hurried passionate hours, the distress of their parting. And with every meeting, because of its very half-fulfilment and danger, their mutual passion grew more intense.

Now, as always, their words were fragmentary and concealed. As, in the movements of the dance, they encountered and separated, they whispered, their lips not moving. They were unaware of the lights, the colours, and performed the figures mechanically, not knowing what they did.

' I could not send a message . . . I had intended . . .'

' I think he goes North ten days from now . . . Alice can meet your Thomas a week to-morrow. We go to my father's . . .'

' I love you — always. Now — your hand . . .'

They were together. His body was erect, one hand on his sword-hilt. He took her hand and his heart leapt into it, to be enfolded by hers.

' He has said nothing ? '

' Only for the first time to-night he asked about my diamond star. Why I did not wear it now.'

' He is watching us — he is smiling.'

' He hates me — more every day.'

The dance was changing. The movements were faster. Men and women were laughing. The heat was intense.

As he had done again and again, even as he sprang towards her and back, he whispered :

' Come away. Come away. We will go to the Netherlands. . . .'

' He would find you wherever you were and kill you. He has some plan.' Her last word, as the livelier capriole began, was like the cry of a child.

' I am so very unhappy.'

This was the last word that he had with her or with Philip that night.

He danced again and again. Women considered him mysterious. It was said that he was very clever and wrote poetry, although no one had seen his poetry. It was said that he was a Catholic plotter. It was said that the Government used him as a spy among the Catholics. It was said that he did not care about women and was discovering the Philosopher's Stone. It was said that at Rosthwaite he was writing a History of the World.

But, strangely enough, no one as yet said that he was the lover of Irvine's wife, the pitiful little thing who was a gowk at home and beaten by her husband.

It was time for the Masque. Six trumpeters, magnificent in crimson and gold, advanced together and blew on their trumpets. The hall was cleared, the Duchess, the Ambassador and the attendant great ones — Leicester, Sussex and their ladies — seated themselves. After that, with much scrambling and laughing and flirting and jokes, everyone climbed up the tiers and settled down. At the end near the great door, there were some wooden stairs, leading through an opening on to a wide outside balcony that overlooked the town. Through this opening came in the warm night summer air, and Robin, because he was frantically hot, sat, eight rows up, near this night freshness.

So it happened that the Masque, at the far distance, had a misted bewildered look and came to him, through the lights and the long embroidered banks of seated people, as something more real than reality, while the actual life close about him was insubstantial ; the coloured clothes of paper, the eager faces inhuman — and himself, alone, tortured with desire, sick at heart and in some way indignant with life, as though he had been forced into circumstances against his will.

This Masque was the most splendid that London had yet seen and, as he watched it, he thought of that other little Masque in his Uncle Henry's house, many years ago, when he had met Sylvia for the first time. The ship balancing in the child's hair, the child at her first ball !

Masques were ever growing more elaborate and this present one was to be remembered for many years, and James himself would one day say, ' I would have it as fine as the Masque presented to the French Ambassador at Westminster in '81 — the one of the Shepherds and the Centaurs.'

The Shepherds had invaded the world. Green hills of paint and pasteboard were dragged on by lions whose heads

were ferocious and back legs acrobats. Then came the
Shepherds, brown of body and bare save for decency, piping
and dancing and leading six acrobatic sheep that baaed most
truthfully.

This was comedy, but anon there was dragged on by the
same lions and two huge giants with clubs a Castle. Here,
imprisoned by the Giant Impertinence, was a lovely Princess
who looked out of a window and wrung her hands in despair.
The Shepherds tried to rescue her, but were defeated by the
Giants. Then came the Centaurs, whisking their tails, clump-
ing their hooves, and with the beautiful bodies of some of the
most vigorous young men in London. To the blast of the
trumpets they pulled down the Castle, rescued the Princess,
killed the Giant, liberated the prisoners. When the Castle fell,
these prisoners, led by their Princess, raised their hands to
heaven in gratitude, and a lovely silver fountain sprang up
where the Castle had been. Then, all together, Shepherds
and Giants and Centaurs and prisoners danced in triumph
while showers of gold leaves fell from the ceiling, the fountain's
water glittered, a choir sang, and a body of French noblemen
and ladies, most magnificently attired, did a special dance in
front of their Ambassador.

' Mr. Herries,' a voice said in Robin's ear. ' Mr. Herries.'

Robin turned. Beside him, as though he had been conjured
out of the air, was a young man, Francis de Lacey. De Lacey
was a youthful Catholic whom Robin had met twice with
Pierson. He came of a Northumbrian family, was a good
deal of a fanatic, foolish in some things, hysterical a little,
but devoted to his faith and undoubtedly, besides this, a
political conspirator. Robin, who detested the political side
of the Catholic cause, distrusted him and in his heart admired
and even envied his determined single-mindedness.

The boy was in a great agitation. His body trembled, his
eyes shone as he stared in front of him, seeing nothing but one
scene.

' Mr. Herries,' he whispered. ' Campion is taken.'

Robin's first impulse was to look around him. There was
no one immediately near them. Robin felt the summer air
on his neck and a sick choked feeling at his heart. They talked,

not looking at one another, scarcely moving their lips.

' When ? '

' Daybreak on the morning of Monday the seventeenth.'

' Where ? '

' Lyford Grange.'

' How was it ? '

' He was to preach at Oxford and was persuaded to stay the end of the week at Lyford. A big house with moat and drawbridge. Mr. Yate was confined in London, but Mrs. Yate with eight nuns was there. Meanwhile of course the expected sermon was all the talk at Oxford. Oh, the folly ! The hideous folly of it.'

The boy was staring at the Masque where the masked Centaurs, their horse-bodies covered with silver nets, pranced and caracoled.

' Friday and Saturday passed in safety. All the Catholics in the neighbourhood flocked to see him. The whole world knew of it. On Sunday morning arrived George Eliot and Jenkins, two Government rats, to see whether there was a Mass. Mrs. Yate's cook let them in and took them up to the Mass, which they appeared reverently to attend. Eliot took of the holy bread from Campion's own hand. Then Campion preached a most passionate sermon. Afterwards the two Government men galloped off to the Justice. While the others were at dinner in the evening the house was completely surrounded by soldiers. Campion, they say, wished to surrender that they might perhaps spare the others, but no one would allow it and the three priests were hidden in a hiding-place. Later Eliot and the magistrate, Fettiplace, entered and demanded the men. The whole assembly was accused of celebrating the Mass. They denied it and Fettiplace was in confusion because he had only the word of a common informer, but he permitted Eliot and Jenkins to make a raid. All day they searched, found some secret places but no priests. The priests were hidden in a crossbow-maker's workshop, very small with a shelf for tools. Mrs. Yate had her bed made up outside it and during the night Campion came and addressed the household.

' At daybreak the search began again ; Eliot was all but

defeated.   He thought that after all Campion might have
escaped.   But suddenly he noticed a space of light in the well
over the stairs.   With a crowbar he broke the back of the cell
and there the priests were, close together upon a bed.

' Jenkins called out loudly, " I have found the traitors ! " '

The boy had recited this as though it were a lesson ;   it
was likely enough that he would tell it in just these words
many times.

Robin stared at the Masque.   The Castle fell.   The waters
of the fountain leaped up.   The golden leaves showered from
the ceiling.   The whole company ' in colours of a summer
garden ' advanced while the trumpets blew.   All were masked :
a masked world of shepherds, giants, and centaurs.

Robin remembered Campion, like a boy, with his bare
legs under his shirt, and his laugh as he said when Cumberlege
had cried :

' Are Thy Saints to be racked and burned eternally ? '

' Not eternally, Henry.   After the rack — Paradise.'

For himself he knew that this moment was one more stage
on his personal soul's journey.   Which way, fighting soul ?
Which way ?

He cast one more look on the wild dancing masked figures,
then, unable to endure his own thoughts, got up and slipped
out of the hall into the silence of the early summer morning.

THE MARTYR

It had been rainy, off and on, for many days and the roads
of the City were thick and deep with foul mud on this Friday,
December 1st. Robin, wrapped in a thick cloak of Irish
frieze, stood in Holborn pressed with the crowd.

It was a large crowd and excited, which was curious, for
there had been many of these sights : it was no new thing to
see condemned men dragged on the hurdles through the streets.
But Campion had roused interest. There were many stories :
how, under the rack, he had screamed and screamed, crying
out that he denied God. Others said that when he had been
first stripped the executioners had said : ' The flesh is as soft
as a woman's.' They said that his limbs had been twisted
so that he could not stand, and that, whether he had recanted
or no, he was now firm and resolute and as ardent a Catholic
as ever he'd been. Men had argued these weeks as to whether
he were rightly punished or no, for it was clear that he had
been himself no politician even though he had been mixed
up with those who were. It was right enough, of course, that
those who plotted against the Queen should be punished ;
but should not a man have permission to serve his own faith ?
There were those who said that you could not be a Catholic
without being a traitor, but for the most part there was a
sympathy for Campion and a liking for him. But this sympathy
was mixed with a sadistic desire to see him suffer, to see anybody suffer, to hear anybody cry out, to see the waxen paralysed
face and the sudden spirt of blood. Londoners, for many
years now, had been encouraged to see these sights and hear
these sounds. Blood ran through the City, blood and mud,
rain and plague, lice and rats, foul water and dead stinking
dogs and cats. Old women were tortured for their private
hoards, old men had their teeth plucked out and their finger-

nails, small children were debauched, and the bull-baitings, bear-baitings, cock-fights, dog-fights, rat-fights were filled with this stink of stale blood and with the muttered whispers of half-exhausted lechers.

But on a day when the sun shone and the flags hung out and the bands played through the streets and the train-bands marched and the apprentices shouted, all was light and colour and song. London was as clean as a whistle and bright as a new-painted toy. The fresh water gurgled through the gutters, and the jewels and dagger-hilts and mirrors and shoe-buckles glittered in the shops, and the crowd pressed the barriers, and wine flowed like water.

Not to-day though. The morning was bitterly cold, the wind wild, the rain stung like whips, and from underfoot the mud oozed up over shoes and ankles like a live thing. When London was cold it was an agony, for the cracks and crevices of the buildings caught the cold and blew it out into the street in icy gusts. The rain did not only rain : it soaked the very skin. You believed on such a day as this that London was truly built on marshes, and that, let the rain go on long enough, these same marshes would rise and swallow the town, en-gulfing it, so that where Paul's was you would see only a spread of water, a lonely bittern crying above it.

Certainly on such a morning London lost all her splendour and seemed a gimcrack wooden-painted place with boards creaking and chimneys (what there were) rocking, and the shop-signs crashing against the wind. Yet even on such a day the crowds were thick, pressing together good-humouredly, some for love and some for warmth and some for thieving and some for human nature.

Robin, who had not slept at all the night before, here in Holborn, waited in a kind of trance. His lack of sleep made his head all fiery although his hands, in spite of the long gloves that covered them, were icy cold. His fiery head and his burning eyes made the scene a nightmare beyond what it really was. Nothing was quite real ; every figure something of a phantom.

He marked everything minutely as though someone stood at his elbow whispering : ' Note this well. You will remember every detail of this day until you die.' Moreover he himself intended to remember. He stood there weighted with a conviction of sin. It was not only the adultery but also the hatred. He knew, deep in his innermost consciousness, that if there were a chance of killing Irvine secretly without fear of discovery, he would do it. Mixed with hatred was fear. He was sure that Irvine on *his* side was planning his death, and he did not know which way it would be attempted. Mixed with the fear was lust.

The more he enjoyed intercourse with Sylvia the more he longed for it. This was contrary to the usual, when physical intimacy often repeated kills lust. But it might be the furtiveness, secrecy, fear of discovery, that increased their mutual passion. They loved one another now as tortured pursued beings.

But mixed with the lust, the fear, the hatred, the furtiveness, was a deep unceasing consciousness of God. Since he had committed evil against God, God was far more *with* him than He had been before. Not an angry and avenging God but a loving. That was the strange thing. He had never realized God's love for him before as he now did. God's love and God's company. His sense of sin, which had always been very active in him so that, in his childhood, little misdemeanours had seemed terrible to him, while Nicholas, committing the same, had not even been aware of them, was now constant. And he loved his sin. He loved God and he loved the sin against God.

When he had heard of Campion's arrest it was at once as though his own history had taken a step nearer to him.

' I am to be caught in the end. This brings me a step nearer.' He had seen Campion so little and yet he had loved him. He would never forget him, standing like a boy in his shirt ; nor would he forget the enchanting friendly smile, nor the gentle voice. All through these last months he had suffered with him, knowing what it must be to one of Campion's sensitive body to be subject to the rack and screw. His own personal horror of physical pain came in here, and his imagination took him into the very heart of that foul underground chamber with the dripping water, the fire, the dank smell, the naked exposure, and the sudden pang of unutterable agony, a savage animal clawing at your heart. But Campion had his faith to believe in. How far, under torture, Campion had recanted Robin did not know. It seemed to him unimportant how much you might recant under torture. You were not yourself then ; you were a physical animal without a soul.

So it seemed to him that this morning he would be with Campion on his hurdle, almost *be* him. And yet he was himself, himself whom he despised. He stood waiting and taking everything in for ever. Although there were the crowds to see the sight, yet all the regular bustle of the early morning in the street was beginning. Opposite him apprentices were taking down the shutters from a horologer's shop. The beggars were out already and a man without legs was dragging himself past the crowd, holding out his dirty cap.

The criers were already busy, for Holborn was a great place for them and the knowledge that crowds would be there brought them early. ' Whiting, maids, whiting ! ' ' Rock Samphire . . . Rock Samphire ! ' ' Buy a mat ! Buy a mat ! ' and (most appropriate to the day) ' Small coals ! Small coals ! ' They passed up and down, caring nothing for the mud and rain. Coaches, with every month more numerous and a cursing disastrous prophecy for the watermen, were already, early though it was, lumbering their way and throwing up great spumes of mud as they went. They made a terrific clatter on the cobbles and altogether the noise was so great that you must shout if you would be heard.

Robin caught and held for evermore certain fragments : a gilt weather-vane on a roof, two tiny children playing in the water of the gutter, a slob of mud on the face of a merchant who was nailing something to his shop's boards, a stout pursy fellow quite unconscious of his disfigurement, a shabby fellow with one arm making water against the wall of a church to the right of him, a woman in a crimson nightcap leaning out of a window, a small cart piled with odd boots that a crier was pushing, the raindrops jumping on to the eaves and running down on to the hat of a man below. All and nothing. Nothing and all. Where he was standing the crowd was thick. A stout fellow with an ugly merry face, yellow-haired, snub-nosed, dressed in an old leather jacket and soiled yellow hose, pressed against him and, after a while, rested his rough red hand on Robin's shoulder, grinning like a friendly dog as he did so. On his other side was a little thin man with a long nose wearing a gold chain round his neck. The little man pursed his lips and wheezed as though he had an asthma.

As may happen on such occasions, standing and waiting, Robin began to feel as though the stout man and the little man were known to him, had been his acquaintances for a long while. As everything was slightly unreal to him, so were these two larger than reality and more intimate with him than his friends. Because this was so special an event, so were they special too. It was as though they had been given to him for some definite purpose.

' Do you mind, master,' the stout fellow said, ' that I press you close ? There's a woman pinching me to the right of me, and I'll have the skin off you '— he, suddenly fierce, turned abruptly on a tall thin man with a yellow pointed beard — ' if your hand wanders to my purse again.'

The thin man edged away.

' But I like you, master.' He dropped his voice. ' If you are a Catholic, master, and will follow me to Tyburn I can bring you where you will be close to the scaffold and can speak with the holy father. . . .'

He was pressing Robin so closely that his breath was in Robin's mouth, and Robin, who was fastidious, was surprised to discover that he did not resent it. The big merry-eyed fellow seemed a comfort against the filth and the cold and the rain.

' I am not a Catholic,' Robin said. ' But I have known Campion.'

He wondered then whether he had been an especial fool. This might well be some spy of Irvine's put there to catch him. But somehow he did not think so. This yellow-haired fellow was not an enemy and had never been. Had never been ? Robin was indeed fever-headed to-day, for he had never seen the man before.

Nor had he seen the little coughing creature with the long nose on his other side, and yet he did not seem new to him. He was very restless, always straining on his toes to see better, coughing and choking, and when he all but overbalanced he would clutch at Robin's arm.

' They say he called out against God under pressure. I am myself something of a wild Christian, but I would not blaspheme.'

' Under pressure you would do anything,' Robin said contemptuously.

' Maybe. . . . Maybe. It is certainly most bitter cold. What I say and have many times said is that he that is not for the State is against it. It is a State newly blessed and freshly strong, and the Queen in her mercy knoweth who shall be punished and who shall not be punished.'

But the stout fellow on the other side was continuing : ' If you have known Campion, master, at any time, it will be a comfort for him to see your face at the last. He will be in need of his friends. And I can arrange it——'

' And your fee ? ' Robin asked, moving a little away.

' No fee. I do it for love of you, master, and because there is great distress in your face and you are young. I am myself a warder in the Tower. They call me Michael Strongback. My proper name is Roland. But I can bend an iron bar double and carry a cart on my stiffened belly. I can kill a man with my fist, and have done, and I could carry you in my arms, master, as gentle as I were a woman.'

He said all this with the very greatest simplicity, his hand against Robin's shoulder.

' So you were in the Tower. You saw Father Campion there ? '

' No, but I heard how it went with him. And it is not true that he confessed anything. There was one day they took him delirious from the rack and it may be that he said something — not knowing what he said. They had him on the rack three times. They say that the second was the worst, for his knees were dragged out of their sockets. They tried to catch him in every way they might. I would give all the stretched-out women in the world for such a faith. But I have nothing in this world but my strength, my family, and what I do for my daily bread.'

' Are you kind to your prisoners ? ' Robin asked him.

' On a Monday — and then on a Wednesday I snarl. You know how it is, master, we are slaves of our bodies, and when we have been drunken, next day we are not fair men.'

There was a swaying of the crowd. The little man leaped on his feet, giving a kind of screech. The yellow-haired man's great arm went round Robin's waist and held him firm. For they were coming. A moment later they were there. Some officers on horses, someone beating a drum, a rabble of boys and men, and then the two horses, each dragging a hurdle.

The other priests, Briant and Sherwin, were on one hurdle, Campion by himself on the other. The horses plodded along, throwing up mud with their hooves.

But Robin had eyes only for Campion. Clad in a gown of Irish frieze, he was bound with thick rope to the hurdle ; his face, with a splash of mud on one cheek, was raised to the sky, and the rain poured down on it. The edges of his rough gown blew up and down in the wind.

Yes, and this was verily the same man as Robin had seen in Cumberland. Under the ropes and the gown the limbs seemed to be strangely twisted — but that might be Robin's imagination. The face was white and strained, but even now, as the lips moved, there was still that same sweetness in the mouth and eyes. An Anglican who had argued on Justification by Faith in one of the Conferences walked through the mud beside the hurdle, still arguing. But Campion did not seem to hear Mr. Charke at all and answered none of his reiterated questions. Robin caught the shrill nagging voice and saw Charke striding along, his body writhed with irritation. A number of little boys ran through the mud, laughing and singing something out. One of them stumbled in the mud and fell ; Campion turned his head and Robin saw him smile with compassion.

' We must move with them,' his friend Michael said, ' if we are to be close at the end. Trust yourself to me.'

They detached themselves from the crowd and went forward, and the little man with the gold chain ran skipping and jumping beside them. It was not hard to keep pace with the hurdles, for the soldiers in front had often difficulty in clearing the way. The hurdles bumped over the cobbles, and the mud that the horses cast up splashed the clothes and faces of the condemned. Robin ran at a kind of jog-trot and Michael Roland strode beside him clearing the way for them. Robin found that his intentness on Campion was a kind of hallucination. It was as though he himself lay on the hurdle, his arms around Campion protecting him. Robin's lips moved and, in his soul, he seemed to be whispering to Campion with the uttermost urgency : ' I cannot believe as you believe, but, before you go, in spite of my disbelief, bless me, ask God to forgive me and strengthen me and set me on the right path.'

And it seemed to him that Campion turned to him with great gentleness and said : ' Do you abandon your sin ? '

And Robin in deep wretchedness answered : ' I cannot.'

' You must fight ! You must fight ! I have known worse battles than yours, and now, thanks be to Jesus, it is over. So it will be one day with you.'

And Robin answered : ' How you are to be envied ! '

And Campion, smiling, said : ' I have never known so happy a day as this ! '

In reality the little procession was stopped by a coach that had caught one wheel in a rut. The horses were plunging and the hurdle rocking. More mud fell on Campion's cheek. Some in the crowd laughed. Robin was very close to him and taking his handkerchief he leant forward and wiped the mud away. Campion's eyes met his and Campion smiled, but, of course, he did not recognize him. As the fingers of Robin's glove touched the cheek it seemed to him that an icy cold struck through to his finger-bone. Campion's face was dirty, the beard tangled, but it had a wonderful illuminated clarity as light shines through a thin shell. There was a faint odour about his body as of corruption, and his boots were thick with mud into which straw was sticking. Rain-drops hung about his mouth and nose.

When Robin made his gesture one of the guards turned to him roughly. They feared perhaps a rescue. But Michael Roland knew him.

' Hey, Boniface ! . . . This is a muddy business.'

Boniface, who looked a stupid oafish fellow, made no answer but nodded his head in recognition.

They moved forward again. The rain was coming down now in torrents as they neared Tyburn. The fields and bending, whining trees were soaked in rain.

Michael was talking as though to divert Robin's mind.

' There was an odd thing once — in 1447 it was — when five gentlemen were to be executed for having to do with the death of " good Duke Humphrey." They were all stripped for their dismembering when a pardon arrived, but the hangman, being rightly entitled to their clothes, for he had hanged them although they were cut down alive, clung to his rights and refused to give up the clothes. So the five gentlemen, when they were recovered sufficiently, walked their way home as naked as they were born and with the marks of their quarterings yet on their bodies.'

' Yes,' coughed the little man with the long nose, ' and I'll swear the good folk were mad at their missing the dismemberment. It is a rare thing and one to be remembered — a good dismemberment is a rare thing.'

Now, as they approached Tyburn and could even see the gallows in the distance against the rushing muddy clouds, they were separated from the hurdles by the greatly increased crowd. The rain and wind had not stopped the good people of London from coming to enjoy the sight, and here they were all pushing and scrabbling together with mud on their faces and eating stinking sausage and gesturing with their hands in the air, against the wild wind, as though they were lunatics.

There were temporary booths set up as though it were a fair, and they were selling portraits of the priests and their histories together with sweetmeats and pies and coloured birds in cages and lop-eared trembling rabbits.

To Robin, as he pressed forward behind Michael, the scene was like something out of Hell. The rain and wind were suddenly abating and even the grey sky was breaking a little with thin bands, behind the clouds, of promised light.

He perceived now that there were many Catholics in the crowd, men and women praying without disguise, their hands raised, and he saw one fellow knock the hat off a certain devout man. Whether it were by physical force or by some especial influence that he had, Michael drove his way forward and soon they were not far from the scaffold itself. The little man with the long nose managed to keep with them. Then they were stopped by a thick concourse of people who were shouting and laughing and clapping their hands. It was now especially that Robin seemed to be in Hell, for all the faces around him were evil, caricatures with swollen noses and tremendous chins and crooked eyes. There seemed to him a great stench, which well might be from all the rain drying on clothes and the pressing together of so many bodies. He was now near enough to see what it was that the crowd was applauding. It was a thick-set fellow with no arms and no legs. He danced a horrible fantastic dance on the stumps that remained of his legs, his round rather childish face grinning and his blue eyes staring. His arms were gone to above the elbow, but with what remained to him he very miraculously tossed a cup in the air, dancing as he did so, and while he danced he sang verses that Robin soon heard to be fitting.

He did not look himself to be evil, but rather simple and childlike. A woman sat on an upturned drum, waiting patiently until she should go round and collect money in the cup. The crowd here were filled with a blood-lust. They had come on this miserable morning, rising early, travelling from far, to see the hangings and the quarterings. There was nothing of a noble England here, no men were here fit to rule a new world, but animals in a pressing thronging mass waiting for the kill.

Another thing that Robin realized was that, in some fashion, he was in Michael Roland's power. His nerves were so wrought, his imagination was heightened so unnaturally by his sleeplessness, that it was as though he saw visions, a time beyond this present moment, when again he would be helplessly in Roland's power, when he would be closer to Campion than on this day he could ever be.

It was almost as in a dream that he followed that proud back. He had the sense that one has in dreams of moving forward without walking and of people dividing in front of him as though by some magic.

In any case he very shortly found that they were close beside the scaffold and that they had passed through the cordon of soldiers. He looked about him and saw officials of the Court, magistrates and some whom he knew — Lord Howard, Sir Henry Lee and Sir Francis Knollys among others.

Quite close to him he recognized a thin dark-faced young man, Henry Walpole, a very distant cousin of his own through the Gilbert Herries who had, in the last century, married Alice Walpole. He knew Mr. Henry Walpole as a young Cambridge wit and minor poet.

He spoke to no one, however, but drew his frieze coat closer about him. He heard Henry Lee's high-pitched voice arguing quite fiercely about the motion of the sun, that it was natural and obeyed inevitable laws, and he caught Francis Knollys' scornful and elegant laugh.

They broke off their discussion, for at that moment Campion was climbing clumsily into the cart below the gallows. No one had eyes for the other two priests. All thought only of Campion. Indeed he was a pitiful sight, muddy-faced, sadly cold with his Irish coat taken from him. Also, because of his tortures, his legs would not obey him. One knee stuck out unnaturally. He tried three times to climb the cart and fell back, so that one of the men assisting the hangman had to help him. He turned, smiling sweetly, and thanked him. The horrible instruments of the quartering were on the scaffold, the irons and knives and the cauldron.

Campion reached the cart, stood there awkwardly and faced the people.

At once there was a great outcry, shrieks and shouts and laughter until all individual sounds were drowned in a roar. But it was his face that was beautiful. Although he stood clumsily, barely clothed, one leg half bent beneath him, his face had, for Robin, a kind of illuminated glory.

Strangely enough, at this moment the sunlight, pale and watery and struggling, emerged for the first time through the clouds, and the gallows, the scaffold, and all the prisoners on it were washed with a thin cleansing light.

The hangman threw the noose over Campion's head. Campion began to speak, but the noise of the crowd was too great for any but those close to the scaffold to gather his words. Robin heard everything distinctly.

Campion, still with that hidden smile behind his lips, began loudly :

' Spectaculum facti sumus Deo, angelis et hominibus . . .' He went on : ' These words spake St. Paul, and in English, " We are made a spectacle unto God, unto His angels and unto men." ' (At the word ' angels ' he raised his voice and looked upwards as though indeed he saw them there.) ' These words are made true this day in me, who am here a witness unto my Lord God, His angels and you men. I——'

But before he could continue, the shrill high voice of Francis Knollys broke in :

' Confess your treason, man ! Confess your treason, man ! ' he shouted.

Robin turned, raising his fists at the interruption, and it was then that, even in his own absorption, he was able to notice Henry Walpole. He had thought this young man always a light-weighted companion, gentle-minded and amusing, but worth no more than the flick of a coin. He saw that now his face was transformed, his eyes burning above his dark cheeks, his lips moving as though in prayer.

Campion, turning and looking at Knollys and the group beside him, said : ' As to the treasons which have been laid to my charge and for which I am come here to suffer, I desire you all to bear witness with me that I am thereof altogether innocent.'

It was clear that this question of treason was of root importance — the relation between religious belief and plotting against the State — and voices called out everywhere : ' Treason ! Treason ! ' And ' No Treason ! No Treason ! ' — and these cries were, on this grey weeping morning, perhaps the first expression of the new battle for the freedom of the people that was, almost at once, to be fully joined.

A thick heavily-befurred man near Knollys, a member of the Council, cried out : ' 'Tis too late. Treason was proved in the Court.'

Some man in the crowd called out : ' Nay ! Nay ! . . . Not proven ! Not proven ! '

Then Campion's voice, with its patience and sweetness, again was heard :

'Well, my Lord, I am a Catholic man and a priest; in that faith I have lived and in that faith I intend to die. If you esteem my religion treason, then am I guilty; as for other treason I never committed any, God is my judge. But you have now what you desire. I beseech you to have patience and suffer me to speak a word or two for discharge of my conscience.'

There then began a fearful time of agitation. It was as though the nerves of everyone about the scaffold were excited to madness. The gentlemen — Knollys and Lee and the rest — began shouting furiously all together, shaking their fists, especially Knollys, like madmen. Henry Walpole and Robin were drawn close together until they almost touched. They stood, leaning forward, their young bodies strung as though they would leap in the air, their eyes deep in Campion's body.

The great crowd beyond was now lusting for blood. It was roaring for the execution to proceed that it might come to the quarterings. Campion's voice could now only faintly be heard. He asked forgiveness of anyone whom, during his examination, he might have compromised, and he forgave the jury that had condemned him. He turned especially to Knollys, who seemed to be suddenly quiet and sombre, and asked him to spare one Richardson, who had never possessed, as Campion was himself aware, a book that was said to have been found in his luggage.

Knollys, frowning, stared at him and said no word. It was as though he had been apprised of some serious news concerning himself that had taken his thoughts away.

A schoolmaster named Hearne stood forward on the scaffold and read to the crowd a proclamation in the Queen's name, shouting out that this execution was for treason not religion, upon which the crowd broke into every sort of reply. Some of the Council, Lee and others, were still bawling questions up to Campion about the Bull of Excommunication and other points in the trial, but Campion heard them no longer. His face was raised to heaven. He was lost in prayer. The pale sun shone on him a little and on the coarse rope of the noose.

A thin fanatic-looking Anglican clergyman stepped to the

very edge of the scaffold and cried out to him that he might direct his prayers.

Campion looked at him and very gently shook his head.

'Sir,' he said (and now all the crowd was quiet and every word came clearly), 'you and I are not one in religion, wherefore I pray you content yourself. I bar none of prayer; but I only desire them that are of the household of faith to pray with me, and in my agony to say one creed.'

Someone called out to him to pray in English, but he answered, smiling: 'I will pray God in a language which you and I both well understand.'

There were shouts again and the befurred Councillor called out in a thick pompous voice that he should ask the Queen's forgiveness.

Campion said: 'Wherein have I offended the Queen? In this I am surely innocent. This is my last speech. In this give me at least credit — I have and do pray for her.'

But Lord Howard cried: 'Which Queen? Which Queen do you pray for?'

And Campion answered in a firm strong voice: 'Yea, for Elizabeth, your Queen and my Queen, unto whom I wish a long quiet reign with all prosperity.'

At that same instant the executioner gave a sign and the cart was driven forward from under him. The body jerked, and almost at once seemed to be lifeless, the neck broken. But it was the law for the executioner to cut the body down while there was still life in it. One of the twisted legs jerked. The man commenced to climb the ladder.

Then unexpectedly the officer in charge called out: 'Not till the body be dead. I have directions.' There was an awful pause while the body swayed lightly to and fro. There was a complete silence everywhere, save that someone could be heard sobbing. The pause seemed endless: time stood still.

The officer gave the sign. The body was cut down and instantly stripped. It lay there, white and clean, the eyes staring, the head on one side.

The executioner took his knife and began to mark for the quartering. At the first stroke blood spirted. Robin felt something wet on his cheek and he saw Henry Walpole raise his handkerchief, touch his face and then hold the handkerchief, blood-stained, looking at it.

Robin, not knowing what he said nor to whom he spoke, cried out :

' But the body is nothing ! . . . The pains of the body are no matter ! '

He turned, his head bent, and pushed his way, as it seemed, through darkness.

END OF PART II

PART III

THE PRISONERS

YOUNG ROSAMUND

ROSAMUND HERRIES was born in May 1566 and was therefore over eighteen years of age in the early autumn of this year 1584. She had been living now for a whole year as companion to Sylvia Irvine in the little house that the Irvines had near Charing Cross.

That had happened most unexpectedly. As she came in one fine morning from exercising her dogs, her mother had said to her :

' A horseman has left this letter for you.'

' A letter — for *me* ? ' she had answered, incredulous.

But there it was. It was from Sylvia Herries.

MY DEAR ROSAMUND — For so I may call you, may I not ? Many many years ago (as it seems) you told me on our very first meeting that at any time you would serve me. And later, you sent a message by a friend promising the same.

I am now much alone, for my husband is busy much of the time with Mary of Scotland's business. London is none too merry in one's own company and I have had the thought that you might care to keep me company for awhile in this town. There are things that you might do for me. I need a friend. Ask your father and your mother and tell me how they find this. — Your friend and well-wisher   SYLVIA IRVINE.

Rosamund sat looking at this, lost in a dream. So the call had come ! She had always known that it would. She had been aware at the first moment of seeing her in that dreadful house that they were in some way bound together.

She told her mother. This family — Guy, Rosemary and Rosamund — was quite unlike other Elizabethan families. At that time, and for long after, the family discipline was brutal. Children were beaten for the slightest error, girls tied to

273

bedposts, boys fastened to the stable door. All this was, in the strange fashion of English habit and thought, mingled with kindliness, indulgence, laughter, song, dance, and a great deal of eating and drinking : much fine education in Latin, Greek, mathematics, music, sewing, housewifery, outdoor exercise also. But there was a deep gulf fixed between parents and children.

But Guy was an artist. He was of the Bohemian Herries variety and so his wife and child were part of himself. Rosamund's education had been lop-sided, but she had picked up a deal of useful learning both outdoors and in.

Her mother and father said at once :

' They say it is a very unhappy house.'

' I heard of it at Bucking from Agatha,' Rosamund said.

' Poor thing ! ' Rosemary sighed. She was so happy in her own married life that it seemed to her most unjust that everyone else should not be so.

But the issue was settled from the first moment, for if Rosamund wished to go she should go, and of course Rosamund wished to go. Then, at seventeen, she was still coltish and still plain. Her hair, do what she would, was colourless and lack-lustre ; her nose would be for ever snub, and her complexion, although no longer pasty, was that of a girl who lived for ever out of doors — brown and without paint or powder. One evening she had dressed herself in an old Court dress of her mother's, rouged her cheeks and put on a patch in the fashion that Anne Boleyn started. She had come in to where her father was painting and her mother embroidering, and curtsied and flounced about and danced with her long legs. How they had laughed ! There was something exquisitely absurd in this long-legged, brown-faced, snub-nosed girl acting the Court lady. And Rosamund had laughed too. Then suddenly she had burst into tears, knelt down, hid her face in her mother's lap. It was so very rare to see her cry that they had been greatly upset.

She had wiped her eyes, blown her nose, grinned at them, blinked her wet eyelashes.

' I shall never be a Court lady. No man will ever love me. I shall die an old mottled milk-maid.'

Her mother looking fondly at her had thought : ' Her
eyes. She has beautiful eyes. But why *should* she be so plain ?
Neither her father nor I—' And then she had gone up to her,
and, as though asking her forgiveness for some unexpected
infidelity, had caught her in her arms and held her —' My
darling, my darling '— and Rosamund had shaken herself
free, for demonstrations made her feel awkward, and had
laughed and wrinkled her nose in a way that she had, and had
done a very clever imitation of a snobbish Court lady saying
to Rosemary : ' I fear no young man will venture for your
daughter — she has so plain a nose.' And Rosemary proudly
answering : ' Such noses are the only thing at Court. All
Frenchmen wear them.'

It was in fact very seldom that Rosamund was unhappy.
She had not the temperament for unhappiness.

It seemed to have little to do with reason or event whether
she were happy or no. On the most disastrous occasions her
happiness remained untouched by circumstance. There had
been the awful evening when, crossing Hopleet Moor, she
had been stopped by a large man with a sword who had tried
to rape her. She *would* have been raped — he had turned
her on her back in the grass and torn most of her clothes off
her — had the old Witch of Malling not come up, out of the
dusk, her head crowned with daisies, and stuck the man in
the groin with her knife and raised such a screeching that the
ruffian had limped away in desperate panic.

Five minutes after that horrible adventure Rosamund had
laughed because she remembered the terrific scratching she
had given the man with her nails.

But then she was fearless. She really did not know where
fear lay. (She would of course one day know.) Her father,
who adored her, said that she had four great qualities : courage,
fearlessness, humour, kindliness.

Nevertheless her mother and father and one or two villagers
— the Witch of Malling included — were her only admirers.
She did not attract people, and that not only because she was
plain. Very much because she said so exactly what was in
her mind.

As she grew older she visited London. She also stayed

with Agatha and Edward Herries. Agatha told her very frankly that it simply did not do to say what you thought.

'You must learn to be complimental,' Agatha Herries instructed her. 'You must lie kindly and for good fashion's sake. You must have fine phrases set together which shall serve equally for all men. You must encourage a man so he shall make proffers to you and say that he will do anything for you. Of course he will not, but at least you must give him the pleasant chance to say so. You must never exact the performance of his promises afterwards, for that he will think ill-breeding. You must remember that a gentleman wishes to be kind at the first even though you know him for nothing afterward. You must give him his fair opportunity.'

But poor Rosamund was quite out in all this. If a fine young London man was euphemistically exaggerated to her she could not help but laugh, especially if he praised her looks, of which she knew she had none. She did not want lovers because her heart had been faithful for so many years to Nicholas that it could not now change. But, although she did not want lovers, she would not have minded if she were beautiful.

Her common sense was always getting in her way. Her heart was readily moved by distress but never by humbug. And, as she grew, she found there was a great deal of humbug in the world. Thinking her mother and father perfect gave her a severe testing-mark for other human beings, and she found them often wanting.

She had no conceit of herself at all, and when one or another told her her faults she considered the charge good-humouredly, and often acknowledged it. She had a hasty temper, but her fiery quality was never sulky. This fire sprang up in everything — fire of admiration and love and loyalty, fire of indignation, fire of love of beauty, fire of physical energy. She often spoke too quickly so that she offended, and moved too quickly so that she was ungainly and found herself in a ludicrous situation.

She had read a great deal, knew both Greek and Latin well, something of mathematics, something of philosophy. She liked to talk with someone speculatively — her father often

— and had caught a good deal of his free-thinking amoral mind. She passionately loved her country, thought that it could never be in the wrong, and detested all foreigners who plotted, or were suspected of plotting, against it.

With all this, her happiness, her vitality, her eagerness and interest in everything and everybody, she was, in her deepest heart, aware of a constant loneliness. This was, in part, because she loved a man who never gave her a thought, whom, indeed, she scarcely ever saw. But it was more than that. Save for her mother and father she had no real friend in all the world.

It was therefore with all the eagerness of her heart, the vitality of her body, the happiness of her nature that she took up this invitation from Sylvia Irvine. It was the precise thing that her situation needed.

And then what a change ! From the sunlit, open, free, loving life of her own home she moved into this silent, mysterious house. The house itself was neither dark nor silent. Philip Irvine had more wealth now and had left his horrible old mother behind him in the country, showing a callous selfishness to that old woman's melancholy loneliness.

The house was bright with curtains and wall-paintings and handsome pieces of furniture. It was bright — and modern and dead. At once Rosamund detested two persons in the house : one was Captain Winterset, whom she remembered from her old visit ; the other was Phineas Thatcher, whom Philip had engaged after Henry Herries' death. (Henry Herries had died two years before this.) Winterset was falling into the corruption that drink and women and all bad habits produce in a man after middle age. He had a flourish once and again of his earlier, more gallant brigandage. He was haunted now by a real obsession about Nicholas Herries, whom he constantly, in and out of his cups, abused. ' He had once,' he told Rosamund, ' three good men of mine ambushed and falsely slain.'

She looked at him with disgust : ' Nicholas was never false in any act or deed.'

' Well, you ask Philip. It was in the North.'

K

Winterset never resented her behaviour to him. He admired her. She gave some life to the cursed place, he said. He was so often besotted now that Philip would not take him on his expeditions away ; so he hung about the house, sleeping, cursing, calling to the dogs, trying to tickle the maids. He cried sometimes for self-pity.

Phineas Thatcher saw to the accounts and the running of the house. He was also, as Rosamund very quickly found, a spy for Philip. Perversely enough this mean, bitter, slippered, secret-moving Puritan also liked Rosamund. He liked her because she was plain and, yet more perversely, because she was honest. It was perhaps a rest and refreshment for him to find a human being in that house who was precisely the same as appearance. There was another thing. Rosamund was not afraid of him. Everyone else in that house — even Philip — was. It was a relief to him not to be feared although to *be* feared was his constant aim and preoccupation.

However, there were only two people in the house for Rosamund — Sylvia and Philip. Philip was away during her first month there and on the second day Robin Herries paid a visit. Within five minutes of his arrival Rosamund had caught a look between the pair. Before the night was out Sylvia had told her everything : how they had been lovers for years now, how they hated the secrecy, the furtiveness, the falsehood, but how their mutual love did not die but ever increased ; how they had once planned to run away together, but how the plan had been stopped, first because Sylvia thought that she was going to have a child (and did not), afterwards because (this was in 1581) they had tried to part, Robin had gone abroad, but the effort had been in vain . . . they *could* not part . . . now a kind of paralysis seemed to hold them together.

Did Philip know ? Of course he knew, had known since the very first act of infidelity. He had been aware of that at once — Sylvia was sure because he had alluded to a certain jewel she had worn in her hat. Someone must have seen her at the time and told him.

Why had Philip during all this time done nothing ? Because he hated herself and Robin, loved to feel his power over them both, prolonged his vengeance, and was waiting patiently for the time when he would kill them both. When once he had satisfied his vengeance, why, then his power would be over too. Sylvia clung to Rosamund, crying that she, Rosamund, had no idea of Philip's subtle devilish wickedness. Philip *was* the Devil; he was in league with the Devil, and so on and so on. . . .

At first, after all this, Rosamund felt nothing but contempt for both Sylvia and Robin. With her own outright nature she could not understand this secrecy and cowardice. But soon she saw that Robin was not to be despised. There were only two ways out for him : to carry Sylvia away before the world, to challenge Philip. Both, quite certainly, would lead to Sylvia's death, and to a death in some shameful, horrible fashion.

Sylvia was safe only so long as the situation was not exposed. But Robin's nature was deteriorating under the secrecy and subterfuge. He was a most unhappy man.

Then, when Philip did return, Rosamund was surprised to discover that he was no monster after all. He was a crude, ill-brought-up, vain, frustrated egoist. He was eaten up with pride — pride of himself and his looks, pride of his family, pride of his position, pride of everything that was his. He was even proud in a kind of way of Sylvia although he hated her, and proud of his apparent friendship with Robin Herries who knew the Court wits and wrote poetry and was considered 'interesting' and 'mysterious.' He was proud of Sylvia and Robin and of his power over them, and he hated them. But he did not mind their going to bed together so long as it was not spoken of publicly. Oddly, it was *not* spoken of publicly.

He liked Rosamund as everyone else in the house did. He poured out to her his confidences. She listened to him with great amusement. It was clear that this was something quite new to him. He expected fear, reverence, admiration — but amusement !

He had become by now, at the age of forty, a very definite 'character.' He was extremely thin and held himself erect with almost unnatural precision. His very black hair and dark cheeks made him like a posturing Spaniard. He dressed

always in black or silver, with high stiff ruffs, one or two fine
jewels, and a jewel-hilted poniard. He liked to stand, very
straight and stiff, his face a stern mask, only his eyes alive in
it ; his hand on his dagger. If someone then approached him
he would answer in a grave low monosyllable — so low that
some people never heard what he said and complained of it.
He considered himself marvellous in everything that he did —
dancing, fencing, riding, tilting ; he never entered into learned
discussions about the arts, the philosophies, religion. He
pretended to a deep knowledge that he did not wish to expose,
but in reality he knew that such kingdoms were not his to
command.

Nevertheless he was not at all a fool, as Rosamund soon
discovered. He commanded respect from those who served
under him, and his vanity gave him an added quickness in
those things that assisted it. When his pride was offended he
could wait long and patiently for his revenge. It was really
true that he could not forgive an injury, and like all very vain
persons he found it quite impossible to understand that there
should be anyone blind to his merits. The principal reason
(among many) why he hated Nicholas Herries was that he
knew that Nicholas despised him. He hated Robin but felt it
easy and even pleasant to be in his company because he was
sure that Robin feared him, if not for his own sake then
certainly for Sylvia's.

So into his sombre and proud self-centredness there came
this unusual girl who was always moving and laughing, who
was learned and could discuss Latin poets and even herself
write poetry, who was afraid of nobody. He liked her because
he was able to patronize her ; he patronized her because she
seemed to him so plain, even ugly, and he was quite amazed
when Winterset muttered one day : ' Her eyes are fires and
her shape most inviting.'

He posed to her as a weary, deep-bottomed man of affairs,
lonely, but trusted with the kingdom's secrets. He stood, his
thin legs close together, pulling at his little peaked black beard,
while Rosamund sat at a table trying to write to her father.

' I interrupt you ? '

' You do.'

'Then I will go away.' But he didn't move ; only stood looking at her. 'You are writing to your father ? '

'I am.'

'You seem to be for ever busied. I go away for three weeks, leaving you busied, and return and find you still busied.'

She put down her pen and looked up at him, brushing what she angrily called her 'tallow hair' back from her forehead. She was smiling at him as though she mocked him.

'What age are you ? '

'Eighteen.'

'And I am forty — and yet you laugh at me.'

'I laugh at myself also.'

'Ah, that is because you are but eighteen. If someone else laughed at me I should be very angry. Why am I not angry with you ? '

'Because you know that it would make no difference to me whether you were angry or not.'

'Yes. You are not afraid of me. So many are.' He sighed. His sigh was ridiculous, and yet, at that precise moment, she was aware of how evil and how dangerous he might be.

'I am unfortunate,' he went on, almost as though he were reciting a lesson. 'I am a very lonely man. Whether I am here in my own house or about the affairs of the Court it is the same. I have a wife who does not love me and no friend in the world.'

This was the first time that he had spoken of Sylvia to Rosamund. She said quickly : 'You pay Sylvia no attention. She also is very lonely.'

To her surprise he answered quietly : 'It could have been otherwise — had we a child.' He went on : 'I am a tenacious man of what I have. And that is right. I am worthy of what I hold. I have done everything for myself. I am now one of Her Majesty's most trusted servants in the matter of Mary of Scotland. And who has made this ? I, myself. No one has assisted me in anything. I am not vain. I claim only what is right. I know my enemies. I can wait. I am content to be by myself. I am a man on my own legs. . . .' And then he added, almost beseechingly : 'And yet you mock me.'

How strange a human being, she thought, so dangerous and so childlike both together !

' I think you take yourself too gravely,' she answered. ' I say that for your own sake. I find that if one regards oneself in a serious looking-glass the solemn picture is a little absurd.'

' I am misunderstood,' he said, sighing again.

' So am I. So is everyone,' she said, getting up from the table. She went close up to him. ' Look at me ! Am I not plain ? '

He stared at her very solemnly. Yes, she *was* plain : there were two freckles on her right cheek ; her nose was short and rather humorous. But what woman wanted a humorous nose ? She had the complexion of a horse-boy and did nothing to improve it. Her eyes were fine, as Winterset had said — bright as fire, sparkling, both deep and laughing . . . and her shape was comely, her breasts small and firm. He touched her breasts. She moved back, and her eyes that he had admired were, for a moment, angry and threatening. She was virginal. She was not to be touched. Or by one man alone. In that withdrawal she insulted his pride and he hated her. But not for long. He sought her company again. She was the only one in that dreary house who was not afraid of him. Even Winterset and Thatcher were never sure of what he might do to them. He was not sure himself.

It was a strange house for a young girl fresh from the country. Nothing was stranger than the girl's relation with Sylvia. Rosamund's father and mother had been, above all things, healthy and normal. Sylvia was, by now, neither healthy nor normal. That first night at Drunning had given her a shock from which she would never recover. Her love for Robin was noble in so far as it was whole-hearted, self-sacrificing, but it had a quality of madness in it.

The madness came from her fear. Just as Robin was afraid of what Philip might do to Sylvia, so Sylvia was afraid of what Philip might do to Robin. She was afraid too lest Robin might suddenly leave her, for Robin was religious. Sylvia understood nothing about religion at all. She was a complete pagan. If there was a God He would not have allowed her to marry Philip. He would not have allowed most of the horrors and cruelties that she saw in the world and that followed her in her dreams at night.

There was no God, but Robin believed that there was. After Campion's execution Robin had come to her and said that he must never see her again. They had parted and he had gone abroad. Sylvia had thought that she would kill herself or Philip or both. She had done nothing. Robin had returned and they had come together as inevitably as the key to the magnet. But this God-nonsense had not left Robin alone. One day it would be too strong for her. So between the Devil which was Philip and the Devil which was Robin's God she lived in a perpetual fear.

Rosamund had never had closely to do with a haunted nerve-jangled woman who had, nevertheless, sweetness enough to force you to love her. Here her deep-seated maternal instinct helped her. Sylvia became Rosamund's child although Sylvia was twelve years older than Rosamund.

Sylvia poured everything out. There were no sexual reticences. All the horrors of that first night were laid bare ; these and other later incidents soon showed Rosamund that Philip was not merely a posing egoist. That was one reason why she had started away from him at his touch. Girls at eighteen then were often no virgins. They were mothers at fifteen often enough. Rosamund was not shocked by the things that Sylvia told her. Only a great tenderness and solicitude developed in her — a tenderness that was never to die. It extended also to Robin.

It extended also to herself. Shut up in this house with all this sexual smoke making the rooms and stairs murky and heavy-laden, she longed for the other kind of life — the life that was really hers — free, brilliantly clear, strong-winged, with all things open and manifest. Nicholas Herries stood to her for the whole of that. She saw him very seldom. He came, of course, never to Philip's house. She met him with Edward and Agatha. They had two children, Janet aged eight and Martha six, solemn little girls with whom he delighted to be. She went, with Sylvia, on one memorable day to Mallory and saw how he was king of the place. They sat on the lawn, drank syllabub and sang madrigals while the moon like a stamped gold plate rose over the clipped hedges, and the nightingale sang. Even Sylvia was gay and happy that summer evening. But Rosamund had no word alone with Nicholas; he joked with her once or twice, and once he looked at her, laughing, while he stood with Edward's little girls on his shoulders, a giant against the moon. But she saw that he did not regard her separately from the rest.

She was quite content if she could but see him. She did not expect anything apart from that.

Then a miracle occurred.

It happened on a day in summer that a Lady Ferris, a Court friend of Sylvia's, made up a party to go to the village of Islington. This was a place for fashionable people to visit, not only because the gravel soil made it healthy nor because the village was itself pleasantly rustic and picturesque, but because the brick-kilns there attracted for their labour rascals and vagabonds who were sometimes sufficiently tiresome to make the expedition adventurous. On this occasion there were no adventures of that kind, although some wild men with their women did gather and ask for food, but there *was* an adventure for Rosamund. Nicholas was there.

He was of course unmistakable at once, towering above everyone on his horse, and his laugh could be heard from one end of the village to the other.

They picnicked on the edge of a little wood, some dozen of them. There was the usual noise and three men sang madrigals, and afterwards, for the gentlemen, a dog-fight was arranged.

For Rosamund there was only Nicholas. She was sitting a little apart, staring before her at the sun-misted scene; she was sleepy, for they had ridden a long way and had been up early.

She heard Nicholas' voice as in a dream. He had sat down beside her. His hand was on her arm.

She turned, looked at him, took in every detail of him and was never afterwards to forget the smallest thing. He was dressed grandly, for he had ridden out with Sir Christopher Hatton and some Court ladies.

Rosamund looked at his peascod doublet of white silk

banded with gold. He wore a turned-down white collar in
place of a ruff. His venetians were of grey and gold brocade
and set off his thighs most handsomely. He had white open-
work stockings, a short surcoat of black velvet lined with
sable. His hat was black velvet with an osprey and a jewel.

Such grand clothes must look awkward on so big a man,
and effeminate against the ruddy brown of his cheeks and
hands. They were fancy, easily soiled gaieties for a country
outing, but she noticed at once that they suited him as though
they were born with him, and, although he lay on the grass
beside her, he was careful to spread his dark cloak to protect
him.

' I am dressed like a zany,' he said ruefully, ' but, to tell
you truth, I bought these things but last week and was eager
to see how they looked. What do you say, cousin ? '

' I think of you always in a hay-cart with your arms bare
and your neck open. I saw you once at a ball. You were
very grand then.'

She knew that he was looking at her curiously. He was
the one man in the world who could make her confused. She
too was dressed with elegance, and fine clothes never suited
her — only she liked her hat, which had a curled brim like a
man's, a row of small pearls about the bottom of the crown
and a panache of ostrich feathers set at the back.

But his curiosity went further than her clothes.

' Why is it that we do not meet more often ? ' he asked.

' You are at Mallory. I must be with Sylvia.'

' Ah, Sylvia. . . .' He looked across to Sylvia, who was
sitting with Christopher Hatton. ' Poor Sylvia. . . .'

' Why do you say that ? '

' Is she not ? Married to the meanest man in Christendom.'

' He hates you too,' she said quickly. She had an odd
desire to defend Philip : she could not imagine why.

' Of course. We are centuries-old enemies. He sent five
men to murder me once in the North.'

' I have heard of that. Winterset said that you ambushed
him.'

Nicholas laughed. He heaved his great body up and
stretched his arms. ' These clothes pinch me. I dare not

stretch my legs for fear of splitting the venetians. Winterset —'
he repeated reflectively, ' so he speaks of me.'

' Yes. He is always thinking of you. And not with love.'

They both laughed. She wondered how much he knew of
Sylvia and Robin. Everything, she supposed.

' We waste our time,' he said.

He sighed, a terrific sigh.

' I am always wasting my time. And yet once I did not
think so. What age do you think I am ? '

She could not help herself. She stared into his face, which
had always seemed to her the most beautiful face in the world.
It was not beautiful, of course, at all, only frank, sun-tanned
and, even now, like a boy's.

' I know. You are forty.'

' How do you know ? '

' I have always known. I know your birthday and once I
thought I would send you a present for it.'

' A present ? '

' Yes, I had a puppy. A wolf-hound. I thought it would
be the very thing for you.'

' And so it would. Why did you not send it ? '

' I wanted it for myself.'

He laughed at that. It was not the answer he had expected.

' I like you, cousin. We shall be friends.'

' I would be very glad. I have not so very many.'

' Nor I. Not in reality. I am forty and have done nothing.'

She said nothing.

' Well — why do you not tell me that I have done everything ? Most women would. I have made Mallory into the
finest estate in the county. I have two farms, the best cattle.'
He stopped. ' Oh, Lord ! You are right. I have done
nothing.'

' I did not say so.'

He laughed. ' Your silences are most eloquent. Do you
never say what you don't mean ? '

She laughed too. ' I try to. But I am discovered. Agatha
is always telling me that I have no good fortune with strangers
because I am not false enough.'

' Does it matter to you ? '

' No. Except that I am lonely one time and another.' She considered that he might think her self-pitying, so she went on : ' I have my own pleasures.' She said this so primly and like a little girl that he laughed again.

' Tell me what your life is.'

She considered ; then looked away from him out into the sunny air.

' I have two lives — as I suppose everyone must. One works on strings and pulleys and golden wires. You can see it working. That is the life of getting up in the morning, washing, putting on your clothes ; seeing how Sylvia may be, walking with her or riding, talking, laughing, eating again, touching things, hard, soft, seeing colours, feeling your body that it aches, that blood is always moving, that the heart beats, jumps, beats again, that the end of the third finger is numb, that you want to have your waist pressed, that this seat is hard, that your hair is heavy on your head — and so you eat again and take off your clothes, and lie on this side, then on that, and sleep.

' But the other life — it is something very different. It has no material boundary, nothing is hard or soft, there is no time there and space is without limit. You change as you live. You grow and you retract. You have a history under direction, and yet you are free also. You are only conscious of your body as, beyond the wall of your room, you are conscious of the weather, the rain, the sun.

' Sometimes you use your body as a pulley, as time uses the mechanism of a watch to make itself clear. You have there mind but no brain. You are in embryo but a distinct figure. You are You but also timeless and personless — as a fly is in amber, only you are free. As a bird is in a cage, only you also fly in the light. There are two lives. One is eternal. . . .'

She had lost all consciousness of him as she spoke, looking out into a faint blue sky that was the more limitless because of the gold haze that fretted it. She spoke only the result of her childish philosophy after all she had read and thought and talked with her father. She had never, as yet, in all her life, met a first-rate intellect.

Nicholas didn't understand a word of it. He thought she was very clever and in general he greatly disliked clever women because as soon as they showed their cleverness he was sure that they despised him. But this girl was different. She had no bodily attraction for him at all, but already he delighted in her frankness and honesty and directness. She did not know that she was being clever.

He tried now to be clever.

' Of those two selves—' But he stopped, grinning. ' I am only one self and a big coarse one at that. I have no thought except that here I am at forty and am not satisfied. No, by Jesu, I am most *dis*-satisfied ! What have I done but use my body ? ' He took off his beautiful hat. ' Here am I in black and white, but naked I am nothing except for procreation, and even that I cannot do between legitimate sheets.'

She looked at him with great seriousness.

' You must marry for Mallory's sake.'

' Whom shall I marry ? '

' Someone most lovely, with a body like Leda's and the charity and sweetness of Psyche, but not the foolish inquisitiveness, the regality of Juno, lovelier than Venus.'

' You exaggerate my worth,' he said. Then he went quickly on : ' I am going to tell you something I never speak of and no one knows save my brother and my man Armstrong. For year upon year now I have loved someone I shall never have. I have not seen her for a very long time — I do not know whether she is alive or dead. She is the daughter of a witch ! '

' A witch ? '

Rosamund's lips parted and she stared at him with wide eyes, looking a wondering half-frightened child.

' A German witch. She lives in Cumberland in North England where the lakes and mountains are. I think she has herself bewitched me. Such things can be, you know, for I have been a man always to take what I want. But I have not taken her. I have scarcely kissed her. Many a time I will be working in the fields or half sleeping by the fire or kissing another woman and I will see her as though she were at my side. Sometimes I am driven North and I see her, but all to no purpose.'

' And she ? '

' She loves me too, but she says that she will marry no man because there is so much evil in her inheritance. It is certain that her mother is a witch. I have seen her fly through the air . . . or have I ? What have I seen ? It is hard to say.'

Rosamund had an absolute belief in witches like anyone else of her time, and the thought that her beloved Nicholas could be so close to a witch's daughter appalled her. She even put her hand on his handsome surcoat and drew him a little closer.

' Perhaps she will do some evil to you.'

He felt her alarm and touched her cheek as he would a younger sister's.

' Never. Never. She is as good as God's Bread. I think that one day she will save me instead of hurt me.'

Rosamund was aware of a new sensation in her veins — jealousy. She had never been jealous of anyone before. She hated this witch's daughter.

' When they throw spells they make you believe them. She feels herself that she is evil. She told you so.'

He put his arm round her waist and drew her close to him. She could feel his heart thump against her breast.

' Rest quiet, little cousin. If you knew her you would see her as I do.'

Rosamund pulled herself away. She was so angry that she could have smacked his face. She wished to get up and run away. She wished to cry. She wished . . . Then she looked at him and loved him so dearly and so truly that she could only suddenly kiss his brown cheek, turn, spring to her feet and walk, with great dignity, she hoped, across the green turf to Sylvia.

THE BURNING

GILBERT ARMSTRONG showed at times a sudden restlessness which Nicholas, by now, because he knew him so well, instantly perceived.

Gilbert loved Mallory and, now that it was a really grand place with two big farms, cattle famous all over the South of England, wonderful orchards and dairies, he had plenty to do as Nicholas' overseer. Nicholas' overseer? He was part of Nicholas. He too was growing to middle-aged girth and rotundity. His brown face was as Nicholas', his voice had the depth but not the chuckle of Nicholas' voice. He looked, beside Nicholas, a short stubby man, but he was, in reality, six foot in height. He was broad of shoulder and back and thigh, and as strong as any man within fifty miles, but Nicholas could still pick him up and hold him in mid-air with one huge hand. He was easy-tempered as a rule but given to sudden flashes of quite furious temper. He liked women and they liked him, but he showed no tendency to marriage. When, with his blue eye and friendly smile, he looked at a woman she was in his arms in no long time. There were three children in the village he was said to be the father of. But these things were incidental. He was Nicholas' man. No one really existed for him but Nicholas. He was like a one-master dog. Anything that Nicholas suggested to him to do he would do, however criminal. By good fortune Nicholas had no very evil suggestions.

Sometimes, when he was lying in his bed early of a morning, with his arms stretched behind his head, he wondered at this subjection. Until he met Nicholas he had been a very independent man, owning no real master and thinking that he would never own one. It was not that he did not see Nicholas clearly—he knew his faults of immaturity and hasty decisions and lechery (only now that was dying in him) and occasional vainglory. These things were small. To Gilbert Armstrong, Nicholas Herries was simply the king of men. He was perhaps what Gilbert, as a small lad, had dreamed of as the perfect, strong, conquering master of men. But it went deeper than this. Gilbert Armstrong belonged to Nicholas Herries as though he were the beat of his heart inside the jerkin, as though he were the rough hair on his chest.

When they were separated Gilbert was incomplete. His actions were at half-vigour. In his movements there was a kind of blindness. And of course this developed with the years. No two human beings can live for so long together in perfect harmony, trust and friendship without becoming part of one another. Nicholas was kindly to everyone, generous-hearted, incautious, trusting, happy-spirited — all the things that Armstrong loved in a man. But Nicholas was often deceived, and sometimes helpless in a bargain and foolish with money so that he needed someone to protect him. And this Gilbert Armstrong, who was in many ways older than Nicholas and wiser, loved to do. Armstrong felt like Nicholas' friend, his brother and his father, never his servant.

Yet, with all this, there came times when Gilbert was restless and longed for the North. Although he liked the life at Mallory, and enjoyed trips to London, yet the South Country was always foreign to him. The South was for him like something a little artificial, but the North was clean and fresh ; no one had done anything to the North. The mountain streams ran as though they were running for the first time. The turf on the Tops was like soil that God had made only that very forenoon ; even the Herdwick sheep were sheep so real that they had never worried to look handsome or clean their fleece. They had no purpose but to be faithful to the ground where they belonged.

Gilbert would wake of a morning at Mallory and see the red bed-hangings and the pewter jug and basin and the view beyond the window of the herb-garden beyond the lawn. It was all as neat and tidy as a doll's garden. He would smell peat and sheep-dung and see the silver break of stream-water over washed stone. He would see a buzzard beating its great

wings over Derwentwater. He would watch its track from
Upper Eskdale to Grasmere — through the gap between Bow-
fell and Crinkle Crags, or from Tilberthwaite to Fell Foot,
then north towards the Langdale Pikes, by Blea Tarn to the
head of Langdale. Then for Grasmere by Stickle Tarn, over
Pavey Ark, descending by Easedale Tarn. He would say these
names, strengthened by hundreds of years of use, aloud, and
suddenly he would spring out of bed and splash his body with
water and, clothed but not in his right mind, walk off he knew
not where. When such a fit came on him Nicholas sent him
up to Keswick.

For Keswick itself Gilbert had a passion. He had always
thought of the little town as a person, a living being in whose
effort to grow and be a power he had a loving interest. He
knew something of its history, a wise old harness-maker, now
dead, having talked to him when he was a boy. Old Kittlecrop
had hunted up little scraps of history about ' Kesewic,' which
meant ' cheese dairy,' and how in 1276 it was granted a right
to hold a weekly market and how angry the men of Cockermouth were. How also he himself had found remains of an
Ancient British village near Crosthwaite Church and how the
Normans had set that church near the same British village.
There were the Druids' Stones, and Roman coins to be found
in Borrowdale, where the village of Grange was so ancient
that old priests of fearful religions still haunted the tumbling
stream. He liked to sit above that stream with young Gilbert
and show him how every civilization in turn had passed over
that rough strong little bridge.

' The heart of all civilization is here — here in Keswick.
This is the centre of the whole world and there is no place
anywhere that is more congregated by ghosts and devils and
the haunting shadows of great men gone.'

Much nonsense, of course, but all the same Gilbert could
never return to that little grey stone town and stand in the
Square (always making one think, in some way, of a foreign
Continental *place*) without feeling that, from the surrounding
dark mountains — Skiddaw purple and Blencathra ebony ;
Keswick, struck by sunlight, glittering against the dark ; and
the rushing crystal-clear streams — strange presences and web-

grey shadow-forms and huge oak-like bead-hung chieftains thickened the air.

But now there was a more practical question. Was Keswick, at last, after being for so many centuries nothing but a small market town, to become a place of great importance ? The potentiality of growth and power had always been there. Its geographical position made it the ideal centre of three main routes : from Penrith, from the South from Kendal through the Dunmail Raise, and from the western lowlands by Bassenthwaite. It had everything needed to make it an important town — fine corn-land, magnificent woodland, river and lake. Of these last, too much, for the annual floods were the infuriation of the farmers and, although Keswick itself was on higher ground, the peril of many a cottager.

The potentialities were there, but, until the coming of the German miners, never the instrument. Now already ' little poor market-town Keswick ' was a mining centre. There were some ten Lake valleys utilized now by the miners. Money had flowed into the town from Augsburg, and the Morlan Leather Fair and other activities like it were known now far beyond the North of England.

On the people of Keswick themselves this had all had a great effect. Germans were as common as Cumbrians. It was no rare thing at all to see grand ladies and gentlemen from London. But strangely enough the town itself scarcely grew at all, and the dalesmen the men and women in the valleys, were but little affected.

In the heart of the little town the whole world — rich and poor, Jew and Gentile, native and foreign — seemed to meet, but the influence was sharp and narrow — very intense on the people of Keswick themselves but dying as soon as it touched the true country. In fact the real Cumbrian spirit that had remained, with strong and steady obstinacy, unchanged through the centuries, in the valleys far away from any outside traffic, could not be contaminated.

But on the Keswick people themselves it may be said that for that century, from 1560 to 1660, great damage was done. Slow-moving, cautious, distrusting all strangers, living an enclosed community, for themselves, this invasion of German blood and German money had bewildered and disturbed them. They were divided violently among themselves. Some said that this mining adventure was a temporary affair, that it would never gain any true grip on the place, that it would disappear as it had come — in the dark of a night.

Others, the more ambitious and enterprising, said that it was only the beginning of the transformation of a small country town into the most important city in the North. They made every kind of prophecy and saw Keswick stretching, a wilderness of grey-green stone, from Grange-in-Borrowdale bridge to Cockermouth, joining up indeed with that town and submerging it. They saw every hill — Skiddaw, Blencathra, Robinson, the Gavel, Glaramara, Scafell, little Catbells even — emptied and scoured like a hen's carcass, and great volumes of smoke rising to heaven, and iron clanging upon iron, and gold falling in a cloud while silver and copper and tin rose in thundering swirl after swirl from the bowels of the earth.

Meanwhile by this spring of 1586 when Gilbert Armstrong paid this visit that was to be the turning-point of his life, there was the very anxious question of the Germans themselves.

When they had first come to Keswick their significance had not been thoroughly realized. They were regarded as foreigners and disliked accordingly. There had been quarrels and fights and even a death or two. It had been found, after a while, that they were quiet and friendly; the Cumbrian is a just man and, after caution, generous. Then it was seen that they brought money and trade; Keswick and its neighbour-hood was wealthy as never before; there were intermarriages; the Germans had a kind of song-making festive sense; it was thought that they were fitting in very well.

But now, after twenty years and more, there were beginning, as Gilbert found, suspicions that the mining affair was not going to succeed after all. The Queen had deserted the enterprise; the Augsburg money was less constant; some of the Germans behaved as though they owned the town; a few of them were riotous; all of them had that insensibility to feelings not their own that marks their race.

Gilbert lodged this time with one Mr. Pottinger and his lady. Pottinger was a little thin bespectacled man, a student of forestry and botany, serious and silent but good-hearted. Pottinger didn't like the Germans, and his wife, a stout garrulous lady, never ceased abusing them. They were coarse heavy monsters who cheated the Cumbrians and were always boasting of their own country. The mixed marriages had not turned out well. True, they had brought some money to the place at first, but now they were in debt here, there and everywhere. She hadn't a good word for them.

On the other hand he encountered some of his old German friends — Hochstetter, Selzenstollen who had married a Cumberland girl, Hans Loner.

They were gloomy and shook their heads. They longed to be back in their own country. They complained, on their side, that they were cheated and that the climate gave them rheumatism.

There was a further element over which old Pottinger shook his skull-like head. It seemed that unruly fellows from the Coast had been attracted to Keswick by stories of the wealth there, foreigners some of them, disbanded soldiers others. They were for ever drinking, thieving and raping.

' Keswick has become godless and turbulent. I fear there will be ill work one of these days.' He added something that made Gilbert start. ' There's much trouble about a German witch-woman. Her name is Hodstetter. They threaten to burn her. They say she kills the cows with her spells, and flies by night on a broomstick.'

He asked Loner about this. Loner said yes : that there were a lot of women in the town who were urging the men on to do away with Frau Hodstetter. They talked of drowning her in the Lake or even of burning her and he thought that action against her might be taken because she was a German.

At first Gilbert was too happy to be back in his beloved country to think deeply of these things. He shot, he fished, he climbed. Often he was alone, sunk in a deep consciousness of happiness, wanting no one, not even Nicholas, and touching, in this separate silence, depths in his soul that gave him a deep

content and a long wide vision of what life really was. For
he was, at heart, a very serious man.

There was one day when, alone in his boat on Derwentwater, he caught from nature, as it seemed to him, a perfect
reassurance about life and its mysteries. The Lake was swept
with a wind so delicate as scarcely to move his boat, but
enough to act as a voice, a whisper of intimate companionship.
It was spring and on the distant woods the green of the larches
was misted like breath on a glass. The hills floated like clouds.
Everything was moving and yet everything was still. As the
sun sank, a light like an expanding flower, as though the whole
world were slowly, with a secret joy, opening to disclose a
fresh beauty never seen before, drew himself and his boat and
the surface of the Lake into itself, and on his cheek he felt a
touch of warmth like an embrace. He stared at the hills now
washed with the palest violet, and saw brilliant stars against
the ashen-rose sky. Then the little breeze of which he had
been so conscious died and then was a silence of pleasure
satisfied and happiness consummated. The stars now rushed
out in multitude above a vanishing world. The oars of his
boat, as he rowed homewards, confirmed the great silence.

On the following day he met Catherine Hodstetter by
Crosthwaite Church. She had grown now into a magnificent
woman of fine carriage, full-breasted and long-limbed. But
he didn't like her. Even as he had his brief talk with her
he wondered why. Was it a deep unreasoned jealousy?
Perhaps.

' I am glad to see you home again, Mr. Armstrong.'

He fancied that she also did not care for him. He detected
a strong reserve in her.

' Mr. Herries said that if I saw you I was to greet you from
him.'

And at that word her colour flamed. He saw joy shoot
through her like the strength of spring. For a moment she
was radiant like a woman unexpectedly freed. ' Poor thing,'
he thought. ' To love so long and so vainly.'

' Tell him—' The radiance died. ' Tell him I am well
and have not forgotten him.'

' I will. Thank you.'

He doffed his hat and rode on. He didn't like her. He hoped that Nicholas would never see her again.

Within two days after this he was so uncomfortable and out of sorts that he had half a mind to ride south again. A multitude of small things contributed to his discomfort. His hostess, Mrs. Pottinger, seemed to be changed from the kindly good-tempered woman she had been. She was obsessed with her dislike of these Germans and especially she tiraded against the ' witch-woman.' She believed apparently a fantastic story that related how Frau Hodstetter tried to turn two small children into frogs : how neighbours had seen the children hopping across the floor, how they had rushed in to rescue them and there had been in the room only a great brindled cat. The cat's foot dripped blood from a cut and next day Frau Hodstetter was seen to be limping.

' At least,' Gilbert said, ' her daughter is a fine woman having nothing to do with this nonsense.'

' Ah, but who knows ? Catherine Hodstetter *seems* well enough, but, after all, does she not live with her mother and must she not therefore see and hear many a forbidden sight and sound ? She's no better if all were known.'

He had an unpleasant little encounter with Joris Fisher. That erstwhile courtier of Catherine Hodstetter stopped him in a narrow place-way of the town and touched him on the arm. Fisher was bent a little in the shoulder and his white wrinkled forehead hung forward like a lifted vizor. He was trembling as he touched Gilbert, whether with ague, fear, rage, Gilbert could not say.

' Tell her to get away — to go south and carry her mother with her.'

' Tell whom ? '

' Ah, you know well enough. Your master has sent you spying. He hasn't the courage to come of himself because he was nigh murdered here one time and can be *quite* murdered the next.'

Gilbert put his two brown hands round Joris Fisher's white thin-skinned neck and with the greatest pleasure he wrung it. He had been wanting these last days some physical expression of his spiritual uneasiness. He shook Mr. Fisher until all his odds-and-ends were in a palsy. Fisher grunted and groaned, then, as Gilbert released his hands, felt cautiously his stomach, his spine-bone and his knees to see that he was still all together. He drew a deep breath, and then quite suddenly smiled, a pale quivering smile.

'You shall shake in your own good time, Mr. Gilbert Armstrong,' he said and hurried away, putting his hand to his neck, straightening his velvet cap and coughing.

On that same evening Gilbert caught two fellows pressing a girl against a wall. They were intending a quick and very forcible rape but instead received a drubbing from Gilbert that caused them to make off limping into the lanes that ran to the Lake. This disturbed him. The old Keswick would never have permitted such easy rogue's violence. It seemed to Gilbert that a bad lot of rogues and vagabonds were in charge of the place. He spoke to Mr. James Mossop, the principal councillor just then, and he was exceedingly indignant.

'Do you tell me, young Gilbert' (for Mossop had known Gilbert since he had been a bare-breeched urchin), 'that we would not apprehend a drunkard for not standing in the Queen's name? Aye, and for much less than that. Have we not the Bridewell-man and the Beadle? Are we not rising a fair town with a goodly commerce and likely to be the first town in the North? Does not our tin penetrate the dark forests of the Indies, and is not our silver finer than the cups and saucers of the Shah in Persia?'

Mr. Mossop had always talked like that, long before he held a high office, so all that Gilbert briefly said was: 'The town is not the sweet place it was. There are too many disorderly fellows abroad in it.' He was not given to vain imaginations, being a plain practical man, but it was to him now as though a spell had been thrown over the place. One witch? Why, there seemed to him witches everywhere. He had never in any place seen so many women with crooked eyes and double chins and black moles on their cheeks and stiff ruffs like threats and yellow crooked fingers. From every window someone seemed to be watching. He would turn a corner and see a cobbled yard with a head spying round the corner of it. There would be a hush in the market square itself, not a soul to be seen, and yet he would swear that a hundred souls were listening. Even the hills, that hung over the little town, seemed too inquisitively alive and the peak in Skiddaw between its two summits was a black finger raised in warning.

He laughed at himself, took a draught to clear himself, busied himself in Pottinger's dried flowers — all to no good. He was a haunted man. And with justice. On the night of April 14th, 1586, the horror of a dreadful crime lit up the darkness and mystery of all these preceding weeks.

As with so many of the events that mark a life, this came with the slightest sound, an almost imperceptible movement. Gilbert was standing in the door of the Pottinger house, taking a last look before going in to bed. There was a moon, very pale — almost green like a melon-rind — but there was light as there often is in the North — unaccountable light — and the hills were as insubstantial as ash heaped before a grey wood-pile when the fire is dead. The fire of the world was dead : no breeze even to stir the ghosts of daffodils that were so pale in this dusk. In the stillness Crosthwaite Church struck the hour. An owl called.

He had turned away from the door when he heard the steps of a man running from Portinskill.

He wondered why the man should run and he stepped forward to the garden wicket. The man stopped. It was Loner. He was elderly and out of breath. He clung to the wooden gate with both his hands.

' Have you — Gilbert — have you a horse ? '

' Yes — in the shed nearby.'

' Take me with you — to Blencathra — they are burning Frau Hodstetter.'

He stood back, his hand on his heart.

Gilbert said not a word. He ran to the shed. Old Pottinger came to the door.

' What is it ? '

Loner moved forward.

'; On Blencathra. They are burning the Hodstetter woman for a witch.'

' Who are ? '

' I don't know. It may be an attack also on my men. Gilbert will take me on his horse.'

Gilbert had found his horse in the shed at the back of the house and at once he was off with Loner behind him, Loner's hands clasped round his body.

They exchanged not a word. They were both silent cautious men. Gilbert's thoughts were wild and confused. He had known for many days that trouble was coming. You could feel it in this strange country where all that happened behind actual event was more surely felt than the event itself.

It was not of itself, to a man of his time accustomed to pain and torture and the brutality of ordinary good men, a dreadful thing that a witch should be burnt. Witches were in league with Satan and so deserved a horrible death. But this was the mother of the woman whom his master loved more than any other woman on earth. He could not himself under- stand that, but Nicholas was everything in the world to him. It was of Nicholas that he was thinking during their short quick ride. Were Nicholas here he would drive into the middle of them, come what may, and in all probability kill a few of them. That was not Gilbert's habit. He would always wait first to see how things were — unless of course Nicholas him- self were there, when he would do exactly what Nicholas himself ordered.

They had arrived now, on the lower flank of the mountain, as far as they could ride. The mountain's thin ridge — the Saddleback — stood sharp and clear against the faint green sky in which the pared moon was struggling against wispy clouds. There was an unbroken silence : not a voice or a sound.

' You are sure ? ' he asked Loner.

The fat pursy German nodded.

' I am certain. Look. There is a light ! ' and above the sparse brushwood immediately in front of them a pale rosy light hung against the sky, rising and falling as though blown by a bellows.

They pushed forward, climbing through the stubble of roots and branches. They came out on to the clearing and stopped at what they saw.

A thick cloud of men and women lay like a black shadow against the side of the hill, and from the middle of the cloud a great gush of smoke and tongues of flame curled and leapt.

Moving forward again they saw that the people and the fire were on a plateau half-way up the hillside. The crowd was as silent and motionless as though it were dead. It was indeed an odd thing and never again to be forgotten : the moon in the still sky and the stillness of the mountain and the stillness of the crowd.

When they came to the crowd's outskirts they found that the men and women were all listening. Someone was speaking. They caught the voice before they saw the man. Gilbert knew it at once. This was Mr. Stephen Horner, a fanatical Protestant clergyman who preached sometimes in the Keswick streets and had a sort of tabernacle of his own in the wilds of Borrowdale.

Gilbert pushed his way, caring not whom he hurt, to the front of the throng. There was a great fire piled high with logs, bushes, tree-trunks. It was leaping and jumping into the air. To the left of the fire was Frau Hodstetter, her head bare, clothed in a long white gown and bound with strong rope. Beside her, also bound, was Catherine Hodstetter in a grey bodice and kirtle, her glorious hair shining in the light of the fire. On either side of them stood men with pikes. Gilbert knew the men — two farm hands, a drunken ruffian called Katts and a Lake boatman. Opposite them, in a kind of frenzy, pointing a shaking arm and screaming, was Mr. Horner with his long peaked face, huge mouth and skeleton body. Grouped behind him were a number of women.

It seemed that there were no Germans there. Joris Fisher standing a little apart, like a white bone in the moonlight, he saw.

But his whole attention was drawn to the two bound women. What could he do ? What *should* he do ? Little for Catherine's mother : but for Catherine herself ? He must save her if he had to call down the mountains to fall on them all to do it.

' . . . And as the Scriptures have ordered us we shall not soil our hands or our mouths or any part of us by touching the Evil Thing and when the Evil Thing is here in our midst we are to destroy it. Mrs. Martha Eager, step forward.'

A stout elderly woman came out of the crowd into the light of the fire.

Horner pointed at Frau Hodstetter.

' Did this woman not come into your house Tuesday a fortnight back ? '

' She did.'

' And did she not bend over the cradle where your child was lying ? '

' She did.'

' And did she not breathe in its face ? '

' She did.'

' And did not the child from that moment sicken ? '

' It did.'

' And by the end of the week it was dead ? '

The woman began to wail and cry and this seemed to rouse the crowd to a frenzy, for the women rushed forward, shaking their fists and shouting : they had to be beaten back by the men, and Gilbert found himself running forward and crying : ' Let her be asked ! Let her give her witness ! '

From this moment it had the nightmare quality of helpless imprisonment inside fear. A number of men, holding pikes and sickles, formed a guard around the two women so that they should not be torn and killed. Neither woman moved nor spoke. Gilbert saw Frau Hodstetter's face set like a carving, but her body swayed a little from left to right and right to left like a pendulum.

But Catherine made no movement at all. It seemed to Gilbert almost as though she were glad. They were the only two now who had not lost control. There had been a good deal of drinking and men and women were dancing round the fire.

Loner had rushed forward and was speaking vehemently, but no one paid attention to him. Horner, now like a lunatic animal, was shouting at the two women, waving his arms and dancing.

The crowd surged forward and Gilbert was, for a moment,

slung to the side so that the razor-edge of the mountain seemed to catch the moon-rind on its tip and the fire tilted in an extravagance of flame towards him.

Just as he righted himself a group of men, looking huge in the fire-glare, drove back the crowd, and two men, one with bare arms, the other with a black beard, seized Frau Hodstetter. At their touch she began to struggle with desperate silence. Her arms were bound, and with a sudden movement they caught her up, holding her like a mummy. For a horrible moment Gilbert saw her face as though it were his own, the staring eyes, the mouth wide open, and what was most terrible, tears staining her cheeks. Her body heaved upwards in the men's arms. She was straining against her ropes. Still she uttered no sound, but for a moment she seemed in the exaggerated painting of the flames to stand up on the men's shoulders.

Then, with a backward pull of their arms, they tossed her. She fell into the heart of the fire. There was a drawing of breath in the crowd and then a complete stillness.

They saw her rise, her arms stretched out, the flames licking her body. She threw back her head as though to escape them and gave out one dreadful, fearful, inhuman scream of agony. Then she crashed down into the fire.

The crowd stared as though it saw its own reflection in the fire. The flames had now complete mastery and were roaring to heaven. Where the woman had fallen was a lambent jewelled heart of fire.

Some were creeping away and turning down the hill : a consciousness of horror as though some dreadful spirit were looking at them all out of the fire had seized them. But not all. Some drunken women rushed at Catherine Hodstetter and began to beat her with their fists, and the heavy fellow with the black beard cried out : ' Daughter like mother. She must burn. . . . They must all burn — burn ! burn ! burn ! ' The women pulled at her and she nearly fell down, and Horner — who seemed to be seized with a kind of convulsive mania — screeched in a broken treble :

' They shall all perish, saith the Lord ! Root and branch ! Root and branch ! '

The crowd, afraid of what they had already done, seized on this as a respite from their own fear of themselves.

' Burn her ! Burn her ! We will be rid of them all ! Find the witches ! Hunt the witches ! '

The persecution hysteria was rising from the ground like a plague-mist and it was lucky enough for one or two old women there, who, in order to save themselves, had been crying their loudest, that events suddenly swung in another direction.

For Gilbert had fallen on the women who were dragging at Catherine, cleared a space round him and then turned on the mob.

' Have you not enough ? You know you will pay for what you have done as it is ! Go to your homes. What ill has this woman ever done ? You have known her for many years and myself too. Let her alone lest you regret your life long — and the justices have something to say, as they will.'

He was interrupted by Joris Fisher, who ran up to him and cried : ' Aye, we know you, Gilbert Armstrong, and why you do what you do. For you are keeping her for your own master, who has been here many a time sniffing after her like a dog. . . .'

And the others, scarcely having heard a syllable of it but longing to do some foul hurt to someone (although to-morrow they would be decent kindly citizens), cried out that it was true (but what was true they hadn't any idea) and what had Gilbert Armstrong to do with it and the girl must burn because she was the daughter of her mother.

Mr. Horner raised his arms as though he were invoking the Deity, and cried out : ' What have you to do with her, Gilbert Armstrong ? Prove your right.'

Gilbert moved to her, drew her close to him with his arm, and, driven by a desire to serve his master, and by a raging hatred against the lot of them, but mostly by something incoherent that came from that dreadful scream in the fire and his own loathing that his dear country should be so foully shamed, cried, as though he were announcing it to the whole of England : ' She is affianced to me. Catherine Hodstetter is to be my wife. She is mine and I am hers. Burn her and you must burn me — me, Gilbert Armstrong, who have lived among you and am friend to you all. Destroy her and you must destroy me too, and I will fight dearly for my safety.'

There was a pause. Someone laughed. Two or three more. Then another and another. A shout rose, a roar. This was farce. This was what they wanted to heal their sense of sin. The fire now was foul to them. They wanted to run from it and from the ghost inside it. They wanted to run, pell-mell, down the mountainside, and away, away to safety, to the hour before the burning when they had still been innocent. They knew Gilbert Armstrong and thought well of him. He was affianced to the girl. He should marry her. He should marry her now, this very night.

They cried out : ' A marriage ! A wedding ! Crosthwaite. It shall be in the church, the Crosthwaite church.'

They rushed down the hillside carrying Catherine and Gilbert with them. At the turn where the path began there were three horses tethered. They piled Catherine and Gilbert on to one of them. She was now unbound and sat behind him. They had caught brands burning from the fire : they were singing, shouting, triumphing, for they were running for their safety away from that awful witch who, now that her body was burned, was sitting in her white gown, astride of the fire, shaking her arms at them — and soon she would be up and after them.

But now they would be safe, for there would be a wedding at Crosthwaite and the church would protect them.

They ran, singing, singing, waving their flaming brands, shrieking drunkenly, beside the bridal pair. Gilbert spoke once only.

' I had to do it — to save you.'

She made no answer. She stared with her eyes wide-open as in a sleep-walking. She was seeing perhaps — and would always see — her mother burning.

They arrived at the lych-gate and tumbled, some falling over the graves and shrieking with laughter, to the church door.

It was locked. This was no time for ceremony so they broke it down. They rushed up the aisle with torches and crowded round the altar steps and shouted for Mr. Horner.

They sang, they laughed, they shrieked like devils, and in

the middle of the uproar Mr. Horner quickly married Gilbert and Catherine. He did not hear whether Catherine spoke : once she bowed her head. Although no banns had been called they were married well enough.

Early on the following morning he rode with her south-wards.

NICHOLAS ENCOUNTERS THE DEVIL
AND DEFEATS HIM

At Mallory Nicholas was sitting in his workroom doing his accounts.

It was a fine April evening, so warm that the window in front of him was half open. He sat there, his body sprawled over the table, singing to himself a trifle out of tune, scratching his head with the end of his pen and smelling, with subconscious delight, the scents from the garden, and hearing, as though in rhythm with his song, the pleasant splashing of the fountain.

He was making some kind of an inventory of his cattle :

Six keen : Lucy, black with a white star in the forehead.
Red with a white back.
One other red with a chinned face.
One white with a brown face.
Black ambling mare with a white star in the forehead.
Five hog of one sort being about two years old at Michaelmas last. . . .
Twelve ewes, twelve lambs. . . .

And then :

To be bought :
One pillow coat.   Two best brass pots.
One quilt.   A good knyfe.

He scratched his head some more, then pushed the papers aside and began a letter. He made a serious face at this and ceased his singing. He wrote slowly with a good deal of looking out of window, up to the ceiling and across to the fireplace where three dogs were lying.

My dearest Rosamund — There is nothing so strong as the force of love, and to prove it here I am that have all my accounts to do and pots and pans to order. Moreover the evening is as fair as this year has known and, as you are well aware by now, I would always rather be outside a house than in it — so the dogs also, for their eyes are melting out of their heads, beseeching me to give them a little hunting before the sun is gone.

But, dearest cousin, you are, ere this, my good sister and better friend and all the day I have been stopping at my better purposes and looking up to heaven and asking how you fare at Chartley and your impression of the Queen (if one may so call her) and how you are in your personal comfort.

It hits even so thick a head as mine that any letter that enters Chartley may be read by whosoever pleases and so you will have no politics from me — only a most cordial greeting to Philip and his lady my cousin, and the first of these will, I am assured, rejoice to know that I am in grand health of body and mind and my spiritual state progresses.

I am alone, for brother Robin is, I believe, in London and Gilbert is in Cumberland whither I despatched him because his soul was there already and I thought his body might most expediently follow it.

The news here is slight enough. Our dairymaid has a child by the Lord knows whom and the new steward is mighty learned and reads Ovid for his delectation of an evening when he might be kissing the pantry-girl. Last Sunday I went to church and was given two pots of marmalade of quince by the old woman who pulls the church bell of a week-day. I have purchased five new keen and a bull. Marjorie, the bitch you fondled, has six pups and you shall have one — although I suppose they are not welcome at Chartley.

But this is to beg of you your news. Show your letter to Philip before you send it but nevertheless and in spite of it tell me all that I wish to know. Is the Queen a proper Queen? Does she talk openly before her women? What women has she? Remember me, if you will and it is fitting, to my dear Sir Amyas Paulet who, visiting my father, once gave me a clout on the head for an uncivil noise I made. Do they keep you strict prisoners or may you ride? What do you of an evening? What room have you for sleeping and are you alone there? All this, and many things more I charge you to tell to — Your loving cousin

NICHOLAS HERRIES.

Pray, do not forget a special greeting from me to Philip.

He grinned as he finished this and dusted it. He grinned as he fastened it.

Then he sighed. The evening was of an exquisite beauty, and now, he did not know how it was, but beauty in nature gave him a sort of melancholy, a sense of loneliness and mal-adjustment. So lovely was nature and here he was, a solitary man in a solitary house, forty-two years of age and with neither wife nor children. Well enough he knew why. Leaning forward on his elbows he stared forward into the garden. Everything was romantic-sentimental for the occasion. Pale gold washed the lawns and hedges : the last low fingers of the sun caressed the marble pyramid-fountain with the carved birds from whose bills the water cascaded in a flood of crystal. From the narrow beds in purple shadow came the scents of thyme and marjoram. From the pantry-room the pantry-boy (who was a nice lad with a sweet treble) was singing :

> ' Lavender is for lovers true,
> Which evermore be fain,
> Desiring always for to have
> Some pleasure for their pain ;
> And when that they obtainèd have
>   The love that they require,
> Then have they all their perfect joy,
>   And quenchèd is the fire.

He thought to stop the boy. He got up to stride about the room, and the three dogs, with manifestations of delirious joy, as though they had been in prison for months and had not tasted sun or air in a lifetime (although but an hour ago they had been out with him), rose and rushed to the door and stood staring at the panelling and turning their heads to him and staring at the door again.

He opened the door and they all rushed ahead of him.

He walked up and down the pleated lawn while bird called to bird in question and answer and the boy's voice more faintly came to him :

> ' And when that they obtainèd have
>   The love that they require,
> Then have they all their perfect joy,
>   And quenchèd is the fire.'

L

Ah ! but he had never obtained it ! He had never obtained it ! That was why the fire was not quenched — no, rather, although the years passed and distance from the original meeting grew wider and wider, that fire burnt only the fiercer !

If he had had all that he wanted would it have died down ? Maybe not. It might be that it was for him, that of all human experiences the rarest, a love so deep that the very recesses of the spirit are filled. For him of all men ! Good-natured, light, let come, let go ! That to him should come this experience ! If only he could see her now ! If only he could be where Gilbert now was !

He knew that someone was behind him. He saw the dogs running. It was Robin. As always with him what he felt he showed to the fullest of his capacity. He was overjoyed.

' Robin ! Robin ! . . . Oh, Robin ! What good fortune ! I have been wanting you many a day ! '

He caught him in his great arms, kissed him on both cheeks, then held him away from him to look at him and felt at once again, as now he always did, the separation, the barrier. Robin was in riding-dress. He held a riding-whip.

Nicholas, still grinning with pleasure, let him go.

' Ah, Robin, but I'm glad ! Gilbert Armstrong is in Cumberland. I've been alone here these three weeks. I was growing melancholic. I will into the house and tell them about a meal and to prepare a room——'

Robin put out a hand.

' No, Nick. . . . I mustn't stay.'

Nicholas' face fell.

' You cannot stay ? Oh, but you must ! It's a month since I've seen you. You've neglected me shamefully.'

He saw that a deep excitement was holding his brother.

' No, no. Be patient with me. I must ride back to London at once. But I had to tell you.'

' To tell me ? To tell me what ? '

' They have asked me to go to Chartley.'

' To Chartley ? ' Nicholas stared.

' Yes.' Robin took his arm. ' Walk up this path with me I have had a letter from Paulet asking whether I would care to carry out some service for him at Chartley——'

' Chartley ! . . . You ! '

' Yes. . . . The Queen ! At last ! At last ! Oh, Nick, the Queen ! The thing that I have been waiting for all my life long ! My life's desire ! To be with her. To serve her ! At last. . . .'

He could scarcely speak for his agitation. Tears were in his eyes. Nicholas felt how all his body trembled. But Nicholas turned and held his brother in a fierce grip.

' Robin ! You know why ? You know who has arranged this ? '

' Paulet. Paulet sent for me ! '

' Paulet ! You cheat yourself. You are lying both to yourself and me. 'Tis Irvine who has arranged this and you know it. I've heard already that Irvine has Paulet's ear. Someone was needed and Irvine suggested you. . . .' He stared into Robin's eyes, speaking sternly. ' Is it the Queen you wish to see, brother — or Sylvia ? '

Robin said hotly : ' I will not discuss that with you. I have told you that all my life long I have wished——'

Nicholas' temper was also up.

' Aye, I know. All your life long. But for the last ten years it has been someone else — the wife of our bitterest enemy.'

Robin wheeled round.

' Very well then. I am off. I have known a long time that I have no brother any more.'

Nicholas caught him round the neck.

' Fool ! Fool ! What a fool you are, Robin ! Do you think that a love like ours that comes from our mother's womb can ever break, and do you think that I am a man, alone in the world as I am, to let you go ? And what do I care if you love my cousin or if you love a thousand for that matter and go to hell for it so long as you are happy there ? I would fight for you and pimp for you and beg for you — although by my nature I am no beggar — and lie for you and die for you, but for your good, Robin, for your happiness, not for your ruin. Do you suppose that Irvine has not been waiting for just this ? And long he has waited. He has tried me with bolder means — with cards in London, with his servants' insults at a tavern, with five ragamuffins in Cumberland — but with yourself and his wife whom he also hates there must be something prettier than cards or assassination. And here he has it to perfection. Here he will have you both shut up together in one house — nay, in one prison. You will be under his orders and at the service of his spies. He will turn his wife into your arms and will devise some scandalous revenge that will torture not only you but her as well. . . . Ah, do not go, Robin ! Robin, Robin, for Jesu's sake do not go ! '

Robin laid his hand on Nicholas' shoulder.

' Forgive me ! I knew that you would say this — all of it, every word. It may be that you are right. It looks likely. But I am not to be stayed. And truly it is not Sylvia. As it is we have been seeing one another often enough. . . . It is the Queen. Indeed, indeed it is the Queen. I have longed, I have prayed for this chance to come. I had given up all hope. . . . Now nothing, no one, could stop me.'

He embraced Nicholas, smiled into his eyes, turned and almost ran down the path. A moment later Nicholas heard the click of the horse's hooves on the cobbles of the yard.

Nicholas stood there long after the sound of the hooves had died away. Robin's visit had been so sudden and so short that it had risen like an apparition — a shadow seen in transparency against the gold-green of the evening and the crystal light of the fountain-shower. No, it had been real enough. He still felt the trembling of his brother's body under his hand, and in the consciousness of that trembling was aware too of the actuality of the danger.

He took some steps towards the house and said aloud : ' He must not . . . it is ruin ' — then stayed because he knew that he could do nothing to prevent it. It seemed to him at that moment in the dusky garden when the hedge-topiary — the ship and the peacock and the wigged nobleman — stood out like ebony against the faint yellow streak in the darkening sky, that he had never in all his life loved his brother so dearly as now.

' It has all led to this. . . . From the very beginning it

was to come to this.' From that moment when, on the moor, he had pricked Irvine's arm with his sword — and the great reason of all for his love of Robin came welling up in him, his sense of Robin's weakness, his rarity of spirit that made him so easily a prey to men like Irvine, his need for someone like Nicholas, robust, forthright, fearless, to protect him. . . .

' By God, I will go after him. . . . I must be near him. . . . I'll stop that devil. . . .'

By a coincidence, in the village of Wayning, five miles from Chartley, there was an inn, ' The Hawbuck,' where he had stayed twice, breaking journeys. He remembered the place because the landlord had two pretty daughters, twins, one dark and one fair, and he had come, in a very quick time, to know the dark one considerably well.

' When Robin goes to Chartley we'll go to Wayning and see how the land lies. And I know Sir Amyas, old cross-grained faggot. It will be hard but I can watch over Robin a little.'

Remembering Wayning cheered him considerably, and there was the realization too that he would then be seeing young Rosamund, whom (although he was not in the slightest in love with her) he now delighted in for her wisdom, humour, courage and honesty. ' And I hope a good man will love her one day, but with that nose and that complexion . . .'

He was very much more cheerful now that he had decided on action ; he was unhappy only when he was undecided or had nothing to do. So he strode into the buttery asking for his dinner, which should have been at five and it was long past the hour and Mr. Minniples, the educated Ovidean domo, rebuked him in his high melancholy voice ' for it had been ready this half hour but Mr. Nicholas was with his brother,' and Nicholas longed, as so often he did, to kick Minniples' virtuous unshapely buttocks, and instead only made faces at him like a boy and ordered the food to be set before him and then sat on the dais with a book of merry tales propped up in front of him and started on the broth with the hunger of a man a week starving.

In the middle of his meal he stretched his arms, yawning. He was weary. It was those accounts that always fatigued him ; he would read a merry tale or two more, take a walk round the farms and see how the new calf was faring and then to bed so that he might be out freshly in the morning. For the events of this fine day were done.

They were not. The door at the hall-end was open for the food to be brought. Minniples' foolish face appeared in it and, before he could speak, Gilbert Armstrong stood beside him. Nicholas, for the second time that evening, was extravagantly happy. He jumped to his feet, knocking the book of tales to the floor.

' Gilbert ! Gilbert ! . . . Welcome ! Only now I was wondering——! '

He stopped. The two men stared at one another across the hall. For someone was standing behind Gilbert and that someone was Catherine Hodstetter.

Nicholas said not a word. The colour flooded his brown cheeks. Gilbert Armstrong came up the hall, leading Catherine Hodstetter by the hand. She was wearing a hood and a dark riding-cloak. She looked at Nicholas gravely, without any emotion at all. She did not smile or frown, nor did she turn her head.

Gilbert stood by the dais and said at once :

' Mr. Herries, we are married. This is my wife.'

Nicholas leaned on his hands as they gripped the table and stared at the other man.

' What did you say ? '

' We are married.'

' When ? '

' Five days ago.'

' Where ? '

' Crosthwaite Church.'

A long pause followed.

Nicholas said : ' Take her to a room where she can change after the journey. Then return here.'

Gilbert turned on his heel, nodded to Catherine, walked forward, she following. They were gone.

Minniples appeared followed by two men bearing food and dishes. When they reached the dais they began to place the dishes, but Nicholas with a wide sweep of the hand crashed everything to the floor and roared like one of his own bulls. The men hastened to disappear. Minniples bravely stayed there.

' Would you wish——? '

Nicholas in a voice quiet but trembling : ' I will whip you into very small pieces—— '

Minniples, who was always dignified, bowed and marched away.

Nicholas never moved, but still leant his whole weight on the oak table. The gravy of the game pie was streaming down the steps of the dais. Gilbert and Catherine married ? Gilbert had married Catherine and had dared to return ? Catherine, who had refused him time and again ; Catherine, who had told him that she was for no man ; Catherine on the sly had married his servant ! And, after it was done, they had *both* dared to return.

His anger was rising from his belly in a hot surging flood. He could feel it welling in him, through his veins, flooding his heart, choking his lungs, his throat. He put his hand to his neck and tore the top button off his shirt. He lifted his chest that he might breathe better. Behind his anger was an agony which he could feel as one recognizes a pain that will soon be a torment but is not yet acute.

He heard steps and saw that Gilbert Armstrong had returned. He mounted the dais so that they stood close together.

Nicholas turned and looked into his face.

' You were my friend, were you not ? '

' I was and I am.'

' You have married her rightfully and in church ? '

' I do not know about rightfully, but most certainly in church.'

In spite of his anger and although his eyes were misted, Nicholas recognized that look of determined stubborn obstinacy with which Gilbert Armstrong always met every crisis.

' Take care. You are stepping on a dish.'

Gilbert moved a little aside.

' You say you are still my friend ? '

' I most assuredly am.'

' And my faithful servant ? '

' I most assuredly am.'

' And you betray me in the deadliest way of betrayal ? '

' I have not betrayed you.'

' You knew how for years there has been only—' To his own chagrin his voice failed.

' I have known very well.'

' Secretly you yourself loved her and when I was not there you persuaded her——'

' I do not love her.'

' You lie.'

' I do not lie. I never lie to a friend.'

' She loves you ? She is passionate for you ? She persuaded you——'

' She did not persuade me.'

' You have lain together maybe for years, cheating me, deceiving me, my friend whom I trusted more than any man on this earth.'

' We have never lain together — and will not.'

There was a noise like a drum in Nicholas' ears. He did not hear Gilbert's answers. Like any man in a great rage he was preoccupied with catching his own anger.

' Do you know what you are ? '

' I know well what I am.'

' You are a liar, a cheat ; your soul is bawd to your body. You will spoil the best things for your own glory. You are unchaste with your tongue and with every other part of your person. You are false and unfaithful.' Nicholas sought Gilbert's face with a puzzled bewildered stare. ' And yet never did I believe in any man as I did in you. I loved you more than any being on this earth save my brother and — and — this woman.

' You have betrayed my honour in its tenderest part.' Now his rage altogether overbore him. ' And you have the loutish impertinence to return to this very house. . . . But by God's grace,' he shouted, ' this very night you shall walk out of it again — the pair of you.'

He raised his hand and struck Gilbert across the face.

The man never moved. A little trickle of blood began to stain his lower lip.

' I would have taken that from no other man in the whole world,' he said at last. And still he did not move or seek to wipe the blood from his chin.

Nicholas stared at him pitifully, then dropped down into the chair behind him.

' Oh, Gilbert, Gilbert — why did you do this thing ? '

Armstrong, who had still on his face the same look of stubborn obstinacy, said : ' And now you had better hear the story.'

Nicholas said nothing. Gilbert told him everything : of his standing at the gate and Loner calling him and their riding to Blencathra, of the crowd and the fire and the parson, of the two women bound, of the elder Hodstetter's dreadful death, of the danger to Catherine and his saving her, of the ride to Crosthwaite and their marriage, of their coming south.

' I do not love her nor does she love me,' he ended. ' It was the only thing to be done.'

Nicholas' head was bowed in his hands. This was horrible — the deed itself. His own action. The two seemed to be linked as one.

He looked up at last, felt for his handkerchief and proffered it to Gilbert.

' I am sorry.'

Gilbert wiped his lip and chin, laid the handkerchief on the table. His face was yet hard and obstinate.

' You misjudged me. After many years.'

Nicholas got up and laid his hands on Gilbert's shoulders. ' You should know ere now that I never reason when I am angry.' His voice dropped. ' I was not angry so much as unhappy. I never even heard what you said. There was a singing in my ears.'

' You mistrusted me,' Gilbert said again.

Nicholas shook him, pressed him for a moment to his breast. Then, with his favourite gesture to those he loved, holding him off from him and looking into his face, he said :

' Once again I am in your debt. You know well by now that I am quickly fired and quickly laid down again. You are a nobler man in every quality. You have proved it over and over and will yet a thousand times. You must forgive and forgive.'

He looked him full in the eyes. ' I have never struck you before and now I swear, by Jesu's blood and the agony on the Holy Cross, that I will never again, do what you will.'

He turned away and sat down again.

' You have done most nobly, but we are in a pickle of a mess, Gilbert — not now only but for long to come. The Lord knows how I love her and only her ! '

Gilbert said stiffly : ' If I lost the notion of you that I have I would lose my faith with it.'

Nicholas looked up.

' You shall not lose it.'

The two men clasped hands and Gilbert went away.

Later that night Nicholas, pacing his room in his furred bed-gown, had conversation with the Devil.

In Nicholas' time and day the Devil was Somebody, not an abstract principle in which no living man any longer believed. Nicholas, who was simple-minded, considered that in very fact the Devil walked among men. Not in horns and tail as the Miracle Plays had it. The Devil was too clever for that. But in the likeness of a very handsome gentleman with black hair and an olive-brown face — like any sly Spaniard — or even Philip Irvine himself.

But to-night here in front of the wall-paintings in rose and violet — the story of Cupid and Psyche painted for Nicholas by a clever young London man — there crept at his side a bent crook-backed little man, washing his hands and bowing. He was clothed in the long velvet sleeves and porringer hat of an older time and was in fact (although Nicholas was not aware of it) the exact replica of a portrait of Louis XI of France that Nicholas had seen in his childhood and been frightened by.

The little Devil, with his mouth smiling, his bent shoulders suppliant, his long hands rubbing together like flies' legs, his velvet sleeves swinging, said in his voice soft and honeyed :

' You know that she has a room to herself ? '

' Yes, I know it.'

' That she is in bed by now ? '

' Maybe.'

' But not asleep ? '

' I cannot tell.'

' Oh no ! Not asleep, I assure you.'

' Well ? '

' You may go and wake her.'

' I will not.'

' Ah, why not ? Poor thing ! She is distracted, wretched in heart. She will not repulse you this time.'

' Why should she not ? '

' Her mother's horrible death which she witnessed has wrought in her a shock that has altered her. You saw yourself how she was altered. She is laid low, humiliated. If you are good to her she will give you what you will.'

' I cannot take advantage of her helplessness.'

' But at some time or another you must do so. Remember that Gilbert and she are to live with you now for ever. Every day, every hour of every day you will be with her — or could be if you so wished. She loves you. You love her. How can you stay apart ? It is more than poor human flesh can ever endure.'

' He is my great friend.'

' Yes, but he does not love her nor does she love him. He did this only to please you. He will serve you in any way.'

A long silence. Then the Devil said :

' She is very beautiful.

' She has come now to her full maturity.

' She lies there in her bed hoping that you will come to her.

' Having her at last in your arms you will satisfy the ache of many years.

' Her body has always been intended for yours. You belong to one another.

' You have not been so very chaste all these years that you should be a Puritan now.

' If you do not go to her to-night, some time you will go. It is quite certain.

' Your mind is already with her. You have pictured waking

her, climbing the bed, taking her hair in your hands, drawing her head toward yours . . .'

Nicholas' hand was on the handle of his door.

He saw Gilbert's mouth when he had struck him. He took the Devil in his arms and flung him into the stone fireplace, where he became instantly a scrap of feathery dust.

Then he threw off his gown, climbed into bed and at once slept like the seven men of Ephesus.

CHARTLEY : THE QUEEN ENSLAVES HIM

ROBIN was now but ten miles from Chartley, and his heart was beating so thickly that the close heavy summer world was dim before his eyes. He knew this part of England, for he had stayed here on two occasions with the Giffords. Gilbert Gifford, whose father's property adjoined the Chartley property (Chartley Manor belonged to the Earl of Essex), was a sort of friend of Robin's — no close one because Robin did not trust him, but Gilbert was one of the more intelligent Catholics, beautiful to look upon, with the face of an angelic boy.

Robin did not trust him and scarcely knew why, but as soon as he heard that the Scottish Queen had been moved from Tutbury to Chartley he thought of Gilbert Gifford. John Gifford, the father, was a devout Catholic beyond all suspicion, but young Gilbert was known to Walsingham, had already a great reputation for falsehood with women, and had told Robin himself a lie or two.

Worst of all, Gilbert Gifford was a friend of Philip Irvine's. Young Gifford was as vain as a peacock of his beauty and, although an ardent pursuer of women, had something of a reputation on the other side.

Then, only a week or two ago, some gentleman in a tavern had told Robin a story that Walsingham was out to trick Queen Mary into a betrayal of herself, that the Queen was in touch with Morgan in Paris and that Walsingham was 'tapping' all her letters, that some young men (he named Anthony Babington, a foolish braggart called Ballard, and one or two more) were plotting Elizabeth's murder and that Walsingham knew all about this also. According to this gentleman traps were laid now for Mary at Chartley, and into these traps she was incontinently falling. Everyone knew Walsingham's cunning. These foolish Catholic boys were silly mice to his trap — but the real victim would be the Scottish Queen.

It was one of those heavy August afternoons when thunder lies packed on the hill. He had ridden a distance that day and his horse was very weary. The foliage was of summer fullness and was almost black against the white sky. The cows lay panting under the tree shelter, for although you could not see the sun its heat was like red-hot bars against the forehead.

As Robin rode, his servant with his luggage on another horse behind him, his thoughts were of nothing but the Queen of Scots. At last the desire of all his life was to be granted : he remembered how, as a boy, he had heard his father speak of her wickedness because she had married her husband's murderer, and how at once he had been ' up ' in her defence. She had *not* murdered her husband, and in any case Darnley was a wretched creature and had himself murdered her friend and servant.

Nothing that she could do was wrong for Robin, and he saw her shining with a brilliant beauty, his Bright Pavilions around her : he lived so often in visions that he must have some woman as part of them. His passion for Sylvia even had driven him only to a greater love of the Queen in its very contrast. The Queen was unrealizable as a human creature ; here was his earthly love and here his heavenly. For Sylvia and the Queen. One had no happiness in it and must end in ruin ; the other was a selfless service and had, in that way, no end. One was sensual like a padlock on his wrist ; the other set him free whenever he thought of it.

He neither knew nor cared whether this was Irvine's plan to catch him. It would be a relief perhaps if he *were* caught. Irvine had watched them, teased them, hated them for so long. Whatever came of it he would be now with the Queen.

In spite of his physical weariness he was conscious of an almost mystical exaltation. The trouble with his life until now had been that he had been able to bring nothing to consummation : not his intelligence, because he had done nothing at all with it ; not his love, because he had only disappointed Nicholas and ruined Sylvia ; not his religion, because he had believed in God but not followed Him. He had betrayed

everything and everyone, and yet he had only love in his heart
— love of God, love of mankind, love of beauty, love of his
country.

He had too much love. He was soft. He was indecisive,
moving first that way and then this. After witnessing Campion's
death he had thought that everything was clear for him, as it
had been from that moment for Henry Walpole who had stood
beside him. But it had not been clear. His weakness had
dragged him back to Sylvia. He was wretched when he was
away from her, miserable when he was with her. He had
degenerated. He was almost lost. But now perhaps he could
serve this unhappy, deserted, betrayed Queen and so recover
some of his true self again. He would not serve her against
his own Queen, but short of that, would lose his life for her.
It seemed to him now, as he rode along, a small thing to lose
his physical life. His Bright Pavilions would not be less bright
for that. He was in a sort of dream, or hallucination of life.
He straightened his back and saw on the low hills the clouds
clamped down in purple blackness. There was steel rigidity
in the air. The leaves hung from the trees like metal.

Against the hill and the sky Chartley Manor stood out in
pale saffron relief. Even as he looked there was a faint rumble
of thunder. Chartley looked pleasant enough and dead.
Water ran all round it and there was a drawbridge. A flag,
quite motionless, stayed painted on the sky above the tower.
He saw three swans come sailing majestically round the bend
of the moat. They were as haughty as queens.

He rode over the moat with a clatter and rang the heavy
bell. It echoed and someone looked out of a window. A
soldier presented himself. Robin gave his name and said Sir
Amyas Paulet was expecting him. The soldier disappeared,
but soon returned with another and asked Robin to follow
him. Inside the hall an officer of rank met him and said that
he would take him straight to Sir Amyas.

In a room with buff leather walls and leather furniture and
two green birds in a cage by the window, Sir Amyas was
seated at a table writing. He looked at Robin gravely. He
was in appearance the perfect regimented official. His eyes
were cold but his face not unkindly.

' Ah . . . Mr. Herries. This is Irvine's business.'

He said to the officer, who was leaving the room :

' Kindly ask them to send Mr. Irvine here. Tell him his friend, Mr. Herries, is arrived. . . . Sit down, Mr. Herries.'

Robin did so.

' This matter has been less pressing than it seemed when I wrote to you in April, but now Mr. Irvine would welcome your assistance. His particular business is the safeguarding of this place at night. He wished for someone he could trust. He suggested yourself : cousin, I believe, to his wife, who is with the Queen's ladies. We give her rights and titles, by the way, while she is under our charge — a small affair, a small affair. Whom he may trust — Yes, a hard matter. Trust ! Trust ! A changeful word ! . . . You will be at his bidding. You are old friends.'

He looked across the table at Robin with a worried, almost appealing expression. Robin smiled.

' You are very young,' Paulet said.

' Thirty-seven.'

' You appear younger. This is, I need not tell you, a place of desperate responsibility. You are expected, if you hear anything or see anything to the detriment of Her Sacred Majesty Queen Elizabeth, to acquaint me immediately with it.'

(' A spy ! ' Robin thought. ' That is what I am here for — a spy ! ')

' You are to be betrayed into no sympathy whether for or against the lady in question. You are here performing a duty for Her Sacred Majesty.'

' I understand,' Robin said. Then, after a pause, he added, ' My brother wished that he should be remembered to you.'

An unexpected, thin, and rather pathetic little smile broke on Paulet's face. With it his eyes were less cold.

' Ah ! The giant ! . . . How does he grow ? '

' He is as large a size as ever,' Robin answered, laughing.

The door opened and Irvine came in. He went to Robin with hands outstretched. He kissed him lightly on either cheek.

' Welcome, dear Robin. . . . Welcome indeed.'

' I have told him that he is at your charge.'

' Indeed, yes. He will lighten every burden I have.'

He put his arm through Robin's and drew him towards the door. But Robin intercepted in the heavy gold mirror opposite the door a sharp comprehending look between the two men, and he heard Paulet say, ' The Honest Man will be needed no more.'

Irvine made no answer, but took Robin with him into the passage. Outside Robin said : ' The Honest Man — who is that ? ' He spoke rather to rid himself of that first awkwardness that he always felt with Irvine than from any curiosity.

Irvine laughed.

' You have sharp ears, cousin. But I have known that a long time. You must be weary and in this thunder weather very thirsty. Do you drink ale ? '

' But of course.'

Philip laughed. ' We have a very special kind of ale here and a very special kind of brewer.'

Robin stared. ' I don't understand.'

' No. Why should you ? '

Philip, his lean body drawn up to a height as though he were standing on his toes, looked deep into Robin's eyes. They stood close together there in the passage.

' I wonder how much you *do* understand. . . . You must have heard something in London.'

' I heard——'

Philip stopped him, his finger on his lips. ' Not here. These walls are all ears. Another time. At least though I can ask you — Do you know young Anthony Babington ? '

' A slight acquaintance.'

' John Charnock ? Edward Windsor ? Edward Abingdon ? One John Savage ? '

' Yes. Charnock and Abingdon slightly. Why ? '

' You will soon hear. Close your mouth. Open your eyes and ears. I sent for you——'

' Yes,' Robin said sharply. ' Why did you send for me ? '

' Because I wanted someone I could trust.'

' And you can trust me ? '

' In this — yes.'

' One thing remember — I will betray neither my own Queen nor this poor lady here.'

'You are asked to betray no one. Only, if either the Queen or her charge is in danger you are to tell me of it. There is peril here to both.'

Irvine had conducted this dialogue with the cold self-satisfied arrogance that Robin detested. Now at an instant he was genial again.

'They shall bring food and drink to your room. Change your clothes and presently the Queen will send for you.'

An hour later he was sent for. He had dressed himself in his best suit of purple and silver, which set him off very handsomely. He had still very much of the look of the boy about him in spite of his years ; his eyes were a boy's and his sensitive mouth asked for affection and trust as a boy might do before his maturer disillusionment. His figure was now at its most excellent, broad at the shoulder, slim at the hips, and his legs so straight and shapely that even in a Court of handsome men they had been much remarked upon. But it was finally the modesty of his approach that won women, a modesty that had in it dignity and quiet and kindliness. What he had not was humour. He could not be light either about his own or the world's destiny.

Now he stood at the end of a long room, saw a cluster of ladies at the far end and certain gentlemen standing. It was a pleasant room with large glass bowls filled with roses, long gilt mirrors, screens of velvet and a spinet ; upon this last as he came in someone was playing. The player stopped abruptly as Philip Irvine led him forward. He saw for an instant Rosamund's smiling face and, not far from her, Sylvia. There were some eight women in all. Then he dropped on his knee before a lady in black whose auburn hair was covered with a black raised cap.

He heard Irvine say : 'This is Mr. Robin Herries, Madame. He has come to do you service.'

He saw a hand, half covered with a black mitten, stretched towards him and he heard a quiet and gentle but very dignified voice say : 'I have heard of Mr. Herries. And good reports too. It is kind of you to join us, Mr. Herries, for we are not very gay here.'

He raised his eyes and his heart stood still in his breast.

He saw seated in front of him an elderly woman, wearing a red wig of hair, with drawn pale cheeks, one eye a little cast, a painted mouth. The fingers of her hands beyond the mittens were swollen and red with rheumatism. This was the woman of whom all his life he had dreamed, whose picture he had cherished, the Queen of supreme beauty for whom all men — singers and soldiers and kings and robbers — had died because of love, the enchantress, the divine . . .

His heart began to beat again. She was looking into his eyes. Aye, but what a look! He was caught and held. Her eyes were sad and oddly humble, as though she were pleading with him. But they were the opposite of humble, because they were royal. They were eyes that had commanded armies. Her eyes were asking his friendship as any woman in distress to any man she liked at first sight. They were also away beyond him, because they were the eyes of a Queen, because they had witnessed so much horror and had shrunk from none of it, because they had expressed so much love.

Those same eyes had seen the grey wet mist clinging about Leith on that first coming to Scotland, had dared Knox in argument, had watched Rizzio murdered, had stared at Darnley as he lay in bed at Kirk o' Field, had half closed in lust as she sank beneath Bothwell's power, had glared like a mad-woman's from Holyrood's windows at the screaming crowd, had watched her soldiers in their armour gathering around her, had seen Bothwell ride his way from her for the last time, and before that had smiled down at her child in her lap, and now for nineteen years had stared at the grey walls of her imprisoning castles.

Yes, her eyes had seen many things — but it seemed now that they saw only Robin Herries. They seemed to say to him : ' I am no longer young — all my beauty is gone. I have been hunted and scorned for twenty years. My own son has deserted me. They are plotting to kill me. More than ever before, now and here I need a friend. I ask you not to betray your trust or break your word. Only to like me and be a little sorry for me.'

' In any way that I can serve Your Majesty,' he said, ' I will be most urgent.' (He fancied that there was a quick smoky stir in her eyes when he called her ' Your Majesty.' He wondered whether that were forbidden. Irvine had said ' Madame.') At least he was sure that her upper lip, on which the rouge had dried a little, trembled.

' If I have been unlucky in life,' she said almost to herself, ' I have been lucky at least in the men who have served me.'

Suddenly he detected the play-actress. Had it become second nature to her ? Was she acting always ? For self-protection perhaps ? He was a man of deep and penetrating imagination and he saw, even in that very minute as he knelt and was conscious that the wooden floor pressed uncomfortably his knee, that she had been, her whole life long, since her babyhood, in grave peril — always in peril, surrounded from the very beginning by men and women who hated her.

' In my End is my Beginning ' — that was her motto. ' In my end are my enemies. From my beginning they were there.'

Never more so than now. Of course she must act to keep them at bay. Irvine who at this moment stood over him was her enemy. And Paulet was her enemy. And that Frenchman, her secretary, Nau, whom Robin could see out of the corner of his eye, a sleek over-dressed fellow, he was, perhaps, her enemy.

And *she* on her side was Elizabeth's enemy and would fight to be Queen again with every weapon in her power. So she was Queen, Play-Actress, Woman. Three in one. All quite just personalities but all three to be reckoned with, and because one was found to be there it did not mean that the others were not there also. He must remember that. He must always reckon with the three of them.

She had made a motion with her hand that he might rise to his feet again, and as he did so he saw that the knuckle of the thumb of her left hand was blue in colour and that the thumb was hideously swollen with rheumatism. He also caught the flash of the diamonds in the crucifix that swung ever so slightly above her breast.

He stood in front of her and they talked. It was as though they talked in a room alone. He became altogether unaware of the others.

She leaned back, picked up a small square of tapestry that she was working in purple and green colours, and began to labour at it with her stiff awkward fingers. Her voice was low and pleasing and he thought to himself that she must, throughout her life, have done much of her charming with her voice.

' Tell me, Mr. Herries — you are a bachelor, I understand.'

' I am a bachelor.'

' It is not strange to me that men should remain bachelors. It is we poor women who must marry or burn — and sometimes we burn even though we are married.'

' I have a brother,' he said, rather lamely, ' who also is a bachelor.'

' You are a poet, I have heard,' she went on.

' Oh no,' he said. ' A poet by desire but not by accomplishment.'

She nodded her head, smiling.

' We must test that.' She lowered her voice and, although her body did not move, she seemed to come nearer to him. ' Long captivity makes music and poetry — yes, and flowers — treasures from God Himself.' Her voice was sharper. Her fingers ceased to move on the tapestry.

' Why have you come here, Mr. Herries ? '

' I have come because I understood that I could serve — Your Majesty.'

' No Majesty. No Majesty. Not now — later perhaps when I am in my own Scotland again.' She was almost mumbling the words so that he could scarcely hear. ' Or is it my Scotland ? And is my son my son ? And my friends, are they my friends ? I live in a dark world now where I can scarcely see or hear.' She seemed to have forgotten him. But she looked up and realized him again.

' I do not know your age, Mr. Herries, but my ladies I know will tell you that you are handsome. And that pleases me too. And there is a cousin of yours here, of your name. Rosamund Herries. We are good friends, she and I.'

She beckoned with her stiff fingers. Robin saw Rosamund come over to them.

' Well, Robin,' she said.

He kissed her. Mary looked at them both approvingly.

' I was telling Mr. Herries that we are good friends already, Rosamund, *ma mie*.'

Rosamund made a little curtsey.

' She is the happiest person in this place, Mr. Herries. She cannot help but be happy even in such a place as this. That is how I would have been. It was always my intention to be happy. In France I was so, and I was so at the beginning in Scotland. When I see Rosamund I can believe in happiness again.' She was suddenly the Queen. ' If you are to remain with us, Mr. Herries, I must introduce you.'

She summoned people to her : M. Nau, Mr. Curle, Mr. Melville ; Bourgoing, her physician, a man whom Robin liked at sight for the honest clearness of his eye and his strong fearless carriage ; Gervais, her surgeon. Then some of her women : Barbara Mowbray, now Curle's wife, Elizabeth Pierpoint, Jane Kennedy, one or two more.

Sylvia came with the others. The Queen gave her a sharp look and Robin was at once certain that she did not trust her.

' Mistress Irvine, whom you know well.'

Robin kissed her lightly on her cheek. He felt her tremble.

Then something happened. The door at the far end of the room opened and someone stood there. Robin saw that it was Phineas Thatcher.

The Queen no sooner saw him than she cried out : ' That man . . . I said that he should not come into my presence. It was promised me——'

Irvine hurried forward and bowing said something about ' a message.'

She was in a rage. Her whole body was alive with activity. Her voice rang out as though she were ordering everyone in the room to imprisonment.

' Message ! Message ! Aye, we know his messages ! Mr. Irvine, you should not have allowed this. It is one more—'

She stopped, for the man had disappeared as quickly as he had come. She looked at all of them, hating them, even her own women.

' That is enough. I will go to my room.'

She half rose. Her mouth twitched with pain. She leaned forward to Rosamund and Barbara Curle. She rose very stiffly, stood for a moment between the two women, then, freeing herself from both of them, walked with great dignity to a side door and disappeared.

On the way to his room afterwards Robin was lost, and at the meeting of two passages he found Sylvia Irvine.

They greeted one another and at once he knew that all physical desire was gone. For the first time ! For the first time ! Oh, blessed, blessed relief ! He recognized further that desire was gone because she also did not feel it. They had passed to that further stage of their relationship for which he had so constantly longed. It might be because they were here present at a greater tragedy than their own. It might be because they were both now doomed, because the last act of their play had begun. But at last it was truly there — the quiet, the peace, the kindliness.

They stood together, he holding her hand, she smiling at him in the dusk, ghost-like because she was so small and so fragile and her face was so white above her black dress. They both realized that they had very little time, and their sentences were swift, breath-caught. At times he could scarcely hear what she was saying.

' Robin, why did you come ? '

' I had to. I had no choice.'

' It is Philip's plan to have you here. He intends us both harm.'

' For years he has intended us harm. There are deeper, more desperate things here than Philip.'

She put her small hand on the silver of his coat.

' Be careful. Be careful. Every word here is overheard, every movement overlooked.'

' Yes,' he said, catching her hand in his. ' But the Queen — what must I do about the Queen ? '

' Take trouble for her. Help her. She mistrusts me because I am Philip's wife. She knows that Philip is her enemy. But because of Rosamund she may have faith in you. I could see that she liked you. She loves Rosamund and trusts her more than anyone save Bourgoing and Curle, Pierpoint and Kennedy.
. . . No one else. She knows that enemies are all around her.'

' What does she hope for ? '

'For release. For Elizabeth's death. For a rising in
Scotland. And there is more. These last months she has
been of a different hoping spirit. Nau and Curle and herself —
they have been engaged in some plan. I am frightened for
her. I know she has written secret letters, and I fear for what
she may have written. Philip knows. The Queen has been
receiving letters from France in some secret fashion. She
believes that her deliverance is quite near, but I think they have
been laying a trap for her——'

'Yes,' Robin said. 'I heard something of it in London.
Walsingham has spies in every place.'

'Keep away from it — you, Robin — my dear, my dear.
That is Philip's plan, I think, to catch you. He will have you
either spy for him or be yourself spied upon. Thatcher is
everywhere, and God in His gracious mercy give it into my
hands one day before I die to see that man suffer. . . .'

The words choked her. She looked up at him, speechless,
then raised herself on her toes as she used to do and kissed him
very gently.

'Listen, Robin, while you are here think nothing of me.
I know that I am going to die very soon and I am glad of it.
I have been afraid in the morning and afraid in the evening for
year upon year, and now I am no more afraid. Only for you.
Philip can have had you here only for evil, but you can make
something of it if you can serve the Queen. She is in deadliest
peril. Think of that and that only.'

'Yes. For ourselves,' he said gravely, 'it is a little matter.'

She moved a little way down the passage. She looked at
him and her voice was thin, ghostly, as she said : 'I love you
in a better way than ever before, Robin. And it is not a sin
now. It would be a fine thing if we could do some good
before we die.'

Her retreating steps made no sound. He stood there
listening, but there was a dark silence. He might have been
already dead.

TIXALL TRAP

' THIS is perhaps the moment. This . . . the moment ! '

He tried to be reasonable, for in the past so often the moment had not arrived. But now, at last, within an hour his whole life, what he had learnt from it, what, after all, he had gained from it, might be put to the test.

It was the bright warm shining morning of August 16th. Robin had been up early, for soon after six he had met Nicholas two miles away. When he saw his brother, his brother warned him. Nicholas was watching over him like a mother over her young, gathering every piece of news that he could, trying as well as he could from that distance to shadow Irvine, taking all that Robin had to tell him and transmuting it into his own cool common sense and so handing it back to Robin again.

For Robin's imagination was on fire now with all that he could do for the Queen. It was as though his whole wasted life could be redeemed by some great sacrificial act. He was hampered always, though, by : first, the fact that Mary's inner party in Chartley did not as yet trust him, knowing that he had been Irvine's choice ; second, that Irvine kept a constant watch on him ; and third, his own rooted determination that he would do nothing against Elizabeth. He would not be disloyal to the one Queen, but he would gladly die for the other.

During this last week he had told himself over and over that some wonderful deliverance was at hand for Mary. He noticed how the Queen herself and Nau and Curle, Bourgoing and Melville, Rosamund and Barbara, all the Queen's intimates, had in these last days carried a certain new confidence in their hearts. Their faces, their words betrayed it. The Queen had grown marvellously better of her rheumatism in this last fortnight. She had been gay, had sung her old songs, and had

333

charmed himself, Robin, with a wonderful girl-like simplicity and kindness and tenderness.

' Something, Nick, that you don't know is on foot. I tell you it *is* so.'

' And I tell you, Robin, that all their plots have failed. They have been betrayed by Gifford and by a brewer here, who are working for Walsingham.'

Robin remembered something that Sylvia had told him on his first evening there. He had been afraid then, but now he was confident.

' Nick, I tell you it can't be so — Men like Nau and Bour-going would not be so sure——'

' Nau — Bah ! I don't trust him a step. Curle even may be betraying her. And Irvine — do you not think him clever enough for anything ? Why is he there with Thatcher but to trap her ? She has always been a fool in that. She has plotted and plotted her life long and always badly because of her impetuous will and her sensual body——'

Robin broke in fiercely, but Nicholas held him.

' No, no, Robin. I must speak what I know. Why am I here at this wretched inn but to watch for you and guard you ? What do I care for any Queen, or indeed for any woman for that ? All women are false and treacherous and betraying. I wish your plotting Queen no harm so long as she does our country no ill, but she may go to the stake and be burnt ten times over before I will have you hurt. You are a romantic poet, Robin, and have lived all your years in the air like a skylark, and have handed yourself over to a black hawk as well. Hist, I must be gone. This same place and time to-morrow morning.'

But Robin, if he had known it, would not see his big brother for another fortnight.

As he sat his horse there in the Chartley courtyard with the others, waiting for the order to be off, his heart beat with a fierce joy and pride. Dear old Nick, he was always cautious and warning and sensible. What could he know, living those miles away and depending on the gossip of the district and his acquaintance with a man or two in the village who did odd services at the manor ?

But the Queen knew and Bourgoing and Curle. He could see their faces now, bright and hopeful in the sunshine. Last evening while they had been sitting together listening to Curle's reading from Skelton's poetry, Paulet had appeared and, awkward and stiff as ever, had suggested that to-morrow, if the weather were fair, they should ride over to Sir Walter Aston's Park at Tixall and hunt the buck. It was a distance from Chartley only of nine miles, not too far for the Queen, and in any case her rheumatics were so much the better now. The Queen was like a young girl : she clapped her hands that were now unmittened and less sadly swollen. Any pleasure was fresh and exciting to her even after nineteen years of imprisonment.

So here they were, in the glittering sunshine, all on horse-back — Paulet, Irvine, Sylvia, Curle, Nau, Rosamund, Robin, Melville, Bourgoing, Bastien Pages, Annibal her archer, Lawrence who held her reins, Elizabeth Pierpoint.

The Queen was in a green riding-dress with a feather in her hat and sitting her horse as though she had never known the name of rheumatism.

They started and when they had ridden a little way the Queen half turned in her saddle and, smiling at Robin, showed him that she wished to speak to him. He rode up to her and then they went on, side by side, for a while, a little apart from the rest.

He was astonished to see her. Her face was young again. She had never been, perhaps, in the strictest sense handsome, but he could see to-day for the first time what it was that had made her, for so many men, so bewitching. She was alive with very life itself ; and this sparkling fire of vitality gave her eyes and mouth a shape and form that they did not have when she was weary or sad.

She was older now, but still even yet there was that appeal of her throwing herself on your kindness, on you and only you, of a gentle surrendering tenderness, though behind the sweetness there was a fierce assertion of independence so that you might say to yourself : ' I can see that with many she might be a tigress, but with me she is an understanding friend.'

She turned her laughing face to him.

' I am gay, Robin, I am gay, for the first time for weeks.'
(She had not called him Robin before.)

She lowered her voice. Irvine, as stiff as an ebony rod on
his horse, was not far away.

' Are you to be trusted ? They have told me not. They
say you are Irvine's friend, but I have watched you. I am no
ill judge of character, although, by Jesu, I have been, once
and once again, in error. But you have a good face and a
kindly. You said on that first evening you had come to serve
me.'

Robin answered passionately : ' So, by Christ's body, I
have.'

She spoke quickly, her bosom panting, her eyes playing on
his face like fire.

' If now, if in half an hour, it is suddenly a question as to
whose side you are on, you will be with *me* ? '

' In anything — in everything — if it is not against Queen
Elizabeth.'

' No. No. How could it be ? Why are they for ever
taunting me with that ? What do I want but my freedom ?
Oh, Robin, I have had year upon year of prison and when I
gave myself to her she promised me my freedom. And yet I
bear her no ill. If they allow me I will go to her and at last
face to face she will know how all my enemies have wronged
me.'

(' In half an hour,' he thought. ' What is she expecting
in half an hour ? ' He thought, too, ' She hates Elizabeth.
Under her voice there is another voice. Too deep for her to
prevent its echo.')

' I will trust you,' she said softly. ' Now. Always. I
know that I have made a true friend.'

He had noticed during this fortnight that her eyes were
everywhere. She was always on the watch for her enemies
and now she had seen Irvine draw closer to them, so she
spurred her horse on a little and rode alone, but as she
quickened her pace, Paulet and Irvine did likewise.

Instead of the Queen, Rosamund was at his side. He had
not liked the girl overmuch and even now, after this time with

her at Chartley, he did not altogether like her. He felt that she laughed at him. He was solemn and serious, he knew, and Rosamund mocked him as she mocked everyone. But this morning she was serious enough. Her horse was very close to his.

'Robin — has Philip said anything to you?'

'No. Why?'

'I am uneasy. The Queen is too confident. Paulet has something in that narrow wooden head of his and Philip is like a black snake.'

'What do you fear?'

'I can't tell. I have been afraid for weeks. . . .' She grinned at him like a boy. 'No matter. I have been shut up too long. Did you see Nicholas this morning?'

'Yes.'

'How did he look?'

'Oh, as fat as ever.'

'He would do better to see me than you. I could tell him more.'

'He asks for you — nearly every day.'

'It is a week since I have seen him.'

But to-day her mind was not set even on her dear Nicholas. She was looking ahead, watching the bend of the road, her sensible honest face wrinkled a little against the sun. She rode beautifully, like a man.

They must have gone some eight miles and been not far distant from Tixall when quite suddenly a group of horsemen appeared, waiting motionless at the end of the road.

That moment would be bitten into Robin's mind while life lasted. His instant thought was : 'These are Babington and some of his friends.' He knew enough to be aware that it was just such an occasion for which the Queen was prepared. He turned instantly towards her and saw her erect on her horse, her face illuminated with joy. He thought : 'There look to be fifty of them at least. How dared Paulet come out into the country with so few?'

His imagination did not carry him forward to consider what would be done after the Queen's rescue. He had been practically shut in Chartley for more than a week, and it might be that in this time all the Catholic gentlemen of England had risen.

Their own party had ridden a little forward and now paused, the sun shining down on them. A lark was singing in the sky, sealing that perfect silence. They could smell the faint hot odour of the corn, poppies stained the fields, and from some other road came the lazy rumble of cart-wheels.

No one spoke. Then they saw from the farther group a horseman detach himself and ride towards them. As he approached, Robin heard Curle, not far from him, murmur : ' God's pity, it is Sir Thomas Gorges.'

Robin's eyes were still on the Queen, and in that awful moment he saw her face change, a look of horror narrowing her eyes, her mouth drawing into a thin tight line. He fancied that he saw her shiver.

Every detail then was marked for Robin as though against the blue cloudless sky.

Sir Thomas Gorges, a man of about fifty, dressed in green serge ornamented with gold, came quite near to the Queen, dismounted from his horse, bowed politely, and in a voice so clear that every word came sharply across the rustling corn, said :

' Madame, the Queen, my mistress, finds it very strange that you, contrary to the pact and engagement made between you, should have conspired against her and her State, a thing which she could not have believed had she not seen proofs of it with her own eyes and known it for certain. And because she knows that some of your servants are guilty, and charged with this, you will not take it ill if they are separated from you. Sir Amyas will tell you the rest.'

There was a dreadful moment of silence. Robin heard a new voice, shrill, furious, a cry of anger.

' It is a lie. I have in no way conspired against the Queen.'

The soldiers behind Gorges had meanwhile drawn closer.

Sir Thomas bowed again.

' I am but the Queen's servant. I do as I am ordered.'

The Queen looked down at him as he stood there, his gold-embroidered cuff gleaming against the hand on his horse's rein, as though she would ride her horse at him.

She cried : ' I know no order. There can be no order. I am innocent of any charge.'

Robin saw a wonderful effort at control discipline her whole body. She swayed a little ; in a cold sharp voice, regal, as though she were commanding in her Holyrood Palace, she said : ' I would have you know, and all the world know, that I have never thought of such things. Had I wished to undertake them it would have been easy to do so. Your Queen has received information from a lying quarter. She has been bitterly misled. I have always shown myself her good sister and friend.'

Gorges regarded her but said no more. He mounted his horse again, then rode slowly, his face impenetrably grave, to Nau, to Curle, to Melville, who were all drawn in a group together behind the Queen. He spoke to the three of them.

' I regret extremely, gentlemen, that by Her Majesty's orders you are not to continue in this party but to follow my officers.'

At that all the Queen's servants broke out into cries and bitter exclamations.

The Queen, frenzied, turned her horse back and shouted, waving her arms :

' To me, my friends ! To me ! Draw your swords, for it is now or never again. These are our enemies declared and open ! For your Queen's safety and protection. Your swords ! Your swords ! '

But it could not be. Bourgoing rode to her, leaning over, putting his hand on her arm, whispering to her as to a child. Her hat was on one side, pulling her wig a little with it.

Nau, Curle, Melville, said no word. Two officers had detached themselves from the soldiers and started down the road. The two secretaries and Melville followed. They did not look at the Queen. The two secretaries were never to see her again.

Paulet had taken no part in any of this, and now when the party moved forward again he was riding slowly ahead. At a group of trees he turned to the left.

Bourgoing said loudly to the Queen, ' We are going a new way. We are not returning to Chartley.'

The Queen pushed her horse forward to Paulet, driving it a little across his own horse.

' Sir Amyas — where are we going ? Is this a short road to Chartley ? '

Robin had noticed from the first that whenever the Queen was angry Paulet was afraid. After all, his responsibilities were frightful. No one, even now, knew how affairs might ultimately turn, and his duty to his own Queen, loyal and faithful though he was, warned him that he might have, any day, duties to a quite different Queen if things went oddly. There was something in Mary, too, when she was angry, that was inhuman — there was none of the Juno about her, but something not altogether mortal, something of the witch who knows spells.

His eyes sought hers now, and then shifted.

' Madame, we are not returning to Chartley.'

' Where do we go then ? '

He stammered a little.

' To a good place — a fine place — finer than Chartley — finer than my own. I fear, Madame, it is impossible for you to return — it is forbidden — I have my command——'

She dismounted. She stood there on the rough path between the ranks of sugar-burnt corn.

' I go no farther. I can see that my end is determined on. I would as well die here under God's sky as in a stinking dungeon.'

Some of the irritation that creeps into all men at sight of an obstinate woman stole now into Paulet's beard.

' I am sorry. We must proceed. I shall be compelled to send for your coach, Madame, and have you conveyed. . . .'

Mary had moved to a flat white stone placed like a seat under the deep shadow of an oak tree. She sat down on it like any other abandoned helpless woman, her hands clasped so tightly that the knuckles shone, staring before her, over the corn, into the summer-misted dove-blue of the morning. Bourgoing had jumped from his horse and now ran to her. He knelt in the dust beside her, taking her hands in his own. The women, Elizabeth Pierpoint and another, were crying. Rosamund also had dismounted and stood, her face unstained with tears but her mouth set as though, at the first word from her mistress, she would leap at Paulet's throat. The soldiers had pushed their horses back out of earshot, but to the others the words came clearly enough.

Bourgoing in his soft tender French, looking into her face, cherishing her hands, made Robin love Frenchmen from that moment to the end.

'My lady! My lady! Take heart. Your friends are here. We are with you.'

'It is the end, Bourgoing. They are going to kill me.'

'No. No. It may be other—' His voice dropped. 'It may be that Elizabeth is dead and your friends choose this way to save you.'

Her eyes sought his face. How old, how old, Robin thought, she seemed!

'No. It's my murder they intend. But I will die here. They shall kill me here with the skylark singing. Better this than more of prison.'

Bourgoing put his broad arm around her. 'Ah, Madame, how we love you! How we love you! Do you think that we will not see justice done? Are we not proud of you and should you not show them that you are not afraid? Go on. Go on. They will not dare to touch you. Up with your head, my lady, and let them see your high courage.'

She turned to him, unexpectedly smiling. She laid, for an instant, the back of her hand against his forehead.

'It will be off with my head, not up with it, my poor friend.' She stood up. 'Very well, we will go. They shall not say that I fear them, hurt me though they may. But first, under His own sky, I will pray to God, for who can tell when I will see this sky again?'

Then, beside the stone, under the oak tree, she knelt down and prayed.

'O God, the Father of Jesus Christ, I pray Thee to have tenderness on all these my people who so faithfully have remained with me through every adversity. I pray Thee also to pardon all my faults, which indeed are heavy and grievous. I merit chastisement and Thou wilt give me endurance to bear it, under Thy commanding mercy. Remember, O God, Thy

M

servant David whom Thou didst deliver from his enemies when it had seemed that they were too many for him, and, in like manner, extend Thy pity to me who am the least of Thy servants.   But do with me as Thou wilt, for I desire no longer anything, neither goods, honours, power, nor worldly sovereignty, but only the honour of Thy holy name and Thy glory, the liberty of Thy Church and of all Christian people. And so I offer Thee my heart and Thou well knowest what are my desires and what is my intention.'

It was her recognition before God and the world that her soul knew well that at last she was given over to her enemies.

There was no sound but the sobbing of the two women. She rose from her knees, and, assisted by Bourgoing, remounted her horse.

She turned her head, and, in a voice perfectly calm and controlled, said to Paulet, ' And now, sir, you may take me where you will.'

THE CHRISTENING

SYLVIA, her small face puckered like that of a naughty child, slipped back through the long avenue, now closing darkly together as the summer night fell ; the church from the village struck ten, there was a sleepy bird twittering and the splash of the fountain with the two Cupids on the west terrace. Did she but reach the Cupids she was safe. She had stayed longer than she had intended, but no one, she fancied, had seen her.

She had spent a whole hour with Nicholas in the barn near the London road, and oh ! what a comfort he had been to her. Nicholas was always a comfort, showing at every crisis that things were not so bad as they might be, kindly, reassuring, and so strong, not only of body but also of spirit.

She regarded him as an inferior creature. He could not understand the joys and miseries of subtly-tuned natures like hers and Robin's. Had he ever known what love really was ? She could not believe it. In his huge arms he had crushed this woman or that, but with the same immediate necessity and vigour with which he enjoyed his food and drink. She looked down upon him, but in such a dreadful crisis as this present he was the very friend she needed. And then he hated Philip. She loved him for that.

He had consoled and comforted her, but that had not been his purpose in meeting her. All he was interested to know was of Robin, and of Robin he knew no more than she did. For he had skirted round Tixall, a miserable place, he told her, compared with Chartley, but had never won a sight of his brother. Robin, Rosamund and two others — Bourgoing for one night only — had remained with the Queen. They had been at Tixall now for a fortnight.

At Chartley it had been truly terrible. First Barbara

Curle, in an agony of distress for the Queen, had given premature birth to a child, and if that were not bad enough, Barbara was in terror also for her husband, who, with Nau, had been conveyed to London.

At Chartley gentlemen had arrived from London and, with Paulet and Philip, had turned the place into a ' mop-fair ' by going through all the Queen's papers, upsetting drawers, taking up boards from the floor, and putting Sylvia, Pierpoint, Bourgoing, Annibal through monstrous questionings.

Philip had been truly in his grand place and had grown, with every minute, more self-pleased and commanding. Sylvia told Nicholas that she thought that he was another two feet in height since a fortnight.

She shook with terror on her side when Nicholas informed her that Babington, Charnock, Ballard and others were caught and held to torture in London, that a dreadful plot had been discovered for the murder of Elizabeth by gentlemen of the Court, and that it was said that Queen Mary was implicated in this.

' If it is proved,' Nicholas said, ' it means her death.'

She reached her room in safety, lit with trembling hand the two tall candles by the bed, and she saw Philip sitting there in the crimson velvet chair, his long black legs stretching out in front of him.

She gave a cry and put her hand to her mouth like a little girl.

' And what did Cousin Nicholas tell you ? ' was his first question.

She did not lie to him. She never could. When he had her cornered as she was now, her terror of him was so great that she was emptied of all subterfuges and conceits.

She rested her small hand on the bed that he should not see how she was trembling.

' How did you know ? '

' Thatcher is aware of all that big bully's movements.'

' He wished to know about Robin.'

' Of whom you also wish to know.'

Deep in the heart of Chartley a bell struck the hour. Irvine raised his hand as if to have silence until the strokes were ended. Then, looking at her with sombre meditative eyes, he said quietly : ' It is finished.'

' What is ? '

She moved closer to the bed and grasped the hangings. She had never been so deeply terrified of him in all their life together as now.

' Mary. And you. It is the end at last for both of you.' His voice went on in quiet satisfaction : ' It has been a long game. Mary is caught past redemption. We have found papers in this fortnight that even our own good merciful Queen will not be able to resist. The end now is certain. I have myself played a good part in this. The brewer, that honest man, was my notion. You have not heard perhaps. They placed their letters in the ale-barrel, the brewer gave them to Gifford, who sent decoded copies to Walsingham. Then the letters were sent forward to Mary's friends, who most hand-somely replied in the same manner. That honest man, the brewer, was paid by both sides — young Gifford too.'

He recited these facts, not as though it interested him to tell his wife anything, but as though his exalted self bent over the chair and patted the back of his other exalted self sitting in it. He suddenly raised himself and leant forward as though he would force her better attention.

' Nevertheless the once-so-proud Scottish Queen is not my interest now. Nor yours.' He said gently, ' It is ended, Sylvia. It is ended.'

' What is ended ? ' she asked again.

' You will never share a bed with young Robin any more. Never, never again. The first time was in Cumberland, was it not ? You never thought, either of you, as you rode away the next morning, of the little gentleman you passed who noticed the jewel in your hat. It was incautious, that jewel — and when he told me accidentally in London of that little episode I knew where I was — and where you had been and what you had been doing——'

She sat on the edge of the bed. Her knees would not hold her.

' Why —? ' she said. ' Why —? ' But she could not go on.

' Why have I not ended it before ? Because I was kindly
intent on giving you an opportunity. An opportunity for
what ? For realizing the remarkable quality of the husband
you had married. You were of no value in bed to me, having
neither the arts nor the semblance of good manners. You
could not even pretend to care for my body, which is as handsome and strong as any other man's. When I saw that you
were blind to my body I thought that your eyes might become
open to my soul. For I have the character of no ordinary man,
Sylvia. I am a man in a thousand, nay, in a million, and I
will rise yet to the top of the world when you — Well, I will
not say where you will long have been by that time.'

Her teeth chattering against her will, she said : ' What
will you do ? '

' What will I do ? Nay, first I was telling you what I *have*
done. Your cousins, priest Robin and bumpkin Nicholas, I
have hated, and do hate, as I hate no other living men. Years
gone booby Nicholas interfered with my duty, stabbed me
treacherously in the arm and named me with insults. I am
so remarkable a man that once I set my hold on a thing or a
man I never let go. Nicholas, his time and place will come.
But it was like you, being the stupid slut that you are, to choose
Nicholas' saintly brother to bed with. . . .'

' I knew him before you — I knew him before you ! '

' Aye — knew him and loved him, I don't doubt, but it
was myself that you married. On the first night we were at
Drunning, as certainly you remember, you refused my embraces
and even scratched my thigh with your nails. For years you
have been unfaithful to me, choosing a lecherous bed rather
than a virtuous one, and I have waited with a Christian
patience. I have said to myself : " Let her but recognize me
for the man I am and I will forgive her everything." But you
did not choose it so. You could not, for you have neither
brains nor taste nor eye nor wisdom nor knowledge. As the
years have gone I have learned to hate your miserable white
face, your " Yes, Philip," " No, Philip," " Please, Philip," so
that there is no pain I would not have you suffer. Your
Robin also. And he *shall* suffer — even as Babington and
Charnock will suffer, who will be hung on the gallows for a

breathing second, their bodies cut down and marked for their quartering, their privities cut off, their bowels——'

She broke in with a throttled cry : ' You shall not touch him ! He has done nothing ! It was I——'

' Your sufferings shall be shorter. So brief that you will scarce mark them — But soon. The end shall be soon.'

He looked at her mockingly. With a light laugh he said as he rose : ' Oh, Sylvia, had you but known and confessed the rare man you married, all, all would have been forgiven you.'

He stood looking at her, and she knew that her doom was fixed. Yet, even at that moment, she realized with an acute perception that it was not his wickedness but his vanity that was speaking. No son of man is wicked, for if he boasts of his evil, he is blind, and if he is sorry for it, there is mercy.

' What will you do ? ' she asked again.

Before he could answer there was a loud knocking on the door and his name was called. He went to it and opened it.

A man stood there and cried, ' The Queen — the Queen has arrived. Sir Amyas is calling for you.'

Philip hastened down and Sylvia followed him.

In the hall there was a wild scene. The great door was open and torches were flaring at its entrance. In the hall itself Paulet, Bourgoing, some men and some women were gathered peering from the dim candlelight into the torches.

In the doorway stood Queen Mary, a little in front of Robin, Rosamund, and one or two more. She was wearing the green riding-dress and hat with which she had set out. Her clothes were dishevelled and disordered, and her face, in that wild light, as white as a bleached bone. She carried a riding-whip and looked a fury.

She cried out to Paulet : ' So you have allowed me to return ! After the filth and neglect of a dirty fortnight you have shuffled me back to my old prison, Sir Amyas. And now whither, pray ? '

Paulet very quietly answered that he was sorry if Tixall had not been at its best. The time had been short, accommodation lacking, but for his part—

' For your part,' she broke in on him, ' Sir Amyas, you lack the courtesies of a common gentleman. But I excuse you. Men cannot be what they are not bred to be.'

She swept forward into the hall, her face working with rage, that strange rage that carried beneath it a running power so strong and so vital that it shook her own spirit. Then she saw Bourgoing, and her weariness and anger turned to a smile.

'Oh, my friend, my friend. How is it with you? How I have needed your kindness and understanding.'

Holding his hand in both of hers she went on, the words pouring from her, as though no one else were present but they two.

'Why did they not let you stay? And after you had gone that first morning I stood on those dirty stairs and saw the beetles crossing the floor and the wind shook the cracks in the wall. I thought "They have taken him as they take all my friends and I shall see him again only in heaven." But it is not heaven for us yet, my friend . . . And you are well? . . . that pain in your shoulder — Oh, but I must tell you — Our friend here, Mr. Herries'— she turned back and stretched a hand out towards Robin —'Rosamund and he — what should I have done without them? We must be good to them while we may. Rosamund has a slight ague — that place — ugh — it is fortunate for us it was summer. . . .'

Her eyes passed over his shoulder and caught Sylvia. The sweetness with which she had greeted Bourgoing did not leave her. Sylvia had come to her, curtsied, and the two women looked into one another's eyes.

'I am glad that they have allowed you to remain with us. I wish—'

A curiously intimate gaze was exchanged between them. It was as though they knew, both of them, that sentence had been passed and in that knowledge was born a new relationship.

Sylvia said softly : 'While I may there is no service that I will not render, Madame.'

The Queen moved to her and surprisingly touched her cheek.

'I believe it. Poor child — you also have suffered. I had not known it when I was here before.'

She turned and cried out to Bourgoing.

' But Barbara ? My poor Barbara — why is she not here ? Has she had news of him from London ? Why is she not here to tell me ? '

Bourgoing hesitated, then, lowering his voice, said : ' My lady — the sudden shock of your leaving, her fears for you. . . . She was ill on the evening of that day. A child was born to her that night before its right time. She is weak and must keep her room, but the child is healthy.'

The Queen was instantly in a trembling agitation.

' My Barbara ? A child ? . . .' She cried out in French and started for the stairs, running.

She ran up them, still crying out. Paulet followed her, expostulating. After them Bourgoing and Rosamund.

The Queen at the stair-head turned to the right, ran forward crying, ' Barbara ! Barbara ! My poor Barbara ! '

Paulet followed, calling out, ' Madame ! Madame ! She is not well. To-morrow — I beg you—'

Before she opened the bedroom door she turned on him, as he hurried down the passage, like a virago.

' Christ's body and blood, Sir Amyas, but if you stop me I will call down God's justice on your head ! You have caught me, you and your spies, and trapped me and held me, but the end is not yet, nor has the time come when Mary of Scotland can cry false to those who love her. Aye, and who have served her with a loyalty and devotion that your spirit cannot conceive of. This is not your place, Sir Amyas. Go back to your papers and your documents and your spider-spinning. 'Fore God, but I will shame you before every woman in this country if you prevent me.'

She threw open the door, ran forward, crying ' Barbara ! Barbara ! ' saw the loved, familiar face against the pillows, fell on her knees beside the bed, throwing her riding-hat to the ground. She forgot in that moment her rheumatics, her ceremony, her watchfulness for her own safety, and spoke, tears filling her eyes, her hand stroking Barbara Curle's hair.

' My dear — and I was not here. You have suffered and I was not here — See ! I have come back. They have not killed me yet, nor you. We are two strong women together. The child — where is the child ? It is a girl. I know that it is a girl.'

Barbara, raising herself against the pillow, smiling, whispered, for she was very weak : ' Yes, it is a girl, Madame. If you allow, it is to be called Mary. And we have waited for the christening until you came.'

The Queen had risen and was bending over the cot beside the bed. The baby was not frightened, but smiled and raised its tiny hand, doubling it into a fist. The Queen caught it up, took it from the cot and stood there, looking at it, murmuring to it, embracing it.

She turned, laughing, towards the bed. ' See, Barbara ! The bonny bairn ! The bonny bairn ! And it has Curle's eyes, I swear but it has. No other man fathered you, my bonny — you were made in legitimate sheets.'

She held the child aloft, then very carefully replaced it in the cot.

' But you, *ma mie*, yourself. How is your bodily strength ? Was it fear for me that hastened the birth ? Ah — that touches me, and if I had my way it would touch *them* also to the heart — if they *had* hearts.'

She turned from the bed and saw the doorway crowded with people. She stamped with her foot.

' Is this a lady's private chamber or is it not ? This at least, Sir Amyas, is a common courtesy. They would see us naked, us poor women, nursing our babes in our shifts—'

She caught the eye of the unlucky secretary of Paulet, Gervase Ellis, and, fixing him with a furious eye, she went on :

' Pray, Mr. Ellis, come forward. Come forward. Examine the bed lest there are red Catholics hidden in it. Never mind Mistress Curle — for duty is duty—'

Paulet ordered briefly everyone to leave the room. The Queen asked for Rosamund, Bourgoing, Robin to remain. When they only were there and the door closed, Philip Irvine was standing at Paulet's elbow.

' And Mr. Irvine ? ' the Queen said. ' Has he no urgent affairs elsewhere ? '

(She hated Irvine above everyone in all this business.)

' I need him,' Sir Amyas said shortly.

' Ah, yes, you need him,' she retorted on him fiercely. ' It is such as he and such servants as the vile Thatcher who best serve your purpose here.'

She gave Philip a look so furious that his brown dark face flushed, but he had great powers of control, his vanity helping him, and he said nothing.

The Queen behaved then for a little as though there were no one in the room but herself and Barbara Curle. She pulled back the dark orange bed-curtain and sat near the pillow.

' Now, Barbara. Tell me. You have heard from Curle ? '

' Not a word — Oh, Madame, not a word ! '

' Aye, but you will.' She began to stroke Barbara's long brown hair. ' You shall, you shall. He is waiting doubtless until he can get word of some certain news to you. I will myself discover——'

She stopped, raised her hand and let it drop, smiled whimsically.

' I ? What can I do now ? They do not respect even your birth-chamber, *ma mie*.'

Barbara caught her hand.

' Madame, what will they do ? What *can* they do ? I am afraid. The Tower. The rack. He has always been so kindly, loving the world and his horse Caesar and all children. He has only served you, Madame, as a faithful servant. He intended no harm to any living person. But now there has been a fortnight's silence and no word——'

Mary drew her towards her.

' There, there. . . . I know what it must be for you. I too have suffered . . . years . . . years. . . . When Bothwell rode for the last time——'

She could not go on. She was sobbing convulsively. Weariness, the fears of the last fortnight, the rough treatment at Tixall, the pains of her body, her own secret knowledge of what they might have found, all these causes at this moment roused in her a fever of excited emotion and hysteria.

She checked her sobbing. She caught Barbara's hand in hers and fondled it.

' I swear to you, Barbara, that all Curle I take upon myself
— aye, the whole of him. They cannot charge him with anything that is not my fault. If anyone is guilty in any case it is
I.' She stroked Barbara's hand. ' There ! There ! Dry your
tears.   There are men here who joy to see us weep ! '

She stood up, staring at the cradle.

' But the child. It has not been christened, you say ? '

' They took Father du Préau that day a fortnight ago.'

She glared at Paulet again.

' So I have no priest now ? Even my own priest I am not
permitted.'

Paulet, who clearly detested this whole scene, bowed. His
voice had a high rather breaking note that was sometimes
absurd. It broke now.

' Madame, I had no alternative.'

' Well, God be thanked *we* have one,' the Queen answered
briskly. ' What of your own chaplain, Sir Amyas ? Against
him you have nothing, for he hates me as though I were
the Scarlet Woman herself.   Nevertheless he can christen like
another. Summon him at once. The child shall not be without God's grace a moment longer.'

Paulet still hesitated.

' Well, sir ? '

' It is, Madame, that I understand that the child is to be
christened Mary and after yourself.'

' Well ? '

' In that case ' — he hesitated again, then straightened his
shoulders — ' I fear that my chaplain cannot perform the
office. It is condoning——'

' Condoning ! Condoning ! Condoning what ? '

' Condoning—' he ended foolishly.   ' I cannot ask my
chaplain to perform it.'

' You cannot ? . . . You will not ? Well, then, I will be a
priest as good as another for this poor neglected child. God
listens from His heaven and hears the desperate prayers of his
persecuted children. This He shall hear and perceive and will
not reject.'

She again lifted the child from the cot, moved to where
there were a silver ewer and basin, tipped some water into her

hand and, sprinkling the child's forehead, murmured most reverently :

' Mary, I baptize thee in the Name of the Father, of the Son, and of the Holy Ghost.'

She held the child for the mother to kiss it, then herself embraced it, and laid it back in the cot again.

She bent over Barbara.

' Be patient. I will get news of him.'

She straightened herself and walked through the room. At the door she summoned Rosamund and Bourgoing, then she turned down the passage. Paulet and Philip Irvine followed them.

She pushed open the door of her own room and stood there rooted, staring.

The room was in the greatest possible disorder. Drawers of her cabinet, her wardrobe, of a table near her bed, were pulled open, letters and papers hanging from them like dead tongues. Papers were scattered on the floor, there were ashes of papers in the fireplace.

She moved without a word quickly about the room. She looked into every drawer. She found her crimson writing-case that had her crest in gold on it and the gold lock burst. A small toy spaniel, adored by her, ran from the basket near the fireplace and began to yelp and spring on its hind legs, but she neither saw nor heard it.

She looked for a long time at the drawer in the table by the bed and at the papers still remaining in her writing-case.

At last she turned and spoke to Paulet, who waited near the door. Her voice was very quiet and courteous.

' So *this* is why I was taken to Tixall ? '

At once, at the tone of those words, Rosamund knew that the Queen was aware of the truth — that, unless one of God's miracles occurred, her fate was sealed. With that absolute knowledge she passed into another world of experience. At that instant when she looked into her writing-case and saw that certain letters had been taken she crossed the narrow bridge and walked into the valley of Death.

All was not yet over. She could still fight and she intended to do so, for with her follies, her blindness, her impetuous falsities, her crude plottings, her trusting to her charms, her spells, her wizardry, she had, to the very end, as great a heart as beat anywhere in the world. Just as her hated sister Queen with her vanities, meannesses, disloyalties, falsehoods, had as brave a heart also.

But Rosamund saw death in her eyes as though a thin veil had been drawn across her face, which was, at this moment, almost that of a wizened old woman.

' What have the robbers done with my papers ? '

' Certain documents have been taken for the perusal of Her Majesty in London.'

' Ah — so that is why Nau——'

She checked herself.

' Is not this a criminal thing — to rape my body under a lie to Tixall and to steal, like any common thief, what is mine and mine only ? '

' The State comes before all.'

' Yes. It has been a pretty plot. For months you have been at it.'

She took some steps towards him.

' Sir Amyas, Sir Amyas, a day will come when your cheeks will be hot with shame of this.'

But he answered her bravely : ' Never, Madame — except at disloyalty to my own Sovereign.'

' Nevertheless,' she answered him, ' some of you ' (and she looked at Irvine, who would remember that look) ' will one day be sorry for this.' And most solemnly she went on : ' Two things you cannot take from me, however you may wish — my royal blood and the Catholic religion, which both I will keep until my death.'

At that last word she gave a little start and stared beyond them all as though she saw visions.

She ended quietly : ' Now leave me.'

All at once left the room save Rosamund and Bourgoing.

When the door was shut she swayed as though she would fall. Bourgoing moved to catch her.

She lay back against his breast, closing her eyes as though she were infinitely weary.

THE INN AT FOTHERINGHAY :
THE STAIRCASE

FOTHERINGHAY CASTLE sat humped like a black and brooding beast on the lowly floor of the sparse winter country. There were witches, seers, prophetesses enough in the England of that day, and it might be that, as night fell, a tattered creature with a skinny finger rose from the stubble and before the yellow-grey horizon darkened shook that finger and muttered her curse : ' For the many evil deeds that your walls have seen, for the tears that have been shed, the cries of agony that have beaten against those thick damp walls, be you accursèd, be you for ever accursèd. The day will come when men shall search for you and find you not. A hump of undistinguished ground shall be all your pride and the lonely blowing thistle your banner.'

Within the Castle on the afternoon of November 19th, 1586, everything was grim enough. Even among the kitchen servants and the men-at-arms no one sang with out-of-tune laziness — no dog barked. Words were little more than a whisper. Suspense was in every heart, even in the most hostile. Even in the Queen's although, deep, deep in her spirit, she had known ever since that night of her return to Chartley what the end must be.

She had known it yet more surely on the day of her arrival at Fotheringhay. Fotheringhay was of ill omen to all prisoners, royal or common. Katherine of Aragon had refused to be imprisoned there, declaring that ' to Fotheringhay she would not go unless bound with cart-rope and dragged thither.' A grim dreadful place with a double moat, a great gateway like the entrance to Hell, a keep dark and thick-set and a vast courtyard that seemed of itself a prison to the inner building where the apartments were.

Sylvia also knew how dreadful it was. As they approached it she would have uttered a cry had not Philip been at her side. For she had dreamed of it. Twice at least she had seen it floating in air above a black stagnant water, thick with green weed, filled with snakes, toads and slimy worms. In her dreams she had been clinging to the battlements as they swung in mid-air. She hung desperately with her hands to the stone. Philip leaned over, laughing, loosened her hands, and she fell screaming into the moat.

She knew every detail of it and said to herself, as they passed under the huge gateway : ' Here in the courtyard there is a stone well, and to the left a horse-block and on the wall by the door a heavy black bell.' These were all there.

There followed the days of the trial when the Castle was filled with gentlemen from London and a great coming and going.

At the trial Mary bore herself like a great Queen, but they all — her friends and supporters — knew that there was no hope. Barbara Curle, Jane Kennedy, Rosamund Herries, Bourgoing — no word passed their lips, but they all knew that among her letters were some so indiscreet that they must destroy her.

After the trial the gentlemen went away and the Castle was horribly quiet.

It was in these days that Sylvia discovered an entirely new relationship with the Queen. She herself was now concentrating all her thoughts on Robin. Whenever he was out of her sight — and he was so during most of the day — she was wondering whether Philip had got him. Philip or one of his men. It would not be Phineas Thatcher who would do the deed — strangling or stabbing or drowning or riding down — but he would be behind it : the arrangements would be his. From the very beginning he had hated Robin and Nicholas as deeply as did Philip.

She suffered a torture that was entirely selfless unless her love for Robin could be called selfish. That torture was increased now because they loved one another at last happily, with a deep unphysical passion that would have been perfect companionship and utter contentment in normal life.

But life now was not normal. For Sylvia life had been crazy since that moment when Philip had picked her up and carried her into that horrible bed at Drunning. Soon that crazy life would have a crazy end, and seen in that colour this Fotheringhay was crazy, with its black bell and its dungeons where words were scrawled with a bloody finger on the wall, and its high hall that in spite of its space stank of close air, and the many little stone staircases such as you see in squirrels' cages.

Everything around Fotheringhay was crazy — the double moat where two swans swam, the fields of stubble, the village where ragged children played in the mud, and the inn called ' The Cock and Rabbit.' This last was of all inns the blackest, meanest, most deserted. You could step into it and call ' Landlord ' for an hour and nothing would come but the wheezing, half-starved hens. From its mis-shapen door you could see the dark Castle squatting on the landscape and smell stale oats, rotten cabbage, stagnant water. Here was a place for the plague. There was a host of the inn, a stout stomachy fellow who often in the coldest weather had his chest bare with the thick black hair clustered between his breasts ; his chin was black with bristles, his eyes small under black eyebrows, his fist covered with black hair. He was dirty and drunken and a villain. Half the children in the village were fathered by him. Sylvia, when she was in the village, thought he watched her with especial attention.

She told Nicholas about him as now she told him everything For Nicholas, when the Queen moved on to Fotheringhay, moved there too — not because of the Queen but for his young brother's sake. He watched over him like a mother, Sylvia thought, and what an infinite help and comfort to her that was.

Nicholas said very little. Quite openly he had hired little Chilcote Manor, two miles from the Castle, and stayed there, shooting, hunting, fishing with his man Gilbert Armstrong and his man's wife Catherine. He paid his duties to Paulet, to Gorges, to others known to him. Rosamund and Barbara took dinner with him ; Gorges went shooting with him ; and ceaselessly, without resting, without, it seemed to Sylvia, closing an eyelid, he watched over Robin.

This was one of Sylvia's comforts. The other was the new relation that she had with the Queen.

The Queen had not at first liked her, had distrusted her because she was Philip's wife. Then while she was at Tixall the Queen had heard something about Sylvia that had altered her view of her. Had Robin told her some story ? Or Rosamund ? Sylvia did not know. But at Fotheringhay the Queen's attitude was altogether changed, and at length, one day, just before the trial began, the Queen said to her :

' Come here, my child.'

Sylvia came to her. They were alone. Sylvia had been reading aloud. Sylvia stood by the Queen's chair. The Queen put up her hands and cupped Sylvia's chin.

' You are dreadfully unhappy.'

' Yes, Madame.'

' Because you have been — how shall I say ? — ungratefully married ? '

' Yes.'

' It is a thing I know by my own experience. To have a man whom you hate — not only his body but his soul — come and lie close to you, take you in his arms, it drives women to madness — worse than madness. The world never blames the man. Women, it says, are intended for such things — as though they had no nerves. No nerves ! No nerves ! God — they are all nerves, a skein of them, and the man puts his hands in and tears them as you tear webs.

' And the other — true love — is a just and lovely harmony. Those same nerves are on fire with longing, desire. And then when the body is satisfied there is a perfect peace, riding on your lover's breast. . . . I am an ageing woman and I have the rheumatics and I wear a wig — once I had most beautiful hair — I am an old Queen whom everyone has deserted, whom her own son — her own son . . .'

She broke down, sobbing into her sleeve like a child. Sylvia, staring up at her, thought : ' I can't be sorry for her. I don't know how much she is acting, even now, and in any case where is Robin ? Is he safe, shall I see him this evening ? '

In spite of herself she was, a moment later, touched and

moved, for the Queen, tears dry on her cheeks, stroked Sylvia's forehead and said very quietly : ' I have been drawn to you these last weeks because I feel that we are joined by the same fate. Only you in all this Castle. We are sisters in trouble, and we must be brave together.'

She thrust up her head and cried scornfully : ' I shall show them, the whole pack and their old painted virgin, how it becomes a Queen to behave. It shall never be forgotten.' She suddenly chuckled like an old woman who remembers a bawdy story. ' Which is a great comfort, my dear, if you *have* to die. For a Queen to die with the drums beating before the whole world, that is something. I have always had fear they would strangle me in a dark ditch. I know now there will be drums.'

From the time of that conversation there seemed to be a special relation between the two. They lived in that dark grim place as though they shared a secret between them. The Queen was a help to Sylvia because of her audacity. She moved and behaved as though she were only at the beginning of life instead of nearing the end of it. In the damp unhealthiness of Fotheringhay, and encouraged, it might be, by her own forebodings when she was alone, the rheumatism returned, and especially in her legs. She was forced to stay in bed for days together. But she was a woman now whose mind was made up. She was gentle and even kindly with Paulet ; to Philip she was as haughty and sarcastic as ever, but idly, lightly, as though she knew that nothing could penetrate his vanity. She was right ; nothing could.

Sylvia's feeling for her grew to something like worship. She spoke of her to Robin. She saw very little of Robin, for he was on duty every night and slept in the day, but they met without disguise, as though everything were settled at last between them for ever.

Robin sought to serve the Queen in every way that he could ; he performed offices for her in a thousand indirect ways, brought flowers and fruit to her, read to her (for he had a very beautiful voice), and she told Rosamund that he was nearer to the men of her youth than anyone she had seen for a long time. ' He is beautiful and a poet. He is unhappy and he is reticent. He is spiritual and he has a most tender heart. He longs for some country he sees dimly and may one day reach. He will be satisfied with nothing on this earth. He serves me, but he does not worship me now as for so many years he did. It is better so. Men who have worshipped me have come to dreadful ends. I am not fit to be worshipped. But how happy I was in those other days when they did so ! '

No, he did not worship her any longer, for she had lied to him. She *had* plotted against Elizabeth, steadily, persistently and foolishly. These weeks in Fotheringhay were a kind of waiting endurance. Sylvia was near to him. Nicholas was not far. He held himself taut, performing his duty, waiting for the event. And the event came — that dreadful day of the Twentieth of November.

On the evening of November 19th, Lord Buckhurst arrived from London at the Castle.

As Sylvia was climbing the staircase to her room for bed someone (she could not see his face) started from the shadow of the stair and pushed into her hand a paper. In the candlelight of the room she read it. The letters were in printed style. The message was :

I must see you on a matter of most urgent import to us both. No one must know of it and I have arranged to be alone to-morrow from six of the clock at the ' Cock and Rabbit.' Tell no one.

ROBIN.

She could not tell, of course, whether it was in his hand. She stood for a long while examining it under the candle and listening too for any sound that might mean Philip's approach. Robin had never once since their arrival asked for a secret interview. They had been meeting always in the most open fashion, for there was no longer any physical relation between them. Philip knew all and there was nothing to hide from him. Moreover their love for one another was so great — so very much greater than it had ever been — that they needed no secret meetings. They were always together now in spirit. And yet it might easily be that Robin had something very important and secret to tell her. Their common fear of Philip was not for themselves but for one another, and it might be

necessary for them both to know of some move that Philip
had made, of some words that he had spoken, against which
they must guard.

Sylvia had not seen Robin at all during the last three days.
Two nights ago Sylvia had woken to see Philip, half undressed,
standing over her bed. All he had said was : ' Did you mark
Beale's attention to me this evening?'

She had said yes.

' He said that he had heard me well spoken of at Court
in this last week.'

She said that she was glad. He stretched himself, raising
his brown arms, pushing out his strong lean chest. He looked
at her so strangely that for a moment she thought that at last
the time had come. He would kill her now, as she lay un-
resisting in the bed. She felt little fear — almost a kind of
relief. She hoped that it would be speedy. She saw, more
distinctly than ever before, how restlessly his vanity hated
her. But he only said : ' I wonder — do you ever look at the
calendar ? '

' No,' she said. ' One day is like another.'

' Nevertheless you should count every day.'

When he lay down beside her he drew a deep breath of
self-satisfaction and in a moment was asleep.

She wanted to tell Robin of this. Whether this message
was from Robin or no she must give it the chance. The
thought of seeing him to-morrow, and alone, delighted her
heart.

The morning of the Twentieth of November was dark and
sombre. Rain fell with a dull obstinacy as though it had been
falling for centuries and was infinitely bored with the necessity.
The moats were covered with raindrops as though pitted with
disease. A rat ran across the floor of the great hall. The
soldiers on guard gathered in groups and told bawdy stories.
The rain hissed down into the courtyard. A prisoner in one
of the dungeons — a soldier caught in bestiality and condemned to a beating and a month's imprisonment — climbed
a way up the wall and put his hand through the grid of his
little window to feel the rain on his palm.

After dinner, about six o'clock, Lord Buckhurst, Sir Amyas, Sir Drue Drury and Beale were granted an audience by Queen Mary.

Dressed entirely in black, the diamond crucifix her only ornament, she was seated in a high gold and crimson chair near the stone fireplace, in which a log fire was rather feebly burning. She was attended by Rosamund, Elizabeth Pierpoint and Bourgoing. The gentlemen stood in the doorway. Lord Buckhurst was a handsome fresh-coloured gentleman with a voice a little too carefully modulated. He had a habit of raising his right hand and studying a fine emerald ring on his finger.

He stepped forward now from the other gentlemen and said that he regretted it greatly, but what they had to say was for her ear and hers alone.

Mary inclined her head. A thin sarcastic smile played about her lips that were brightly red in contrast with the pallor of her cheeks.

' Go, Bourgoing, my friend. . . . You, too. I am safe with these gentlemen.'

Bourgoing kissed her hand. He and the two women retired by a side door.

Mary was quite alone on her side. She seemed to realize it, for she rose a little in her chair, re-seated herself, and with a back absolutely erect and a defiant carriage of her head she waited for their move.

They came forward, Buckhurst in front of the rest. They said nothing and the whirring of a gilt and enamel clock on the table filled the room.

At last Buckhurst spoke in his soft, gentle, too-courtly voice.

' I am an envoy, Madame, from my Sovereign Queen Elizabeth, and I beg leave to deliver a message from Her Majesty to yourself.'

Mary's hand tightened on the crimson arm of her chair. She said nothing, only bowed her head. Her dog that had been hidden under her skirt came out and growled at the gentlemen. She bent down and took him up on to her lap, stroking his silky ears with one hand.

Buckhurst, with a little ahem, spoke of the trial. Mary's eyes never left his face.

' Her Majesty has known the deepest sorrow of her life at finding beyond peradventure that you, Madame, whom she thought her dear sister, were not only consenting to the horrible fact of rebellion in the country against her person and State, but were also the author and inventor of it.'

Mary, her body stiff as though frozen by the determination of her will, said : ' I have repeated again and again, before my trial, at my trial, after my trial, that I have plotted nothing against the safety and happiness of Queen Elizabeth.'

' Letters in your own hand, Madame, have persuaded Parliament to the contrary. Therefore Parliament has sent me hither to acquaint you with the fact that it has pronounced sentence of death against you.'

There was no stir, no noise, no voice in the room — only the whirr of the clock and the rain beating against the window. But the word ' death ' in its starkness created nevertheless its own movement, a movement in the hearts and minds of those present. Paulet, whose duties were nearly over, who, a martinet by spirit and training, had faithfully served his Queen, nevertheless was not untouched, during all these months, by something grand and strong in this other Queen who could be false, foolish, vain, but was, at the last, a greater woman than any he had ever known, save only her rival. At Buckhurst's sentence he dropped his head as though in prayer. But he was not in prayer ; he was only uncomfortable, as though someone had committed a social indecency.

Buckhurst, looking at his ring, and then fixedly at the Queen, continued : ' My mistress has not yet given her consent to this measure, but urged as she is by Parliament it is impossible that she shall not yield.'

Still Mary said nothing. Her eyes looked at Buckhurst gravely and a little scornfully, as though he were performing a poor duty and knew it.

Buckhurst continued. ' The person of the Queen, the State, and religion are no longer safe. It is impossible for you both to live and therefore one must die. For this end, then, in order that you should not be taken by surprise, Mr. Beale and

I have been sent to warn you to prepare for death, and we will send you the Dean of Peterborough or the Dean of Lichfield for your consolation : they are both men of learning and understanding.'

Buckhurst spoke as though he were delivering a learned lesson. He was the complete cultured, polished official. It was as though, too, he were aware that he was in the presence of Mr. Beale, who was noting every word, watching for anything wrongfully omitted or carelessly spoken.

Mr. Beale was a spare modest-looking man in a simple suit of black, and he stood carefully behind Paulet near the door. Nevertheless it was he, and not Buckhurst, who dominated the room, and it was as though he had now stuck a pin in the backside of Lord Buckhurst, for that nobleman moved forward a little and raised his voice.

'Take thought of your conscience,' he said, with considerable unctuousness, 'and acknowledge your fault, repent and make satisfaction before God and man. If you know anything concerning this conspiracy further than what has already come to light, you are bound in Christian charity to unburden your conscience, being, as you yourself say, nearly related to the Queen, to whom also you are indebted for many favours. And if you know of any other persons who have had a part in this undertaking, it is your duty to declare it before your death.'

Mary turned her body round in the chair towards the door and, as though she knew by perfect long-trained intuition who was her real interlocutor, she looked over Buckhurst's head to the modest but very attentive Mr. Beale.

Mary began her reply in a quiet low voice, so that those by the door could scarcely hear, but as she continued her voice became stronger and more fervent.

'I expected only this,' she said. 'This is the way in which you generally proceed with regard to persons of my quality, those nearly related to the Crown, so that none may live who aspire to it.

'For many, many years now I have known that this would be the end and have expected it. I have loved the Queen and the country, and have done all in my power for the safety of both. The offers which I have made are the proofs of this, as Mr. Beale ' (she raised her eyes and stared directly at him) ' can bear me witness.'

She coughed a little, looked down at the dog, stroking his silken ears as though she were thinking deeply, then looked up sharply again.

' I do not fear death and shall suffer it with a good heart. I have looked forward to it for many a year. I have never been the author of any conspiracy to injure the Queen——'

' The author — no,' Beale broke in with a sharp, high querulous voice, ' but the abettor — the aider and abettor.'

She paid him no attention, but went on : ' I have several times been offered my freedom, and have been blamed for refusing my consent. My partisans have abandoned me and troubled themselves no further with my affairs. I am quite alone save for these my few friends.'

She paused and waved her hands as though Bourgoing and the others were there with her.

' To prevent this I have attempted to obtain my deliverance by gentle means, to my great disadvantage, till at last, being repulsed on the one side and pressed on the other, I placed myself in the hands of my friends, and have taken part with Christian and Catholic princes, not, as I have before declared, and as the English themselves can bear witness by the papers which they have in their possession, through ambition nor the desire of a greater position : but I have done it for the honour of God and His Church, and for my deliverance from the state of captivity and misery in which I was placed.'

She looked up to the ceiling. Then, turning back to them, her face was proud and her voice exultant.

' I am a Catholic — of a different religion from yourselves ; it is for this reason you will take care not to let me live. I am grieved, however, that my death cannot be of as much benefit to the kingdom as I fear it will do harm ; and this I say not from any ill-feeling or from any desire to live.

' For my part, I will tell you frankly, I am weary of being in this world ; nor do I, or anyone else, profit by my being here. But I look forward to a better life, and I thank God ' (her voice gathered into it almost a note of ecstasy) ' for giving me this grace of dying in His quarrel. No greater good can come to me in this world ; it is what I have most begged of God and most wished for, as being the thing most honourable for myself and most profitable for the salvation of my soul.'

She was now on ground where she was happiest. All defiance was gone from her voice. She spoke quietly again but with a happy assured confidence. The Queen was gone, the actress was gone. She was never in all her turbulent life more honest than now or more perfectly at peace. All in the room felt this.

'I have never had the intention of changing my religion for any earthly kingdom, or grandeur, or good whatever, nor of denying Jesus Christ, or His name, nor will I now. You may feel well assured that I shall die in this entire faith and with my good will, and as happy in doing so as I was ever for anything that has come to me in my life. I pray God to have mercy on the poor Catholics of this kingdom, who are persecuted and oppressed for their religion. The only thing I regret is that it has not pleased God to give me before I die the grace to see them able to live in full liberty of conscience in the Faith of their parents, in the Catholic Church, and serving God as they desire to do. I am not ignorant that for long certain persons have been plotting against me. But I have spoken sufficiently of this before the Commissioners.'

She seemed to have said all that she had to say, and sat back in her chair with a little sigh. She pressed the dog against her with her hand. The absurd lively face as of a lost child looked up into hers. The feathery tail wagged.

Mr. Beale broke in with his high voice. He talked for a long time, conceitedly, about treaties and conferences, saying he knew of what he was talking because he had been employed as envoy between his mistress and Queen Mary.

Mary looked at him sharply. 'We know you, Mr. Beale. Have no fear.'

Beale went on so hurriedly that the words tripped over one another. He said that when Queen Mary had been in danger from her own subjects she had fled to his mistress for protection, and his mistress had arranged for her to retire to Carlisle to be in greater safety.

Mary, her eyes flashing, answered : ' I was taken there by force and against my will, and well you know it.'

' It was for your good, for your good,' Beale answered fiercely.

It seemed as though there would be a sharp and very unseemly altercation between the two of them, but Mary suddenly held up her hand.

' Hush. . . . Did you not hear ? A cry ! '

They all listened.

' There ! A woman crying for help ! '

There was another silence and then Paulet said : ' The wind — the wind in the chimney.'

But Mary was still listening, her head set towards the window. She turned at last and bowed as Lord Buckhurst and Mr. Beale left the room.

Sylvia, protected from the rain by a rough cloak, hurried from the side door of the right wing of the apartments, slipped through the bare sodden gardens, showed herself with a timid smile to the guard at the western gate, who at once allowed her to pass into the road. It was very dark now and the rain had shredded into a thin drizzle, but the wind was blowing furiously and made the only sound on the surface of the earth.

She was happy : she was thinking of nothing but that she would see Robin alone again. For weeks they had not been alone. She did not care who knew of their meeting, but it was like enough that no one would know. Neither she nor Robin was watched. She because she was Philip's wife, Robin because his loyalty and sense of duty had been thoroughly tested during this time.

She wondered a little what it was that he wanted to tell her. On her side all her mind and endurance now were given to the business of reassuring and comforting him. She had a dim but gradually strengthening hope that when this business was ended and they were back in London again, Philip would allow her to go away somewhere by herself, and so, gradually, they would separate for ever. After all, he hated her, the very sight of her exasperated him. He would have been rid of her. long ago were it not that his vanity was afraid of any public scandal. But this separation might be managed very quietly. If he did her any physical hurt, that would be a very much greater scandal.

Only to be away from him, to be by herself, to be free of this constant fear that pursued her into her very dreams and was making her a cowed, nervous, speechless creature, only half a human being. At this she thought of the Queen, who had been so very good to her during these last weeks. Poor lady ! The coming of Lord Buckhurst and Mr. Beale to the Castle could mean no good. Oh, poor lady ! poor lady ! How eagerly Sylvia would do something for her if there were an opportunity ! By that she might recover a little of her own self-respect : the loss of it, the contempt she felt for herself, the knowledge of the wastage and wreck of her life, all this was, after her fears for Robin, the worst of all her burdens. One glorious deed, one act of noble self-sacrifice, one *thing* that would prove to herself and to the world that she was not the poor defeated failure that she seemed !

She sighed ; she wiped the drizzle from her face with the edge of her cloak. The village street was deserted. It was so dark that she stumbled among the pools and pitfalls of the road. She saw one dull misted yellow lamp. That was the ' Cock and Rabbit ' and, at the same moment, the church clock struck six.

She had never been inside the inn and she wondered what she would do if the central room were crowded with rough and drunken men, farmers, soldiers from the Castle. But Robin would be there, waiting for her.

She was surprised to find the door ajar. She pushed it back and entering found herself in a passage with rooms to the right and the left. There was a dank smell of rotting matter and she could hear the noise of the rain like a whisper. From the passage there rose a twisting black staircase that led to an upper passage, and on the top of the stair there was set a horn lantern in which a candle was burning.

There was no sound or sign of any living being. She looked up the staircase half expecting to see Robin at the head of it, and as she looked she shivered. She did not know why. The rain had wetted her and the dank smell of the place was alive as though there were rotten straw about in which animals were crawling.

At last she called ' Robin ! Robin ! ' very softly. There was no answer.

Very fearful, she turned the handle of the door on the left and saw faintly that she was looking into a room quite empty, with a wooden bedstead and a table. She opened the door on her right and saw that it was the customers' room ; there were shelves filled with bottles, a glass upset on a table, stools and a bench. Seated on a stool, his head fallen on the table, a guttering candle beside him, fast asleep and snoring gruntily, was the landlord, whom she knew by sight ; an unpleasant picture, for his chest was bare, his hair wildly disordered and his fist clenched.

Very, very quietly she closed the door and wondered what she should do. She called ' Robin ! Robin ! ' once more, this time more loudly. The fact that there was no answer made the silence more insistent. She dared not call more loudly still lest she should rouse the man in the room. She knew well that he was an abandoned brute with women, especially when he was in drink.

At last she began to climb the stairs and, with every step, her fears increased. She hated this staircase. She felt that she had seen it before and been frightened of it before. Half-way she called again : ' Robin ! I am here ! Where are you ? '

At the stair-head beside the lantern her fears grew so that she began to shake and quiver. Why was Robin not here ? What if the message had been a trap either for herself or him ? She had accepted it without a question and yet she had no ground for believing it. Her eagerness to see Robin alone had overridden all her caution. After all why should he choose such a place as this ? And if he had chosen it he would have taken care to be here before her.

In a panic she moved about the passage. She opened one of the doors and saw that it was an empty stinking bedroom. The smell of the place gained on her and it was as though the walls were closing in on her.

She must go. It *was* a trap. She had been a fool to call Robin's name. Someone had heard her. At first she had thought that it did not matter, their meeting anywhere before the whole world, but now, in her alarm, it seemed to her that calling his name aloud had betrayed him.

She turned to hurry down the stairs, when a sound paralysed her. Someone was there. She caught the balustrade of the stair.

'Who is there?' she cried out.

She heard the movement again, and at once, as in a most horrible nightmare, hands were laid on her shoulders.

She did not turn or struggle. In a flash of the bitterest, most agonizing realization, as though a voice had whispered in her ear, she knew that this was death.

For some strange reason she thought of the Queen. She was caught up and lifted and, as her heart turned and was constricted, she uttered one wry, trembling scream.

'Oh God, have mercy — this is death!'

One vast overwhelming fear, again as many times before in her dreams, seized her brain and killed it as with a shot from a gun.

She saw, her last sight on earth, the lantern toppling over. She crashed, in absolute darkness, on to the stone floor.

THE LAST DAYS ON EARTH

ON the evening of the 7th of February, Rosamund Herries stood waiting in a room so small as to be almost a powder-closet off the big salon. This small room was framed in red leather, stamped with gold studs, and Rosamund, standing rigid, listening, counted the gold studs over and over, and the grey stripes in the dress of the Madonna in the little Italian picture over the fireplace.

She knew what the Lords Kent and Shrewsbury had come to say. How long would it be before the dreadful climax to these months of agonized waiting? They would surely give her time for preparation, the poor lady. Rosamund might doubt many things now, after these months, about the Queen, but she never doubted her religion.

She, Rosamund, was full of warmth of heart but had no sentiment. She saw everything always in the clearest light — even the things that hurt the most, as that Nicholas did not love her, that no man had ever desired her, that all men and women were false again and again (false of action, not necessarily false of soul).

She thought that she knew now this woman, Mary of Scots, through and through. She knew her insatiate vanity, the lusts that even now were active in retrospect, the charm that was put forward like a piece of acting in a theatre, the sudden malice, the lurking cruelty. She was a woman who had been brought up in the Medici Paris, a woman who, from birth, had had to fight for her life. Those two facts said everything.

Rosamund knew every turn and twist in that woman's soul. Mary had said to her once : ' Rosamund Herries, no man or woman has ever seen me as clearly as you do.' And yet Rosamund loved her, loved her more every day that she was

371

with her. She asked herself now, as she stood there waiting, the game almost ended, why she loved her so much. She loved her because she *was* so easy to understand, because her faults were all as clear as early summer morning. Her virtues too. She was like a woman whose fair flesh was glass. Her bravery, her pugnacious defiance, her single-track persistence, her very lusts that had led her to such public humiliation, her contempt for a fool or a coward but her generous warmth of heart so that she could protect a Chastelard or champion a Rizzio, her childlikeness so that to hear her laugh at a game or sing a song or dance on a happy evening was a joy for anyone, her sense of humour suddenly jumping out, her courage in physical pain, her deep unswerving devotion to God, her caprices, her wonderful regality when she chose to put it on, her womanly sisterliness at a private hour — for all these things Rosamund dearly loved her.

Rosamund was as honest about herself as about anyone else, and now, looking at the studs that swam before her eyes in the red leather, she murmured half aloud : ' As grand as she has been these last months — I could not . . .'

Could she not ? For her father, mother, Nicholas, anyone she loved, she could endure everything, but for oneself, as lonely as the Queen was, hemmed close in by her enemies, betrayed by her very closest such as Nau and, possibly, Curle — no, no. Rosamund would have shrunk in this case into a trembling, thin, white-lipped woman waiting for death.

But the Queen, ever since November, in spite of rheumatism, the shock of Tixall, Sylvia Irvine's death, the realization that Nau had been one of her betrayers, the awful death of Babington and his boy conspirators, the full realization that she brought ruin on to all who tried to help her — in spite of all these things and the dank chills of Fotheringhay she had grown grander and grander.

It was as though now when she knew that she had lost the game she was determined to win it. ' In my End is my Beginning . . .' Nevertheless how loathsome Fotheringhay was, and Paulet and his merry men, including Irvine. . . .

Rosamund's face darkened. Philip had not murdered Sylvia, but someone sent by him had. Poor child, poor doomed helpless child! And poor Robin, in whom something now was hopelessly broken, so that he walked like a ghost.

Rosamund was no necromancer. She was as normal a woman as ever was born — but it did seem like a wizard's spell to find, at that very moment, as she turned towards the door, the long, skeleton-grey, bone-dry figure of Phineas Thatcher standing behind the cedar-wood writing-table across the wall of the little room. He had been there all the time watching her, without moving or speaking, and she had not turned sufficiently to find him there. Unlike all the others round the Queen she did not hate Thatcher. She knew what he was, a selfless bitter fanatic, and, more far-seeing than the others, she foresaw that it would not be very long before men like Thatcher were powerfully strong in England.

Full of pleasure in physical delights herself, she yet understood the sensual temptations of total abstinence, the tremendous force that such abstinence gave you. Puritans were not foreign to her : in any case she liked them better than humbugs ; she did not, of course, foresee that it would be this very humbug hypocrisy that would in the end destroy them.

She was always greatly interested in Thatcher : he was a kind of prophet to her, cold, remorseless, who, had he the power, would come down like Moses from the Mount and condemn the people to awful torments because they worshipped the golden calf.

'If men like him,' she had sometimes reflected, 'ever have control of England . . .'

She thought it might be so. She understood so well why to him a woman like Mary of Scots must seem a horror in God's sight. Why she and Sylvia Irvine and Barbara Curle and Nicholas and Robin must stink so in his thin, red-lined, distended nostrils.

This evening, nevertheless, perhaps because of the tension to which her nerves were strung, she appeared to have double-sight. She knew, quite certainly, staring at his bony hands close to his black-clothed sides, that it was he who had thrown Sylvia down the stairs. She knew so certainly that she said, staring at him with a kind of fascination : 'Why did you do it?'

Thatcher liked her the best of the Queen's women. For

N

one thing she was plain. He knew instinctively that she had no sensual lure for men. But she *had* (so curious is human passion) some sensual lure for him. Her honest fearless gaze, the absence of all coquetry, her strong body — his half-crazy, whirling, nervous brain could understand the cool, restful relief of lying in the arms of that unagitated strength. He had thought sometimes vaguely that he would talk to her about himself, for he was very lonely and had mad dreams and had done things that haunted him at night. Most especially he was afraid that God might one day punish him for the imaginations of his mind that, lying alone on his bed, he often could not prevent. He was sometimes afraid that he was crazy and sometimes proud that he was.

He made her no answer. Still staring, Rosamund said again :

' Why did you do it ? . . . Why did you throw her down the stairs at the inn ? '

He did not attempt to deny it.

' She was an adulteress.'

Rosamund felt tears sting her eyes. She had not yet cried for Sylvia, although the death had been months ago. Now a tear fell and she put up her hand against her cheek.

' To murder anyone so helpless . . .'

Her voice caught. Thatcher, without moving, said coldly : ' Some things are right. God commands them.'

(He saw her with her body pressed against his hard ribs and his chill lips on her warm ones.)

She would have answered that, but the door opened widely and she saw Bourgoing beckoning her.

' We are to come. . . . It is time.'

They were to go to the Queen's bedroom. Bourgoing told her that Kent and Shrewsbury had desired to speak with the Queen, that she had answered that she was in bed and begged for a little time to dress herself. They replied that they must see her immediately.

When Rosamund reached the Queen's room she found that she was seated in her chair at the foot of her bed, and quietly dressed in black with a lace cap on her head. Her women — Kennedy, Barbara Curle — were with her, and several others.

When Rosamund came in, Shrewsbury was saying to her that she must prepare herself to hear her sentence read.

The Queen sat there, her head raised, very dignified, her hands on her lap. Every now and again she rubbed the thumb that was so especially swollen with rheumatism. Beale (whom Rosamund detested) began to read a document from which the Great Seal of England in yellow wax swung to and fro.

Rosamund listened intently and yet for some reason of agitation could hear little. She understood that Shrewsbury disliked his office and was making an attempt now, at the long desperate last, to offer some show of courtesy. Rosamund heard him say at last : ' I would have greatly desired that another than I should announce to you such sad intelligence as that which I now bring on the part of the Queen of England, but he and I being both faithful servants I could but obey the commandment she gave me. It is to admonish you to prepare yourself to undergo the sentence of death pronounced against you ! '

At that word something seemed to happen to Rosamund as though a great wind had blown through the door and the candle-flame had leapt in the air. She had, but now, been studying this Queen dispassionately. When Shrewsbury, ashamed a little, spoke the words ' sentence of death pronounced against you,' Rosamund had to dig her nails into her palms and hold her arms rigidly against her sides that she did not rush forward, fling her arms around the Queen, call to all of them that they touched her at their peril. Looking stead-fastly at that woman with her wig, her mouth drawn with physical pain, her swollen hands, she loved her as, for the moment it seemed to her, she had loved no one else. She would, at that instant, have sacrificed Nicholas to her. The Queen's quiet dignified reply called her back to control.

The Queen, looking at Shrewsbury a little sarcastically, said : ' I thank you for such welcome news. I am very glad to go from this world. I am quite ready and very happy to die, and to shed my blood for Almighty God, my Saviour and my Creator, and for the Catholic Church, and to maintain its rights in this country, for the welfare of which I have always done everything that has been possible, loving the

376 THE BRIGHT PAVILIONS PART

Queen, my good sister, and this island as dearly as myself, as I have often shown. I have constantly offered to arrange matters peacefully and to bring things to a happy issue, but have always been rejected and put aside. I have been held a prisoner without having merited it, for I came into this country of my own free will in hope of succour, according to the promise of the Queen. We should have agreed very well, and would together have arranged matters so well as to satisfy everyone if I had at once been permitted to speak to her.'

After this she suddenly drew herself up, looked at them all with the utmost solemnity, and drawing a Bible on the table near to her, laid her hand on it.

' I swear by God,' she cried, as though she were challenging the whole world, ' that I have never either desired the death of the Queen or endeavoured to bring it about, or that of any other person.'

Kent stepped forward, crying out : ' Madame, that is a Catholic Bible, the Pope's false version of it. Your oath is then meaningless.'

Mary gave a little sigh as though she were truly sick unto death of the subterfuges, the twists and turns, the manœuvrings, in all of which she had truly had her own share. It seemed to Rosamund that, at the moment she had heard her sentence of death, everything, every lie, every plotting trick had fallen from her. She had a lightness, almost a gaiety.

' My Lord of Kent, this is the translation approved by the Church and if I swear on the book which I believe to be the true version, will not your lordship believe my oath more than if I were to swear on a translation in which I do not believe ? '

Kent, whose eyes and mouth were tender towards her so that she could see that he wished fervently to help her, had nevertheless now to urge her to think of her soul and prepare herself for death which was so near.

' It is the Queen's wish that you should be comforted in this time of stress by a divine. We are charged once more to offer you the services of the Dean of Peterborough. He is one of the most learned of God's ministers and from him you may learn much of the true religion.'

On this Mary started up from her chair so sharply that she was caught by her rheumatism and bit her lip against the pain. Then she cried out 'No. No. . . . My Faith . . .' and sat down again, bending forward a little and holding out her hand as though for strength. Rosamund caught her hand and pressed it.

The Queen withdrew it and, now altogether mistress of herself, she answered : 'I have been for long sufficiently instructed in my religion. I know well what I ought to know of it. When I came to this country, being in the house of my Lord of Shrewsbury, in order to satisfy everyone and to show that I acted only by conscience, I listened to the most able Protestant preachers for nearly the whole of one Lent, but at the end, finding no edification, I withdrew.'

She paused, looking at both Kent and Shrewsbury almost with supplication. Then she half rose, resting her hands on the chair arms, and her voice was exultant as she cried : ' Having lived till now in the true Faith, this is not the time to change, but on the contrary it is the very moment when it is most needful that I should remain firm and constant, as I intend to do. Rather than be unfaithful to it I would wish to lose ten thousand lives, if I had as many, and, if it were possible, shed all my blood several times over, and endure all the most cruel torments you could threaten me with.'

She dominated Kent and Shrewsbury as though there were something in her divine.

' No. No. No. . . .' She softened her voice into petition. ' For my consolation I beg you to let me see my own priest, so that he may help me to prepare the better for death. I wish for no other.'

Shrewsbury answered hastily : ' It is our duty always to prevent such abominations which offend God. We beg you, Madame, to see the Dean of Peterborough.'

The Queen cried out so that the whole room echoed with it : ' No, I will do no such thing. I have nothing to do with him and I neither wish to see him nor to listen to him.'

She quieted then, and bent her head again as though in prayer. No one moved. No one spoke. The small wood fire had died down and the room was very cold.

She raised her head and asked Shrewsbury whether the other Powers had interceded for her. Shrewsbury said yes, they had done so but had shown no sufficient reason why she should not be executed.

Her voice broke and faltered : ' My son . . . he has not . . . he has not as a loving son . . .'

Kent answered softly : ' He did all that was in his power, Madame. You must die in charity.'

She said softly, as though to herself : ' I forgive every one and accuse no one.' Then quite fiercely, like someone at bay against her foes, she continued : ' At least like King David I may pray God to confound and punish His enemies and the enemies of His divinity and religion.'

She asked sharply : ' What has become of Nau and Curle ? '

Shrewsbury answered : ' We do not know.'

' Is Nau dead ? ' she asked.

' No.' Drury, speaking for the first time, added : ' He has not escaped. He still drags his fetters.'

She murmured almost to herself : ' He has accused me so that I die.'

Then, as the Commissioners turned to the door, she asked very calmly : ' When am I to die ? '

Shrewsbury, bowing his head, said very compassionately : ' To-morrow morning at eight o'clock.'

At that there was a terrible scene. Barbara, Jane Kennedy, Rosamund, broke into cries. Barbara Curle even ran forward and caught Shrewsbury by the arm. The Queen tried to restrain them, rising clumsily, but their cries were more vehement. ' No. No. It is too soon. . . . It is cruel. . . . Time to prepare . . .' Barbara Curle, who was very hysterical from the premature birth of her child and the uncertainty about her husband (her worst fear that he might, under torture, have betrayed the Queen), hung on to Shrewsbury's sleeve, screaming. Bourgoing, dreadfully disturbed, came to Shrewsbury and in the greatest agitation said : ' My lord — remember that I cared for your lordship. I would not remind you, but when you were ill I took every care——'

The scene was horrible. Barbara was on her knees ; everyone was talking and crying together. The Queen herself,

staring in front of her, repeated ' Eight o'clock. . . . Eight
o'clock.'

Shrewsbury, finding it hateful, could only shake his head
to Bourgoing. He could not move, for Barbara Curle was
clasping his ankles and crying : ' No. No. It is cruelty— So
soon.'

Bourgoing pressed him.

' You have shown much compassion on other occasions,
my lord. You cannot be condemned for a little common mercy
now.'

But Shrewsbury had had enough. He moved abruptly,
almost kicking Barbara Curle from him, and shouted : ' I
have no power to grant the smallest delay. I have no power,
I tell you.'

He motioned to Kent and Beale. There was some confusion
near the door but they broke through and the door was banged
sharply behind them.

After the door closed the others all crowded round her,
kneeling at her feet. She put her hand on the soft hair of
Jane Kennedy.

' There, Jane Kennedy. What did I tell you ? I knew
they would never allow me to live. I was greatly in the way
of their religion. Now, now, no weeping. Tell them to
hasten supper. You should rejoice, for I am now on a good
road. I am of no good in this world any more, but by dying
I may do good to our dear Church. . . . I return thanks to
God and thank Him with a very good heart that it has pleased
Him to call me at this hour.'

After a while she asked the men to leave the room. They
brought in supper — a cold pigeon-pie, marzipan tartlets,
cheese and apples. The Queen helped with the laying of the
table. The four of them sat to it — the Queen, Jane, Barbara,
Rosamund. They tried to eat to please her.

The Queen was suddenly malicious. ' I would see Nau
have a piece of this pie with poison in it.

Bourgoing had remained behind when the other men had
left and now was acting as steward, handing the plates with a
trembling hand.

' My last supper,' the Queen said. ' Strange. Strange. So

many suppers in so many places, and this my last.'

She caught Bourgoing by the arm, drew him close to her.
' Did you remark, Bourgoing, what Lord Kent said to me? He
said that my life would have been the death of their religion,
and that my death will be its life. How happy that makes me !
What a glorious end that is only a beginning ! I would not
change, even at this moment, with any life in the world for this
one thought.'

She released him and pushed at the tablecloth with her hand.

' Call in my servants. All of them.'

They came, including Robin Herries, who stood, his face
like a mask, his body stiff as though no blood flowed in it.

The Queen looked on them all very kindlily as they stood
sobbing and crying about her. She spoke with great sweetness,
telling them that she was to die at eight in the morning and
bidding them live at peace with one another and surrender,
for her sake at least, all bitterness and quarrelling. She told
them that she was herself perfectly at peace and was dying
for her religion.

When she had dismissed them again and only her maids
and Bourgoing remained, she leaned her elbows on the table
among the bread-crusts and the apple-skins and, raising her
glass, drank to them all in turn.

' Jane — dear Jane Kennedy, whose heart is too tender for
a prison.

' Barbara — who shall be the mother of a child more
worthy than mine.

' Rosamund — of steel and fire, England as she is truly,
never as she is falsely.

' Bourgoing — (here her voice broke) — my friend . . . my
friend.'

She raised her glass.

' I drink to the health of all of you. Drink now to mine.'

They raised their glasses and drank.

She went back from the supper-table to her chair and,
taking the spaniel on her lap, said in a warm, cosy, chuckling
voice : ' Gather round now. Jane and Rosamund, go to that
wardrobe and the chest beside it.'

The girls went.

' Bring the chest. Bourgoing, help them. . . . The things in the wardrobe too.'

They piled up on the floor beside her, hats and kerchiefs, dresses and jewelry, portraits, miniatures, silver daggers. The spaniel grew excited and barked shrilly.

' Now, Bourgoing, I charge you. Certain things that I will show you are for the King and Queen of France, the King of Spain, my cousins of Lorraine. I charge you with these. And for yourself' (he was kneeling on the floor and she bent forward and touched his cheek) ' these rings — that is a favourite of mine — these lutes and my music-book bound in silver, for I know what love you have for music. No, no. . . . Stay, my good friend. You must not weep. You know how I love you and love also to give you anything.'

She seemed now quite miraculously happy. She was as gay as a little girl.

' These pearls for you, Jane ; and Barbara, the diamond pendant. This tablet, Barbara, with the portraits of myself, the King of France — my son — my son.' She took the gold and enamelled tablet in her hand and gazed at it. After signing she put it into Barbara's hand.

She looked up at Rosamund who stood above her. ' And you, most faithful of all women. This miniature of me and the ring with the red stone and — and — this gold chain for your son to play with.' She laughed. ' Nay. Do not shake your head, for I am " fey " to-night and you will marry and bear a son. Round his fat neck hang you this chain and look back, with your steady eyes, to this hour and know that all is well with me.'

The night was wearing on. It was intolerably cold. The Queen asked for her fur cloak. With this huddled about her shoulders she sat at a little table near the embered fire and wrote to her chaplain :

To Préau

I have been attacked to-day concerning my religion, and urged to receive consolation from the heretics. You will hear from Bourgoing and the others that I at least faithfully made protestation for my Faith, in which I wish to die. I requested to have you with me in order that I might make my confession and receive my Sacrament, which was cruelly refused me, as well as leave for my body to be removed, and the power of making a free will or writing anything except what shall pass through their hands and be subject to the good pleasure of their mistress. In default of that, I confess in general the gravity of my sins, as I had intended to do to you in particular, begging you in the name of God to pray and watch with me this night in satisfaction for my sins, and to send me your Absolution, and pardon for the things in which I have offended you. I shall try to see you in their presence, as they have allowed me to see the steward, and if I am allowed I shall ask the blessing on my knees before all. Advise me as to the most appropriate prayers for this night and to-morrow morning, as the time is short and I have no leisure to write ; but I will recommend you, as well as the others, and especially your Benefices shall be spared to you, and I will recommend you to the King. I have no more time. Tell me in writing of all that you shall think best for the good of my soul. I shall send you a last little token.

Very briskly she fastened and sealed it and motioned to Bourgoing, who came over to her.

' Go, my dear friend, find Préau, deliver him this ; have an answer if you can.'

He kissed her hand and went with it.

She started then about her will and wrote for a time, and then suddenly began to cry. She continued to write, blinded by the tears that fell on the paper.

Rosamund ran across to her, knelt beside her, looking up into her face.

The Queen was sobbing wildly. She was incoherent.

' The last . . . alone . . . if I am not brave all history will hear of it. . . . The last night . . .'

Two hours rang from the hall bell.

' Never that hour again . . .'

She caught Rosamund's hands, looking into her face.

' Your eyes are brave. So steady. I shall be free, with God, let them say what they will.' She lowered her voice to a whisper. ' Would you be frightened ? '

' Yes,' Rosamund said. ' But no one must see it.'

The Queen sat back, nodding her head.

' What I do now will be remembered for ever.' And then, still nodding her head, to herself : ' Many have loved me. How much more must Christ then, who is all tenderness, and knows my weakness ! '

She was quite firm again, finished her will with a steady hand, then wrote to her brother-in-law :

To Henry III, King of France

MONSIEUR, MY BROTHER-IN-LAW — It is now almost twenty years since I — by God's permission, and for my sins, as I think — came to throw myself upon the mercy of this Queen, my cousin, where I have had many trials ; and now at last I am condemned to death by her and her Government. I have asked for my papers — which were taken by them — in order to make my will, but I have obtained nothing that can be of use to me, nor have I permission to make another will ; and they have even refused the desire I expressed that my body should, after my death, be removed to your kingdom where I, your sister and former ally, had the honour to be Queen.

To-day after dinner it was announced to me that to-morrow, without fail, I must die like a criminal, at eight o'clock of the morning.

I have not had leisure to write a long account of all that took place, but if you will please to believe my Physician and those others my sorrowful servants, you will know the truth and that, thanks be to God, I despise death, and faithfully protest that I suffer it innocent of all crime, even were I their subject, which I can never be.

The Catholic Faith and the maintenance of the right which God has given me to this throne, these are the two points of my condemnation ; and yet they will not allow me to say that I die for the Catholic Faith, but say that I die because I am dangerous to their religion, and the proof of this is that they have taken my chaplain from me. Although he is in the house, I cannot obtain leave for him to hear my confession, nor give me Holy Communion at the hour of my death ; but they made great efforts that I should receive consolation and religious instruction from their minister brought here for the purpose.

The bearer of this and his companions — chiefly subjects of yours — will testify to you of my deportment at this the last scene of my life. It remains only for me to implore you, as Most Christian King, my brother-in-law, friend and ally, who have done me so much honour as to love me and protest of your affection, that under this blow you should show proof of your virtue in these matters by charitably aiding me in that which it is impossible for me to do without your assistance, namely, to reward my desolate attendants by giving them their salaries, and by having prayer made to God for a Queen who has been called Very-Christian, and who dies a Catholic and destitute of all means.

Regarding my son, I commend him to you inasmuch as he shall merit it, as I cannot answer for him ; for my servants I beg your help with clasped hands. I venture to send you two rare stones, valuable for health, the which I desire you to have in perfection, as also I wish you a long and happy life. You will receive them as from your very affectionate sister-in-law, who in dying desires to show her affection for you. I will again recommend my servants to you in a memoranda, and you will command, if you please, that my soul shall benefit by a portion of that which you owe me, in honour of Jesus Christ, to whom I will pray for you to-morrow at my death. I beg you to grant sufficient to found an Obit, and to make the desired Alms.

This Wednesday, at two hours after midnight.—Your very affectionate good sister,

MARIE.

She sat for a long while staring in front of her across the little table.

Bourgoing had not returned. Jane Kennedy was reading, Barbara Curle sewing some child's garment : only Rosamund sat staring into the embers of the fire.

'Thus it is,' she thought, 'to be dead in four hours, to *know* that I will be dead. . . . This is reality.' She felt a compassion almost overpowering so that she must hold her hands hard not to go to the Queen. 'Life is so short. The Queen is alive, her blood in her veins, her heart beating ; hunger, thirst, weariness, cold — she is conscious of them all. In four hours all that reality will be gone. Another reality perhaps. So, at any moment, it may be with myself. The only thing that matters is that I make something of my life. Make something I will. For the Queen's sake. For the Queen's sake. I love her as dearly, but in another fashion, as I love Nicholas, and I swear to God that after this night I will lead a true life before God, be compassionate to all and re-member always how fleeting this life is.'

She repeated the Lord's Prayer to herself and even as she finished it the Queen got up and came over to them.

She looked at them and realized that while she had been writing they had gone and dressed in mourning garments. She asked Jane Kennedy to fetch the silver bowl and wash her feet, which Jane Kennedy did. Then saying that she was tired she lay down on her bed. Jane Kennedy always read to her at night and the Queen asked her to read now.

' Read of some saint who had once been a great sinner.'

Jane Kennedy read of the repentant thief. The Queen said that he was indeed a great sinner but not so great as she had been. Then she remembered that a handkerchief would be needed to bind her eyes and they found a beautiful one with gold embroidery.

After that there was complete silence. Barbara and Jane fell asleep. Rosamund sat on, feeling herself drawn into the very soul of the Queen. It was as though she herself were to suffer and she had no fear. She knew by that that the Queen had no fear.

Five o'clock sounded from the hall and the Queen sat up and beckoned to Rosamund.

Rosamund came over and sat on the bed-edge. The spaniel was curled up against the Queen's thigh and was fast asleep. The Queen spoke very softly, almost in a whisper.

' Rosamund, I have been thinking of that poor child Sylvia Irvine. I fear she was done foully to her death. It is a strange thing, but a while ago I was suddenly aware that we were, the two of us, doomed and at the same time. Poor child . . . poor child ! So young. So hopeless. Her death has broken Mr. Herries' heart, has it not ? '

Rosamund said : ' He has suffered for it most deeply. He thinks he should have prevented it.'

' That is not yet the end of that story,' the Queen said. ' Help him as you are able, Rosamund.'

Her eyes were half closed.

' How we may cheat ourselves ! I think that I see God on His throne waiting for me, and Jesus Christ at His side, and Mary the Mother of Jesus. . . . Of one thing above all in my life I repent myself. But I was very young. He tried me hardly. And now, in Purgatory I shall suffer as I indeed deserve . . . O Mary, Mother of Jesus ! . . . O Mary, Mother of Jesus . . .'

She turned a little on her side, taking care not to disturb the dog.

' These rheumatics — I see now why I was charged with them — for with their twists and cramps they make death a pleasanter, more desirable thing.'

She stayed in great peace, her lips moving in prayer.

Quite suddenly there came into the silence of the room the noise of hammering. Then the heavy tramp of soldiers. The hammering grew louder and more insistent.

The Queen's hand moved, sought Rosamund's and held it tightly.

THE CRUCIFIX

ROBIN HERRIES, guarding the door of the Queen's room, heard six o'clock strike, then half-past six. The deep gong-like note had scarcely died away when the door opened and Bourgoing, his face pale and lined like a map, summoned him.

He stood exactly inside the door. The Queen faced him, her women behind her; Bourgoing, Jacque Gervais, Pierre Gorion, Didier, ranged on either side of her.

She was superb, the Queen of all Queens. She was dressed as a Queen-Dowager. The skirt and bodice of black satin were worn over a petticoat of russet-brown velvet; while the long regal mantle, also of black satin, embroidered with gold and trimmed with fur, had hanging sleeves and a train. The Queen's head-dress was of white crêpe, from which fell a veil of the same delicate material, edged with lace. Round her neck she wore a chain of scented beads with a cross, and at her waist a golden rosary.

Before Bourgoing had opened the door he had read the Queen's will aloud, after which she had signed it and given it to him to deliver to the Duke of Guise. She had then distributed little purses of money; she took farewell of her friends, embracing the women and giving her hand to the men to kiss.

She looked now at Robin, and suddenly out of her dignity smiled at him, a little childishly.

' I pray you, Mr. Herries,' she said. ' Excuse me a moment in the Oratory that I may make my last prayers.'

He bowed his head, then followed her and her company into the ante-chamber that had been arranged as an Oratory. The bedroom door was closed and even locked.

She knelt before the altar and her people knelt about her. They all began to weep and to implore God in passionate tones. Mary's pale face was raised upwards to the ivory crucifix on the altar. Her lips moved and now and again her body trembled. She must have been in pain from her rheumatics, kneeling there so long in that position.

Robin stood between the ante-chamber and the bedroom. He was a slain man. Nothing could touch him any more. Not physically slain. His bodily functions continued ; even at supper last night, with Paulet, Irvine, Beale and others (yes, at supper, much drinking, bawdy talk, only Beale, Paulet and Irvine were grave and steady-eyed, while, upstairs, the Queen had *her* supper also, pushing, with her swollen hand, the apple-rind, the bread-crusts away, as she prepared to write her last letters on earth) — even at supper Robin had called out 'Excellent tender tongue. More mustard.' That was the dead man crying as ghosts cry from the graves in the church-yard. 'I was there. I saw her fall. Her husband murdered her. Excellent tongue. More mustard.'

But not her husband, not that brown black man, picking his teeth with his dagger-end, Philip Irvine . . . Philip Irvine. . . . For he was here when she fell, here in this dark, dangerous Castle where men die and no one knows that they are dead. Here, in Castle Perilous, Philip was alive, for even (we think ; we cannot be sure of the time : only one man knows) as she fell he was playing at chess with another officer, who trapped his queen and beat him in ten moves. (And now the Queen writes her letter and the tears fall on it and stain it. A pain shoots up her arm as she writes.)

Robin woke every morning (for he was sleeping mightily well) to the same emptiness of air and water in which for many weeks he had been moving. After the chess Irvine had been speaking to Robin at that very moment on the staircase, speaking to him friendlily as he always did, and Robin replying friendlily although he hated him so deeply that he could see how his thin finger (for Robin's fingers were very slender) would lengthen like a gimlet, would pierce the silver-trimmed doublet, the coat of mail, the silk vest, the brown smooth skin, the pulpy fat, the bone and sinew, would turn and turn in the breast until the blood, black like his traitor's heart . . .

'It must have been weary for you, Robin, this night-watching for so many weeks, but it will soon be over, I understand.' Philip's smooth, self-satisfied, ambition-devoured voice.

And then the man running up the stairs to them, pausing half-way.

'Sir. . . . Sir . . . your lady . . .'

And Philip's sharp : ' What ? What ? What about my lady ? '

' They have found her, sir. . . . At the inn. She is . . .'

Robin had known at once that it was Philip's deed, yes, even though Philip had run down a step or two, caught the soldier by the arm and shaken him.

' *What* do you say ? At the inn ? My wife . . .'

Robin had stood in the shadow against the wall, straight up as though he were being crucified. He had remained there for a long, long time, so long that he was there, staring down into the hall, when they brought her, illuminated with torches, lying, her face covered, on a plank which four men carried. They laid the plank down on the floor of the hall, and someone brought candles. They blew out the torches, and the wind through the still-open door was bitterly sharp and cold. He felt the wind and was inclined to call out to them to close the door. His body shivered as though with an ague.

He could see into the Oratory and the bed-room also. From under the chair near the fire crept the spaniel. It stood there, greatly dejected, shivering a little, raising up to him large brown melancholy eyes. It was as though it asked permission of him. It seemed to realize that he was a dead man, for it went past him into the Oratory and lay down beside its kneeling mistress.

Robin saw her face and its extreme pallor. Bourgoing saw this too, for he went to her, whispered, turned back into the bedroom, where on the table by the bed there was some red wine ; also a plate with some thin slices of white bread.

He poured out a little wine and took a piece of the bread, returned into the Oratory, helped her to rise and offered her the food and wine.

She rested a little against him, and Robin heard her say : ' Thank you. . . . You bring me my last repast.'

She knelt again, but at once there was a loud knocking on the bedroom door and a high-pitched voice crying : ' The Lords are waiting. . . . The Lords are waiting.'

Mary, from the altar steps, half-turning her head, said very low : ' Mr. Herries — pray request them for a few moments more only that I may finish my prayers.'

Robin went to the door and said : ' A few moments only.'

As she spoke eight o'clock had sounded from the hall below. There was a slight pause, then the voice called more roughly : ' The door must be broken if it is not opened. Eight o'clock was the latest hour permitted.'

The Queen, turning, nodded to Robin, who opened the door, and when the messenger stood inside the bedroom, the Queen was waiting for him.

He was a very young man with red hair and a pale face, and he seemed confused by the great majesty of the Queen and the weeping women. He stammered and said it was the order of the Lords. She was standing in the opening to the Oratory. She turned to Bourgoing with a smile and said : ' Yes. Let us go.' He turned back to the altar and removed from it the ivory crucifix there. She took it gladly, kissed it with eagerness and gave it to her groom of the chamber, Annibal Stuart, to carry for her.

At the door of the bedroom, Bourgoing, bowing, his voice broken with emotion so that it was hard to distinguish his words, said : ' Madame, neither I nor any of your servants can bear to offer our arm to deliver you to your executioner. . . . But we will follow you to our last breath.'

The Queen, whose left knee plainly hurt her because she had been kneeling for a long while in the Oratory, said : ' You are right, my friend.'

She spoke to the sheriff, who was preceding her, a tall stately man with a grey beard, and said : ' My servants do not wish to lead me to death. I cannot walk without help ; pray let me be a little assisted.'

Two soldiers came and, with great reverence and even tenderness, assisted her, one on either side.

They had walked a little way down the passage when they were met by Philip Irvine, who, dressed entirely in black, seemed of a great height and exceedingly handsome. Robin perceived how supremely delighted he was with his importance on this historic morning. In a cold clear voice he said : ' Madame, I regret, but none of your servants must attend you.'

At that they all broke into desperate cries. Rosamund opposed Philip, her body almost touching his, and with passionate, angry words said that they could not take the Queen away alone, that princesses even must be always attended, that she had always, even for the last nineteen years, had someone to assist her, that her rheumatics made her movements difficult for her, that she must not be shamed before all the world, that it was right that some of her servants should be present to see that all should be properly done. She caught his arm and cried : ' Philip ! Philip ! You cannot do this.'

He made no answer at all, but moved his hand, and two soldiers with pikes came forward and began to drive the men and women back into the bedroom. But it was a piteous scene, for they clung about their mistress, knowing that this was the last time they would ever see her on this earth, holding her hands, her dress, her arm.

She was deeply tender with them, murmuring words of love, but she gently detached them, only saying one word to Philip Irvine, whom of everyone in the Castle she most detested : ' You do wrong, Mr. Irvine, in preventing my servants from assisting at my death.'

She walked on alone, Irvine and the sheriff in front, Robin and some soldiers behind. They could hear the sobbing and crying from the bedroom.

Before she left them she took from Annibal the ivory crucifix and from Jane Kennedy the gold-embroidered handkerchief that she had prepared on the previous night.

' Yes,' Robin thought. ' This is the perfection of Majesty.' His dead self remembered how his living self had asked at the very beginning : ' Queen. Play-actress. Woman — all three together ? ' Now (for he did not care any more : he cared for nothing at all) she was acting a part on a stage before all the world, but behind the actress was the Queen who was dying for her Faith, and behind the Queen was a simple woman whose rheumatics pained her, whose heart was lonely, whom no man would love in physical fashion ever again.

Strangest of all she was a Martyr, and it is quite possible that in a literal sense she saw Heaven opening, angels in glistening array waiting to carry her to the Mother of God. For she had not slept and had eaten very little. In and out between these things moved the frightened question : ' Will it hurt ? '

She descended the great stairs slowly, supported by Paulet's guards, and her left knee hurting her more than it had ever done before. Perhaps at a sharp twinge she thought almost with relief : ' Within an hour I shall not feel this.'

Kent and Shrewsbury were on the first landing waiting for her, and although they had not intended it they bowed low, so superb was her majesty and so calm and tranquil her expression.

Then at the bottom of the staircase her beloved Melville, her devoted master of the household, who had been kept apart from her for three weeks, was waiting. This for a while quite unmanned her. She spoke to Melville ' Thou,' which she never did to any of her servants. He knelt on the stone floor. She rested her hand on his shoulder. His voice was broken. ' After having been so long separated . . . to meet now . . . to endure . . .'

' Thou hast always been a good and faithful servant to me. So I beg thee to continue towards my son. He shall recompense thee as I alas am unable to do. Tell him to keep me in memory. As I pardon all in Scotland who have offended me so would I wish that they would pardon me. May God enlighten my son, and send him His Holy Spirit.'

Melville, sobbing, his voice choked, raised his head as though to speak more clearly, caught his ruff with his hand, pulling it a little.

' Madame, never shall I bear a more sorrowful message than this when I report my Queen and Mistress is dead.' He repeated the words. ' My Queen. . . . My Queen.'

But the Queen, patting his shoulder, then letting her hand rest for a moment on his head, said that he was not to grieve,

for to-day he would see ' the end of Mary Stuart's miseries.'
She raised her voice and gazed out in front of her as though she
were speaking to the whole world : ' My good Melville. Be
the bearer of this news, that I die a Catholic, firm in my religion,
a faithful Scotswoman and a true Frenchwoman.' She said
again : ' Commend me to the King my son. Take him my
blessing.' At this she made the sign of the cross as if to bless
her son.

One of the Commissioners, a wizen-faced, pock-marked
little man, had been growing impatient through all of this,
and pushing past Shrewsbury he said roughly : ' The hour has
struck.'

The Queen bent forward and kissed Melville on his forehead. She had great difficulty in speaking but looked at
the pock-marked Commissioner who had interrupted with a
wandering smile, as though she did not see him.

' Adieu, good Melville,' she said, ' till we meet in the next
world — and pray to God for me.'

She was about to move forward, having recovered all her
dignity, when William Fitzwilliam, the Castellan of Fotheringhay, advanced, knelt down and kissed her hand.

The Queen smiled almost a gay smile, for Fitzwilliam had
been her friend, showing her courtesy and deference in everything. He had been often at words with Paulet over her and
had been regarded by the Government with grave suspicion.
All that he was, however, was a large-hearted, tender-natured
man. He was a great friend of Nicholas Herries'. The
Queen had remembered him on the previous night, leaving
him a gift.

It may have been this meeting with Fitzwilliam that caused
the Queen to feel that this would be a right moment to make
her requests. She looked with great sweetness at Kent and
Shrewsbury.

' My lords, I have two requests.'

Shrewsbury bowed.

' The first is that you will intercede with Queen Elizabeth
for the safety of my secretary Curle, who indeed was a man of
the guileless sort, like a child, and could plot against no one.
There are also certain moneys due to him.'

The two lords made no reply.

The Queen went on : ' The other, my lords, is that you will permit my servants to assist at my death that they may bear witness that I persevere in my Faith to my last breath.'

At this Kent and Shrewsbury stood aside and Beale joined them. They consulted together for a brief while and then Shrewsbury said : ' Which of your people would you wish to be with you ? It must not be more than five or six.'

The Queen seemed surprised at this courtesy and said eagerly : ' Messieurs Melville, Bourgoing, Pierre Gorion, Jacque Gervais, Didier ; two of my women, Barbara Curle and Jane Kennedy.'

They were now at the entrance to the hall. Shrewsbury, speaking with great courtesy, said that the men would be permitted but not the women, for they would create disturbance with their cries.

' Alas, poor souls,' said the Queen. ' I give you my promise, my lord, that they shall not cry out. Your Queen, who is a maiden Queen, cannot have given this cruel order to refuse to the women of another Queen the consolation of assistance at her death.' She became greatly agitated. ' She cannot. . . . She cannot. . . . To be alone without anyone of my sex . . .' She put one hand to her face, the other holding the crucifix, to hide the tears that began to fall. She seemed in danger of absolute collapse, her knees trembling, and the soldiers had to hold her between them more firmly. She saw that Kent and Shrewsbury were hesitating, so, checking her tears, she recovered her dignity and proudly asked : ' Do you then forget, my lords, that I am cousin to your Queen, that I am of the blood royal of Henry VII, that I am Queen-Dowager of France, and anointed Queen of Scotland ? '

Shrewsbury said in a low voice that the two women would be permitted and they all waited while they were sent for.

They came, poor things, expecting that the Queen was already dead, and when they saw her, they ran to her, and then, perceiving the great hall entirely hung with black, the raised platform, the block and the executioner, they cried out piteously.

The Queen said gently, as though speaking to her own

children : ' Now ! Now ! You must not. I have passed
my word to these lords that you shall be quiet and not offend
them.'

At once the two women were quiet and gravely composed.

So the procession entered the hall : the Queen, holding
the crucifix raised up, walking as though she were in command
of the whole world, Melville carrying her train.

At the upper end of the hall — near the large Gothic
fireplace in which a great fire was burning — stood the scaffold,
raised two feet above the ground. This was twelve foot
square and covered in black serge, as were the stool and
cushion prepared for the Queen, and was made low enough
to allow the spectators to see all that passed. At the side
towards the end of the hall, the scaffold was approached by
two steps. The block, made of oak, and covered also with
black, was placed near the chimney-piece. By it stood the
executioner and his assistant, both in long black velvet gowns,
with white aprons, and both wearing black masks. The
executioner carried a large axe mounted with a short handle.

In front of the block, chairs were placed for Kent and
Shrewsbury. Two other chairs, placed higher up the room,
outside the scaffold, were for Paulet and Drury. Round the
scaffold was a guard of halberdiers, the men of Huntingdon.
Three hundred spectators were allowed in the hall.

Robin Herries was near the fire, not far from the scaffold,
but standing closely pressed with men whom he did not know,
servants possibly of Kent and Shrewsbury. He stood as
though his body were one long bone upon which heat was
burning. He gazed into blackness. Everywhere was blackness
except the red leaping light of the fire. He noticed little things
as a man in a trance may yet notice, although he cannot
move, the sun-shadow on the wall, the blowing of a spray
against the window. He had seen, as they came down the
staircase, the spaniel keeping its place close to its mistress,
and he saw it now, as the Queen mounted the scaffold, moving
beside her. Why had no one prevented it ? Only he had
realized it, and he had a crazy impulse to step forward, catch
it in his arms, fondle it, and turn its head close to his breast

when the dreadful moment came. But it was a dream impulse, when you wish to leap, to run, to fly, and are held by a vice.

He heard above him a twittering and a fluttering and, looking up, saw above the beams in the far distance of the ceiling, a bird that flew, uttering little cries, from corner to corner. It could not get out and its sound was like a beseeching whisper in his ear urging him to wake.

The man next him was stout and wheezed between every breath. His eyes were bulbous and stared at the scaffold as though they would never have enough.

All these trifles meant nothing to Robin — only far, far away he seemed to hear his own voice saying : ' Once, long ago, I prayed that I might serve this Queen. It was my dearest wish. I have been given a handsome opportunity and have done nothing, nothing at all. Somewhere — at some time — some other cried to me to save her. She fell and her neck was broken. There too I did nothing.'

But a man who is dead does not care for broken vows. That is the blessing of being dead.

He could hear all that was said. The Queen was approaching the scaffold. She had raised the crucifix in front of her and moved with the greatest dignity. But at the moment before mounting the scaffold she paused, as though listening.

Everyone in the hall could hear the cries and shouts, many of them insulting, from the courtyard, but more insulting were the strains of music, for musicians placed in the courtyard were playing a mournful dirge which was frequently played at the execution of witches.

The Queen must have known this well, but she gave no sign, climbed the steps and seated herself on the black stool. Kent and Shrewsbury stood on each side of her and at once she begged them that she might have her own chaplain. This was refused her. Beale then ascended the scaffold and read aloud to everyone the royal commission for the execution. At the end of this everyone shouted ' God Save the Queen ! '

Shrewsbury turned to her and said : ' Madame, you know what we are commanded to do.'

The Queen answered : ' Do your duty.'

She moved on her stool, looked about her, up into the roof

where perhaps she saw the constant flight of the bird, then in a clear quiet voice that everyone could hear, said :

'My lords, I was born a Queen, a sovereign princess, not subject to laws, a near relative of the Queen of England, and her legitimate heir. After having been long and wrongfully imprisoned in this country, where I have endured many pains and evils, no one having any right or power over me, I am now, through force, and being in men's power, about to close my life.

'I die a Catholic. As to the crime which they have fixed upon me — the death of the Queen — I never suggested it, nor consented to it, nor to anything against her person. I have always loved her and the country also. I forgive each one, whoever he may be, who may have offended me, or done me harm, as I beg all to be so good as to forgive me. I accuse no one any more than I have done previously ; my tongue shall do harm to no one.'

The air was absolutely still and clear. Someone had closed a door, and no sound, whether of music or voices, came from the courtyard. So still was it that a log falling in the fire startled everyone. All held their breath. Only, as she ended, the wheezy man next to Robin muttered : 'Poor lady ! . . . Oh, the poor lady ! '

Out of the stillness something stirred in the soul of Robin Herries, the first life in him since Sylvia died. Life — very dim, only half conscious, came to him from the face — the high forehead, the eyes, the mouth — of the Queen.

She seemed, sitting there with so straight a back on that stool, holding the ivory crucifix in front of her, to be in an ecstasy of exaltation. Far, far away Robin heard the incoming of a fresh tide of consciousness across the dry sterile plains of his spiritual experience.

Now all saw the Dean of Peterborough, Dr. Fletcher, come and place himself, very self-importantly, in front of the Queen. He bowed and said that, by his mistress' command, he had come to prepare her for death.

The Queen sighed as though she wished for all this to be over, then very gently said : 'Peace, Mr. Dean ; I have nothing to do with you. I do not wish to hear you. You can be silent if you please and go from hence.'

He continued to speak, raising his voice, but Mary, raising hers, cried out : ' You gain nothing ; I will not listen to you ; be silent, please,' and she turned right round on the stool so that her back was to him.   But the Dean was urgent.   He even laid his hand on her arm, telling her to think of her crimes, but at this Shrewsbury was shocked and told him to stop.

Then Kent, out of nervousness and the strain of this dreadful business, seeing that she made the sign of the cross with the crucifix, cried out : ' Madame, what does it avail you to hold in your hands this vain image of Christ if you do not bear Him in your heart ? '

And the Queen answered sharply : ' How is it possible to have such an image in one's hands without the heart being deeply moved by it ? '

Everyone in the hall was now feeling a nervous uneasy excitement, as though the scene were being drawn out beyond endurance.   A young soldier in full armour near the fire fainted with the heat and was pushed to the outskirts of the pressing crowd, where, propped up against the wall, he uttered little muttering groans.

Shrewsbury cried out : ' Madame, if you will not listen to the Dean we must all pray in common.'

To which Mary answered : ' Pray if you wish.   I will pray also.'

So Fletcher began to pray loudly in English and the Queen in Latin, repeating some of the penitential psalms —' Miserere ' and ' In te Domine speravi '— and as she did so she beat her breast with the crucifix and kissed it.

Then she began in English and it was strange how her voice, which she did not appear to raise, was clear above the hubbub, for now they were all praying — Shrewsbury, Kent, the Dean, men crying out in the hall, some women (neither Kennedy nor Curle) weeping hysterically, men moving and pushing against one another.   It seemed, if this suspense continued very long, that there would be some dreadful outbreak of violence.

The Queen prayed : ' Send me your Holy Spirit, Lord, that at the hour of my death He may enlighten me and enable me to understand the mystery of your Passion. . . .'

She prayed for peace between Christian Princes, the conversion of England to the true Faith, for the Pope, for her enemies, for Queen Elizabeth, and for her son's conversion to the Catholic Faith.

When her prayer was finished there was a sudden extraordinary silence. All men looked at her. Raising the crucifix high she passionately kissed it and exclaimed : ' As Thy arms, my God, were extended on a cross, so receive me into the arms of Thy mercy. Extend to me Thy mercy and pardon me all my sins.'

She turned to her servants and embraced them, rose and reseated herself.

A man's voice from the back of the hall cried out : ' Have done ! Have done ! . . . Put an end . . .'

Kent and Shrewsbury approached her and asked her whether she had any secret matter to reveal to them, but, clasping the crucifix to her bosom, she answered : ' I have said all.'

She looked about her, and then, with a shy smile as though she were timid about entering into new company, she rose and began to prepare herself for death, for she saw that the actual moment had at last come.

She laid the crucifix upon the stool. Bull, the London executioner, approached and offered to remove her outer dress, but the Queen, smiling, shook her head : ' Let me do this. I understand this business better than you. I never had such a Groom of the Chamber.'

Then she took the pins out of her head-dress, but her fingers were sore and swollen, so she called softly to Jane Kennedy and Barbara Curle, who were on their knees praying.

They came to her and began to assist her to disrobe, but they were both sobbing and crying now like frightened children. The Queen bent forward and kissed Jane Kennedy's wet cheek.

' Do not weep any more or I shall think that I should have had Rosamund Herries with me for this. I am very happy to go from this world ; you should be happy to see me die in so good a quarrel. Are you not ashamed to cry ? If you weep any more I will send you away, as I promised for you.'

She looked at Jane Kennedy with great intensity, then she

took the gold cross from her neck and was about to give it to the girl when Bull pushed his way in, saying, ' This is mine,' and he roughly took the chain from her.

' My friend,' the Queen said, ' you cannot make use of this. As my last request I pray you leave it to this lady. She will give you good value for it, for it is worth to her very much more than money.'

But Bull shook his head, muttering, ' It is my right,' and dropped it into his shoe.

The Queen, quite joyfully, with eagerness, had helped in her own disrobing and now stood in a brown velvet skirt and black satin bodice with long sleeves.

It was a stormy wild morning. The rain was beating against the windows and the hall was smokily dark. The great fire in the stone fireplace near the scaffold was leaping wildly and illuminated the Queen with a crimson light so that some thought that her undergarment was crimson.

Once more, and always smiling, she bade farewell to her men-servants, Melville and the rest, then embraced and blessed the two women, making the sign of the cross on their foreheads.

She said in French : ' Adieu, for the last time. Adieu. Au revoir.'

Jane Kennedy fastened the handkerchief with the gold embroidery over her eyes. The Queen moved her own hands up to it and adjusted it. She asked the two women to go down from the scaffold.

The executioners fell on their knees asking her pardon, and the Queen, moving with her hands a little as a player does in blind-man's-buff, said : ' I forgive you with all my heart.'

She was seated on her stool again, holding the crucifix, and it seemed that she thought she was to be executed then, for she stretched out her neck. She thought that she would be beheaded with a sword as was the privilege of royal personages in France. But the executioners came over to her, helped her to rise (she stumbled in her blindness, caught Bull by the arm and smiled at him as though in apology), and then conducted her to the block as though they were leading a little child who was learning to walk.

The drums began to roll. The executioners made her kneel

down by the block, and as she knelt upright, still thinking she was to be beheaded with the sword, they made her lie flat, Bull pushing her in the small of her back, with her head on the block.

As the Queen repeated the words ' In te Domine speravi,' Shrewsbury raised his wand to give the signal.

The drums rolled.

Bull raised his axe high, but stopped, for his assistant showed him that the Queen, in order to enable herself to breathe, had placed her hands under her chin. The assistant bent down and held her hands behind her back.

The drums had ceased. There was a deep, fathomless silence in the hall made vocal only by the twittering of the bird in the rafters. Mary's voice came out loud and very clear, ' In manus tuas Domine commendo—' They were her last words on this earth.

Bull struck, but with an ill aim. He wounded the Queen on the side of the neck but she neither moved nor spoke. He struck again and the head was severed. He raised the head, holding it by the grey hair, for the red wig had tumbled, and cried in a coarse rough voice : ' God Save the Queen.'

A low ' Amen ' sounded through the hall.

Kent came to the front and shouted ' Amen ! Amen ! May it please God that all the Queen's enemies be brought into the like condition ! '

The headless body lay there stretched out. From beside the skirt the spaniel, its golden coat stained with blood, stole out, its whole body trembling, its large eyes pitifully looking for someone, but it uttered no sound.

The drums rolled until, with the wild leaping of the fire, their sound filled the hall.

END OF PART III

PART IV

THE ENEMY IN FLIGHT

ASHES OF LETTERS

CHEVELEY, Robin Herries' fat, dough-faced servant, paused on the bridge beside Rosthwaite before mounting the hill to his master's house. He was not a great lover of nature, but it did strike him on this October day that the hills were on fire. He raised his large gooseberry eyes, and then, with his distended nostrils, sniffed the blackberry-chrysanthemum sky-flavour as though he were embalming his nose with an immortality of crystal-scented air. Very good! Oh, very good! And he walked up the hill with that extra stride and that added straightening of the shoulders that had come to Englishmen since the defeat of the Armada.

It had not as yet, however, he reflected, come to his master. And then he saw him, like a thin ghost in ebony, standing quite motionless in front of the courtyard, the gate being open and the autumn sun sparkling on the weather-vane as though the Bird of Fire were perched there.

So his master was a ghost and had been ever since that awful time at Fotheringhay. Cheveley had not been with him there. He had left him before that to marry a baker's daughter in Islington. And *that* had turned out most unfortunately, the baker's daughter deserting him for a soldier from the Low Countries. So Cheveley had returned to Robin in the summer of 1590 and was with him now for life.

Robin had a power over Cheveley that he had never had before. Cheveley had never really approved of Robin's illicit pursuit of Irvine's wife. He had been at times a letter-carrier, a go-between, and this had distressed his morality, for, in spite of his occasional somewhat doughy debaucheries, Cheveley was a Puritan at heart. Then Robin had been, in those days before Fotheringhay, moody, unhappy, restless. Now he was as quiet and restful as a ticking clock. And his

O

courtesy ! He spoke to you as though you were Leicester himself and was considerate about everything. He was a grown man now in his self-control, his dignity, and he was like a dead man in his passivity.

This was the kind of post that Cheveley enjoyed : an easy life with a good master, no women to order you, good wages, not too much heavy labour, and plenty to eat. A sort of love for his master had crept into his slow-beating heart. Cheveley was distressed when others demanded emotion of him, which was, perhaps, why the baker's daughter left him for the Low Countries soldier. But this remote, still, controlled English gentleman asked nothing of him but service. It was as though Mr. Herries were waiting for some call, Cheveley thought, as he looked up the road and saw him standing at the gate. He was always like that, as though he were listening.

Robin was staring, as he often did, at the scene before him and seeing it as a vision. The ridges of the hills were hard and sharp against a pale green sky. The afternoon was closing in. Already the shadows were gathering over the valley and the white mist lay like ruffles of lawn over Borrowdale. Above the mist were the flaming bastions of rock and fell, a dim sparkling gold with a movement in it, as when someone, very gently, shakes a cloth. Little valley sounds came up to him as though cows and dogs and sheep were rejoicing in the loveliness of the evening. A blind man, belonging to the valley, who had been at Watendlath, came down the path past Robin. He was ringing a little bell. He wore a high-peaked shabby white hat and had a red muffler round his skinny neck. His dog, a big sheep-dog, walked behind him. Robin knew him. He stopped, scenting that someone was there.

' Good night, William.'

' Good night to you, Mr. Herries. A fine night.'

' Yes, a fine night, William.'

Cheveley came up and they both went indoors.

This was the hour that Robin always dreaded, the hour before he could settle into his work. He tried to defeat his fear sometimes by starting to work at once, and so he did now, drawing the high-backed chair in to the table, kicking out his long legs and feeling the last rays of the October sun hot upon his head.

He was translating the elegies of Propertius, and now, leaning forward, gazing at the open book, he repeated to himself the famous lines of the twenty-sixth elegy of the Second Book :

> ' Vidi te in somnis fracta, mea vita, carina
>   Ionio lassas ducere rore manus,
> et quaecunque in me fueras mentita fateri,
>   nec iam umore graves tollere posse comas,
> qualem purpureis agitatam fluctibus Hellen,
>   aurea quam molli tergore vexit ovis.'

Smiling ever so slightly, he repeated over to himself the lovely, smooth, marmoreal words :

> ' qualem purpureis agitatam fluctibus Hellen,
>   aurea quam molli tergore vexit ovis.'

He began, quite eagerly, to consider how he would begin the translation of this verse, giving the very quality of Propertius, so different from the light humorous play of Catullus whom also he loved.

These lines are part of a description of a dream wherein the poet sees his beloved drowning in the sea, her hair sinking with the weight of the brine, crying to him to help her. . . .

To help her. To help her. Robin suddenly began to tremble through all his body. For more than four years now these trembling fits had constantly seized him. All his limbs shook and his heart hammered and his eyes filled with tears. There seemed to be no reason behind them, but because of them and because he could not sleep he had come to live, alone except for Cheveley and an old woman, in his little house at Rosthwaite. He did not wish anyone else, not even Nicholas, to see his helplessness. And while he trembled, deep down in his very reins a voice seemed to say to him : ' Traitor ! Traitor ! Traitor ! '

The country round Rosthwaite slowly comforted him. Its wildness and remoteness, with its woods, the sudden clearings where cattle were, the unexpected streams, and more than all, the unchanging friendly hills. All these alone in the world seemed not to accuse him, to understand his failure to save his Queen and his lady.

At one moment only he had seemed to spring to life : the night on the Seascale sands when he had seen the reflection of the Armada fires. Until the Armada it had appeared to him that the country was sinking into absolute ruin. His hatred of Elizabeth had grown so frenzied that if, during those months between Fotheringhay and the Armada, he had been tempted by the Catholics he might have joined in some hidden plotting.

More and more he had loathed her meanness and parsimony. Her meanness towards the States of the Netherlands and her plotting with the man she knew to be her enemy, Philip of Spain, against them, her lies and subterfuges, and then, when the danger from Spain was clear to all, her parsimony to Drake and Hawkins so that Hawkins must pay his men out of his own pocket, her refusal to provide ships, her constant going back on her word, her supplying such filthy provisions that half the men died of dysentery from the foul beer and bad peas and beans — yes, right up to the moment of the Armada itself.

And then at that instant when, the sea murmuring in his ear, his thoughts miserably set on that little house where he had spent the night with Sylvia, he had seen the sky redden with the fire from Skiddaw, his heart had suddenly leapt up. He knew that he had a passion for his dear country.

Afterwards he had realized that he was living in a new country. Three hundred and fifty years later Englishmen were to go to war once again with a great lifting of doubt at their country's courage from their hearts and souls. So now Robin felt. Almost his life long he had watched the uncertain policies of England's statesmen. Was England to sink into a lower place among the nations of the world ? Were the days of her greatness over ? He had not shared in the congratulations over the piracies of Drake and the others. He had wanted something quite different for England. And now he had it. God, in spite of her sins, had been after all on England's side. He had raised His great winds and the enemy had been scattered.

Robin had even come to see that there might after all have been some wisdom in Elizabeth's caution and parsimony. Men like Philip Sidney had not died altogether in vain.

He loved his country in a new way : ' aurea quam molli tergore vexit ovis.'

He raised his head and listened. This was a trick that took him often. It was as though he were expecting some signal. He listened. The dusk was quickly falling. There was the twittering of a bird. Yes, and there was a hurried tap on the window.

He turned on his elbow and stared. Even as he looked the golden light seemed to vanish from the sky and a grey dusk sweep to the walls of the house. Against the grey was a darker shape. Robin knew at once that it was Anthony Pierson. He undid the clasp and threw back the casement. Pierson was over the sill and, without looking at Robin, gasped :

' There must be a fire lit . . . somewhere . . . not here . . . deep in the house . . .' He caught at the high back of the chair for support. He was dressed as a farm-hand in a smock and leather breeches. As he talked he began to throw off his clothes.

' I have half an hour at most. Can you get me some of your serving-man's things ? And I'll do my hair. . . .'

He bent down, kicking off the breeches. He stood up again, his chest heaving, the cords in his thick neck swelling. He was still breathing like a running man.

' Quick. Quick, Robin. Cheveley will have something, stout though he is. Don't tell him the wherefore though. I know he's faithful but better not. And see that a fire's lit. They mustn't get the papers though they get me.'

He was recovering himself. He stood there, his arms folded across his broad chest. He suddenly laughed.

' Oh, Robin, it's good to see you — even in this flutter.'

But Robin was gone. Pierson watched the window. He passed his hands up and down his thighs, stroked himself friendlily.

Robin was back in a few minutes, carrying some clothes. He laid them on a table, vanished and returned again in a moment or two with a flagon, bread, a meat pie, some fruit.

Pierson had clothed himself in the plain doublet and hose
that were too big for him but could serve. He was trussing
his hose. Suddenly he stopped, went over to Robin and
embraced him.

'I may be bringing great trouble on you for this.'

Robin, whose eyes were shining with happiness and pleasure,
answered :

'Tony, I haven't seen you for a year. Nay, it's more.
The afternoon at Baddicombe was the last. But what is it?
Why are you here? Who's pursuing?'

Pierson went quickly to the window. The curtains had
been pulled across it and he drew an edge and looked out into
the dusk. Robin had brought silver candlesticks and now the
candlelight shone on the table. Pierson sat down close beside
Robin and began to eat and drink.

'It's Irvine.'

'Irvine!' Robin cried out.

'Yes, Philip Irvine. He has a man Thatcher who has been
up here some months nosing out Catholics. He had Chamberlain at Lasting Manor and Forster at Breeding as you heard.
I have been in the Low Countries, but I came over a month
ago, bringing letters to — well, never mind who. It's better
for you if they question you that you shouldn't know. I have
them with me now and we must burn them before I go. . . .'

He stopped, caught Robin's arm and gazed into his face.

'Robin, it's dangerous for you. Very dangerous. If they
come and question you and find that you have burnt papers —
and Irvine hates you, doesn't he?'

Robin was staring at the wall opposite him in a sort of
exaltation. It was as though he had not heard his friend. But
he had, for he turned back to him.

'Perhaps my chance has come at last, Tony. I have been
waiting a long time. I had failed in everything through a kind
of inanition, an indecision. I knew what I should do but I
could not. Now in this last ten minutes everything has cleared.
I am happy as I have not been for years.'

Pierson put his arm round his friend's neck and drew him
closer to him.

'Yes, but, Robin, this is truly dangerous. You know what

they do to anyone concealing or helping a proscribed Catholic priest. But just now I was desperate. They have been after me for two days and nights. I had got to the Isle of Man where I had business. Then, two days ago, I landed on the shore between Seascale and Whitehaven. I should have gone straight to Lancashire, but I caught at the chance of seeing you. . . . I hadn't, you know, for over a year. You are the only human being left in my life, Robin. I — I— But no matter. I came to Keswick. I lodged last night with a man and woman — good folk who knew me. This morning I started off to walk to Rosthwaite, and there, outside the inn, I saw Irvine sitting his horse. Thatcher came out of the inn and spoke to him. And Thatcher saw me. He knows me well and is longing to have me by the tail. He saw me and knew me. I was away across the bridge to Portinskill and then along the path to Manesty. I was safe in the woods there, I thought, but early in the afternoon there they were riding the path on the Catbells slope above me. I slipped by the Lake and over the bridge and so along the valley here. But I fancy they sniffed me. But I came here, Robin, because I thought Irvine and Thatcher would find it the most unlikely place, just because it was so likely. And — because — I had to see you. I *had* to. But it was wrong. I have brought you into this. . . .'

' It was right, Tony,' Robin cried, jumping up, ' the rightest thing you ever did. I have been expecting, waiting for something like this — something that would take some of my shame away.

' I loved a woman and deserted her, Tony. I had longed for all my life to serve a Queen and when I came to serve her did nothing. I love you more than anyone else alive now save Nick, and I can serve you — at last I can serve you ! '

He seemed in a frenzy of happiness.

' Come, I have lit a fire myself. In Nick's room. I call it that because he sleeps there.'

' How is your brother ? '

' Nicholas ? Well enough. Not so happy as he was. There is a queer business with a German woman who has married his man. The three of them together are at odds — I don't know how or why. He has grown up, my brother.'

Pierson stood looking at Robin. ' I have never had anyone
to love me like that. I am a priest and must not permit
myself such indulgences.' His voice was unexpectedly bitter.
' Suppose if, after all, God is not there — only vacancy —
clouds and behind clouds space — a Nothingness. And my
body — all the happy lasciviousness that I have not known —
prayers to Our Lady who perhaps is not there. This strength
of body, these parts, this heart. I was meant by nature to
know love. Is nature God ? Can God hear ? I tell you,
Robin, for more than twenty years now I have sweated in
disguise, lain in hedgerows and ditches, starved and shivered,
run day by day the risks of the torture as even now I run them.
My body has been virgin, my seed sterile. Most of all I have
held myself from *you*. Why ? If there should be nothing,
and the Christ an idle tale.'

He was trembling and, Robin thought, on the edge of
tears.

Robin said : ' Remember Campion. I saw him die. He
too was afraid, he too was lonely, and yet I would rather have
been Campion than Drake or Leicester or Burghley. As he
rode on his hurdle there was a vision before him that for him
was a certainty. The Bright Pavilions of which you were the
first to tell me, Tony. That was *real* that Campion saw.
And if we have been kept apart, at least we have not lost one
another, which, if we had come closer, we might have done.
We love one another as greatly as on the first day we met.

' I believe, Tony, that all the real things are the things we
possess with our souls but not with our bodies. The weakness
of my bodily courage has kept me out of the world where I
would be. Perhaps I may do something for you that may
bring me there.'

They went quietly into the other room, which was a small
place hung with red and gold paper, a design of flowers and
birds. There was a trestle bed, a fireplace and a cupboard.
Pierson had with him a wallet, and kneeling down he took
out a bundle of papers and burned them in a wood fire.

They both watched them burn to ashes.

' And now I must be off.'

He embraced Robin and held him so long in his arms that

at last Robin, freeing himself, said, laughing : ' You are more of a bear than ever, Tony. It is as though you will never see me again.'

' I think that I shall not,' he said, climbed the window-sill and was lost in the darkness.

Robin sat thinking. So Irvine was in Keswick. Irvine . . . Sylvia . . . Fotheringhay. The moment on the stairs when they had stood together and the servant had come saying : ' Sir, your lady . . .'

Phineas Thatcher had done that. He had confessed to Rosamund. And Thatcher also was in Keswick. Robin summoned Cheveley.

' You have seen no one here either coming or going ? '

' No, master.'

' You had no suit of clothes that I borrowed from you ? '

' No, master.'

' How many suits have you ? '

Cheveley paused, his heavy white face expressionless.

' Three. The black, the brown with silver . . .'

' Good. You have the same number as you had before ? '

' Yes, master.'

' And you have seen no one this evening either coming or going ? '

' No, master.'

Robin pointed to the plates and flagon.

' I have had my supper early this evening. You may take them away.'

' Yes, master.'

He took them away.

Robin brought out his Propertius again, but although he stared at it he could not attend to it. His whole condition of life seemed to have been changed now that he had served Pierson. His long passivity was over. It would have been almost better had he done a service for someone he did not love — even for an enemy like Irvine. Now that he was passive no longer the activity must continue. He would not work for the Catholics because he was less a Catholic than ever and he would not act against the Queen. But there were other things that he could do. He would go down and stay with Nicholas. He might help him in this queer business about this woman he loved who had married his man Armstrong. There were those in London he could help : the poor, the crippled, the prisoners. He rose, stretching his arms. Yes, his passivity was over. It was as though he had wakened out of a long, horrible sleep.

He started. He heard voices. The door was flung open. He saw Cheveley's frightened face ; behind him Irvine, and behind Irvine, Thatcher and soldiers.

Irvine looked at him as though he had never seen him before. He took a step forward and the soldiers closed in at the door.

' In the Queen's name——' he said.

Robin had risen and, smiling, answered : ' How can I serve you ? '

' I regret — this house must be searched and all inside it. My soldiers are at the gate. No one may leave.'

' May I ask why ? '

' You know well enough. A recusant priest, Anthony Pierson, carrying treasonous papers has been here within the hour.'

Robin said : ' No one has been here within my knowledge.'

Irvine turned to Thatcher.

' See that they search the house — everything, everywhere. Every cupboard, every hole. And all the servants.'

Robin laughed.

' There are only Cheveley and one old woman. The hostler, gardener, what you care to call him, left for his home in Rosthwaite two hours back.'

' How long have you yourself been here ? '

' The whole day. I have not left the house save to walk to the gate an hour back.'

' You have been entertaining that beggar priest — an old friend of yours.'

' I have seen no one all day save Cheveley here, Martha the cook and Hoggs the gardener. I saw a blind man go down the path an hour back.'

' You are lying. You gave the priest a meal here.'

' I had my own meal here half an hour agone.' Lightly

he pushed his book across the table. ' I have been translating Propertius,' he said.

Irvine stared at him, frowning still as though he did not recognize him. He turned to the two soldiers who were still beside him (one of them had his hand on Cheveley's fat shoulder) and said : ' Take that lout until I can examine him. Leave me.'

So soon as they were alone Irvine's expression changed. He drew a chair and sat down at the table opposite Robin.

' So at last, Robin, I have caught you.'

' Caught me, dear Philip ? '

' Oh, I could have done it often enough before. Love, politics — you have often been sufficiently careless. But with you, as with your hobbledehoy brother, it has been pleasant to suspend. An act such as this has a finality. For indeed, Robin, you are ended. There is pain ahead of you — much pain of the body — and then your release. You have been in my hand — for how long ? — ten — twenty years — and now, at last, I close it.'

He suited the action to speech, opening his thin brown palm, closing his thin brown fingers upon it.

Robin said easily : ' I am not aware that I have been in your hand. You flatter your power, but indeed you are the most vain and dissatisfied man I have ever met.'

Irvine drew a little breath.

Robin had not seen him for over a year (the last time had been at the Court in London) and, within these twelve months, he had grown most amazingly thin — not only thin, but behind the dry brown skin there was almost a transparency as though you could see the veins and the pulses of the body at work. His large dark eyes stood out in his bone-dry face as though with an almost frantic urgency. When Robin looked at his eyes he fancied that Irvine had in the last years become a little crazy.

His next words emphasized this. He spoke with hurried gravity.

' It was our Sylvia's fault,' he said softly, ' that she could not recognize the man who was her husband — his great qualities, I mean, and exceptional virtue. If I have a vanity

it is of the highest order. And it was yourself murdered my
poor wife.'

Robin said : ' Ah, no. That, Philip, is, and will always
be, your own companion.'

Irvine leaned forward, the knuckles of his right hand so
thinly fleshed that the bone shone in the candlelight.

' Who told you of that ? How do you know ? If she is
with me it is not by my wish. I never saw her fall and if she
cried it was not I that heard her. And so I tell her, but she
has a fashion now of not hearing. She can look but she cannot
hear, and her right arm is broken — at the elbow. She is
very still and quiet and younger than she was. And I think,
when you are dead, Robin, she will be more quiet.'

He changed his tone ; he leaned back, folding his arms.

' Come then, Robin. The priest was here. We followed
him all day. Where have you hidden him ? We will pull the
house down to find him.'

' I have seen no one. I have been here since the afternoon
with my books.'

Irvine went on : ' You know what it will mean ? I have
seen others suffer — many times. You saw what they did to
Campion before they executed him.'

A very slight trembling ran through Robin's body. It was
as though he saw, in an instant's vision, the things that lay
ahead of him.

He discovered, to his own intense joy, that he was not in
the least afraid.

Thatcher was in the doorway. Robin looked at him
steadily, remembering so many things. Those hands had
killed Sylvia. Thatcher was greatly aged, bent a little, and his
lean face deeply furrowed. He looked as though he were
made of a tough, ugly, shabby grained wood. He came
forward and spoke privately to Irvine, who jumped to his feet.

He spoke to Robin sharply, now quite without any personal
contact.

' It seems that some papers have been burned. The ashes
are yet warm. Would you come with me ? '

Robin followed him into Nicholas' room. The little place
was filled with soldiers. Cheveley, his hands bound behind

him, was held near the bed. From the ash-heap they had recovered fragments of a letter with writing.

Robin thought : ' We were fools. Thinking of ourselves and being together.'

Irvine examined them, and with a smile, triumphant, but at the same time morose, he said to Robin : ' This is important. You were not thorough enough. Now will you say that no one has been here ? '

' I have seen no one, heard no one.'

' What is the use ? Your man has confessed to everything.'

Cheveley called out with surprising anger : ' I have not, master, I have not.'

One of the soldiers kicked him in the groin. He bent forward, groaning.

' I am afraid, Mr. Herries,' Irvine said, ' that you are under arrest. Make your arrangements as quickly as may be. You must go with us.'

Irvine permitted Robin to ride unbound. As they crossed the little bridge and turned right, through the woods, towards Keswick, Robin saw all the tree-tops frosted with the light of an infant moon that seemed to gambol like a lamb of silver in the brilliant sky. In daylight these trees just now were of radiant colours — crimson, saffron, amber, orange, gold. Now, under a night breeze, they stirred like white-shadowed waters. Robin looked around him. He knew that he would never see this valley, which he loved with all his heart, again. But he remembered what Nicholas had said on that day long ago when they had ridden to visit their uncle — namely, that his descendants would ride here, and that this place would be their home.

He waved his hand, bidding farewell, and then they were swallowed up in the woods.

THERE SHALL BE NO PAIN THERE

THE room was more pleasant than he had expected. He was alone for the first time for more than a week, and this loneliness was inexpressibly pleasant. Yes! beyond expression! He could say nothing — and, blessedly, there was no one to whom he should say anything.

He sat on his plank bed. He was still in the same black suit of clothes he had been wearing when they caught him at Rosthwaite. After they had stripped him (a soldier had done it, alone with him in Nicholas' room, and had apologized most friendlily) they had allowed him to resume all his clothes, seeing that no pistol or dagger remained with him. They had taken his translation of Propertius with them to search it for secret writing.

He had succeeded during the ride south in persuading them to release Cheveley's bonds. Cheveley was his one overwhelming anxiety — not for anything that he might reveal under torture, but that he should be tortured at all.

This room in the Tower was small and exceedingly bare. There was a grated window high up and, if he stood on the plank bed, he could see through the window and watch the clouds race through the sky or catch threads of gold at sunset. Beside the plank bed there was a stool and there was a bucket.

He found that he could eat the food they gave him, that he could sleep. As he sat there or lay there he thought continuously, uninterruptedly, of three people. Sylvia, the Scottish Queen, Nicholas. He did not think of himself at all. It was as though he were disembodied. But now for the first time for a long while he could think of these three persons with happiness. He was not ashamed to be in their company any longer.

On the fourth morning he woke abruptly to find the sun

pouring into the little room and a new gaoler standing beside
his bed. He knew him immediately. It was the big man with
the yellow hair who had been with him at Campion's execution.
The man was looking down at him, had been, maybe, while
he slept.

' Do you know me ? ' Robin asked, looking up and smiling.

' Yes, I know you, sir,' he answered. ' I have never forgotten you. I knew that you would come here.'

' How did you know ? '

The man was very quiet, not moving his big body.

' I cannot tell how I knew. But when I touched you that
raining day I knew.'

And then, quite suddenly, Robin's heart seemed to stop its
beating for an instant. He felt the constriction in his throat
and put his hand there. His eyes could not meet Roland's eyes,
for the man was looking at him with a tender pity. This man
knew terrible things.

' See, master, they haven't asked me. I do it from no order.
But I know the case. By telling them all you can, master,
you will spare yourself — the questioning — your life, it may
be . . .'

He spoke in broken sentences.

Robin could look at him now and he did so. He thought
that he was honest. Was he ? Who could say in this world
of lying and spies and torturing ?

' My man — Cheveley — do you know anything of him ?
See — tell me — I have forgotten your name.'

' Michael Roland.'

' Ah, yes — Michael. We were friends that day of
Campion's death. You placed your arm around me and
protected me. Tell me — my man. Where is he ? Here in
the Tower ? Have they tortured him ? '

' They say,' Roland answered slowly, ' that he has confessed
everything. So you see, master, it's of no use. Tell them what
you know. The priest has safely escaped — is in France or
Holland by now, I shouldn't wonder.'

Robin broke out joyfully : ' God be thanked ! There is
news.' But he looked at Roland suspiciously again. ' Is it
really so ? Are you instructed——? '

The two men stared at one another.   Roland shook his head.

' They have not instructed me.   They may at a later time. I would spare you the suffering.   Do you know it, master ? You have not seen it as I have — the rack, the boot, the glove.'

He bent forward and put his large hand on Robin's shoulder.

' Tell them all you can.   If you speak to them they will spare you the torture.'

He went, very quietly, from the room.

Robin lay down, his arms behind his head.   So it had come at last.   All paths led at last to *this* path ; even that act, so many years ago, when Nicholas had heard on that northern moor the unseen man breathing at his feet, had led to this. And, in the confused metaphysical world that his mind at this moment inhabited, it did not seem that Irvine was a man with blood, bones, passions, but rather the Hostile Spirit that every man must challenge, encounter, defeat, if he is to touch experience and see reality.   He saw so many pictures as he lay there : Sylvia at that first ball with the little ship in her hair, Sylvia coquetting with him at Mallory, Sylvia as he watched her praying by that dreadful bed in that dreadful house, and then Sylvia sleeping on his breast in the Seascale room, his ears soothed and charmed by the murmur of the sea, Sylvia giving little sharp cries of ecstasy, sobbing cheek against his cheek, dressing in the early dawn, silent and unhappy, joyful at the first sight of him, loving him always, loving him, loving him . . . Her place was taken by the Queen, and always the Queen in those final hours, kneeling for the last time in the Oratory ; walking, like all the Queens who had ever sat on thrones, down the broad stairs ; kneeling, the executioner moving her hands from under her chin. . . .

How odd it was !   He could think of them now without shame, as though he saw them standing near him, waiting with confidence for his Test.

His Test !   At that the tender commiserating look in Michael Roland's eyes came back to him, and it was as though a door swung back and a draught of hot dry air struck his face.   Reality !   Reality !   The reality of the stripping, the damp air on his flesh, the ropes of the rack, the . . .

He was amazed. He felt no fear. His heart was not beating faster, there was no sweat on his brow. He smiled. He turned on his side and fell asleep.

He woke and found Nicholas standing there. He cried aloud with joy and threw himself into his arms, and Nicholas folded him round and held him close to him, his great body defending him against the world. Robin sat on the bed, looking up at him, laughing.

' Brother, you are as vast as ever.'

But Nicholas didn't laugh. He sat down on the pallet beside Robin, and looked at him with so much love and agitation that Robin said hurriedly : ' Now see you, Nick. There's nothing to grieve for. We'll come out of this to safety. Do not grieve. Do not grieve.'

' Tell me the truth of it.'

Robin told him the truth of it.

' I said always that that fellow Pierson would be no friend. No. No. I would not hurt you, but if you had kept from him there would be none of this.'

' Except for Irvine.'

' Yes.' Nicholas' eyes narrowed. ' And Sylvia. You had betrayed Irvine, remember, Robin. It does not make him the less my enemy, but it gives him a kind of justice.'

Nicholas hurried on to tell Robin of all that he had been doing to help him. He had been even to the Queen. He had seen the Queen three times and she had liked him. She had loved his size and strength. She had even pinched his arm. She had promised him this and that, or half promised him. You could not tell where you were with her. She would not give a clear answer. Everyone had been kind to him, but, he must confess, he had not obtained very definite help from anyone.

Irvine seemed to have his power and it was known that this was his case. It was also known that Robin had been his wife's lover. It was said even that Irvine had strangled his wife, finding her in bed with Robin. Moreover, Pierson was an old thorn in the Government's side. For many many years he had carried treasonable letters from abroad. Once again he had escaped them (Robin gave a little cry of joy at hearing this confirmed), and by Robin's aid.

Nicholas poured all this out, thinking to disguise none of it. It was never his way to disguise anything. Nor did Robin wish that he should.

'I have failed with them all, brother. Edward and Sidney have also tried. They have been good beyond my expectation. I am going now to Richmond where the Queen is.'

Robin laid his hand on Nicholas' huge thigh. 'Do not take this trouble, Nick. I know that there is nothing can be done. I know it as though I foresaw every movement of the next days. And what is more than that, I am not sorry. All my life long I have failed to be a man of action. I think both ways and so never move. But now at last I think only one way and know just where I must go. It is right, too, that Irvine should have some reward. I wronged him, and although I would do it again, still — I wronged him.'

Nicholas sprang to his feet.

'You shall be out of this. Within twenty-four hours — you shall be free. Wait. Wait. The Queen *shall* listen . . .' And he hurried from the room.

But Robin was *not* out of it.

On the following day at about ten in the morning Roland and another man came to fetch him.

He had made himself as presentable as he could and he walked, with his head handsomely up, ahead of the two gaolers and behind a pikeman, along a narrow worn passage, down stone stairs, along a further passage, down more stairs (they were damper now. He saw snail-slime on the wall), and through a heavy door that creaked as it was pushed.

He was now in a high wide room with bare stone walls. There was a door in the end wall; no windows. Braziers in tall iron stands both lit and warmed the room. Behind a black table six men were seated, and one of them was Philip Irvine. He did not look at Robin, but bent forward busily writing. Robin looked at his judges and recognized Sir Humphrey Casselet, an officer about the Court, elderly, stout and paunchy, plethoric. The man in the high chair, the principal seat, he did not know at all. He was thin and exceedingly handsome, with a delicate almost feminine face and kindly grey eyes. Robin noticed his hands as they stayed folded on the table ; beautiful, long-fingered, exquisite hands, and on the little finger of one a large turquoise ring.

Most of the questioning came from this man, and he was most gentle and even tenderly friendly. He told Robin that he had nothing to fear if he would inform them of the truth. There were penalties, of course, for shielding and abetting a Catholic priest, and they were severe ones, but Robin had powerful friends and he thought that, in his case, the penalties might not be harsh.

He was bound to say that in this instance the affair was more grievous because the priest in question, one Anthony Pierson, was a notorious rogue, and would have been taken by the heels this time had not Robin succoured him.

Robin broke in here demanding to know by what court he was being judged, to which the gentleman with the turquoise ring answered him with gentle politeness that he might be quite sure that they were acting under the Queen's orders and according to her wishes.

Irvine then rose and gave his evidence : that he had heard that this priest, Anthony Pierson, was in the neighbourhood of Keswick, Cumberland, and was carrying papers dangerous to the State ; that all the time they had him shadowed ; that at last they were directly on his track ; that he took refuge in the house of Mr. Robin Herries ; that they arrived, owing to some miscalculation, an hour too late, found Mr. Herries working at his books, denying altogether that he had seen anyone ; that they searched the house, found burnt ashes of paper in the fireplace, recovered certain pieces not burned and sufficiently incriminating. He continued that Mr. Herries was then arrested and brought with his servant to London ; that the servant had confessed everything.

Irvine then sat down ; once he flickered a swift passionate glance at Robin.

Robin was then asked what he had to say to such evidence. Robin replied firmly that it was true that he had been sitting at his books on that day in his house, but that he had, from first to last, seen nothing.

' Your servant has confessed to everything.'

' I shall not believe that until I hear it from his own lips.'

' Bring in the man.'

The door in the far wall instantly opened and Cheveley was led in. Robin had much ado not to cry out. Cheveley's face was grey like a snake-skin ; his mouth hung loosely. One hand was bandaged. One foot seemed to turn the wrong way.

At sight of Robin he burst into tears. He sobbed : ' Master . . . master . . .'

Robin went across to him and Cheveley leant his head on Robin's breast, crying like a child.

Robin consoled him, patting his cheek.

' You have done me no harm, and it is another of the wrongs that I must cure to have brought you into this.'

Cheveley, still bitterly crying, was led away.

' You see, Mr. Herries.'

' I count nothing as evidence that is taken from a man under torture.'

The handsome gentleman said nothing to this, but began most delicately to persuade him.

' I would wish you to understand, Mr. Herries, that there is no unkind feeling towards you here. Her Majesty, who has been placed in full acquaintance with this affair, has especially charged us that we are to deal with you tenderly — that is, of course, if you answer the questions put to you with a full heart and mind.'

Old Casselet broke in here, puffing and blowing out his mouth : ' By Jesu, that is the truth.'

Robin noticed the fine lawn cuffs to the sleeves of the interlocutor. Under the light from the braziers they were of a sparkling whiteness.

' Nor can it serve any purpose, Mr. Herries, that you should refuse answers to our questions. We *know* that the priest, Anthony Pierson, an old acquaintance of your own, visited you, ate and drank with you, and burned important and incriminating documents in your house. All this is known to us beyond a peradventure. You are not, Mr. Herries, yourself a Catholic. If you refuse our questions it must be only because you would defend this priest. He is, for all we can tell, now beyond the seas. You are therefore serving no purpose at all in obstinacy.'

(Was Pierson safe? Robin, with a quick look at the interlocutor, believed that he was not.)

' If,' the interlocutor went gently on, ' you refuse our questions, Mr. Herries, I fear that in spite of Her Majesty's care and our own desire, pressure must be put upon you.'

There was a silence. Robin said nothing.

The interlocutor asked : ' Did you, Mr. Herries, on such a day receive in your house at Rosthwaite in Cumberland a disguised priest named Anthony Pierson ? '

' I did not.'

' Did he not remain with you, telling you that he was in flight from the Government officials ? '

' No such person was in my house at Rosthwaite.'

' Did he not eat and drink with you ? '

' No person ate or drank with me on that day.'

' Did you not go with him while he burned documents in the fire ? '

' No documents were burned in my house on that day.'

There was again a silence. Then the interlocutor said : ' I beseech you, Mr. Herries, to reconsider the matter. You do no good to anyone by your obstinacy.'

(Robin knew that Pierson was somewhere in hiding in London, and not far away. It was as though he heard him whispering in his ear : ' Robin ! Robin ! ')

He started and stood with his head a little on one side as though listening. For a space he did not hear the interlocutor's remarks. He saw the Queen kneeling at her little altar and himself on guard. Then he caught the soft gentle voice again.

' For the last time, Mr. Herries . . .'

He broke out quite passionately : ' I know nothing. I had no priest to visit me. I saw no papers.'

He was walking through the door in the far wall, the two gaolers one on either side. The door closed behind him. It was much darker here. They must go down steps and he caught at Roland's arm. He heard the man's hoarse whisper :

' Ah, for the sake of Christ's virtue, tell them what they ask.
Return and tell them.'

At the bottom of the steps they passed a door and entered
a long broad room. Braziers were burning here also. He
saw at once two men stripped to the waist, and under the
breast of the stouter there was a large brown mole. In a stone
fireplace a fire was burning. He saw the instruments of
torture : the rack, the thumb-screws, the boot, the gloves, the
spider. He saw that the interlocutor and Irvine were present.
The two gaolers were close beside him.

He stood still, not knowing what he should do. He heard,
as though from a great distance, the voice of the interlocutor :
' There is yet time. Give me only a sign, utter one word, and
you shall leave this place, never, I trust, to return to it.'

Robin was surprised at the firmness with which his voice
answered : ' I have nothing to say.'

In the half-light he saw that Irvine's eyes were fixed steadily
upon him.

The interlocutor raised his hand. Roland came to him
and very gently began to undo the ties of his doublet. Robin
assisted him. He found that he was to be quite naked, but
he had always understood that even here the privacies were
respected. Words of a protest came to him, but he thought :
' Of what matter is it ? '

He saw the two men who were stripped to the waist roll the
rack a little forward. He felt quite suddenly an insufferable
heat. His body was burning and when they laid him down
and stretched him out their rough hands were cold.

He felt his feet brought together and attached to an iron
hook fixed at the rack end. They then pulled his arms out-
wards, and this was their first piece of roughness, for they
jerked them fiercely. He realized, coming out of them, the
beginning of their lust for their business. It seemed as though
in the sharpness of this crisis he was given an extra acuteness.
He turned his head and saw the stout fellow with the brown
mole fastening his arm to a hook fixed in a roller at the opposite
end. His eyes were screwed up. His belly was already shining
with a glistening sweat. But perhaps the most terrible thing
about him was his practised air. He hissed a little between his

teeth, as when you groom a horse. He paused in his business for a moment to scratch his breast. He was quite impersonal, so many hundreds of times had he performed this same office, and yet he had pleasure in it too.

He stayed and stood up, straightening himself. He stood, his hands on his big strong buttocks, looking down, approving his work.

The voice of the interlocutor came again : ' There is even now time. It is our urgent wish that you should be spared.'

Robin said nothing. His whole being now was strung to meet the first onslaught of pain. All his life it was this that he had dreaded ; his dreams had been haunted by it and even on the softest summer afternoon at Mallory he would see the face of the Tiger between the trimmed hedges. The Tiger was waiting to spring. It was in truth, in the lurid smoky light with the musty smell as of caged animals (the stout executioner as he stood over him smelled of sweat, of dung, of straw), exactly that — as though from the darkness a tiger were about to spring and fasten its claws . . .

He stared upward, praying that he might not fail. He heard the turning wheezily of cogs in a wheel, and instantaneously with that came an agonizing pain that belonged to no particular part but ran like fire through his body. The impulse was, as it would have been had he been struck by a stone or a fist, to cry out, but only a little ' Oh ! Oh ! ' came from his lips.

As the general fiery flood receded he was conscious of acute sorrowful pain at the shoulders, the wrists, the ankles. Yes, ' sorrowful ' was the true word, for he could have burst out sobbing at the wrongs done to his body which he loved and had cared for so long, the body that had done no one any harm. It was a great commiserating pity that he felt for himself and his body, for his wrists and his ankles that were crying out to him to help them. Silly, loose tears rolled out of his eyes and down his cheeks.

He heard the voice of the interlocutor : ' Confess only that the priest was with you . . .'

A dreadful civil war began then in his body. All his members were meeting round his heart, some were crying out for mercy, some were angry rude fellows protesting against this treatment, some were wailing sufferers from pain, simply crying out ' It hurts ! It hurts ! ' some were beseeching that they should not suffer more, and, beneath all this, with a steady deep refrain, was a voice telling him to endure and that in this battle he would win a great victory.

Then quite suddenly there was nothing but fear — sharp-fanged, biting fear — for, close to his brain, he heard the wheezy turning of the cogs. This time he screamed indeed, for the pain swung like a bell up through his body and rang in a high shrill note at his lips. It was not he who cried, but the very figure of pain itself, a sad screaming creature, all teeth and eyes.

The distended torture of his torn muscles shot, in regular beats, darts of fire into his heart. ' One. Two. Three. Four.'

If the ropes could be removed and the body allowed to tumble into a heap. The extremity had been reached. His dry tongue moved between his lips. He would confess anything, true or false. But he did not speak, for still there was that voice saying, ' Be of good cheer. . . . Be of good cheer. . . .'

Now once again he heard the cogs turn ; a wave of sunlit fire smote him in the face and he fell comfortably, with a happy ease, into cool darkness.

He sank, rose, sank again, not attempting to battle against the soft stirring sea that enclosed him. Whether he moved or was quiescent, pain was constant, and any active mind that he had was given to the prevention of movement. If, against all his will, there *was* movement, the animal floating beside him bit into his flesh, and with that stab of agony he rose to full consciousness, saw the bare walls of his own little room and the bar of light where the window was.

No one must touch him and he would murmur : ' Spare me. . . . Prythee . . .' But Michael Roland could move him, most gently, as a mother her child, and would change the linen bandages and perform the humblest offices, holding him up a little against his breast, taking the cup to his lips, caring passionately not to disturb his shoulders, his wrists, his ankles, which were all dislocated.

He had, for some days, a violent fever, and saw always

Sylvia eluding him, and the Queen bending her head on the block. She would bend it, then raise her head and smile at him, then bend it again.

Behind the dreams, the pain, the floating in the clogging water, were intervals of absolute consciousness. Then he would lie on his pallet bed, and a curious happiness, such as he had never known in all his life, would pervade his whole being. He thought that he had never in all his life been happy before.

He was happy because he had kept his word. His mind returned to the scene of the torture. He avoided that. But he knew that he had, at last, overridden the two fears of all his life — one the fear of physical pain ; the other, that he would never be resolute enough to take definite action.

It was as though his whole personality had been cleared of poisons that clogged it. Aside from the physical pain and not part of it his thought and mind and purpose were free and light. He rose above his body, and new horizons of whose splendour he had never before been aware seemed to invite him.

For many days he saw no one at all but Michael Roland. The agony in his body began to pass, the torn flesh set about its healing, the fever left him. Nevertheless the dream of the water and the fierce waiting animal floating at his side sometimes returned, and it was from one such dream that he woke with a cry one day and saw Nicholas kneeling on the floor beside his bed. His first impulse, still clouded, was to cry : 'Do not touch me !' ; then he saw that Nicholas' broad brown face was drawn with such anxiety and distress that he loved him more, perhaps, than he had ever done before. He had also now a stronger capacity for love.

'Nick ! Oh, Nick ! How glad I am !'

Nicholas smiled. 'I have been twice before, brother, but you were in fever and did not know me. Why, this is most handsome ! We shall soon have you from here !'

His pleasure in seeing his brother made Robin very weak, and he said faintly : 'I fear they will never let me from here, Nicholas. They wish me to speak, but I have nothing to tell them.'

Then Nicholas began, with all his heart and soul, to implore him to speak and have done.

'What harm is there ? Pierson is abroad long since. They have all the information. They need only your submission. It is their *wish* to let you go. The Queen herself has said that, once you have made your submission, there is to be no more of this.'

'Are you assured that he is out of the country ? '

'I am assured,' Nicholas answered, but Robin, who knew him so well, looking into his eyes, was sure that he had no certainty.

'No,' Robin said. 'He is not abroad. He is hiding in London and it is because they think I know more and could lead them to him that they keep me and will question me again.'

Then Robin saw what he had never seen, Nicholas standing with the tears pouring down his face. He could not stop them, but blubbered, choking to stop his sobs, turning at last to the window with his back to the bed.

When he returned he said again : ' Submit ! Submit ! This man is nothing to this . . . to this . . .'

'Dear Nick,' Robin said. 'It seems to you more of a torture than to myself. It is a great thing to me to discover that I can endure these things, for I had always the fear that I could not. That fear is killed now : it is the greater of the two fears. Moreover, even if I would I cannot guide them to Anthony Pierson, for I know nothing. All I know they already know. . . . And I think, too, that Irvine will see to it that I do not leave this place.'

Then Nicholas, standing there, now dry-eyed, swore that, from this time on, he would pursue Irvine wherever he might be, and would not rest day or night until he had killed him. ' By the precious blood of Jesus Christ, this shall be so.'

But Robin, suddenly weary, turning his head against the bolster, said : ' I feel no bitterness against Philip, for I betrayed him as you yourself have said. Nor against any man. Only I live in a great peace and happiness.'

The weeks passed, Nicholas came and went. The wounds healed. The torn flesh was restored by Nature ; only, one leg was permanently twisted so that Robin would limp for the remainder of his days and he would never write with his writing hand again. Spring passed into summer. Robin was allowed books and worked once more at his Propertius.

During this time Roland served him with a fidelity, a humour, and a gracious perfection of manners that made Robin wonder.

' Where do you come from, Michael ? ' he asked him one day. ' And why do you love me ? '

' I am Norman William who won the Battle of Hastings,' Roland said, pulling his flaxen hair. ' I am resurrected and can eat a calf whole as well as any man. That's what they did in those days. And as to loving you, master, love something or someone I must because of the maggoty wife I have at home and two daughters as evil. She's French extraction,' he added as though that summed up everything. ' When the Queen, God save her, was after marrying that French monkey with a honey-taste for boys I tried to beat the French blood out of my wife's body, but the more I beat her the more the Duke pranced it at Court, so I abandoned the beatings and now she pulls my hair.'

During this time Nicholas had no end or aim but to get Robin out of the Tower. He had influence of the highest, sometimes the ear of the Queen herself, but he moved in a fog. Something or someone always stopped him.

Nevertheless as the summer waxed hotter they began to hope. Soon Robin would be forgotten enough for it not to be difficult to slip him away. And it was said that Pierson had died of fever in Antwerp. Then quite suddenly on a July afternoon Nicholas heard that Pierson had been seen in London again. Two days later he was told that he must be prevented from seeing his brother.

On that late hot July afternoon Robin, his foot resting on a pillow, was sitting, looking up at the white-blue sky, hot and limpid, that hung like a flag across the window. Yes, like a flag, for the summer heat dazzling it seemed to make it quiver as a flag stirs in a breeze. A bird, like a gold ball, was thrown across it and was gone. The door opened and he turned. A new gaoler, a man whom he had never seen before, thin and black, with a heavy bunch of keys at his girdle, stood there.

'You are summoned to attend . . .'

Then Robin's cheek did indeed contract as though a hand had pinched it. It had come, then? And so suddenly, when he had thought that he was almost safe. Again. . . . Again. . . . The torture again. . . . His body was shivering all against his will. But he *could* not endure it again. He *could* not, he *could* not. He would not. He would tell them anything. But he had nothing to tell them. His news was old news, old, old, stale news. He could not endure . . .

He raised his head and looked at the sun-white sky.

'Where is Roland?' he asked.

The man did not answer. He seemed a very surly fellow. He moved into the room and was followed by two halberdiers.

It was then that Robin felt, like an icy wind, his loneliness, his utter abandoned loneliness, wrap him round. There was no one — no one. Not Nicholas. Not Roland. Only the space of sun-white sky.

He put the book down on the table and followed them out.

He was in the same room as before. The interlocutor was there with his turquoise ring and his white gleaming cuffs. Only three others were with him and Casselet and Irvine were not among them.

It was the same business as before. The interlocutor asked him to tell them what Pierson had said to him about his future movements, what names he had given of his friends, what were his purposes in England.

Robin replied over and over that he knew nothing. At the last the interlocutor spoke to him like a loving father.

'Mr. Herries, I told you on the last occasion and I tell you again that no one wishes at all that you should suffer. You bring this upon yourself. You have but to tell us in a few brief words the things that we would know, and you leave this place within half an hour to return to your friends and your home.'

He was looking at Robin very attentively, and perhaps the look of suffering in the thin drawn face, the twisted leg stuck forward (for they had allowed Robin to sit), touched his heart. He spoke very gently indeed.

'We do urge you to save yourself. We urge you . . .'

Robin only steadfastly replied : ' I know nothing.'

When he stood once again naked, resting on his right foot so that he might spare the twisted left, and looked about him he saw again the stout fellow with the brown mole, and he smelt again the musty warm air as of an animal's cage. He heard again the interlocutor's soft voice, and then to his surprise found his hose put on him again. He had a wild desperate notion that he was after all to be spared.

He was asked once more : ' Will you inform us ? . . .' And, with a clear strong voice, replied : ' I have nothing to say.'

He was led forward, his hands were raised and his thumbs placed within two iron slots. He heard the iron bar being screwed on to the slots. His body murmured : ' I cannot . . . I cannot.'

His soul answered : ' You can. . . . You are able ! '

A great triumph rose in him. ' I am able ! I am able ! '

He heard the screw turn in the iron bar, and the agony was such, as his thumbs crushed like fiery water, that he cried out, but oddly his scream was : ' I can ! I can ! ' His whole life was in that cry. His heart, already overstrained with the sad pressure of the last months, fought frantically in his body. The screw turned again, but now he felt no pain, for he was away, away, and the Bright Pavilions were in sight at last, standing in the sun-white sky. All was light, air, and a vast endless space of freedom.

His head dropped. The executioner swore an oath and quickly unscrewed the bolt. He caught Robin's body in his arm.

' He is gone, masters,' he said sulkily, for this had happened against the plan.

NICHOLAS IN ARMOUR

SOMEONE brought Nicholas the dirty piece of paper as Rosa
mund Herries had risen up to go.

He read it, then turned it in his fingers, thinking. The
scrap was thus :

I am dying and have something to say to you before I go. You
will find me at the Mulberry Tree in Cutting Lane.

P. THATCHER.

He put it in his pocket and said to Rosamund : ' Stay
another quarter-hour. I wish to ask you a question.'

She had ridden from a house ten miles away and was in a
riding-suit that was a good fashion, as anything was for her
that meant a definite purpose and not a mere lolling around.
She was no doll. As she sat on the settle by the fire, her back
straight, and her good strong legs swinging, her honest kindly
face contented (for she loved above everything to be with
Nicholas), she looked what she was, a fine friend for any
man.

Nicholas, holding a whip in his hand, was wearing a kind
of country smock and was still flushed with his work. He had
been ditching with his men.

He said gravely : ' Rosamund, you will call it nonsense,
but yesterday there were some gipsies in the Long Field. I
gave them settlement for the night, and an old woman with a
beard like a man told me my fortune. She said I should
marry and have a son, but that not until my great-grandson
would there be a descendant of mine of my own kidney, and
that he would be a rogue and a rascal with every man's hand
against him. What say you to that ? '

' Why,' she answered lightly, ' that it is a pity you will not
care for your own son.'

' Yes, but — but . . .' He bent his head. ' There is only
one I love with sickness and longing or would ever have
loved, and her — I cannot.' He came over to her, close to her.
He towered above her, almost, as it seemed to her, enveloping
her. ' And now I will say what will offend you, maybe, for
ever. Will *you* marry me, Rosamund ? '

She looked at him, smiled, shook her head.

' No, Nicholas. I am not a woman to marry.'

He went on urgently. ' But listen, there is so much merit
in it. For my part, since Robin's death I have known a terrible
loneliness. I am growing into a hard man and shall be one
shortly. I have a purpose to fulfil, and only one in my life.
Before I set out on it it would make me happy to have you for
wife, for indeed I love you dearly as my best friend, my constant
counsellor, my merry companion, the most wise and pleasantest-
hearted woman alive. So much for myself. This house needs
a mistress, has needed one sorely for many years. It needs a
son of mine, too, that it may go on with the family. And on
your side I know you care for me, that I am the best friend
you have. I know, too, that you are lonely, that you are never
so happy as when we are together. And I know that you, too,
would have a son and that it should be mine. If I am arrogant
in this——'

' No, no.' She put out a hand. ' Dear Nick ! Of course
I have loved you all my life. But we could not. *You* do not
love *me* ; could I live here and she in the house ? '

' She could leave me,' he said thickly. ' Armstrong should
take her back to the North.'

' And I ? Divide you from Gilbert Armstrong who is, I
think, half of yourself ? '

He stared at her, his brows knitted, the old, old problem in
his mind again.

' It is beyond belief. . . . No one would believe. . . .
For all these years I who have never minded what I did and
have taken, I fear, so many women. . . . And now, all this
time we have lived in the same place, scarcely speaking. And
she is still a torture to me as ever she was, perhaps because
I have not had her. But for Gilbert's sweetness, his fidelity,
his generosity, how would I have fared ? '

He had for a moment forgotten her, staring in front of her, his right hand clenching and unclenching.

She kissed him lightly on the cheek and went away, but as he stood with his hand on the neck of her horse he said very earnestly : ' You *are* my best friend, Rosamund, and so — if you hear within these next days news of me, remember that I thought of you and cried your name.'

' Where are you going ? ' she asked.

' North,' he answered and went indoors.

Catherine Armstrong that had been Hodstetter knelt arranging logs on the hissing fire and was aware that he was standing close behind her. She turned and rose, her face flushed with the fire, her flaxen hair lit with it. She was now a magnificent woman, broad-shouldered, deep-breasted. She had the face, he sometimes thought, of a woman royally born.

' Stay a moment,' he said. ' I have to speak to you.'

She sat down on the stool near him, her legs set wide apart under her dress of dark blue. Her breasts heaved partly because of the logs that she had been carrying, partly because she loved with heart, soul and body this man who in the rough country smock stood looking at her.

' Listen, Catherine. You have lived all these years in this house and I have never kissed you.'

' No,' she said.

' And now I will.'

He knelt down beside her, took her in his arms, and they kissed as though they were one soul, which perhaps they were. She put her hand up and stroked his hair. He cupped her right breast with his hand. Then, as though by mutual unspoken agreement, they parted.

' Well, then —' he said, breathing a little hard, ' this is the first kiss for a long while. Have I been fair to you these years here ? And to Gilbert ? '

' Yes. You have been very fair,' she answered, smiling.

' The first night you were in the house was the hardest, but it has been all the time difficult, and would have been impossible altogether had I not known always two things.

One, and the most important, that if I once climbed into your bed and had you there I lost you for ever. Two, that Gilbert Armstrong your husband is the noblest, most honest friend that any man has ever had.'

'Yes,' she said, 'that is true about Gilbert. How good and kind he has been only I can say, for he does not love me at all and never has. In his third and deepest heart I think he hates me.'

She slowly rose and stood, her hand in her hair, turning her body first this way and then that.

'Have you been unhappy here?'

'Not unhappy.' Now she looked truly a Queen, he thought.

'If you wish I will tell you. You do not know — how should you? — what it is all your life to see two worlds. Always two worlds, one a looking-glass for the other. When I was very, very small I knew that if I closed my eyes and walked with my hand out it would touch something warm and furry, and that when I opened my eyes there would be nothing to see. As a babe I knew that. They burned my mother, but she was a witch truly enough. She could not help herself. I have seen her stir milk in the bowl and the flame leap up and a cat burning in the flame. I have heard one talk to her with a voice like the screech of a mouse and have heard the evil things he has said and there has been nothing and no one to see. . . . But she was good too, mother was, and would heal the sick and give money to the poor. But they would not allow her. They burned her. But that is not why I tell you. It is because this thing has been always close to me, to my ears, to my eyes, to my breath. I have not wanted it, but it was there with me from birth. I have known always that I need only take one step, say one word, look with one glance, and I would be *there* as my mother was. That is why I must be always apart, by myself, with *no one*, and in especial not with you, Mr. Nicholas Herries.

'Once, when I was a girl I told you. Now I am a woman whose mother was burned for a witch, and you and Gilbert have taken me here and sheltered me so that no word has ever gone out against me, and I have had rest. It is as though I have been asleep. I shall wake very soon, do one thing for you, dear Nicholas, and then cross the Border where there is no Border.'

She seemed to move but not to move. In the dancing firelight it was as though she rose upwards into the air from the floor. But it was not so, for he caught her hand and they stood there close together like two great friends.

' No woman in all the world's history,' she said, ' has loved a man more than I love you.'

She laughed as she picked up a wicker basket loaded with apples.

' I will take these to the loft. . . .'

Half-way down the hall she looked back at him.

' So we are riding North, you and I and Gilbert.'

A little farther away she said : ' I shall see Keswick once again, and for the last time.'

When Nicholas rode with Gilbert Armstrong it was a clean sun-swept late October day.

' Do you know why I am happy again ? ' Nicholas asked.

' Because we are away from women.'

' Does that make *you* happy then ? '

' I am weary of women. The only way to be with them is to be with them in the light of a candle, have them quickly and go to your own place before they can stay you.'

' Well, it is not for that reason that I am happy to-day.'

' Why then ? ' Gilbert asked.

' Before I tell you I will ask you something more ? I trust you more than any man alive to tell me the truth. Have I seemed to you changed in the last years ? '

' Yes,' Armstrong said. ' Since your brother died.'

Nicholas nodded. ' Since then — and before that too. In what way have I changed ? '

' What was young in you—' Armstrong paused. He was not clever at analysis. ' That has died. You were always before more like a boy than any grown man I have been with. I have seen you,' he went on, ' mowing in the fields with other men and the scythe has moved as though it were alive, and you have been tireless, laughing without knowing you laughed, and you have flung off your clothes and sprung into the stream at the Long Field end before the men, calling to them that the sun would be down, while they wiped their scythes on the wet grass, and you have come back into the field, the water dripping from your body, and have caught the flagon from one of them, flung your head back and drunk as though you would never have done, and the sun has fallen until the scythes blinded your eyes. You will never mow the fields like that again, master, nor sing as you did then. You will never sing again so without care.'

This was eloquence for Gilbert, but the sort of scene where his heart was.

' When we have ridden to the North, Gilbert, finished a long quarrel and ridden back again, I shall sing once more.'

' We go North ? ' There was great joy in his voice.

' Yes. You, I, Catherine.'

' What has Catherine to do with this ? '

Nicholas had never in all these years asked Gilbert Armstrong one question about his wife. Now he guided his horse closer, put his hand out and let it rest on Gilbert's bridle.

' Would you be free of her ? '

Gilbert looked ahead of him.

' I would be free of everyone but you, master. I was not meant to be anything but free. She is a good woman, but I have never come near to her. She is a woman all alone, by herself. I have slept, as you know, for all these years in the pallet bed in the same room with her, and I have heard her cry in the night as though her heart would break, and I have seen her walk, when she thought me sleeping, beating her breast, and I have heard her cry out as though someone were persuading her and she would not listen. . . . She is the most alone woman in all the world, I think. I am sorry for all created things and for her more than any other perhaps, but I have never loved her, and without love I cannot comfort her.'

' It has been a marred life for all three of us all these years,' Nicholas said.

' It has been a wrong life, master, and I was never born for such a life. How was I born ? For a direct word and to be a man's friend and ride a horse and love a woman, and one day to have a wife of my own and children at my own table. And yet,' he went on, ' I suppose I could not have found, had I travelled the world with Drake and his men, as I think I was made to do, such a friend and a master as you have been and are,' His voice rose. He cried out : ' Ah, that should have been the life for you and me, away across the sea with the cities of gold and the Indians and the giant serpents and the Spanish ships heavy with treasure. We were not intended, you and I, to be tied to a woman who is a witch's daughter, poor thing, and cries in the dark. Love, to my thinking, is a foolishness if you want it and cannot have it, and a foolishness if you get it too easily, and a foolishness if you marry it.'

' But you said,' Nicholas answered, ' that you wished for a home and a wife, and children at your knee.'

' So every man dreams when he is single,' Gilbert answered, ' but I suppose there is no perfect state in the world. God arranges it thus that we may be surprised with delight when we come to Paradise.'

Nicholas stopped his horse.

' Listen, Gilbert, I am happy because Irvine is in the North and at last — at long, long last — I go to kill him.'

Gilbert nodded gravely. ' That should have been done long ago.'

' In London,' Nicholas continued, ' Phineas Thatcher is dying. He has sent to see me, and I shall get from him something about Irvine that I must know — how nearly he was concerned in my brother's death. After that we will go and finish it.'

' You have hated him a long while,' Gilbert said reflectively.

' Because I have hated him so deeply and for so long, I have waited. For I would not kill him unjustly, and my brother did him a wrong. But now it is ended — at last it is ended — and my mind will be healthy again.'

As Nicholas and Armstrong threaded their way through the narrow little streets around Paul's Church, Nicholas reflected that maybe, after all, success had done England some harm.

He had visited this quarter of London but little in the last few years and there seemed to him to be a new spirit of

noisy, bullying ruffianism unfelt by him before. In his youth
the London Strand had been a place of uneven cobbles, spouting water-pipes, stinks and crying, bawling voices. But there
had been few coaches, and walking along the middle of the
street had been chiefly a matter of elbowing and cursing with
your hand on your sword-hilt.

But now the hill up to Paul's Church was crowded with
coaches lurching through the mud, and carts and hand-barrows.
Even to his steady and tolerant ears the noise was a frenzy
and a babel. He saw too here a new phase of gentleman :
effeminates with extravagant hair, jewels on their gloves, and
roses behind their ears, and boots so ridiculous that they could
scarcely walk with them.

The bullies also were of a new fashion. There had always
been bullies, but, in the old days, they were out-of-work, half-
starved soldiers, and servants of the wealthier houses Westminster way.

Now there were bullies in little bands, stout fellows and
almost gentlemen, who, moving four or five together, pinched
young women, pricked stout merchants in the thighs, swearing,
singing and roystering and taking always the middle of the
street. And what contrasts !

Outside Ludgate Gaol little boys and hungry gaunt women
were screaming, ' Bread and meat, for the tender mercy of God,
for the poor prisoners of New Gate,' holding baskets into
which passers-by dropped stale husks of bread and meat-bones,
while from the windows of the prison itself fearful faces looked
out and you could hear cries from within ' as of the damned.'
Then, as they turned towards Cutting Lane, the cry was
suddenly raised of ' Clubs ! Clubs ! ' a woman running and
men with truncheons striking at one another and a man with a
bleeding face leaping on another man and cracking his head
with a wooden stump.

The back streets were so filthy and of such a stench that
Nicholas must hold his nose, and he could not but think of
the Court, the flowers, the jewels, the gardens at Richmond
and the Queen herself, old and yellow, but her gown stiff with
jewels. Here were two worlds, and he who, in the simplicity
of his heart, wanted every man and woman in the world (save

Irvine) to be happy, felt dimly that something was very wrong with all of this and thought of Gilbert's description of the mowing and the sun shining on the field and his own body glistening with the fresh water of the stream.

Since the Armada England had become great, but was this greatness, this huddled body with the naked arm stiff and dead lying in the gutter, the children on the doorstep like little animals picking at one another's hair, and the drunken woman clinging to the wooden posts of the horologer's shop, her breasts bare and grimed with filth ? ' There are others wiser than I,' he thought, ' that should attend to these evils.' But he could not think of anyone who did so attend, no divine or grand lady of the Court, or philanthropic gentleman. He thought with a sigh of his friend, Philip Sidney, and wished he had not died at Zutphen.

They found the ' Mulberry Tree,' and a mean enough hostelry it was. Inside the low-raftered drinking-room Nicholas all but touched the ceiling, and the landlord, who had but one eye, could only stare at him with it as though he were a pheno-menon out of a fair.

But Nicholas had a way of commanding anyone he wished to command, and the one-eyed beer-barrel fellow was soon guiding him up some dark and stinking stairs and showing him and Gilbert into a dark and stinking room. When their eyes became accustomed to the dim grey-smoked thickness they found the wretched Thatcher, his body emaciated to a skeleton, restlessly dozing on a straw bed.

Nicholas had last seen this fellow at Fotheringhay, had hated him there as he had hated him everywhere. But now he was dying and in extreme neglect, so the two strong men busied themselves with straightening the straw and folding Gilbert's cloak under the thin-haired skull and bringing him a draught of water.

Thatcher, however, showed a surprising energy. When he saw that it was indeed Nicholas he stared, wiped his eyes with the back of his hand, and stared again. He nodded his head as though satisfied.

' Before the morning I shall be standing by the throne of the Heavenly Grace. The Lord is my Shepherd and He will lead me. You wish to know where he is. In Keswick, Cumberland, with four of his ruffians. He turned me off with a kick and a blow, but his brain is broken like a clock with the key lost. You must find him, Nicholas Herries, and send his soul to the Devil where it belongs.'

His voice had a crachitty whistling note and he laid his hand to his bare breast where his ribs were like the bent staves of a barrel.

' How did he turn you off ? ' asked Nicholas, bending close to him and catching the nauseating sweet smell of his breath. ' You have served him long enough.'

' I have served him as the Devil's own hireling, but only that God may, through me, have His own way on His evil servants. God's Triumph is at hand, Mr. Herries — make no error — and God's Saints, his Puritan children, will rule this land——'

' Yes, yes,' Nicholas interrupted impatiently, for although the man was dying he still hated him. ' But I would know something. My brother — when he was in the Tower — was it Irvine's responsibility that they took him that second time ? Would they have let him free, after the first time, had it not been for Irvine ? '

But Thatcher's mind now was wandering. He started up and, waving his skinny arms, was like a scarecrow in the wind.

' I saw her ere she saw me. How she screamed when she felt me behind her, my hands on her throat ! She called out, I remember, and then I threw her, tumbling her head against the middle stair and breaking her bones to a jelly. She was a little pitiful thing and it was an evil thing that I did, but she went whoring with the young man whom afterwards they racked in the Tower. Irvine saw that and will be haunted by it until he has that sword between his ribs. That sword the Almighty is even now sharpening against him. . . . Aye, she screamed, and she fell and her head struck the floor so that her brains were dashed out.'

It seemed that he could not escape from Sylvia's light childish spirit, for he twisted his fingers and drew back his head in the straw telling her to keep from him. He opened his eyes as though he woke from a sleep, stared at Nicholas, sighed and rubbed his bony forehead.

' The Saints of God are the Chosen of the Lord and this land shall be in God's hands under their guidance.' He shook his head, looking at Nicholas with great solemnity.

' You go North, Mr. Herries, and you will find him. He is a lost man, for ever since he saw your brother racked he has been a ghosted fugitive flying from God's wrath. And he has the Sons of Belial with him, as evil as himself.'

Nicholas put out his great hand and held the bone-jutting, sweating shoulder of the dying man.

' Now tell me, Thatcher. There is only one thing I would know. Did Irvine persuade them that my brother must be tortured the second time ? '

He motioned to Gilbert, who went over and fetched water from the ewer. The man drank savagely. He pushed against Nicholas' hand impatiently, but his voice now was clear and low and he was in all his senses.

' You are not to hold me, Mr. Herries. You cannot keep my soul from its Maker in that fashion. But because I am the Lord's messenger and His instrument for punishment I will answer your question. That evil man did, of his own will and determination, go even to the Queen herself and persuade her against her true will, which was to give your brother his liberty and to release him from a second torture. But he had a Devil and, besides, your brother had lain with his wife. So he was persuaded to do him a hurt to the very last crushing of the finger-bones. And under that your brother died, even while the thumb-screws were on him.'

Nicholas straightened himself, drawing a deep breath.

' Ah,' he said, ' that is sufficient.'

He looked down at Thatcher as though he would be tender with him, but he could not. He hated him dying as well as living. He turned on his heel and with Gilbert behind him strode swiftly down Ludgate — swiftly because a great purpose was now in front of him.

FLIGHT FROM A PHANTOM

PHILIP IRVINE, on that dark, dim, sky-waterlogged morning in that early November day, as he looked out of the dirty window of the Ulpha inn, allowed to pass unnoticed three things. The first thing that he did not notice was dark little fingers of cloud driven by the wind from Ulpha Fell ; the second thing was the ill-temper of one of his henchmen, Harry Steelshaft. And the third and most important thing was a woman riding in on to the grass-cobbled forepiece to the hostelry.

Because he missed these things he would miss more before that day was ended. The black-fingered clouds portended snow : the ill-temper of Steelshaft meant rebellion : and the woman, walking now towards the inn door and knocking on it with the butt of her whip, meant destiny. She was so finely made, regal in her carriage, and had, under her green-feathered hat, so rich a crop of gold-spun hair that Irvine's other attendants — Roger Bones and Wilfred Portal — turned their heads on the bench where they were sitting and stared as one man.

But Irvine had seen neither the sky nor the lady. He saw at that moment nothing. His business was that he and his men should get their horses and ride by the coast to White-haven, where he had, he fancied, some Government business. Or did he now invent that for himself ?

For many months he had been wandering with these few rapscallions in Scotland and Northern England, doing he knew not what, going he knew not whither. For his trouble was he could not stay in one place more than a day. So soon as he stayed he dreamed evil dreams. To prevent the dreams he drank, but it was one of the strange elements of his personality that he was deeply fastidious : it did not please his humour to be a sot, and it offended his pride in himself.

What he wished to cure was his loneliness. He had fled from London with Winterset (who at this moment entered the inn parlour) and some rascals for company. For he had never in all his life been so lonely as he now was in London. He had neither mother nor wife. Nor had he friends, for he was so inordinately proud that he could not endure correction or mockery.

In former days he had not minded a certain loneliness, for after all he was a unique creature, and unique creatures must be alone. Now his dreams made his loneliness dangerous. He would keep Winterset and Steelshaft gambling with him late into the night because he must not dream. And it was the worse for him because he dreamed as evilly waking as when he slept. Pictures formed, passed before his eyes like smoke held down on a still day, drifted and vanished.

With an irritable nervous movement of his whole body — he was thin now as a black skeleton — he turned from the window to see Winterset entering the parlour. Winterset was fat as an over-ripe pumpkin and everywhere seedy, his nose swollen but at the flat tip dead-white, his cheeks blotched and his eyes rheumy. He was an old ruffian swollen with evil living, no good for anything any more, no good at wenching, at fighting — not even at sleeping, for like an old sick dog he snapped in his sleep at his pursuing enemies.

Irvine beside him looked as clean and delicate as an ebony cane, lissom, dark-shadowed, with an angry, haughty discontent in the eyes and mouth. But the gold buttons on his black sleeves sparkled even on this smoky day as though they were alive.

Winterset said that a fine, handsome woman had just ridden off away across the moor, after alighting here for a bare three minutes. What did she want to take all the trouble of dismounting and then mounting again for, without even a word to the landlord ?

' I could have tumbled her.'

' You—' Irvine began, but his contempt was so sharp that it was not worth the while to finish the sentence. Winterset fingered his shabby wrists and tried to draw himself up straight in indignation. But he could not. He had forgotten the way.

Irvine had no time to waste. Calling out of the window to Steelshaft, the most intelligent of his ruffians, he summoned him into the room. Steelshaft was broad of shoulder, thick of thigh, and had a brown neck as corded and dull as grained wood. His head was round as a bullet, with little peepy blood-shot eyes. He was the true animal of the party, for his passions were altogether animal. He killed without reflection either before or after.

Irvine laid out a map drawn in red and black on the table.

' Here we are,' he said, pointing to Ulpha, ' and we can sleep to-night at Muncaster where I have a friend. I have talked with the landlord, and from here by Holehouse Gill we can take our horses. It is wooded then to Woodend. After that there is a small lake, Devoke Water. Thence across the Esk to Muncaster. The landlord tells me there is a path there.'

Steelshaft looked through the window at the sky.

' There's a storm coming and a cold wind blowing up.'

' What of it ? Have you never been cold before ? '

' They say here that there may be snow.'

' It's early for snow — or snow of consequence. Besides, what of it ? '

' You can be lost in this cursed moorland. Many a time men have been lost for days and died where they fell.'

Irvine was remarkably patient. He had a strong opinion of Steelshaft's instincts, for he, being an animal, could sniff weather, and danger too, earlier than a man could.

' Why are they lost ? Because they are alone. There are five of us.'

But Steelshaft persisted.

' I mislike this country. It has a life of its own, hostile to us. We had better take the road to the sea and then ride on a good foundation to Whitehaven.'

But Irvine felt in himself a strong disposition to cross the moor. It would be quicker and at Muncaster was a good warm house where he could be with gentlemen again for a night or two — gentlemen to whom he could boast of his powers at Court, his great work for the Queen. And so he might sleep afterwards in a soft bed without dreaming. He called his troop together and they set out.

But he felt, in the first few yards, a strangeness in this country. In the first place the great ebon hump of Black Combe hung over them against the grey skyline and seemed to follow them as though it were alive. When they were on the open moorland Black Combe began to stride forward, shaking its dark head. It had about its top, but not obscuring it, a wreath of pale grey cloud like a helmet.

They did not know it, but the land around them was filled with history. This country is in many ways the most curious in all England, being timeless and scornful of mankind. At Swinside there is a great circle of stones, how ancient no one knows ; at Standing Stones is the Giant's Grave of Kirkstanton, and nearby the Giant's Chair. In many places are the foundations of small dwellings, garths enclosed by dykes, very similar to the old type of Icelandic farm, and there are remains of many Roman settlements.

All this country suggests a no-man's-land where for century upon century the outlaws and fugitives from society have found refuge. The soil is almost vocal with the shouts and cries of hunted men, outlaws, sea-rovers, refugees and Vikings. At Barnscar there have been found the remains of what many think was a Danish city, although it may well have been a Bronze Age settlement. Time is not here, and individual man is of no account. The ragged, rather nondescript little cavalcade rode slowly forward. It was no easy going for the horses : there was a path of a kind, scattered with stones, but the sward on either side of this was boggy, with patches of bright and dangerous green.

They were a silent company, being in any case churlish and ill-tempered because they hated these waste places where there was no drink nor fat wenches nor any fighting. They could not conceive why they followed Irvine thus about the country except that he paid them regularly their wages. Perhaps also they caught something of his own gloom and melancholy and, from the first, on this ride felt something foreboding and dangerous. The hills against the skyline were soft, grey, mouse-coloured, and the land itself was tawny, brown, suddenly green, and a real no-man's-land in its suggestion of endless waste, in its sudden revealing of cold swift-running streams, in its silence which nevertheless was vocal with little sounds of a rustling plant, of a rising bird, of running water, of a melancholy cold whisper, of a wind that threatened storm.

They were not beauties at all. Roger Bones was fat and lumpy with a scar silvering his right cheek, and arms like hams. Wilfred Portal was a thin, gaunt man with eyes opened in perpetual surprise and a mouth with a broken lip. Steelshaft rode, his thick body set purposefully as though longing to kill.

Irvine, riding in the rear, felt growing in him a strong impulse to return to the inn. He did not know why he felt this, because it had been his own impulse that had started them on this path ; but it was as though there were an enemy behind him. He was no coward, but for a long time now his dreams had mingled so closely with his actual life that he could often not distinguish between them. He seemed often to be in some other place than where he really was.

One dream especially haunted him, and that was of Robin Herries on the rack. He could not understand why this should be so, because he had seen so many men on the rack, and their groans, cries, agonies, had meant nothing to him. But the sight of Robin's long white body stretched, the sound of the turning screw, the faint crack of the yielding muscles, the red blotches that stole into the white skin, and, above all, that strained intense face, the eyes staring into the smoky roof, the sweat gathering on the forehead and pouring down into the eyes, these were always present with him.

It was not that he felt any conscience in the matter, for Robin Herries had lain with his wife, and that for any man was justification enough. It was rather that these two men, Nicholas and Robin Herries, seemed his life long to have been in his way, and were in his way yet, although one of them was dead. He hated them with a hatred that made him shiver, but this hatred did not comfort him because he could not satisfy it with vengeance. They for ever eluded him.

As he rode he felt for himself an intense, almost dreadful pity. He was a man above all ordinary men, of great beauty, exceptional talent, daring courage. Many men of far slighter gifts had come to the greatest glory, but he, by some ill pursuing fate, had come to this, that he was riding, on a bitter morning, with rapscallions across a lonely moor with no friend in the world. He might search and search but could find no blame in himself. He had been, when he thought of himself, always alone — with his mother, his wife, the men and women at the Court — and that loneliness came from his great superiority, his uniqueness ; he had been too proud to explain this to anyone.

He looked behind him hastily. It seemed to him that someone was at his shoulder : but there was nobody.

The sky grew darker. To the right of them was Ulpha Fell, black now under a white, smoky patch of sky. Beyond Esk Force was the valley bounded by Scafell, the Pikes, Great End, not to be seen now in detail, but, when they came to a rise, dimly, like mysterious unattached shadows moving, it seemed, because the dark clouds above them moved.

The men themselves already felt that they were lost. There was no determination, no boundary in this great waste of tufted, turfed, inhuman land and the wind was rising while the black-fingered clouds gathered into fists of darkness.

After some hours of slow stumbling riding they saw a little bunch of trees and a farm-house beside them. Steelshaft said grumpily that it must be Birker Moor they were on, and this must be the farm of Crosbythwaite that the man at the Ulpha inn had told them of.

Here they drew up their horses and looked at the gloomy scene. An altercation began. Irvine, for some reason, wanted to push on. He felt within him that a great danger threatened. Although it was an ordinary farm enough and peaceful he hated the sight of it. He felt like a fly in the web and with every struggle of his body his feet stuck faster. He might have cried to his men : ' I will not enter that farm. There is danger for all of us,' had it not been so foolish and reasonless. But unexpectedly old Winterset was determined to stop. When Irvine cried, ' What are you staring for ? It is only midday. We shall be at Muncaster by dusk,' Winterset deliberately urged his horse down the slope towards the farm and cried out over his shoulder : ' Warm drink and a fire, come what may.'

Irvine would have gladly shot him in the back, and he moved his heavy gilded pistol in his holster, but the other men were following Winterset and he suddenly knew, as though he expected now that every move in the game would be against him, that he had no power over these rascals any more. It was as though they realized that he was doomed.

So they all moved on to the farm, led their horses into the court and dismounted. They pushed open the farm door and looked in, crowding together. A stout elderly woman, dressed in home-made hodden grey, was busy at the fire stirring ' crowdy,' the soup made from the liquor of beef and oatmeal. The smell of the ' crowdy ' was exceedingly good, and the whole kitchen was clean swept and the brass and copper brightly shining. It was warm and comfortable after the cold moor.

It must have been frightening to the woman to see that parcel of ruffians in their shabby bits of armour, swords and pistols, crowding about her door, but she asked quite calmly what they wanted. A splendid sheep-dog that had been lying stretched in front of the fire, his nose on his paws, rose, growling, on his haunches. She told him to be quiet, naming him Ranter, and asked them again what they wanted.

Irvine advanced, bowing courteously, and the others pushed in behind him, looking curiously around them and sniffing the ' crowdy.' Irvine must have seemed a strange figure to her with his great thinness and darkness, but she could see of course that he was a gentleman.

' We wish,' he said, ' that you would be so kindly as to allow us to rest here for a while. The wind is rising and there is a storm coming that will blow across the moor and then will be gone again.'

It was plain that she suffered from great uneasiness, and they guessed that she was alone in the house. With the black-white sky beyond the window the room-light was dark and also lurid from the fire, and against this the brutal Steelshaft, the fat and loose Roger Bones with the silver scar on his cheek, the gaunt, broken-lipped Wilfred, the ancient, evil Winterset, were no reassuring figures. Wilfred was already fingering the shining pewter flagons, and Steelshaft sharpening his dagger on the edge of the oak table. So she said that they could remain, turned her back to them and continued to stir the ' crowdy.' Ranter, the dog, rose on his four feet and, with hair bristling, walked about sniffing at the legs of the men.

Steelshaft approached the woman.

' That's good broth you have there.'

' Aye,' said the woman, bending lower over the pot.

' 'Tis for your own dinner ? '

She straightened herself and looked at him bravely.

' My man will be home and the others with him.'   She turned and, her arms on her hips, looked at them all.   Then she spoke to Irvine.

' He'll want the room and his own company,' she said.

The longing to be gone was growing with Irvine at every moment.   ' We'll ride on,' he said to the rest of them, and moved to the door.   But the men never stirred.   They were all staring at the woman and the pot.

' Come, we'll be going,' Irvine said again.

Winterset turned and made a step or two towards him. Out of his blurred eyes he looked at Irvine with an almost crying hatred.

' You are my master no longer,' he said.   The others stood and stared.   Irvine, drawn up to his full height against the moon-faced clock on the farm wall, stared at his tumble-down henchman as though he were too proud to see him.

Winterset spoke thickly, drunkenly.   ' I have no fear of you any more, and I am free of you.   For year upon year you have mocked me and spat on me.   What have you had round you always but rotting medlars like myself and these here ? And why ?   Because you were too proud to endure your own kind who could answer you and show you in your own velvet-backed mirror.   You sent me once to this very country to strike a man better than you, but he stuck his big back to the wall and beat you.   You have made me crawl like a dog and stand in the dark with a sword while your fine Puritan threw your wife down the stairs and broke her neck.   You forced me to spy on a Queen who died nobly.   You have stripped me and beaten me, and fed my lechery and stolen from me any pride I had. I am free this very day in this place and I will not go with you — no, not now — never, never, never ! '

His voice rose into a scream and it appeared as though he were demented, for, drawing his sword, he ran at Irvine who was straight against the wall. Irvine made one movement to his side, raised his gold-mounted pistol and shot Winterset square in the body.

The man half turned : his face, swollen and surprised, stared amazement, then he coughed, a froth of blood rose bubbling in his mouth, and he fell on his face, his legs kicking and twitching like a hen's scratching.

The woman gave a cry and rushed to the window. The men looked at Winterset and then at Irvine. Steelshaft knelt down, turned Winterset over, tore open his doublet and pushed his hand against his heart. He looked up at Irvine.

Irvine, still not moving, said : ' He had been provoking this. What was he but a drunken sot ? ' Then he stepped forward convulsively and they all drew back.

' *Now*,' he shouted at them, ' will you come from this cursed place ? '

He strode up to the table and said to the woman : ' It will be better for you to keep quiet about this. Better for you, do you hear ? You do not know how he came by his death, do you hear ? '

' But I *do* know,' she said, staring at the body and the pooling blood. ' I *do* know.'

' You are *not* to know,' Irvine repeated. ' I am the Queen's servant on the Queen's business, and what I did I did because I must. But you saw nothing. You were above in the upper room — in the upper room, do you hear ? '

She looked at him with terrified eyes and could not speak. This irritated Steelshaft, who came up to her and caught her arm : as he did so Ranter, the sheep-dog, was at his back and tore his hose, showing his bare flesh. Steelshaft, cursing, drew his dagger, but there was a man's voice at the door telling the dog to come to him.

A broad-shouldered, stout, bearded farmer stood there — a fine man with a clear brown forehead and strong grey eyes.

It must have been for him an odd enough home-coming, with his wife trembling in the window, Irvine with his pistol still in his hand, and the murdered man crumpled in his pool of blood on the floor. He went straight to Irvine.

'What are you doing here? Who killed this man?'

'He was my servant, and I shot him for disobedience,' Irvine answered quietly. 'I am the Queen's minister on the Queen's business.'

'How do I know that?' the man asked. His big body was trembling with anger, for he had seen Steelshaft's hand on his wife's arm.

'You know it because I tell you that it is so. This shall be reported in the proper place.'

He strode to the door: the others began to follow him. But the farmer caught Steelshaft by the neck. It was he who had touched his wife.

'Wait,' he said. 'There is more to be said. This matter——'

But the touch of the man's hand on his neck brought Steelshaft to a frenzy. The sight of Winterset's blood was like hot smoke in his nostrils. He flung himself free, the farmer raised his arm, but Steelshaft was under his guard and had plunged his dagger into the man's belly before he could move again.

As he tottered and then fell with a crash the woman screamed, and at the same moment Irvine cried, 'Out! Out! The horses!' and they all bundled through the door, mounted and galloped on to the fell. They could hear the woman screeching from the door and men shouting.

Irvine's horse was pushing along the fell-path beside Steelshaft's and he cried: 'You fool! Fool! Dummerer! We'll have the whole country up. This is a public trouble.'

Steelshaft, who was never a man of words, said nothing, but licked his lips with his tongue. He was turning over in his hot brain the moment when his knife squirted the tight belly, and it was good — the dagger like a live thing, hesitating a moment at the stuff of the jerkin and the shirt, then, at the touch of the skin, gathering energy and flighting onwards through the skin, the fat, the muscle like a happy bird.

So he said nothing, but he felt something wet on his face and he put up his iron-gloved hand. It was snow. Although it was only the middle of the day the sky was dark like an inverted saucepan and a cold mean wind carried snow in its arms and flung the flakes, scattering them like food to chickens.

Steelshaft pushed his face near Irvine and gruffed at him : ' He was swag-bellied. The knife was as gay as though it were but cupshotten.'

But Irvine felt nothing but a frantic and crazy disgust. What had happened to him since he had risen that morning ? This day left him unguarded, as though at ordinary times you were protected by a screen of safety, intangible but felt and sometimes almost touched.

Every man knows this quick apprehension that comes from the suspicion that the screen is withdrawn. ' To-day I am helpless.' Well, that was what he knew, and Winterset had known it, too. Why had he killed him ? The poor devil had been with him for so long. And now this fool stabbing the farmer. . . . He half handled his pistol, thinking that he might kill Steelshaft and then wait with his body until the pursuers came up, declare himself a minister of Her Majesty's peace and urge that he had done this in his own justice. But no. . . . He could not tell what the others would do ; they had a kind of admiration for Steelshaft.

They had stopped. Roger Bones was on a little height above the others and he was listening. They all listened. Quite clearly they heard the calls, disembodied, high in air, of the pursuers.

They rode on again, and through the driving snow, thicker now, they saw the round dark shield of a little water, or tarn as the name was. It was very black under the grey snow-thickened sky.

' Devoke Water,' Irvine said. He looked across at it as though he had seen it before. Then he heard the high, shrill voice of Bones : ' They're after us. There's a world of them.'

So in the mist behind them it seemed, for shadow was crested on shadow, and when the horses were for a moment pulled up they appeared to be of a gigantic size.

' To the level ground ! ' Irvine cried and pricked his horse towards the tarn. The others followed him, and, at the sight of them moving, the farm-hands and others who had come after them gave wild halloos and spurred their horses on.

By the tarn the ground was marshy and the horses clogged. So the four of them — Irvine, Bones, Wilfred, Steelshaft — left the horses and ran back to a clump of three trees, waiting with sword and pistol.

It was a strange enough scene, for the snowstorm swirled like mad and a little hiss and froth struck the Devoke Water so that it was as though it were alive.

The pursuers came riding and running along the flat, shouting and waving clubs and sticks. Steelshaft, with quiet relish, took aim, fired, and a boy running with the rest gave a cry like a bird and fell.

After that there were ten of them at least pressing the four. Steelshaft's head was beaten into pulp ; Wilfred had his neck half severed with a butcher's knife ; Roger Bones had a knife in his side.

Irvine, after firing wildly into the wind, his eyes blinded with snow, turned and ran. He reached a hillock, looked down, but quite suddenly seemed to be shut off from all sight and sound.

He was alone in an icy, breathless, top-spinning world.

He ran on into the heart of it.

END IN STORM

NICHOLAS HERRIES had reached Keswick with Catherine and Gilbert Armstrong in a thoroughly poor temper. The North Country in November did not seduce him.

In this year, 1592, he was forty-eight years of age and, although he felt himself as strong as ever, there were times when he was weary and other times when he was simply out of temper.

All the journey he was hard to please, but as Catherine spoke but seldom, and it mattered nothing to Gilbert what Nicholas' mood might be, there was no harm done.

In Doncaster, coming home to his inn on a night as dark as black velvet, three robbers set upon him. He killed two and wounded the third, but this meant that he must stay there an extra day. The little fight, however, pleased him, and he was not in the sulks again until they came to Penrith, where his horse, Snowdrift, so called because of her perfect whiteness, went lame.

He was not cheerful again until he heard in Keswick that Irvine had been seen at Cockermouth. At that news he was as merry as a fighting schoolboy.

He knew well in himself why it was that he had been sulky : he could not get Robin from his mind. His love for Robin was even stronger now that he was dead. He forgot now, as we all do with the dead whom we love, the little irritations. He did not care any more that Robin had been a dreamer and a poet, or that he had loved Sylvia and companioned Papist priests. He saw him, either slender, on guard at Fotheringhay, or on that last time when, limping to the door of his Tower room, he had bidden him gaily farewell, laughing and telling him that soon he would be free and back at Mallory with him again.

And so he would have been, but for Irvine! But for Irvine! But for Irvine! This murderer, this dark enemy who had been, his life long, in fight with himself and Robin . . .

He knew that Robin, who accompanied him always on that ride North, did not care whether he put an end to Irvine or no. Robin had been set on another task, had another vision. But for his own selfish peace Nicholas would know no comfort or quiet until he had paid his enemy full quittance for that long quarrel. There had been always something in himself that was lacking. He had lived actively and well; he had known physical pleasure to the full, but that was not sufficient: to live for oneself was not enough.

As they reached the North, and the dark hills with the tawny shadows of amber still lying about their flanks closed them in, he remembered that old fight with Winterset and his shabby men. Always Irvine had been in the background, never meeting him face to face. Now at last it would come to a true encounter for Robin's sake.

There was another irritation too on that night, namely, that he had never loved Catherine with such savage desire as now. Her nearness to him was a torture, the remoteness an agony. He was fierce with her, abusing her that he might bring her nearer, but he could not touch her because she loved him so deeply. When they slept at the inns he withdrew himself altogether from Catherine and Gilbert, and lay awake by himself cursing the slow hours.

But when he knew that Irvine was not far away, then all was well.

He became infected with a kind of berserk joy. There is a portrait of him in Norris's *Anatomie of Politeness* (1598) which must have been written almost exactly at this time:

'*Nor must I omit Mr. Nicholas Herries of Mallory Court in Sussex who was, by all odds, the largest gentleman I ever set eyes on and yet no monstrositie. He must have been, at the time I knew him, some forty-six or seven years of age. He stands taller on his own bottom than any man I ever did see, being more than six foot and four inches, but his breadth of shoulder and width of his limbs makes his height unnoticeable.*

*You would say by his countenance, which when I knew him was
ruddy but brown in shading rather than red, that he was a man
quickly fired, but not so, for an English gentleman more amiable
of spirit there never was in all the Queen's time. His hair
brown and curling has retreated from his high forehead. His
eyes are bright and staring, so bright that they resemble a dog's
seeing his prey a mile off, but then suddenly neighbourly and
of immediate friendliness with wrinkles at the corner of them.
His mouth, too, although large and filled with white teeth (many
of our gentlemen and ladies too suffering from teeth of a most
wretched and stinking badness), but he is for ever laughing unless
he is angry, and then he will puff and blow and shake his shoulders
and frowns will gather in his forehead like waves in a storm at
sea. When he shakes your hand you must be careful of your
fingers, and he can lift an ox over the nearmost hedge. They
say he can wrestle three men of good size and can carry a cart
on his belly. But with all this he is beloved through all the
southern parts of England for his generosity, practical wisdom
and courage. We may say that Fortune, a fickle jade, may kill
him but not deject him — for he is altogether above the world
and its drudgery.'*

He was most certainly above the world and its drudgery
now that he was assured that Philip Irvine was in his neighbourhood.

Gilbert Armstrong soon had him supplied with Irvine's
movements : how he had been in Cockermouth on some
business, then to Carlisle, then to Kendal, then Coniston
Water, and now was somewhere in Eskdale ; and that he was
attended by several ruffians who made themselves most un-
popular wherever they went by their bad behaviour.

Nicholas was now joyful, ebullient, singing, chucking the
Keswick girls under the chin, and impatient to be gone.

Before he went he saw Catherine and told her that she must
remain in Keswick until his return. She, standing against the
door of his room in the inn, looked at him with a curious,
loving humour.

' I am back in my own country again. No one is my
master here.'

He was polishing his sword and hissing like a hostler.

' It is no question of master.'

He was in his shirt and she watched, from the door, the muscles of his back moving gigantically beneath the silk.

' No,' she said. ' I have no master. I have never had one. If I ride into Eskdale it is the business of no man. Where you go, I go also. But it may be that you will not see me.'

She went up to him, put her hands on his shoulders, turned him round towards her, laid her hands on his warm breast beneath the cool silk and kissed him on the mouth.

' Look at me.'

He was already looking at her. He had never seen her more beautiful, in a long dark riding-suit, with breeches like a Turk, a sword at her thigh, her bosom tightly bound by her dark-shadowed velvet tunic, her hair of so brilliant a gold under the little square riding-hat that it dazzled his eyes.

She had the bright, bright blue eyes, the fair soft cheeks, the full mouth of a German woman, but he saw her now, staring at her, as the incarnation of splendour from no earthly country. Himself, he was wearing only his silk shirt and hosen fitting as tightly to his person as a second skin.

She looked at him and saw his love for her. She pressed against him, pushing her hands against his breast as though she would drive him backwards. She raised herself and folded her arms around him, and they became for a great moment of time, mouth to mouth, breast to breast, thigh to thigh, one flesh.

Then, while he sighed and his knees trembled and his spine was cold, she was gone. He heard no movement — only stared, shuddering, at an empty room.

He did not, however, shudder long, and that same day, by the evening, was with Gilbert Armstrong at Boot in Eskdale. That night, before he went to bed, he stood in the courtyard of the inn snuffing the wind.

' To-morrow there will be snow,' he said.

Next morning they rode into Ulpha half an hour after Irvine left it.

When Irvine ran up the fell from the Water he was lost

at once. He could see in front of him, around him, behind him, but this free space was for ever changing. A clear line of fell, lit with a strange light that was thin and yet dense like opaque milk, stretched into distance, but even as he ran forward into it a web of driving mist and snow swept around him as the wind drove it. Then, quite suddenly, everything was clear. He saw the fell stretch on every side of him, and even a line of hill beyond it, but it was ground of a gaunt ugly darkness, surfaced with knobs and globules of humps of earth and piles of rough stone. Against one of these stone-heaps, as the snow-mist closed in again, he struck his ankle and stumbled to his knees, spreading his hands against wet cold soil that seemed to stick to him and hold him.

He stayed there for a moment, trying to clear his brain, staring in front of him into the whirling snow that was alive and personal, flicking his eyes, his mouth, his chin, with soft melting dabs of wetness. He could hear no voices : he was utterly alone in the whole world. He had no sense of direction, but he hoped that, in a little while, the storm would clear. But his brain refused to concentrate on any future. If the storm *did* clear how should he find Muncaster ? Or would it be wiser if he moved downwards to the sea ? Was all the countryside out after him ? And Nicholas. . . . He must escape Nicholas. . . . He repeated the name over again, almost sobbing with a sort of wild terror. Terror was alien to him. He was not a coward and had never been one, but he did not want to fight Nicholas Herries on this disgusting moor in this chilling storm, where a man could not see, where he might imagine that others, who could not be here because they were dead, kept pace with him, standing even now over his kneeling figure — Robin Herries, Sylvia, his old mother, even the Queen at Fotheringhay.

With a great effort he pulled himself up, felt for his sword and dagger, shook himself, brushed the teasing snowflakes from his eyes. As he walked forward he realized something here that he had never known in any place before. The hillside was alive. It was not the stream whose fall he could hear, nor the stinging activity of the storm, but the actual soil itself that moved with him as he moved. So lost was this land, so deeply pressed with the bodies of lost and wandering men who had walked on it, that a great current of eternal never-dying life ran through its veins. These stones, these tussocks of rough grass, sudden splashes of marshy clogging mire, hard surfaces of pebble, unexpected hillocks that he could not see, quick blind descents, climbs that fought him at every step, all these seemed to be the movements of a breathing, hostile creature that felt him an encumbrance as a man will feel a fly on his eyelid.

He might, as he had heard men lost in a storm often did, be walking in a circle, and the wind seemed to whistle in his ear : ' You cannot escape from this ! You will be held here until the pursuers find you. They are gaining on you with every whistle of my dance.'

He stayed dead still, listening. He could see a little way now behind him and he was not sure that there were not figures there, a group of men, silent and still as he was. He called out : ' Who is there ? ' but to his terror could not hear his own voice.

' If anyone is there I am waiting.'

He thought that he saw a white horse and seated on it a great rider, but the storm wrapt aside its veil and there was a heap of stones there, and voices that he thought he heard were the echoes of a leaping stream.

He was soaked now and water ran down from his chin under his clothes against his thin breast. He began to run, quite madly, leaping along, half tumbling, jumping, calling out. He was going uphill and splashing through some kind of swamp. He stood with his back to the storm, recovering his breath. A kind of despair seized him. He would die here, a miserable, soaked, buffeted death, alone, not even in the fighting company of his enemy. Tears welled up in his eyes for sorrow at himself, that so great and remarkable a man should die all alone, storm-choked, snow-battered, on a desolate moor.

The storm, in the beating of a second, lifted. The wet mist shrivelled as into a clenched hand. He could see the moor everywhere a wasted dreariness. Close to him, only a yard or two away, was a thatched hut with an open door.

What a relief and a comfort was the roof over his head! He sat down on a pile of straw against the rough stone wall, clapping his hands to warm them, huddling his body together against the wet cold that had soaked into the very marrow of his bones.

After all, things were not so bad! If need be he could remain here for the night and in the early morning find his way over to Muncaster, secure protection there and frighten local authorities with Her Majesty's vengeance for his murdered men. Not that he cared for their deaths. It was even a relief to him, and especially that that old doddering wine-soaker Winterset had sopped the dust! He had been tired of Winterset for many a day. He had been chained by men and circumstances, but now, on returning to London, he would associate himself with Essex or some new favourite, work his way to the Queen's very footstool. She was ageing — he could work on her — work on her! And so, with the straw warming his legs and the stone at his back, he stared into the wild grey waste beyond the hut door and envisioned his own fine spirit, bare as a bodkin, in black velvet and silver, a man alone, but gazed at by the whole Court, a man of deep sorrows but of a remarkable unique being, so that the Queen herself . . .

He stared and saw a woman standing in the doorway. She was tall and dressed in a man's riding-habit of black velvet and she had deep gold hair piled beneath her hat. There was a sword at her side. She stepped inside the hut and bowed. He climbed clumsily to his feet and bowed also. He saw that she was an exceedingly fine, opulent woman, and was immediately amorous.

' You take shelter from the storm, madam ? '

She shook her head and answered, ' No ! '

There was something peculiar about her and he did not know what it was. But, as he stared, he thought that there would be nothing better, in this cold and dismal weather, than to take this rich and opulent woman in his arms and so secure a radiant, rewarding heat. Did she prefer storms, then, that she would rather stay out in them ?

No, not that. Her horse was tied to the wall. She had expected to find someone in the barn.

To find someone ? He was surprised. On such a day to find someone ? And then a thought struck him. Of course, of course, it had been she whom his men had seen in Ulpha that morning. Yes. She nodded her head. It had been she.

The storm was dying. Outside the barn-opening only a little wind sighed and whispered. He could see a broken bar of pale silver light above the dark fell-line. He felt a profound and self-pitying melancholy. There would now be nothing more consoling than to lie in the straw with so handsome a lady, to stroke those cheeks, to unbind that golden hair, to unpin that deep dark velvet. . . .

He asked her to share the straw in his company : ' For it is cold and we will warm one another. . . .'

But she did not move, only looked at him with an odd intensity.

He moved towards her, holding out his hand.

' Come. I would be warm.'

And then, as she did not stir, he added : ' I am a gentleman of Her Majesty's Court whose fellows have had some trouble with a farmer down the hill. I was lost in the storm. After we have warmed ourselves we will go down——'

' I know you,' she said quietly.

He felt a small, wondering terror, like a little arrow, touch his heart. It was there and was gone. Who was she ? Why was she there so motionless and regarding him with such fixity ? He suddenly did not desire her any longer, but only that he might be gone. He found that he disliked her company. So with a quick, new haughtiness, he drew himself together, feeling, however, that he was a shabby sight with his lank hair and soaked clothes.

' I will wish you good-day then. I will find my way alone.'

She stepped into the doorway.

' No,' she said. ' You must wait here. That is why I came. Someone will join us.'

She seemed to him then no real woman. He could not see her shape clearly as he had done before. He wanted nothing now so much as to get out of this place and be free again.

He stared at her as a man whose sight is dazed stares to clear the blurred outlines. The light was ghostly, the air most bitterly cold, and snowflakes fell now behind the barn in slow heavy fragments, white against grey, white against tawny brown.

' Who are you ? I have nothing to do with you.'

She made no answer but only stood in the doorway. He drew his dagger, but she did not move.

' Let me pass. I have no dealings with women.'

Then he heard a voice calling, quite clearly through the now freezing air : ' Catherine !   Catherine ! '   He was trapped. They had sent that absurd woman to hold him. He caught her arm. She eluded him, drew her sword.

He saw the sword, her neck white and warm above the black velvet, her eyes, blue and hard, driving him back with more than human force. But he would not be driven back and, more than anything else in this filthy world, he must be free of this place. He saw her against the stormlight. He snatched his dagger and stabbed her deep to the heart. Then he pushed at her as she fell, and ran out on to the moor.

On the height of a little knoll he stopped, turned, looked back. The light was clear. The hut was outlined and emphasized. In the open doorway he saw Nicholas Herries stand, move forward, return with the woman in his arms.

The great figure remained there motionless, holding the woman as he would a child. He looked across the space and upwards. The two men stared at one another, then Nicholas bent forward, kissed the woman's cheek, stood motionless again ; at last, after what seemed an infinite time, moved back into the hut.

Irvine waited.

Nicholas returned, now alone. Once more the two men regarded one another but without speaking.

Irvine started running. It was not fear now. He knew that the encounter was inevitable. He was not in the least afraid of it. He felt rather a great relief as though, at last, after a lifetime of waiting, this issue would be settled.

He must find a good vantage-place, and very soon he found it, a rise of ground, two torn and twisted trees behind him, and to his right a precipitous decline that ran to a little valley where there was a noisy, chattering stream. He looked

all around him, studying the ground. He could see clearly
now to a great range of hills.

He did not know that those watching, waiting mountains
were Scafell, the Pikes, and, just emerging, Great End. He
did not care what they were, but he regarded them curiously,
feeling how alive they were in that cold, grey light. The land
seemed vast, unending fell, rising and falling with a rhythm
that, in the stillness, he could hear. But it was perhaps only
the voice of the stream in the valley.

He was, it might be, a little crazy, for he never ceased talking
aloud, while he drew his sword and his dagger, feeling their
sharp edges. ' You will not fail me. It has come at last. But
he cannot touch me. How was I to know that it was *his*
woman ? How bright her hair was ! I have never seen such
bright hair in a woman. . . .'

He saw Nicholas approaching. When he was close it
seemed to Irvine that this was a man he had never seen before.
He had always regarded Nicholas as a clumsy, overgrown
clown, laughing, witless, a fool. Here now was a man whose
face was so sorrowful that Irvine might have pitied him had
he been able to pity any but himself.

When he was at the foot of the slope Nicholas, his sword
drawn, stopped.

' This also you must do,' he said. After a pause he added
very gently : ' Why must you kill her ? She never did you
any harm.'

' I wished her none. She would not let me go.'

' *That* was not the quarrel between us. Had she been there
or not been there we must have met.' He said, as though to
himself : ' Robin, Catherine——'

Irvine cried out in his shrill, angry scream : ' Get back,
you fool ! Get back to your woman.' And in a rage that
came from some intense exasperation and the bitter cold and
a deep loneliness, he jumped from the little rise and hurled
himself on Nicholas.

Nicholas moved sideways. Their swords rasped. Irvine
had almost fallen, but the touch of the other sword transformed him, at an instant, into the skilled, cool fighter that
he really was. He steadied himself, held himself on guard,

recovering his breath, ordering, by old practised command, his whole body, from head to heel, into a disciplined, pliant weapon. Only, with a quick gesture, he pushed his wet black hair back from his eyes.

When their swords met again, the joy of skilful fighting overcame all other feeling. The ground upon which they stood was here marsh and here pebble, not an easy foothold, and the small icy wind blew against their faces, swinging the sky with it like a torn scarf.

At first it was as though they were practising in a friendly fencing match. Their swords kept guard, one against the other, like living things, running up the blades, meeting as though by some joyful arrangement. Then, with a little cry, Irvine passed Nicholas' guard but only touched the neck. And at that they both paused for a moment, stepping back and regarding one another.

Irvine was worried now by the light. Great bastions of heavy cloud were coming up over the hills and the wind was once more rising. He was standing with his back to the paler, whiter sky. He turned, faced round and swept his sword through the air, dancing and giving little cries like a man maddened by excitement. His sword-hand was now towards Nicholas' thigh, but Nicholas, keeping guard with his blade, turned towards him, leaning forward ever so slightly on his toes, and digging his heels for a moment into the higher ground. His great height and length of arm gave him now an advantage and, as the wind was rising, his bulk of body strengthened him against it while Irvine was buffeted across open moor.

Irvine was now more cautious, stealthy, agile in his attack. His onslaught was so furious that Nicholas could do nothing but defend. Irvine's brilliance as a fighter had come always from three things : his quick intelligence, his knowledge of the art of fence, and the litheness of his body. He was angry now with the rage of a vastly proud man who had expected to win in the first moment, and his brain was cold and hard. He was moved to a fury also by the set, angry gloom of Nicholas' round boyish face. This was a new man born within the last half-hour, and there was something so deeply purposed and of so large a size in him that Irvine, beset with ghosts, felt that if he killed one Herries there would be another in his place, monumental, grieving, oafish but impregnable, as this foul moor and those sulky, watching hills were impregnable.

His disgust and his anger together drove him into a passionate, flashing attack. His sword responded to his brain ; again and again it beat Nicholas' guard and he saved himself only by miracles of adroitness that his heaviness should have forbidden. Now Irvine's blade ran up the other's like a leaping tongue, now it darted and, as Nicholas' sword was up to meet it, flashed down and was an eyelash only from his belly ; now it was straight and hard, independent of Irvine's body as though it were launched from heaven, now it spat again and again and yet again like a serpent's tongue, now it was languid, almost asleep, lazily creeping towards Nicholas' sword-arm, now it was moving with the swaying litheness of Irvine's body, and Irvine stood tip-toe, was back on his left foot, straightening and bending his arm.

Nicholas, in all his long life of swordsmanship, had known nothing like this. Irvine was so thin and so active that it seemed there were a dozen of him there, all spitting hatred as though Nicholas had stepped upon a nest of vipers. Also, he himself was heavy with the shock of Catherine's death. It did but make him the more implacable, but it closed a sort of grip about his heart so that his fire, his vigour, his passions, were fastened in a cold chamber. He felt his breath come drily. His eyes began to be blinded with the swiftness of Irvine's blade. It was almost as though the weaving of its pattern cast some spell upon him.

Irvine moved forward. Nicholas retreated. Fiercely he beat down Irvine's blade, but he struck only the edge of it, and a second later knew a sharp bite in his left side. Irvine had struck home. But it was just that bite that was needed. He turned half-sides, swept his sword round, caught Irvine's hand and pierced it ; Irvine's sword dropped, but the swiftness of Nicholas' own movement, and the chillness of the bitter cold, had loosened his hold, and his sword flew high, circling into the air, and swerved down to the turf ten paces away, and stuck there quivering.

It was Irvine's left hand that had been cut, but his right had his dagger and was at Nicholas' throat. They were almost breath to breath.

At the same moment, as though with a shrug of impatience because it had waited long enough, the storm swirled down upon them. The snow fell now in great moving webs of choking fragments. The wind rose from the ground as though it would tear the rough grass from the soil.

Blinded, deafened, the two men swayed together. Irvine had his thin, long, bleeding hand on Nicholas' throat while his right curved, trying to be free for the dagger-blow. But Nicholas' hand was on that right wrist, his other hand round Irvine's waist. They were clutched like lovers, meeting at last after these many, many years, as it were in a lovers' embrace.

Relentlessly Nicholas' iron hand tightened on Irvine's wrist. The dagger quavered and fell. Then Nicholas' dagger rose. Irvine flung his face back, his eyes staring upward. He cried once. Nicholas struck deep into Irvine's throat. The blood spurted into Nicholas' eyes as water from a released spout. But, as Irvine fell back, Nicholas caught him, gathered him to his breast, raised him high, and with a great cry flung him down, over the hill, into the stream below.

He could not see, for the storm was boiling above the valley. But he stood with his arms raised, as though acclaiming heaven, and he shouted : ' Hulloa ! Hulloa ! Hulloa ! '

The hills, the whole waste of fell, the spirits of all the lost men wandering there, repeated, echoing : ' Hulloa ! Hulloa ! Hulloa ! '

Q

THE SUMMER WEDDING

ROSAMUND HERRIES was thirty-three years of age on the fifth of May in that year 1599. She spent the three days around her birthday at Mallory Court with Nicholas. This was altogether by chance. He did not know it was her birthday and she told no one — only her father and mother knew.

To be thirty-three and still unmarried was not a thing to tell the town-crier of. Rosamund did not mind in the least that she was unmarried. She had loved Nicholas since she was a baby — the sound of him, what she was told of him — and would love him until she died. After that? Who could say? She had heard her father say once : ' Every man is immortal until his task is ended.' Loving Nicholas had never been a task, but her father had explained to her then that the word ' task ' must be used in the sense of an ' art '—' something created.' Her love of Nicholas was ' something created,' something that grew, year after year, under her hands. And would it ever be done? Love was a growing thing, and sometimes in this life you saw only the beginning of it. Was it so absurd to fancy that it continued? But — without the body? Why not? Rosamund had longed for many years to lie in Nicholas' arms, longed often enough, crying on her bed with longing. But it was not his body that she loved. Cover him with sores, give him a split nose and a cleft lip, and she would love him just the same. Once, perhaps, it would not have been so, but, in true love, you work slowly beyond the body, until at last you are interwoven with the spirit. For a woman this contact with the spirit of anyone she loves is her constant pursuit, whereas a man is busy about too many things to search so determinedly. When a woman reaches the spirit of her lover and finds that the man knows not that he even *has* a spirit, the woman is so deeply exasperated that she would kill

470

him if she did not console herself by remembering that he is a child.

Rosamund had been often thus exasperated by Nicholas, or would have been exasperated but for her sense of the comic. As she sat, on this May afternoon, in the Mallory garden near the fountain, she was thinking about Nicholas and what a ridiculous man he was.

Her sense of the comic was always saving her from bitterness. If you find *yourself* comic you really cannot object when others find you so. She lived, she considered, in an exceedingly comic period. England was a most comic country. Elizabeth a most comic queen. She had lived for so long in and out of the Court that she had seen enough comic characters close at hand to fill a country town. Her mother and father also were comic, but she loved them so dearly that she could never laugh at them, only with them. And that she couldn't do with her mother, who had no sense of humour. Her father and she laughed at themselves incontinently.

She saw through everyone, including herself. These ridiculous, posturing men in their gold braid and diamond buckles, turning their calves, twisting their necks, driving their swords into another's stomach for a trifle, at Court intriguing for the Queen's smile as though they did not know that she was a black-toothed, ill-smelling old woman, furious at her barrenness. Not that Rosamund did not admire the Queen — she thought her simply the greatest tyrant the world had ever seen, the saviour and maker of her country. But Elizabeth's greatness did not make the men's servility the less absurd. They thought of only two things in the world : advancement and lechery.

Rosamund, although she had never been a beauty, had still received offers, but she was yet a virgin and would remain so unless Nicholas proposed otherwise. Beneath her raillery, her sharp-sightedness, her realism, she had a heart that bothered her far too often. When she loved she loved for ever, which everyone knows is as foolish a thing as you can do.

In the sunlight now she was thinking of Nicholas. No one (save possibly Gilbert Armstrong) had known what occurred in that November in the North. Philip Irvine had been last seen alive, moving, with his men, out of a farm on a stormy morning on a Cumberland moor. Two months later the snowdrifts had melted from a valley a mile or so from Devoke Water and his body had been found, his neck and legs broken and a dagger-wound through his neck. No one had cared very much.

Long before that Nicholas had returned south and resumed his life at Mallory again. Only it was known that the German woman, Gilbert Armstrong's wife, had died in the North.

Rosamund had seen at once that the death of that woman had killed something in Nicholas : he was another man ; the days of his adventurous life were over. When she had heard of Catherine Armstrong's death a wicked joy had leapt in her heart. She knew that it was wicked and cherished it. For what good had this witch-woman ever done with her golden hair, her foreign remoteness, her unhappy silence ? But, afterwards, when she saw that part of Nicholas was dead now, Rosamund almost wished her back again : anything that Nicholas might be his old, happy, careless self again. But that he could never be any more ; Robin and Catherine were dead.

In her own rather dry, practical fashion she did all for him that she could. They were companions now as they had never been, were constantly together, having jokes, riding together, sharing ' sights ' in London. She had, at least, the satisfaction of knowing that she and Gilbert Armstrong were everything to him.

He liked to talk constantly of Robin, of his brilliance, of how he might have been a great poet, of his sweetness of nature, of his gentleness, of something he had that Nicholas would never have, of how his eyes were always staring into a world that he, Nicholas, would never have a sight of. Nor she, Rosamund, either. There were two sorts of mortals : one plain, the other coloured. She and Nicholas were of the ' plain ' kind.

But even in the ' plain ' world all was not well with Nicholas. He was fifty-five years of age and growing ' over-heavy.' He was not proud of his appearance as once he had been. He wore his old clothes too long. A man of his size must take especial care of his person. There was no woman at Mallory to see to that. The servants were old and presumed on his kindness and laziness as once they would not have dared to do. He would sit for long hours before the fire, his great legs stretched out in front of him, his hands folded on his belly, or pulling the ears of his dog, thinking of nothing. There was yet time for him to be saved, for his body was as strong, his eyes as bright, his smile as contagious ; and there was always Gilbert to care for him, and insist on his exercise and to see that the servants did their work.

She sighed and saw Nicholas sitting on the garden seat beside her. He put his arm around her and drew her close to him.

' And of what are you thinking ? '

' I was thinking how aged I am. I am thirty-three years this very day.'

He sprang up.

' I will go into the house and fetch you a gift.'

She pulled him down again.

' I want nothing but to be here with you.'

He looked at her, his blue eyes speculative ; the colour slowly flushed his cheeks. He stammered, stuttering, until she wondered what was the matter with him. He took her hand.

' As it is your birthday you shall give *me* a gift.'

' Anything, Nicholas.'

' That is a promise. You shall marry me.'

She said at once : ' Yes. Of course.'

He held her tightly in his arms, kissing her even passionately, which surprised her. This hour, for which so many years she had longed, had come at last. She was so wildly happy, but wished so ardently that he should think her calm, practical, wise, that she allowed him to talk.

' I have wished it again and again. But I am twenty-two years the older. I have waited for you to have some other man, younger, more handsome. But I fear you will grow an old maid, and it is lamentable to me that you should die a virgin.

' Moreover, I think that I will live to a long old age, and

when I am seventy and you fifty there will be nothing between us. I have loved you for many, many years — not with that strange, mad love that I had for Catherine. I asked you once before and you would not because she stood between us. And she did. She stood between me and all other men and women in the world. But now I love you, and you alone. We are the best company there could be, I think. And I would have a son and heir by you to carry on our family.'

She laughed, she clapped her hands like a child.

' I have wished for this moment my whole life long.'

' And there shall be other better moments,' he said with glee.

There seemed to be no reason for waiting. The very months for wedding were April and November, but April was over and November was a long time away.

Rosamund Herries was married to Nicholas Herries of Mallory Court, Sussex, in the church of St. Mary Breding in the village of Mallory on the 8th of June 1599.

From the old yellow-paged family book kept first by Nicholas and Rosamund, and after by their son Robert and his wife, Margaret Blaikie, and after that again by *their* son Matthew and *his* wife Frances, members of the family present at this joyous wedding were :

Edward Herries.
Agatha, his wife.
Janet and Martha Herries, their daughters.
Sidney Herries.
Very old Lady Courthope.
Guy and Rosemary Herries, father and mother of the bride.
Barbara and Tobias Garland.
Rashleigh, Lucy, Peter, their children.
Carey and Somerset, sons of James and Constance Herries.
And Alicia Turner with her sons Matthew and Paul.

It was, it seems, the most radiant of June days. There are several accounts of the affair from contemporary Journals and Diaries, and all agree that it was a glorious, happy occasion, without a shadow in any sky.

A great, great affair it was for the whole countryside, for

Nicholas had lived at Mallory all his life and was the most popular Englishman in the whole of Sussex. From the hour of dawning country people poured in, coming from miles distant, walking or riding. The whole of Mallory grounds was thrown open. On the Long Field and away through the meadows to the stream tents were set up and there was every sort of jollity and feasting.

But that was all for later. The immediate business was to get the bride and bridegroom to church.

When Rosamund appeared in the doorway of Mallory, before the flagged path that led through the garden, across the meadow, by the wicket gate to the church, an ' Oh ! ' of admiration went up from the crowd of villagers and sightseers. Janet Herries, who had caught a grudging nature from her mother, murmured to her sister Martha, ' Anyone would look something on such a day.' And, indeed, the lawns and hedges glittered under the June sun, the roses and pinks savoured the air with their scent, the church bells were ringing like crazy bells, the sky was blue without a cloud.

But it was her character and her happiness that gave Rosamund her beauty that morning. She would never, perhaps, look so beautiful again until she was an old woman.

Her dress was of white (white or russet were the wedding colours) and on to the sleeves and body and skirt were stitched the coloured favours. These were ribbons tied as true-lovers' knots, and after the ceremony they would be fought for by the young men of the party. Rosamund wore her hair down about her shoulders, and on her head was a wreath of fresh flowers. Her hair was combed, and the favours stitched to her dress were of every colour — flame-colour, peach, blue, orange, red, tawny, but not of gold, for that signified avarice, nor flesh-colour which was lasciviousness, nor green which was wantonness.

Before her was carried, with a great deal of pomposity, by fat Tom Boulter the steward, a bride-cup of gilt and silver, and sticking out from it a fine branch of rosemary gilded and hung with silk ribbons of all colours.

Rosamund walked between two ' sweet-boys ' very gaily dressed with bride-laces and rosemary tied to their silk sleeves.

These two ' sweet-boys ' were Carey and Somerset, the sons of James and Constance.

In front of her went the village musicians, playing for all they were worth and somewhat discordantly. Behind her came the bridesmaids : Janet and Martha, wild, dark little Lucy, and daughters of neighbouring gentlemen friendly to Nicholas. They carried bridecakes and gilded garlands of leaves.

Beside her and very close to her, as though he could not bear to lose her, walked her father, very handsome in plum-colour and silver.

The path all the way was strewn with flowers and rushes, and the clanging of the bells, the huzza-ing of the people, the discordance of the musicians, made a noise that could be heard almost as far as the town of Lewes.

Everyone said, as everyone always has and everyone always will, how very beautiful the bride looked, but it was only her happiness and goodness that made Rosamund beautiful — and they were quite sufficient for the occasion.

The crowd about the church door was so pressing that the musicians had to push with their trumpets, and Tom Boulter, very self-important, handing the bride-cup to one of the household, went about with his stave pulling people back and telling them that ' they must be ashamed of themselves.'

The little church was, of course, crowded to a hot agony, people standing on the boards of the font and hanging over the gallery to their desperate danger, and even two bad boys perching themselves on the portly stomach of the effigy of Sir Bertram Fanshawe, a Crusader of local fame because his ghost was said to walk.

Near the altar Nicholas was standing resplendent, his black velvet jerkin edged with strands of gold bullion, his sleeves of rose-coloured satin, slops of the same colour, his hosen and the feather to the cap which he carried in his hand of the same colour. This black and rose suited him admirably, and he looked, in the opinion of everyone, twenty years less than his real age, although his face had the grave concerned look of a boy before his elders, and he was for ever moving his hand towards his sword as though he feared an attack.

Nevertheless when he saw Rosamund appearing up the church his broad face broke into a full grin and he nodded at Gilbert Armstrong, just behind him, as though to say : ' All is well. She is here. And now I care for nothing.'

The ring was of two hands in gold clasping a heart that was a fine ruby, and when he placed it on Rosamund's thumb they exchanged a look of such perfect happiness that it astonished old Lucy Courthope, who, a bent and wrinkled misanthropist, nevertheless was in the front row and bent forward so as not to miss a thing.

After old Mr. Martindale, the clergyman, had pronounced them man and wife, Rosamund knew a moment of miraculous vision. All time for her was rolled into that one moment. She saw herself as a small, ugly girl in the country, watching her father as he painted, and hearing for the first time of this giant cousin who could carry a cart on his belly and yet was so gentle with his dogs and horses. She had loved him, she fancied, from that first moment of hearing. But there had been so many, many years when she must put away from her altogether any hope. She had learned to love him as an ' unattainable.' But there had come that moment at the great London ball when she had spoken to him, the party in the country when they had had their first real talk together, the strange, dangerous years when she had lived with Irvine and Sylvia in London, and at last, those months at Fotheringhay, when, under the shadow of that tragic history, under the horror of poor Sylvia's death, they had grown into true friends.

After that had come the obstacle of the German woman : it was then that Rosamund, although she did not realize it, had developed true character, wanting nothing for herself, caring for him, making him happy when she could, reconciling herself to the truth that she would never be nearer to him than she was.

All this seemed to present itself to her in one flash of burning joy. She turned the ring on her thumb. She placed her hand on his arm. She was Nicholas' wife.

Before they left the church a great cup of muscadel with sops in it was presented. First the bride must drink in it, then the bridegroom, then the reverend clergyman, then the father and mother of the bride, and, after that, as many of the company as could get to it, for it meant the greatest good luck to have a taste of it. It was the old custom that everyone stood in the church there where he or she might be and the cup was passed from hand to hand.

After this the musicians struck up again outside the church, and down the churchyard path went the bridal pair. Nicholas towering over everyone and grinning on this country friend and that, shouting a word here and a word there, struck in the face by flowers and not minding it at all. Catching Rosamund's hand in his, then, as they turned into the meadow towards the house, putting his arm around her waist, looking for a long moment across the fields, sniffing the summer grasses, thinking how good life was, and how lucky he, at so advanced an age, to secure so perfect a bride.

When they were returned to the house they sat on a raised dais in the great hall and received the congratulations of everybody. This was a long, long business and Nicholas, sitting stiff, upright, with a studied smile on his face and saying again and again, ' I thank you. We thank you. I thank you. We thank you,' caught wistfully through the high open windows the merriment and gaiety from the tents on the meadow. Indeed, outside the house there was a concatenation of disharmonies ! Women screaming with laughter, men shouting, cows lowing, miniature guns popping, trumpets and whistles and flutes, dogs barking — above all, everyone singing. The whole world singing. Already, thus early in the afternoon, dancing had begun.

At last, God be thanked, these stiff ceremonies were over and the married pair might retire to wash their hands and faces, attend to nature, and breathe for a space by a cool-aired window. Even now they could not be alone. The bridemaidens must be with the bride, the young men with the bridegroom. Nicholas did all the same take advantage of the moment when he could claim reason for solitude to have his arm round Gilbert Armstrong's neck, pull his ear and chaff him about his grand clothes of white and orange.

' You are glad of this, Gilbert ? '

' This is the happiest day of my life, master.'

' Why — when you think marriage a disaster ! '

' Not thus. You need a steady woman.' He stretched his arms. ' And now, too, I can go away for a time — hunting my own game — and know that you are in safe charge.'

' Have I imprisoned you all this while then ? '

' No, but I had no life of my own any more. Now I shall have it again. And we are old friends, your wife and I. I say what I please to her. Only, master, watch——'

' Yes ? ' asked Nicholas.

'— that in a year's time you are not altogether at her command. She has that character. . . .' And he hurried, chuckling, from the room.

Later, at the feast in the same hall, Nicholas and Rosamund were once again side by side on the dais.

As the customary hour for the meal of the day was between eleven and twelve, now that it was near mid-afternoon all were ravenous. And there was food enough for a village : vast sides of beef, mutton, veal, flavoured with the oddest sauces of musk, ambergris, saffron ; oysters, wild-fowl, geese, deer in pasties, barley and rye brown bread. And, to wash it all down, beer, ale, sack, muscadine, Rhenish, alicant and charneco. But most of all had they a sweet tooth (which was partly why the teeth of so many of them were so sadly decayed), and none more than Nicholas himself. There was that most delicious of all sweetmeats ever invented by man, marchpane, made of pounded almonds, pistachio nuts, sugar and flour. There were sugar-sops, Eringo, kissing-comfits. And at last, set in front of bride and bridegroom, was a magnificent construction in green and white and gold sugar of the Long Field itself, with the stream and three fine cows whose bellies were full of sweetmeats — all standing on a cake of sweetened and spiced bread — powdered sugar with the juices of oranges was used to flavour it.

But, of course, by now the sack and alicant and charneco had risen into people's heads and everyone was merry indeed. Only Nicholas and Rosamund kept themselves sober, for they longed for the time when this might be over and they, the bed-curtains drawn, lying in one another's arms. They were both weary, for they had been up with the dawn.

Nevertheless Nicholas was awake enough to cast his eyes over his guests and speculate over one or two of them. Time moved so swiftly that those who, only a minute ago, were howling in their cradles were already here howling in their drink ! He had not for many a day seen so many of the Herries family gathered together, and he, as head of that family, must study them with considerable interest.

Old Lucy, Lady Courthope, was already fast asleep, her peaked chin sunk into her plate of marchpane. The best of them all was his own father-in-law, Guy Herries, who even now had the most flaxen hair, the bluest eyes, the straightest back of any of them. Here was a man of sixty-three who had, it would seem, a whole life of vigour and goodness yet in front of him.

For Edward and Sidney, both now portly and heavy-eyed, he had a feeling of kindliness. But what about the people who died long before physical death took them ? Was it our arrogance that made us think so ? Well, they did not *know* that they were dead, so no suffering could ever come to them.

Close to their passivity was someone so vital that she constantly caught his eye : the strange child, Lucy Garland, daughter of Barbara and Tobias, niece of Edward and Sidney. This child could not yet be ten years of age : she was a little thing, as thin as a wisp of cord, dark, gipsy-faced, with eager sparkling eyes. Now and again he caught her excited voice, shrill, piercing. She was dressed in ill-judged finery with a large ridiculous feather in her hair. Poor Barbara, her mother, had never had any taste. What made Nicholas single this child from all the rest of the company ? He felt in her some element of tragedy, something in common with Robin, with Robin's Sylvia. Looking at the plain, matter-of-fact faces of Janet and Martha, the daughters of Edward and Agatha, he thought to himself that it was strange that the same family should hold such opposites. But had not he and Robin been examples of it ? Fact and poetry — the two strains in the family, blending to cover the whole round of life. Had not, years ago, Philip Sidney been of one sort, was not Burghley's son of the other ? Had not Leicester been the one, was not Essex the other ?

And his gaze passed kindly to the boys of the family : Carey and Somerset, grandsons of old, blinking, blear-eyed Lucy Courthope, fine and handsome boys, representing the new self-confident, arrogant, courageous England that was everywhere developing. . . . Matthew and Paul Turner, also grandsons of old Lucy, but of quite another kind from Carey and Somerset, already grave in spite of their childishness, middle-class business running in their veins. He was glad that Turner himself had not come, for he did not like him with his narrow-lidded eyes and his intention never to allow a bargain to slip.

Here in front of him was a growing, conscious, composite English family. To what would it come ? What service might it render England ?

He looked at Rosamund and thought of the gipsy's prophecy — that the first of his body resembling himself was to be his great-grandson and that he would be held by all the world to be a rogue and a vagabond. Well, no matter. There would *be* an heir — that was the principal thing.

Afterwards real weariness confused him to the end. After all, he was fifty-five years of age ! All he wanted now was to be alone with Rosamund, not first to make love, but rather to feel her close to him, to know that she was to be his companion until life should end, to feel that wonderful security in her loyalty, her friendship, her humour and good-nature. To be alone with her ! To be alone with her !

The hall had been cleared for dancing ; the musicians played from the gallery. Nicholas did his proper duty and danced with Agatha and Janet and Martha and Barbara and little Lucy and Alicia Turner. And how his legs ached and his back, and how very hot he was, and how absurd that, on this night of his own wedding, he should scarcely have a glance of Rosamund !

But at last the moment came. To the shouts of the whole company he was conveyed to his room by all the men — Gilbert, Edward, Sidney and Tobias — and Rosamund was taken to hers by the ladies.

He was undressed and teased and jested with while the night-rail was thrown over his head. Then, with singing and the lights of candles, he was taken to Rosamund's room, and there, with the women around her bed, she sat up in the big four-poster with the brown and red hangings waiting for him.

He climbed in beside her and they both sat up against the pillows while the last cup was drunk, improper jests were made, the final Marriage Song sung. All the candles were blown out but one. With this at their head the company moved to the door.

This candle also was blown out.

As they lay in one another's arms, Nicholas suddenly said : ' Gilbert has it that, in a year's time, you will have the say in all things.'

Rosamund answered sleepily : ' In a year's time I shall not be thinking of you at all — but only of our son.'

THE QUEEN WAS IN HER PARLOUR

ROBERT PHILIP HERRIES, eldest son of Nicholas and Rosamund Herries, was born at Mallory Court in Sussex at five o'clock in the morning of April 10th, 1600.

On the morning of January 21st, 1603, when Robert Philip was two and a half years of age, the Court moved to Richmond. The weather was bad, extremely cold, a foul north-east wind.

Elizabeth, who had now entered on her seventieth year and had been more than forty-four years a queen, protested in the icy winds at Richmond that ' furs could not withstand winter cold,' so wore none, and suffered. Then her cousin, and closest friend, the Countess of Nottingham died, and grief of spirit, cold of body, brought her low. At the beginning of March she had a fever and could not sleep. She refused both to eat and to speak. She sat silent, thinking on her extraordinary reign, on Leicester perhaps, on Essex most certainly, on her loneliness, her grandeur, the misery of her body, her longing for death, her pride in England.

Her coronation ring had to be sawn off because it had grown into her flesh, and this distressed her greatly because she had a superstition about it.

A year before, at least, Robert Cecil and others had entered into communication with James in Scotland and assured him of his succession. Already history had passed over the great Queen's head and left her behind. She sat, looking into the air, wondering at her loneliness, angry and silent, baffled by approaching death.

Nicholas and Rosamund had, by now, a little house close to the old Banqueting House in Whitehall, and there they lived until the Banqueting House was burned down in 1619. Near there were the old Hall of Westminster and the ancient buildings of the Exchequer, and near these again, the Star Chamber of such evil memory. They were, in fact, at the very hub of the universe.

Not that this, of course, was their real home — Mallory Court would always be that — but Nicholas now had a considerable amount of business on his hands. Old Lucy Courthope had died in the preceding year and left him as her man of affairs. Then Turner was for ever trying to drag him into this business and that. Rosamund also liked London, had many friends, enjoyed a dinner, a play, a ball, as much as any one. They enjoyed almost anything when they were together, and, indeed, hated to be apart.

There was a truth, though, in what Rosamund had once said, for she adored her baby to madness and would perhaps have neglected Nicholas had it not seemed to her that he was her child as well.

Nicholas, too, was dreadfully proud of Robert Philip, and the baby would have been spoiled to destruction had it not been that he proved to be a child entirely without imagination. He was good, solid and full of chuckles. Anything that he saw exactly in front of him he could grasp, and grasp it he did, but it never occurred to him that anything existed that he did not see with his own eyes. He already realized his father and mother thoroughly, and once he had seen them he would remember them, but ask him to credit a horse that he had *not* seen, even though it stood in an adjoining stable and you had just come from it, and he would look at you with mild blue-eyed scorn.

He was sturdy of build and most equable of nature. When his nurse, Mrs. Margit, told him about Robin Goodfellow he roared with happy, mocking laughter. Fairies ! Pixies ! The very idea !

On a day early in March Nicholas was going over his accounts with Gilbert Armstrong in his London house, when the servant came to the door and said that Sir Hubert Chichester was in the outer room and must speak to him.

Nicholas sprang to his feet.

' Chichester ! From Richmond ! What can he want ? '

He hurried into the outer room, where he found a grave, black-bearded gentleman, very much younger than himself.

'You are to come at once to Richmond, Mr. Herries, if you will — and I fear even if you will *not*. It is the Queen's request.'

'The Queen?'

'It seems that last night when Her Majesty could not sleep she suddenly remembered " a man like a giant — a man who had come one time about his younger brother who was in the Tower." At first no one could recollect, and then Lady Bracy recalled that you had been — in the year — what was it? — no matter — on a number of occasions to the Court to get Her Majesty's interest for your brother.

'It must be you, of course, that she intended. So I was sent off in the morning hour, and beg you to return with me. I am certain that it will not be to detain you — a half-hour at the most. It may be that by your arrival there she will already have forgotten. Nevertheless, we must do what we can for her.'

As they rode, through Chelsea village and the woods beyond, and at last the fine free Common and Park, they had a pleasant conversation.

Chichester, although grave and a little consequential, had a wise knowledge of the world and showed a very decent respect to Nicholas. He talked frankly about the state of the country.

'It is all settled for James' succession. It will be a strange business, after all these years, to be under another monarch, and there are many odd stories about him. I would have feared for the country at one time, but I fancy that it is too settled now for any change in the Crown to affect it.'

Nicholas asked about the Queen. Did she realize her approaching end?

'We cannot tell what she realizes. She will not speak or eat. I think first the tragic business of Essex and now the other day the death of the Countess of Nottingham have broken her.'

He asked Nicholas something about his own life, and said

that, when he was a young man, he had heard often of Nicholas' feats of strength.

Nicholas laughed. ' I am all but sixty years of age and it is not for an old man to boast. But I have had a happy life, never seeing more than was under my nose, which is, I think, the easiest way to be happy.'

Chichester, after some hesitation, spoke about his brother : ' He died, I think, in the Tower ? '

Nicholas turned towards him.

' You must pardon me in all courteousness, but I would prefer not to speak of that. I loved my brother as I have loved only one other creature on this earth. His death was the work of a villain, and, having revenged it, I have buried it in my heart.'

Chichester hesitated again. At last he said : ' You will think me, I fear, impertinent, but I have a message to you that I must deliver. I offered myself indeed to come to fetch you to-day so that I might deliver it.'

He went on again : ' Last summer I was in Antwerp, and one evening I was asked by the landlord of my inn if I would visit for a moment an Englishman who was there and was dying. He could not die in peace, he had said, without seeing me. Wondering what this could be I went into the room where he was. There was a man in a bed dying. He had all his sense about him and spoke clearly. He asked me whether I knew a Mr. Nicholas Herries. I said that I did not, but that I could easily communicate with him. He said that this illness had come suddenly upon him and that he would never be in England again. He said that his name was Pierson, that he was a Catholic priest, and that it was because of him that your brother had been tortured in the Tower and that he had died there. He wanted me to tell you that he would have saved him by giving himself up to the authorities, but that he had been prevented by the orders of his Church that must be obeyed absolutely, but that he wished me to convey to you that your brother must have welcomed such a death as affording him a victory that would wipe out his other defeats. That he wished to tell you this so that you should not in any way grieve. He added that he had loved your brother more than any other man or woman on this earth, and that it had been his chief temptation that he should put your brother before his God. That he could not help it, but that now, in dying, it was his first thought that soon he would be with your brother again.

'I left him, and early in the following morning he died. I thought to write this to you but considered it better to speak to you when the opportunity occurred. I made this opportunity to-day.'

Chichester spoke as though he were reciting something that he had repeated to himself very often that he might not forget it.

Nicholas did not speak for a little while. At last he thanked him for his considerate courtesy, but said no more, and they rode through the wild, wintry morning in silence.

Nicholas, as he thought over it, was very happy that he had been told this. It was true, as he had always known, that Robin had won some victory at the end and had been happy. He realized now how, all his life through, he had looked up to Robin and adored him as being of some much finer spirit than himself.

He heaved his big body up on his horse as though he would shake it off into space. But it would not leave him yet. And feeling the sharp wind on his cheek and hunger in his belly, for eleven was the hour when he dined, and realizing that it was his body that had created young Robert, he thought that after all it was well enough and had done him much service in its time. But he shook his head over Pierson. He was glad that at last he was dead.

At Richmond he found the whole paraphernalia of Court life and ceremony (which had, before now, seemed sufficiently absurd) in operation. In the presence-chamber there was a gathering of gentlemen, ladies, the Bishop of London, and Archbishop Whitgift whom the Queen called her 'black husband.' Everyone stood about and whispered while the green and gold tapestry shook and rustled in the wind.

At the door was a gentleman in velvet with a gold chain.

While Nicholas was standing there alone (Chichester had

left him to go and see about an audience) a door behind him opened. He stepped back, lest he should be in the way, and found himself in the dining-hall.

While he looked, two gentlemen, one with a rod, the other with a tablecloth, entered, knelt three times, spread the tablecloth and retired. Then two more came in, one with the rod again, the other with a salt-cellar, a plate and bread. These also knelt three times, placed the things on the table and retired. Then came an unmarried lady and a married lady, the latter bearing a tasting-knife. The married lady approached the table and rubbed the plates with bread and salt.

After a moment the Yeomen of the Guard entered, bareheaded and clothed in scarlet with a gold rose on the back of the scarlet. These brought twenty-four dishes, most of them gilt ; these were placed on the table by a gentleman in black velvet and then the lady-taster gave to each of the Guard a mouthful of the particular dish he had brought. This was to guard against poison.

Now this ceremony was not new to Nicholas, and would have in no way attracted his attention had it not been for an incident. All the entries, the laying of the table, the tasting of the food, had been carried out in absolute silence ; even the voices of the talkers in the presence-room were in whispers.

Quite suddenly a small page, who had been following the two ladies and carrying a gold plate with a fork on it, burst into loud crying. The effect of this upon the silent careful atmosphere was extraordinary. He was a very small boy, not more than ten years of age perhaps, and he simply stood there crying his heart out, while the Yeomen of the Guard, big grim-looking men, stood in a line and had much to do not to burst out crying also. For it was like the lamentation of the whole of England. All in the presence-chamber were transfixed by it, and especially some, perhaps, who were already considering in their minds that there was a new King in Israel and they must take advantage of it.

The small boy stood there and would not be comforted. The ceremony around the dining-table seemed almost insultingly hollow. One of the ladies put her arm around the little boy and carried him out.

Almost immediately after, Chichester touched Nicholas on the shoulder.

' You are to come,' he said.

All eyes followed the huge, dignified man, with his grey curly hair and brown cheeks, as he crossed the big room. Everyone knew that he was going to the Queen.

Chichester led him down passages, through an empty hall on whose surface their feet most dismally sounded, past a yeoman usher, and so into the privy chamber itself.

Nicholas stood just inside the door and saw a strange sight. He had been before to Richmond to see the Queen, and once, in this very room, he had pleaded for Robin's safety. He remembered how it had been then : the Queen, loaded with jewels, on her dais, the room blazing with lights, filled with ladies and gentlemen, the musicians playing dance music.

Now there was so thin a light that he must accustom his eyes to the dimness. Against the far wall two musicians were standing, and nearer the centre of the room a gentleman and two ladies. There was the dais, but no one was sitting on it. On a pile of cushions, her back against the lowest step of the dais, was an old woman. He could only tell it was the Queen by the yet fierce brightness of her eyes.

As his eyes became more accustomed he saw that she was wearing a dress of white taffeta. On her wig was perched a little crown bristling with jewels, but both wig and crown were awry. Her cheeks were yellow and drawn, her teeth discoloured, her lips thin and violently red with paint. Her bosom was half bare, and around her bony scraggy neck were three heavy ropes of pearls. She sat, all huddled up, clasping and unclasping her hands.

Nicholas did not know what to do. Chichester went forward and spoke to the Queen. She paid no attention. He spoke again.

She raised her head sharply. ' Where is he ? ' she asked.

Chichester came and brought him forward. He knelt and she gave him her hand to kiss. A heavy decaying odour was in the air and the heat from the fire was great. But she shivered.

' I cannot be warm,' she said. ' I cannot be warm.'

Someone brought a heavy cloak of dark red velvet trimmed with ermine. She huddled in this, her haggard yellow face with the brilliant eyes sticking out from it like a monkey's. He saw that she was in her perfect senses.

She said : ' Mr. Herries . . . Mr. Herries.' Then called out sharply : ' Bring a chair.' Then she motioned them to lift her on to the dais, and there she sat, twisting and untwisting her jewelled fingers against the crimson gown.

She ordered Nicholas to sit close to her, which he did. She wiped her dry, cracked lips with a handkerchief. She spoke, with perfect, quiet, ordered dignity : ' Mr. Herries, you came, I remember, once or twice about your brother. I hope that he is well.'

' He is dead, Your Majesty.'

' Ah.' And then, as though to herself : ' They are all dead. They are all dead.'

She looked at him curiously. She even smiled a very little.

' Once I had a liking for a fine man. I can recollect one or more. There was something about you that I have never forgotten.'

She stayed. She looked steadfastly at a ring on her finger.

' I am sure,' she said, ' that you would serve me in any fashion——'

' With my life.'

She shook her head so that the little sparkling crown rolled on her wig.

' Ah, but now there is no more need. It is all ended. . . . I am very ill.'

He was touched most deeply. He did not think of her as a Queen but only as a sick, ailing, very unhappy woman. Most of all he felt her unhappiness. He hated this room with its hot fire, its waiting people, this wretched sitting on the floor, the stale smell. Had it been his mother or some other relation he would have carried her in his arms to a bed where the air was fresh, where she might rest.

He ventured : ' Were Your Majesty in a cool bed——'

She darted a fierce look at him. For a moment he thought

that she would, even now, break into one of her famous rages. But all that was over.

She murmured, like any sick old woman : ' I cannot sleep. I cannot eat. I am very ill.'

She sighed. She looked at the ring on her finger. ' Nay, I am not well — not well.'

She remembered her dignity. She spoke like a Queen : ' We have been happy to see you, Mr. Herries, and we wish you good fortune wherever you may be.'

She held out her hand, and as he bent to kiss it he looked for a moment into her face. What sadness he saw there ! What deep, deep unhappiness ! Not only the unhappiness of her consciousness of approaching death, of her loneliness and weakness, but an unhappiness far more deeply rooted, that came from some old, long-lived-with sorrow. As he kissed her hand he thought of that other Queen whose execution he had seen in the hall at Fotheringhay : of her majestic proud entry into that hall, of her happy consciousness that she was dying, before all men, as a true Queen, of her deep enjoyment of that consciousness.

As he bowed his way out he saw Elizabeth huddle down among the cushions again, and the little crown fall on to her lap.

Later he sat in his parlour, in front of his fire, in great content. Rosamund, his wife, sat near him, working at tapestry. On the floor his son and heir, Robert Philip (whose bedtime it was), played with a Fool who had silver bells, a red cap and a long hooked nose.

Nicholas felt a great comfort. His visit to the Queen, the ride home through the cold air, the crackling fire, cast him into a mood of half-sleepy reminiscence.

He saw all his life as a happy thing. How young he had been at that first encounter with Irvine on the moor, how jolly afterwards had been the meeting with Robin at the Keswick inn ! It did not seem to be long ago. How proud he had been on that day when his father had told him that he would be overseer in charge of Mallory ! Dear Mallory, with its old dark rooms, its scent of honeyed wood and beeswax and dried flowers. How he had cared for every inch of it : the garden, the lawns, the hedges, the flower-beds, the meadows, the stream, the farms, the horses and cattle, the men and women under him. He stretched his arms and yawned contentedly, for next week, God willing, he would be there again.

He became more tenderly reminiscent. That first meeting with Catherine at the fair in the Keswick street, the later evening out at the mines when she had so nearly been his . . . a strange business, a strange business. That evening when he had first seen Gilbert Armstrong, wrestling on the table with all the lights and the mirrors askew.

And Robin, Robin, Robin! How he had loved him, and loved him still! Robin, who saw a kingdom that he would never see. Robin, who was so weak and so strong, and always to be loved. Robin had told him once that there were bright pavilions in the sky and that they must be found or life had no meaning. He, Nicholas, knew nothing of bright pavilions, but if dear Robin desired them he prayed to God that he had found them at the last.

From Robin his thoughts passed to England. His life had been parallel with England's greatness. He had seen her grow from a weak, undefended country to a rich and mighty Power, and that poor, sick old woman he had been with to-day had been the engine of her greatness.

He thought of her quiet and rich and deep loveliness that he had learned to worship because he, himself, had worked on her soil, digging and planting, sowing and reaping, bathing in her streams, climbing her hills. He thought of the South, his own Sussex with the rolling downs and the sea on the horizon, and he thought of the North which he also loved, with the rich changing skies, the streams of pure cold water, the hills guarding the valleys, the springing deep turf so strong beneath your feet.

So many various beauties in so small a space! He was no poet as Robin had been, but the English sky, the English fields, the English hills, were part of his very blood.

He was almost asleep. He jerked himself awake, murmuring, as though someone had challenged him : ' England is a lovely place. I would have no other.'

His wife heard him, looked across at him and smiled. It

was time for his son to be in bed. He stretched out his arms.

' Come, Robert,' he said. ' Come ! '

Robert Herries looked up, staggered to his feet and, chuckling, started across the floor towards his father.

THE END

MALVERN, *August* 4, 1938.
BRACKENBURN, *October* 24, 1939.

THE HERRIES FAMILY

IN

'THE BRIGHT PAVILIONS'

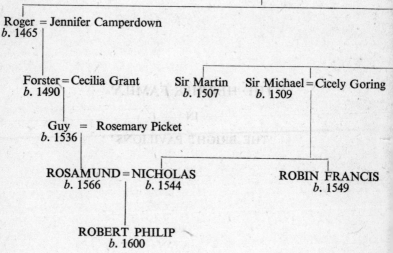

Roger Herries
b. 1430

Roger = Jennifer Camperdown
b. 1465

Forster = Cecilia Grant
b. 1490

Sir Martin
b. 1507

Sir Michael = Cicely Goring
b. 1509

Guy = Rosemary Picket
b. 1536

ROSAMUND = NICHOLAS
b. 1566   *b.* 1544

ROBIN FRANCIS
b. 1549

ROBERT PHILIP
b. 1600

```
                    Humphrey = Margaret Wade
                      b. 1470

              (1) Mary Trowneer = Henry = (2) Grace Clyde
                                  b. 1510

Edward = Agatha      Sidney      Barbara = Tobias      SYLVIA = Philip
b. 1536   Still      b. 1540     b. 1548   Garland     b. 1554   Irvine

Janet    Martha           Rashleigh    Lucy      Peter
b. 1576  b. 1578          b. 1588      b. 1590   b. 1591
```

Printed in Great Britain by R. & R. CLARK, LIMITED, *Edinburgh.*